ALSO BY ANGELINE FORTIN

Time Travel Romances:
A Laird for All Time
Nothing But Time
My Heart's in the Highlands
A Time & Place for Every Laird
Love in the Time of a Highland Laird

The Questions for a Highlander series:
A Question of Love
A Question of Trust
A Question of Lust
The Perfect Question
A Question for Harry
A Question Worth Asking

Pride & Penitence

A Time & Place for Every Laird

ANGELINE FORTIN

Copyright © 2013 Angeline Fortin
All rights reserved

Names, characters, and incidents depicted in this book are products of the author's imagination or are used fictitiously. Any resemblance to actual events, locales, organizations, or persons, living or dead, is entirely coincidental and beyond the intent of the author or the publisher. No part of this book may be reproduced or transmitted in any form or by any means, electronic or mechanical, including photocopying, recording, or by any information storage and retrieval system, without permission in writing from the publisher.

Published by

ISBN-13: 978-1492753841
ISBN-10: 149275384X

DEDICATION

For my baby girl.
May time never keep you from want you really want.
.

Prologue

The Drumoisse Muir
Near Culloden, Scotland
April 16, 1746

It was a colorful battlefield. The green of the springtime moors and the Highland kilts contrasted with the turbulent grey-blue of the sky and the vivid blue of the regimental flags. But mostly there was red. The red coats of the Hanovarian army, which vastly outnumbered the supporters of the bonny Prince Charlie, offered a bright counterpoint to the duller red of the Highlanders jackets, whose kilts of green, blue, and red were stained by the sickening hue of their bloodshed, washing the moors of Drumoisse.

There was also the red of anger, veiling the Highlander's vision as he watched the carnage. More than a thousand of his countrymen—brothers, clansmen, and friends—were dead already, fallen amid the vicious hand-to-hand mêlée while many of the enemy who still stood. His mount shifted restlessly beneath him, eager to join the fray as he was, to avenge the lives of those already lost. To spare others a certain death.

The cannon fire from the Hanovarians continued relentlessly until the blasts rang in his ears and rained earth upon their dwindling army as he watched the slaughter from a rise in the distance. Swords clashed and men shouted out their clan's cry for battle or cried out in pain as they were run through.

"Your Highness, we must retreat." The words were neither his own nor directed at him, but as they were spoken the Highlander's jaw clenched in denial. Mayhap they should. If they could not save or avenge, fleeing this ill-conceived catastrophe was one of few options remaining, but he was a Highlander by blood and right. The blood of his ancestors raging in his veins demanded that he not accept defeat.

Their forces on the left flank had not joined the fight that was ripping apart their countrymen by cannon fire and sword. Their main attack had been forced by soft ground to push right and was now pressed from both sides, with no escape from the slaughter, and the combat had waged for no more than half an hour thus far. At this rate, the battle would be lost in the same amount more.

He couldn't stand for it. He hadn't wanted it. This Jacobite cause wasn't his own, but he was a man who supported his clan, supported the uncle who had called him to arms. Nay, he hadn't wanted this, didn't believe in it, but he would not stand by and be an observer to bloodshed and death… his own pristine jacket red as well but not dyed so by the blood of brother or foe.

His mount shifted under the clenching of his thighs and

started forward as he unsheathed his mighty claymore.

"Nay, cousin!" a voice shouted over the din. "Ye dinnae hae to!"

"Aye, Keir, I do," the Highlander ground out and spurred his mount into a gallop as he headed into war. Behind him, more of his clansmen followed, including his cousin, and he plowed through the fringes of the bloody battle, swinging his sword left and right at any red-coated soldier he encountered until he was at the heart of the melee. His mount reared against the press of bodies, but he held on and continued to swing, ignoring the scrape and prick of glancing blows and the trickle of blood down his neck and arm.

It was a massacre. Their weary band stood no chance in this fool's errand. They were outnumbered more than two to one. Even at their best they would have stood no chance, but he was proud of the Scotsmen who refused to concede victory, who continued and would continue to fight to the last man. He lashed out again and again, growling viciously when he felt a blade pierce his leg. The Highlander turned with murder in his eyes to face the man who had done him harm, his face not the blue of his ancestors in battle but red with the blood of his foes. The Englishman's eyes widened and he spun about, eager to vacate the area, but the Highlander would have none of it. Kicking his mount, he pressed forward with a fierce cry. His horse screamed and buckled beneath him, falling to its knees with a shrill cry. The Highlander had no choice but to leap away, but he couldn't abandon his enemy. He chased after the fleeing coward on foot, cutting down any who stood in his path.

The ringing of swords faded until all he could hear was the sound of his footsteps striking the ground, his harsh breathing, and the pounding of his heart. His prey glanced over his shoulder and started to sprint in earnest from the Highlander's pursuit. Horns sounded, calling for the Jacobite retreat, but the Highlander ignored the call. Before this was over, this last Sassenach would be his.

A grim smile pressed his lips into a tight line as he focused on the soldier's back, just an arm's length away. He swung his sword and caught the man across one shoulder, and the soldier stumbled and fell… nay, fell and slipped out of sight through a wide hole before them.

Heels digging into the ground, the Highlander tried to turn aside before he met the edge of the abyss, but his momentum was too great and he too slipped over the edge, through the darkness and into the light beyond.

1

Spokane, Washington
Early May 2013

"Dr. Fielding?"

Claire knocked firmly on the office door, only to have it give under the pressure and swing inward with a low moan of the hinges as if inviting her in.

"Dr. Fielding?" she ventured once more, sticking her head through the portal, but found the office empty. Claire hesitated, gripping the stack of folders she carried against her chest, and debated whether to simply leave them or come back later. Finally, with a shrug, she stepped in and went to the desk to drop the files.

As she approached, a small furry face appeared at the door of a pet carrier—a plastic shell with a caged door—sitting on the corner of the desk. A cat? But, no. Little hands wrapped around the bars as it looked out at her with huge blue eyes that blinked at her calmly, almost as if the creature were studying her as she approached. "Well, aren't you a funny-looking thing?" Claire cooed at the animal, which looked to be some sort of monkey, though it was no bigger than a kitten. It had a long tail and long fingers, like a primate, but large, oddly shaped ears on the sides of its head reminiscent a bat and long, shaggy fur. Claire had never seen anything like it and had to wonder if it was perhaps some newly discovered species from Madagascar, where they identified new sorts of primates and small lemurs all the time.

Given that Dr. Fielding was an astrophysicist, the bigger question was what the animal was doing on his desk. "What a funky little mammal you are," Claire whispered, bending to get a closer look. The little monkey leaned forward as well and waggled its fingers, much as she did.

"Oh, how cute you are! Smart, aren't you?"

"*Ssss ba-boo*," the monkey-thing sounded out, reaching through the bars toward her, its little fist opened and closed as if it wanted her to give it something.

"Do you want something to eat?" Claire asked, charmed by the bright-eyed creature. "I wish I ha—"

A high-pitched cry broke the near silence of the room, making Claire almost jump out of her skin as the fine hairs stood up on the back of her neck as the monkey squealed in turn. The sudden noise was followed by other muffled noises, some animalistic and some almost human. All of them close. She jerked around to a door set at the far end of the lab that was standing just an inch ajar.

Curious, she inched closer to the door and peeked in, only to find a darkened lab space. Shiny metal machinery reflected the meager light from the office and outlined ghostly shapes around the white room. Off to one side was another door that had also been left ajar, and from it a ray of light streaked across the floor almost to her feet, creating a path inviting the curious to take a look. And Claire was undeniably curious about the sounds that continued to echo through the room.

Just a peek, she told herself as she slipped across the room. Just one little ... but what she saw through the door startled her so much that Claire couldn't help but stop and stare. Flanking each side of the room was a long row of ... well, they looked like prison cells.

Prison cells that were mostly full of animals.

Her company, Mark-Davis Laboratories, had often been equated to a real-life version of the fictional conglomeration Global Dynamics from the SyFy television series *Eureka*. The company's mission was to be on the cutting edge of technology in many different areas. Though they had their fingers in a lot of pies, as it were, Mark-Davis dealt; first and foremost, in weapons development under contract with the federal government and, for that reason, unlike pharmaceutical companies or even cosmetic companies, they didn't have much need for animal experimentation. In fact, in her two years with Mark-Davis, Claire had never seen an animal on company grounds before.

So, what was Dr. Fielding up to, she wondered as she pushed through the door and stepped inside for a better look at the animals in the first few cages. For what reason could an astrophysicist possibly need animals? And these weren't your standard lab animals, either. There were deer and other small forest animals as well as a kangaroo. An oddly shaggy bear slept on its side in one cage, while another cell held a fierce-looking wildcat that paced its confines restlessly. There were also several species that she didn't recognize, like the monkey in the office.

A shudder passed through her, prompting her to inch back towards the door. Curiosity had not only killed the cat but had cut short a few careers as well. This—whatever it was—was not something she or anyone else was meant to see. Regretting her impulse, Claire knew she should leave and pretend she had never been there, and she meant to, but at that moment movement stirred farther down the line of cages. A figure rose from the floor to stand at the bars.

It was a man, Claire realized with a gasp of surprise. Or, to be more precise, an Indian. Not an Indian as a nationality, but a good, old, straight from the Wild West, feathers and all Native American Indian.

Moments ago, she'd thought that monkey to be the craziest thing she had ever seen, but she had been wrong. This guy looked so authentic! He was dressed in a leather breechcloth. His bare chest was darkly bronzed and covered with scars as well as filth and … was that the dull shine of oil or grease? There was a primitive nobility about him but also a primal savagery that inspired instant fear.

Claire nearly jumped out of her skin when that horrid cry sounded again. From him.

God, it sounded like a war cry. Just like in the old westerns her dad watched on the weekends.

He fixed his gaze on her then with eyes as black and hard as obsidian, piercing her with a shiver of fear. He shouted at her, guttural sounds in a language Claire couldn't understand, but his curt hand motions told her what he undoubtedly wanted.

He wanted out.

Eyes wide, she inched back, shaking her head in automatic denial. There was no way she was going to be the one to release that angry man. And it wasn't based on prejudice against his race or anything at all like that. No, only a madwoman would unlock the door and release someone who looked that pissed off.

He read her shaking head correctly and his scowl deepened even further. He barked at her again, motioning insistently to the door.

A faint terror took ahold of Claire and she edged back another step toward the door. This was all too crazy for words. A thousand questions were crowding her mind, begging for answers. Who? Why?

How?

But Claire knew they were questions she couldn't ask of anyone she met. Her natural inquisitiveness had gotten the better of her this time and she'd stepped into something that was way bigger than a few stray animals.

Backing off another step with the intention of fleeing the room and forgetting what she had just seen, another figure appeared at the bars of a cage farther down the row and opposite the Indian. Another man! This man was larger than the Indian but just as grimy and mangy. His dark hair and beard were long and matted. His face so dirty it was difficult to see that there was human flesh beneath. He was dressed in a bloody, torn tan shirt and ... was that a kilt? Was he Scottish? If he was, he was so dirtied and bloodied that it was difficult to tell.

His nostrils flared and his lip curled ... his heavy eyebrows parted only by the vertical furrow between them when his gaze pierced hers. There was anger this man, just as there was in the Indian, though he was perhaps even more terrifying without the restraint and nobility of the Native American. He was wild, untamed. Claire's heart raced unexpectedly, pounding against her rib cage.

Fear. Panic? She couldn't define what she felt, but even as her pulse quickened, the anger faded just as rapidly from his vivid blue eyes. Frustration remained and maybe a touch sadness and defeat. When he spoke again, his voice grating but soft.

Surprisingly, her first thought was that she'd thought they spoke English in Scotland. Claire couldn't comprehend his words, but neither did she ask him to repeat them. As with the Indian, she knew what he was asking.

Inexplicably, her first impulse was to comply. She even took a hesitant step forward before she realized what she was about. "I can't," she whispered with a shake of her head, not even certain that he would understand her any better than she understood him.

Even if she were to unlock the cells somehow, there was no way for him to escape the facility. There were coded locks, guards, and cameras everywhere. Thinking of the security cameras, she glanced overhead at the camera mounted above the door, aware that both men's eyes followed hers. Were they intelligent enough to realize that they didn't stand a chance?

"Please."

Claire's eyes widened at the sound of the word. Had she heard that right? Was he speaking English now? Glancing back at the Indian, she tried to determine whether he'd understood as well, but that warrior's gaze was still as dark and fiery as the depths of hell. The bigger man waited more patiently but there was desperation in his eyes. Pleading. Claire's heart ached. Whoever he was—*whatever* he was—he didn't deserve this.

"I don't know... I—I'll try," she said, sweeping her

glance around the room once more and taking in the variety of animals and the two men caged as if they were beasts as well. she didn't know if there was anything she could do, but some latent humanitarianism in her couldn't leave them there like that without doing something.

The murmur of voices drifted in from the hallway, jolting Claire back to the precariousness of her situation. It wouldn't do at all to be caught where she knew she shouldn't have tread. Hurriedly, she stepped back into the lab, pulling the steel door shut behind her before hastening as far away from it as she could. With luck on her side, she made it to the main office door just as it opened. "Oh, Dr. Fielding, Marti asked me to drop off those files you needed. They're on your desk."

"Thank you...?"

"Claire," she supplied.

The astrophysicist nodded absently, his entire focus on the folder in his hands, leaving her ample opportunity to inch by without any further questions but for those fairly bursting in her mind.

Inhaling deeply to calm her racing heart, she dashed into the hall nearly tripping on the ragged mop head sweeping across the tiled floor.

"Careful on there, lass." The custodian wielding the mop caught her as staggered forward, steadying her and lifting her away from the pool of sudsy water on the floor. For a such a stooped, elderly man, he had a surprisingly strong arm. "Ye dinnae want to step in something ye shouldn't."

"I'm afraid I might have already."

"Hae ye now? *Och*, it maun be fate then, aye?"

She looked at the old man who'd been working here since before she'd started at Mark-Davis. Many of her coworkers claimed Donell had been there before the company was even founded. With his deeply wrinkled face and haggard appearance, he often gave the impression of being older than the dirt itself. But his dark eyes twinkled with youthful cheer and he always had a kind word or joke to share when he came around to clean when she worked late.

Which was often.

Perhaps she'd been working too much lately and all she'd come across Fielding's lab was a hallucination.

Or fate? As if she were meant to help that terrifying person in there?

That wouldn't be her smartest move ever. She should just forget she ever saw it.

"Nae harm done then?"

"What?" she asked, shaking herself back to the moment.

"If all's well then, ye should get getting on, aye?"

"Yes, of course." She nodded absently. "Have a good day, Donell."

"Ye as well, lass."

Claire shook her head. She had an ugly feeling, all would never be good again.

2

"Claire? Hello?"

Claire looked up to find her friend Darcy Washington looking down at her with a frown. "You've got a mark on your forehead, you know?" she continued when Claire didn't speak.

Reaching up, Claire rubbed her forehead. Of course she had a spot there. She'd been face down on her desk, numbed with shock over her recent encounter.

"Come on, girl! It's time for lunch."

Claire blinked up at her friend and then at the clock in surprise. For more than an hour, she'd been trying to figure out what Dr. Fielding might possibly be working on that had him keeping specimens of any sort in his lab, let alone human ones, but so far had been unable to even hypothesize a single logical explanation. Mark-Davis Laboratories was awash with top-secret activities, but in reality most of them weren't that big a mystery to those working on campus.

Grabbing her purse, she rose and trailed Darcy out of

the building before coming alongside her. Like fictional Eureka, Mark-Davis was a sprawling campus rather than just one building. Since the higher-ups preferred to keep their employees from having reason to leave work, there were places to eat, a gym with a swimming pool, day care facilities, a small medical office, and even a post office housed within the corporate confines. Inside the dozen buildings there was a honeycomb of sectors working on everything from ballistics to bombs.

Claire's sector worked in the development of ultrasonic weaponry, or USW. USWs employed focused beams of sound as a weapon in the form of bullets, grenades, or mines. This was one of the many projects helping to make science fiction into science fact.

As they walked down the sidewalk and around a tiny park surrounded by buildings on their way to the cafeteria, she continued to rub her forehead, trying to rationalize what she had seen, but still couldn't think of a single project in the works that used animal testing … or human. Of course there were many levels of security clearance at play in the company, but regardless of the secrecy of any project in the works, there was always some gossip in the company cafeteria. Whatever secrets Fielding was keeping, he was keeping them well.

Still, she couldn't help but ask Darcy if she'd heard anything. "I suppose you think Todd probably said something," Darcy grimaced, referring to her former boyfriend, who worked in Fielding's sector.

"Did he?"

"Just pillow talk," Darcy confessed in a whisper. "Todd never told me exactly what they're working on but I do know that whatever it is, they are failing miserably. Billions of dollars given to them by INSCOM and nothing to show for it."

"INSCOM?"

"Army Intelligence and Security Command," her friend explained the acronym. "I know, I had never heard of them either but apparently they're like the black ops of Army intelligence. Todd said Fielding's so afraid of losing his funding that each night at Riley's he cries like a baby into his beer. That's what you get for putting an astrophysicist in charge of a weapons division, I say."

Claire wasn't interested in Fielding's decline into academic depression, however. "He never said anything else?"

"Just that it had something to do with surveillance, I think." Darcy shrugged as they entered the cafeteria building, which was similar to a shopping mall food court, with several different choices of foods. There was a grill with burgers and chicken; a bistro with soups, sandwiches, and the like; a bakery with fresh bagels, donuts, and pastries for early morning arrivers; a new sushi bar that had opened just the week before; and even a Starbucks. Claire and Darcy went by rote to the bistro's salad bar, picking up trays, plates, and utensils.

"Surveillance?" Surveillance in military-speak often translated to spying, and with the project being funded by this INSCOM that made sense, but even so, how would that result in a lab full of caged beings? Claire scooped up a small amount of baby spinach onto her plate with a wrinkled nose. It was repugnance that gnawed at her stomach now, not hunger, at the thought that a botched experiment – whatever it might be – had led to the incarceration of human beings.

"Yes," Darcy nodded. "Why do you want to know?"

Shaking her head, Claire halfheartedly tossed on some mushrooms and a little vinaigrette. "I'm really freaked out, Darcy."

"That much is abundantly clear," Darcy quipped. "The question is why?"

They paid for their meals at the register and went to their usual table near the windows. In the distance, Claire could see the mountains of the coastal ranges in Washington State. Even in May they were covered in snow. Clean and pure compared to the unethical practices she'd just uncovered.

Glancing around, she answered in low tones, "I was in Dr. Fielding's lab today and saw some ... animals there."

"What were you doing over there?" was the first thing Darcy wanted to know.

"I was getting coffee this morning," Claire explained, gesturing toward the Starbucks numbly. "I was talking with Marcia— do you know Marcia?— anyway, she got a call from her son's school saying that he was running a fever, and asking her to come pick him up. She's been swamped ever since Big Al disappeared a few months ago and Dr. Fielding was pestering her about some files he needed. So she asked me to drop them off in Dr. Fielding's office so she could leave right away."

"She shouldn't have done that," Darcy pointed out, only to receive Claire's arch look that mutely stated, "no kidding" in response. "Fine. No lecture. What kind of animals are we talking here? Lab mice?" Darcy speared a green pepper before popping it in her mouth but Claire only nudged her salad around her plate.

"Bigger," she mumbled. "What could he possibly be doing that he would need ... specimens?"

"Specimens?" Darcy asked with more focused curiosity.

"More than mice?"

Claire snorted softly and glumly nodded her head.

"Bunnies?"

Darcy's voice had taken on an edge of hope that Claire knew was little more than denial rearing its head. It was nothing compared to the misery that had been eating at her. She'd never considered herself an ardent humanitarian before. She cried for the troubles in other countries, the poor, the hungry, but thought America had enough troubles of its own to focus on. She gave to St. Jude's and to the Wounded Warriors Project, volunteered her time at the local animal shelter, and did what she could to be the change she wanted to see in the world, but had always inwardly acknowledged that the influence of one person was negligible in changing the fate of many—animals or human.

For the first time, she wanted to truly save someone – someone specific. She *needed* to do it. This went beyond wrongful imprisonment. Those men! Claire couldn't even contemplate how they had come to be there, but neither one of them probably had a clue as to what had happened to them.

"Not just bunnies, Darcy." She poked at her salad again before pushing the plate away. "There are men in that lab. Two of them."

"Men?" Darcy squeaked, then lowered her voice to a whisper. "Like, *human* men?"

"Are there any other kind? But not just like the guy next door. One is an Indian. A Native American. You should see him." Claire paused. "Darcy, there's no way he's from… *here*."

"Here, as in Washington?"

"No, here, as in now," Claire said, voicing the truth that

was becoming clear to her, no matter how preposterous it sounded. "He's from a different time. He has to be. No one, not the most brilliant costume designer in the world, could come up with something like that."

"That's ridiculous, Claire," Darcy protested before digging back into her salad. "You're talking about time travel? It isn't possible."

"Really?" Claire scoffed. "Would a time machine really be the most unbelievable thing that came out of this place? Al hinted that there were weird things going on in there. Besides, your projects are right up there with *Star Trek*, aren't they? Why not something out of *Dr. Who?*"

Darcy's team was developing the next generation of orbital weaponry—weapons effective in the vacuum of outer space, should the world ever come to that. Naturally, that division's work was all supposed to be limited to theoretical development, as the United Nations had banned the militarization and weaponization of outer space long ago.

"Come on, Claire!"

"Come on, Darcy!" she shot back, her heart pounding desperately against her chest. "He has them locked up in cages, the Indian and the other one ..." Picturing the larger man, the one whose emotional stare had affected her so, her words drifted off. "I think he's Scottish or something. It's hard to tell. He's all bloody and mangy looking. But even if he is a medieval savage, he doesn't deserve being locked up like that. He has them in cages, Darcy! Wallowing in their own filth. This is bigger than the ACLU or PETA here. We need to do something."

Wide-eyed, Darcy shook her head in denial. "We? No, no, no. I need this job. I can't afford to do something stupid."

"Stupid?" Claire asked incredulously. "It's not stupid to save a life."

"Oh, Claire," the other woman moaned. "You know the kind of security they have in there. There's just no way."

"I know." And she did. Hadn't she thought the same, back in Dr. Fielding's lab? But what else could she do? Just stand aside and let the men rot in those cells? "There must be something, some authority we could report it to."

"Really?" Darcy scoffed at that. "If these two men are really from another time – and I'm not saying they are – who do you think would take them without treating them like a science experiment?"

Darcy had a point there and Claire knew it.

"Go home, Claire. Get out of here before you do something stupid. After a good night's sleep you'll realize that you just need to keep your head down and forget about what you saw."

"I can't just forget."

"You had better, and don't you be calling the ACLU!"

If Darcy was right about anything it was that Claire needed to get out of there and clear her head. Giving up on her lunch, she told her supervisor she was going home with a headache and left the building.

But she could not erase the image of that prison, those two long rows of cages. It was one thing to keep animals for scientific experimentation. Perhaps it was not a PETA-friendly concept, but at least it was accepted. But to keep people? That was something else entirely.

Claire tugged at the edges of her cardigan and wrapped her arms tightly around her midsection with a tremor of repulsion. While the Native American man had seemed more than a little animalistic, the other man, for all his savage appearance, had more in him than anger.

Something had to be done for them. But what?

And where had they come from? What was Dr. Fielding working on? Surveillance? *Bah!* There was something more than that going on. Something had potentially transported not information but two men through time.

    Time travel. It was ludicrous, or at least unprecedented. The two men might have just been in costume. Exceedingly authentic costumes. Geez, she scoffed inwardly, for some reason that sounded far more unreasonable than her time travel notion.

)O(O(O(

    Lost to the mad scramble of thoughts clashing with the questions in her mind, Claire robotically pulled her keys from her purse, absently unlocking the door of her Toyota Prius as she approached. The usual beep-beep and flash of her taillights passed unnoticed but the vice-like grip that wrapped around her wrist as she reached for the door handle brought her back to the present with a squeal of surprise. In a heartbeat, she was yanked to the ground, a rough hand clamped over her mouth, cutting off her cry. For a moment, she froze in shock and denial. A thousand news reports of women assaulted and killed flashed through her mind, sending an icy blade of sickening fear through her gut.

    Then somehow the adrenaline born of panic kicked in, and she began struggling against the arms that held her. She clawed at the hand covering her mouth, trying to pry it away, until her eyes…and her nose…caught up with her mind.

    The arm and hand that held her were large, filthy, and bloody.

    The smell that assailed her held the metallic tang of dried blood, perspiration, and death.

    A harsh voice sounded in her ear, speaking words she couldn't make out, but Claire recognized it immediately. It was hard to forget something that sounded like that.

    Something that smelled like that.

    He spoke again. The rhythm of his guttural words was

familiar but she still couldn't make them out. She tried to speak against his hand, and after a moment he reluctantly lifted it away, his body tensed to react should she dare scream. "I can't understand you," she whispered shakily, wondering if her death was imminent.

"Send me back," came his carefully enunciated reply accompanied by a rough squeeze that nearly stole her breath. His command sounded like "Sen mae back" and was still nearly unintelligible, but Claire got his point.

"I can't," she choked out, quaking with fear as she launched a futile struggle against him once more. The mass of his huge body felt even larger behind her than her short glimpse of him in the cell had led her to believe. His arms were like steel bands around her, making her resistance pointless.

He twisted her about in his arms until Claire was staring up at him with wide, fearful eyes. Up close, he was even more terrifying. His black beard was crusted with blood and grime, as was what she could see of his face and arms and clothes. The whole of him was just as nasty as it had seemed from a distance. "Send me back home," he commanded fiercely once more, his hands rough on her upper arms as he gave her a little shake. Had she truly just been thinking that there might have been a softer side to this man, whoever he was? She was at his mercy and suddenly regrettably sure that there was none within him.

"I-I told you, I can't," she repeated, terror evident in the high octave of her voice.

"Who can? Take me to who can," he growled ferociously, sending a more violent shudder of alarm racing through Claire's limbs, and she began to fight again, pushing against him.

"Stop fightin' wi' me, lass. I mean ye nae harm," he said, enunciating each word slowly to ensure that he was understood.

An incredulous squeak escaped her. "Oh, is that so? Where did all that blood come from then?"

"From me."

Claire's eyes darted over him in disbelief, finally seeing the half-healed wounds on his forearms and one on his neck. His left leg was caked in blood from the knee down. Then she raised her eyes to his vivid blue ones, held them. Of course, they were all she could see beneath his matted hair and beard, but those eyes didn't glow with murderous intent or with cold rage. Instead, they held the same despair and desperation she had seen in the lab when he'd been caged. While desperate men could do desperate things, and logically Claire knew she should fear for her life, somehow she felt the fear ebb just as it had in the lab.

"Are you badly hurt?"

Clearly, the question startled him, much as it had her. His gaze turned to bewilderment for a brief spell before the anxiety began to return. "I want to go home."

Heart pounding wildly against her ribs at his impassioned words, Claire felt her chest tighten with emotion, and tears sprang to her eyes as sympathy rushed through her. She understood that. She knew what it was like to desperately want something you could not have.

To beg and plead, curse and wail at Fate and still be denied.

Suspended by the thought, Claire stared up at him, not even flinching when the wail of sirens and alarms filled the air. He did though, his eyes darting around in alarm.

The Scotsman—if that's what he actually was. Who

knew, really?—looked wildly around, trying to identify the source of the noise, while Claire tried to come to terms with the inherent insanity of what she knew she was about to do. She could hardly believe it herself.

"We need to get you out of here," she said calmly, recalling his attention. "I assume that's for you?" While he stared at her in surprise, she stood and opened the back door of her car. "Get in and stay low."

His blue eyes were easy to read. Mistrust. Doubt. Who could blame him? She was as dumbfounded by her actions as he. "Do you really have any choice?" she asked. "It's them or me."

If she hadn't known better, Claire might have thought he rolled his eyes with something akin to humor before he disappeared inside her Prius. Shutting the door, she opened the driver's door and slid in. Calmly, she started the car and shifted into reverse, backing out of the parking space. Just as serenely, she put the car in drive and pressed her foot down on the gas pedal.

That was about how long it took for her to second-guess herself.

"What am I doing?" she whispered to herself, gripping the steering wheel tightly at ten and two. Doubts and recriminations filled her mind. "Are you insane, Claire?"

Still, she drove calmly through the gates while the big Scot hid in her backseat, glad the gate was unmanned but fearful that the cameras might catch something, some movement, as she passed. Fearful? Her mind whirled. Shouldn't she be hopeful? Hopeful that someone had seen what had happened and was on their way to save her from this savage madman? To save her from herself?

What was she thinking? The guy might be a mass

murderer for all she knew, and she was actually thinking of taking him ... where? To her townhouse so she might be slaughtered in the privacy and comfort of her own home?

A hysterical giggle escaped her as she steered her car through the streets of Spokane. At worst she would be dead by nightfall. At best she would be unemployed by the next morning. "You're risking your life and livelihood here, Claire," she continued to mutter under her breath in self-recrimination. "Why? Why are you doing this? Turn around, take him back, and claim temporary insanity. Kidnapping. Something. Oh, my God, I'm such an idiot. Stupid. Stupid. Stupid!" Claire pounded on the steering wheel with those last three words.

What was she thinking? Was she thinking at all? There was a time and a place for sympathy. This was not it. That man might have a sad story that tugged at the heartstrings, but was she really going to risk her whole life just because ...

"What is this conveyance?" The garble of words from the backseat was barely intelligible.

"What?" she asked, unable to work out his thick brogue, and the Scot repeated the question more succinctly, pointing at the dashboard.

"It's a car," she told him.

"Car," he repeated, pushing himself into a sitting position until Claire could see him in the rearview mirror. He was looking around him with that odd combination of fascination and denial people get when they're subjected to something new. A low, brushing noise told her he was running his hands over the upholstery, as if tactile sensation could prompt belief or acceptance.

"What is this world?" he asked harshly as his eyes took in the scenery passing by the windows, the panic once again rising in his voice, but she had a question of her own.

"How did you get out?"

"Tell me what I want to ken, lass," he barked.

"You first!" Claire shot back, taking her eyes briefly off the road to turn and look at him. His blue eyes were as blazing hot as the pilot light on her stovetop. He was terrifying. *She* should have been terrified, but whether she was doing the right thing or not, some part of her illogically believed that he wasn't going to hurt her.

Or at least he wasn't actively planning on it.

Taking an abrupt left, she pulled into a parking lot behind a small strip mall and threw the car into park even as she twisted around to face her would-be kidnapper.

"What are ye doin', lass?" he gaped in disbelief. Each word was clipped and carefully enunciated so that she could understand him the first time. "We hae to flee 'fore they coordinate a pursuit."

"I'm not going any further until you tell me what happened."

Their eyes locked, warring for position and power. Claire couldn't believe that she was taking such a drastic step as to challenge him so. Her insides were a mass of nerves that shook her until she felt like jelly but she couldn't back down. Somehow she knew that showing any weakness was the very worst thing she could do with someone like him.

Apparently her instincts were correct. A moment later, his fierce frown eased and a grudging respect lit his fierce blue eyes. He fumbled against the door for a moment before finding the handle and deducing its operation. The door flung open, and he was out of the car and into the front seat before she could even think about taking advantage and making a quick getaway. He looked at her as if pondering her state of mind. He crossed his arms over his broad chest, over the bloodied tartan, without thought and Claire could only shudder, wondering what else this savage man might consider with such disregard.

"Well?"

His teeth were practically grinding out his annoyance. "Our jailor came in wi' food an' the savage ..."

"The Indian?"

"Aye, if that's what ye would call the savage warrior, though he dinnae appear to be from that nation, but I willnae argue the point. The guard got too close to his cage and the savage caught his arm and pulled it 'twixt the bars. He broke it rather ruthlessly before taking the guard's keys," he explained, missing her grimace at his unemotional retelling. "I could tell the *Indian* was unfamiliar wi' them but had seen them in use often enough these past days to know their purpose. Cannie lad."

No argument there. "And he let you out?"

"Aye, and the animals as well," the Scot nodded, and Claire thought of the animals she had seen that morning. Many looked harmless, but the bear and the wildcat would have provided additional chaos in the lab. Canny lad, indeed.

"But how did you get out of the building?" she persisted. "Its security is state of the art."

He shrugged. "I dinnae ken yer terminology but 'twas simple enough to elude the roving eye. I had a view from my cage into the outer room, which allowed me to see the mobile portraits staged there."

"The monitors?"

He only raised an impatient brow to indicate once again that he was not familiar with the term. "It wisnae difficult, watching the movement of the eye within our prison walls and the portraits, to ken that they showed only what the eye could see."

So he had some brains. He'd been smart enough to glean information from what he saw and extrapolate that information into usable data. Impressive. But still…

"I can't believe you managed to get out of the building."

"'Twas simple enough," he shrugged once again. Clearly the gesture was a dismissive one, and Claire got the impression that he thought she was wasting his time. Well, impatient or not, she wasn't going any further without answers.

"There are guards everywhere in there," she pointed out. "How did you get past them all?"

"Past them?" he laughed arrogantly. "They were but a wee annoyance."

"But they had guns. Firearms."

"Those puny guards were nae match for us."

Gripping the steering wheel tightly, she blinked at him in horror. "Did you kill them?"

The Scot met her gaze, his humor waning. "Nay, I dinnae. It wisnae necessary to do so in order to overcome their petty resistance."

"Thank God."

"The Indian, however…" he added with another nonchalant shrug. "I fear he dinnae feel the same moral obligation to the sanctity of life."

"Oh, God." Claire rested her forehead against the steering wheel.

"Ye think they wouldnae hae done the same to either of us if they had the opportunity?"

She rocked her head against the upper curve of the wheel. "I think they won't hesitate when they find you now."

"Then I shall hae to assure that they dinnae."

She looked up doubtfully. "Should I even ask how do you plan to do that?"

"Wi' yer assistance."

Rolling her eyes, Claire laughed disbelievingly. Regardless of the effort she had put forth so far in his favor, she would be a fool to continue with this madness. She had put herself at quite a risk already. "You expect me to help you?"

"Ye already hae."

"Because I felt sorry for you," she told him, and the Scot bristled at the words.

"I dinnae need yer pity. I dinnae need anyone's pity."

"Then get out and start walking," she shot back.

He was scowling at her once more, but she could see the respect growing again in his eyes. He probably wasn't used to women talking back to him. Given his attire, he was probably more used to damsels in distress and wilting maidens. Or ... she raised a brow. Perhaps he was just used to clubbing them over the head and dragging them off if they misbehaved.

"I shall accept yer assistance," he said in magnanimous tones.

"I haven't offered it," she pointed out, amazed at his arrogance. "And every bit of logic in me argues against doing so."

"But ye will," he responded with astounding certainty.

Was she that easy to read? Could he see so readily that what her mind knew and what her humanity insisted on were at odds? "What makes you so certain?"

He met her gaze steadily then, and Claire could see the crinkle of the crow's feet at the corners of his eyes as if they were smiling at her. "Ye hae a soft heart."

Claire just stared at him, wide-eyed. "That's what you're

going with?" she snorted, shaking her head. Cautious Claire. The one who never did anything stupid. Damn it but she was going to get the World Cup of awards for Most Momentous Mistake Ever Made after this. "What is your name? I might as well know it if I'm going to help you."

"Hugh," he said, the name surrounded by the soft roll of his brogue. "Hugh Urquhart."

Claire *humphed* and jerked the gearshift back into drive.

"And yers?" he asked. "I might as well know it if ye're going to be my savior."

Twisting her lips to keep from smiling, Claire looked away so that he wouldn't see the reluctant humor. "Claire Manning."

"My pleasure, Miss Manning," Hugh said with unexpected gallantry that had Claire shaking her head once again.

"Oh, it's all mine, you know," she murmured a little sarcastically. "Just so we're clear ... I'll help you and in return you promise you won't kill me. Deal?"

"Ye hae my word," he said solemnly, holding out his hand, and she daringly slid hers into his roughened palm, intent on giving it a firm shake.

But then the strangest thing happened. His hands – dirty and bloody as they were – engulfed hers. They were strong, warm, and rough, and just the feel of them made her shiver. It was not a shiver of fear.

It was something else. Something more.

And apparently he felt it as well. His eyes widened as they both stared down at their clasped hands, his so large and dark surrounding hers.

A metallic bang and a shout sounded nearby and jolted them both. A busboy from a restaurant in the mini mall was tossing garbage into a dumpster behind the building. Hugh moved away and turned in his seat until he was facing forward, but Claire could almost see the questions bursting from his mind.

She had questions as well.

The biggest one was, which of them held more answers?

Shaking her misgivings away, she pulled back into traffic.

"Oh, and it's Mrs., not Miss. Just so you know."

4

Surely this Hugh Urquhart's eyes could not get any rounder, Claire thought as she pushed the button on the ceiling of her car to open the door of the garage attached to her townhouse. As it went up, his eyes widened, much as they had repeatedly during the short ride there. Once the anxiety of their escape had passed, Hugh had begun to look around, seeing perhaps for the first time the world outside the lab if her theory of time travel was correct.

A dozen times he'd lifted his hand—the one that wasn't clinging to the armrest—to point out this or that, his lips parting with the questions forming on them, but inquiries had never come. Whether he was too shocked or simply too proud to ask, she had no idea, though there was a part of her that leaned toward the latter. If she hadn't been so worried, it might have been amusing.

Sadly, she had rounded the bend from worried to pure agitation.

The garage door closed behind them, leaving them in

semi-darkness, and Claire breathed a sigh of relief, knowing the world and its prying eyes were blinded to them at least for the time being. Perhaps now she could relax a little. Getting out of the car, she scooped up her purse and went inside, leaving Hugh to follow as he would.

She was flipping on the lights in her living room when he appeared at the door. Thankfully, she kept her blinds closed while she was at work, so there was no need to race around, closing them. "I don't think anyone saw us."

He only snorted. "Yer people are about as stealthy as a startled stag. Anyone could hae heard ye a league away."

She just shook her head. "You're welcome." Tossing her purse and keys on the kitchen counter, she began to search the cushions of her couch for the television remote. Maybe there would be something on about Hugh's escape.

"Yer no' frightened of me any longer, Mistress Manning," he said with some amusement, crossing his arms over his broad chest.

"I told you my name is Claire," she said absently. "Would being afraid of you do me any good? Would you like me to cower before you?" The urge to do so had certainly been there more than once. She found the remote and pointed it at the flat-screen TV mounted over the fireplace and pushed the power button. Any response Hugh might have made was immediately sidetracked.

"Good Lord Almighty!" he swore in disbelief as the picture came on and sound filled the room.

"I thought you said you saw the monitors at the lab?"

"I did indeed. However …" He waved a hand at the TV. "What images does it capture? Where are these people?"

"Probably on a soundstage in Los Angeles," she said, flipping the channel away from the Ellen DeGeneres show and exploring the other local channels with dread icily gripping her heart. Nothing.

Yet.

With a sigh of relief, Claire turned it off again and turned back to Hugh, who was still staring at the blank TV screen in horror. It was almost a pleasure to see that look on his face, to see some small vulnerability in him. To see him looking as anxious as she had been. He was right. She wasn't afraid of him any longer. Or at least not as afraid, though she was still troubled by what she had done. Still, she would be an even greater fool to throw her wariness to the wind along with caution. "I'll explain the TV later. I just wanted to make sure there were no reports of your escape or mentions of the authorities out looking for you, publicly at least."

Hugh ran his hands over his face with a groan. "I'm sure they will do so."

"I'm sure they will, too," she nodded grimly, once again inwardly questioning her choices.

"So, what shall we do, Mistress Manning?"

"Claire," she corrected again. "I guess you can call me by my first name, if mistress is my only other option."

"Claire, Clara," he said with clear disdain. "A Sassenach name. An English name, just as is yer surname, Manning. In Gaelic, Clara is Sorcha. After my recent dealings wi' the English, I prefer the latter."

"Recent dealings?"

"England wants to rule Scotland. They want to take the lands of my clansmen, take our freedoms, and strip the lairds of their power. And so we fight. 'Tis what I was in the midst of doing when I came to be here." He looked so pensive that Claire dared not ask any of the many questions she had for him.

"If they are in the same shape you are, I guess I should be thankful I'm not English," she said instead.

That made him lift his head. "Yer no' English?"

She shook her head. "No, and since you hate them so much, that's probably a good thing for me."

Hugh cocked his head, clearly sidetracked by her words; his blue eyes alight with curiosity. "Wi' a name such as Manning, I had assumed ... What nationality are ye, then?"

"I'm an American."

"American?" he repeated interestedly.

Holding up a hand, Claire shook her head to forestall any further questions on his part. "I think there's a lot we need to cover before we go there."

He nodded grimly, setting the momentary diversion aside. "Aye, I hae many questions as well."

"Why don't we start with the most basic one then," she said matter-of-factly as she studied him. The kilt was a crumpled blue-and-green plaid with a thin crossing of red that was a few shades lighter than the darkened bloodstains all over it. A blue vest hung open over a linen shirt, which wasn't tan, as she had thought, but simply that dirty and stained. Above his plaid stockings, his blood-encrusted knee looked in need of medical attention. "Do any of those wounds need stitches?"

He looked down at the multitude of crusted wounds covering his arms, shrugging them away as insignificant. "Ye asked me before if I was hurt. I can only say that I shall be well only when I return to my home. This is one question I need hae the answer to now. Who can return me there?"

"I don't know," Claire told him with an apologetic wince at his palpable frustration with her answer. "Dr. Fielding might, maybe, but since he's the guy who locked you up, I wouldn't think that he would help. And I don't know what brought you here other than there had been some issues with Dr. Fielding's project so there's nothing I can do to get you home. I assume Scotland is home?"

"Aye."

Then she asked the question that had been eating at her since she first walked into that lab. Since she had first seen that kilt. "I need to ask this, Hugh, and there's really no way to cushion it at all. What year is it?"

His brows knit in confusion. "What madness prompts such a question?"

Claire waited as his eyes searched the room, seeking answers, and saw the anxiety in his eyes become denial before slowly despondency shadowed it all. "My God!" he moaned, dropping onto his haunches. "What hell is this? What world hae I been sent to?"

She didn't answer. There was no good response to a person whose only hope had been destroyed. Hugh rocked back on his heels, burying his face in his hands. A moment later he rubbed his hands over his face again and again, as if doing so could erase everything he'd seen, and Claire felt another tug of sympathy.

Life was so unfair, she thought. It gave the highest of highs only to follow them with the lowest of lows. She knew from personal experience how it could throw a knockout punch. She knew denial. She knew despair.

She had just never seen them on the face of another person before, had never seen that hollow, haunted look anywhere other than in a mirror.

An insane urge to hug Hugh nearly overwhelmed her before she pushed the impulse away. He would only rebuff her as she had rebuffed so many, once upon a time. Now finally she understood how helpless those on the other side felt, but she had to do something.

"Hugh?" she whispered and waited until he met her gaze. "I know…Damn." Pause. "How about a shower and we can talk later?"

"Shower?" he repeated numbly.

"Come on," she said, jerking her head toward the staircase. "Let's get you cleaned up. We can talk more later."

Claire showed Hugh the shower and towels and promised to find him something clean to wear before leaving the Scot alone. Returning to the living room, she dropped into an armchair and took her turn rubbing her hands over her face. What was she doing? She should find the guards who were probably even now searching for this man. But somehow she couldn't. They would only lock him up again. God help her, but for some reason she couldn't let that happen.

)O(O(O(

He could make the water as hot as he pleased. With the turn of a handle, he could make it so hot that he could hardly stand it, and Hugh did, hoping to scald the misery right off his skin. Raking his nails through his hair and beard, he let the water pelt his face and scalp, the scorching water beating on him until he was almost numb.

And he wanted to be.

The water could not be fiery enough to match this hell. From the moment he'd arrived, he'd been treated and caged like an animal. His attempts to question his captors had been ignored. When Sorcha had met his eye that morning in the lab, it had been the first time in a long while that Hugh felt he'd been seen as a human being.

Escaping the lab due to one guard's lax negligence had

been miraculous. Squashing the feeble resistance of the guards he'd encountered upon his flight had not proven much of a challenge, but in all honesty he'd savored those moments of retribution for all that had been done to him. He'd exited the building to the blinding light of sunshine, savoring the feel of its meager heat on his face and the fresh air that filled his lungs.

Then his eyes had adjusted to the bright light and Hugh had stood frozen in his tracks at the sight that awaited him. Hugh knew he would forever remember the shock and dread that had seized him in that moment. Fields and fields of what he now knew were 'cars' had spread before him. Alien shapes in a variety of colors and sizes. He had crept between them, searching for an avenue to his liberation, fascinated almost to distraction by the smooth, glossy shells. Of course he recognized them as bizarre conveyances of some sort. The wheels told him that much. And had contemplated taking one, but their operation had been puzzling.

Then the lanterns on another car nearby had flashed and a horn sounded, startling him. Hugh had watched with astonishment as a man had gotten into one of the cars and somehow sent it roaring to life. Then another person had come out and merely pointed her hand at one of the cars to set off the flash of lights and the horn that accompanied them.

In his world, such trickery might have been seen as witchcraft, though no one had been accused of such in nearly a century. Nevertheless, it had startled the bloody hell out of him. And then he'd seen them drive away with no identifiable power source, and Hugh had admittedly been petrified. That was when he had seen his savior wading through the field of cars and followed her, determined to force her assistance in freeing him from this strange land.

He'd never dreamed she would voluntarily help him when no one else had ever truly looked at him. He owed her his life, a debt that honor demanded he repay, but what could he offer a woman in this world? Whatever this world was.

It was a world with plain-faced buildings with little ornamentation but extraordinarily large windows set apart from one another only by the large placards that named them. A world with streets of solid black stone to carry the cars that traveled them. A world where women wore clothes like men, clothes that seemed to deny their very gender.

A world where the push of a button was the equivalent of the wave of a wand.

A world where he owed his life to a woman.

Raising his face to the water's spray, Hugh pushed the questions crowding his mind aside. He could not think about Sorcha's question. He would not. He slammed his fist against the smooth white tiles. The pain matched his frustration and he did it again with growl deep in his throat. The minutes slipped by as he let the water wash over him, ridding his body of the blood of battle and the stink of imprisonment. He soaped his body and hair, chafing away bits of dried blood and grime until they disappeared down the drain along with his reason and sanity.

No hell could match this nightmare, he amended his earlier thought. For weeks, perhaps months, he'd sat in that windowless cell, floundering amid the mire of questions to which there were no answers. Now he might find some, and Hugh wasn't sure he wanted them at all.

How long Hugh stood there in the shower, deliberating thinking of nothing, he had no idea. It wasn't until the water grew cold that he turned the handle to stop the flow. Drying off with the toweling Sorcha had left him, he focused only on the soft cloth and the foggy steam of the bath chamber until there was nothing left for him but to open the door and face the strange world that waited.

He set a hand on the doorknob then pulled it away, fisting his hand. What cowardice was this? He who had faced foes armed with deadly blades, frightened by the unknown? Where was his vaunted bravery now?

A humorless laugh broke the silence of the room, and Hugh doggedly gripped the doorknob once again and opened the door to a cold rush of air.

5

His savior did not notice him as he stood at the bottom of the stairs leading to her great room, such as it was. Though her home had two stories, he was surprised that it consisted of only two bedchambers, the bathing chamber, and this single space that housed not only her parlor but her kitchens as well. Though it was not large and was rather stark in comparison, many of the courts of Europe did not sport such extravagances as Sorcha's residence. The bath chamber and privy were extraordinary, the carpet beneath his feet thick and luxurious. The walls were smoothly plastered, with lanterns set into the ceilings that lit with the flick of a switch. His prison had been similarly lit, and though Hugh had contemplated them for weeks, he could not fathom how they worked.

Or how the monitors projected the images caught by the eye. Or how the cars worked.

More than anything, he could not fathom what more might await him beyond these walls. A part of him did not truly want to know, but Sorcha's question troubled him. The truth could not be ignored. Hugh knew nowhere in the world where such things were possible, and the answers—as difficult as they might be to hear—would have to come from her.

It hadn't been difficult to locate Sorcha – he refused to think of her any other way. She sat in a chair, staring into space, apparently oblivious to the constant hum of sound that seemed typical of this place. She was a lovely woman, he thought. He'd noticed so before when she'd come into his prison. Taller than most women he knew, she was willowy with bright auburn hair and large eyes so blue that they were almost violet. Rimmed in impossibly long, dark lashes and a modest application of kohl, her expressive eyes dominated her lovely, delicate face.

He had to wonder at her age. She looked young in years. Her skin was unlined and luminous as a child's, yet she spoke and moved with a confidence that belied youth. Of course, any man, anywhere knew better than to ask such a question. In any case, with her mannish garb, slouching posture, and unrefined accent, it was clear she was no lady by society's standards, though she'd earned his reluctant respect by standing her ground in the face of his anger. "My thanks, Sorcha," Hugh said to garner her attention.

)O)O)O)O(

Claire started and turned to him, recovering her calm enough to offer casually, "You were in there a long time."

He shifted, wishing for some way to avoid the conversation that he knew was looming before them. "The hot water is gone. My apologies."

She frowned. His brogue was really almost impossible to interpret. It was like nothing she'd ever heard on *Downton*

Abbey or in the movies. His *r*'s rolled; "ing" did not seem to exist in his language at all; his vowels were exaggerated, the *e*'s becoming *eh*'s; multisyllabic words were compacted; and on top of that nearly every word was slurred into the next. With his voice already so deep and gruff, the combination was nearly incomprehensible.

Oddly enough, his words weren't what distracted her the most. It was his hair. Now that it was clean, she realized it wasn't black, as she'd thought, but a rich brown threaded with golden highlights that even the best hairstylist couldn't duplicate. The once stringy, crusty locks now looked soft and curled only a little before they reached his shoulders. Even the full, shaggy beard looked better on him. She could still see nothing of his face but for those blue eyes peering from beneath his thick brows, but Hugh looked infinitely more human, if not exactly civilized.

But still impatient... particularly when she only looked at him blankly.

"I'm sorry. I have a hard time understanding you," Claire explained.

Hugh repeated his words more slowly.

"Oh," she waved a hand. "There will be more later."

"And for the clothing," he added. The shirt was simple and unadorned, snug but soft, and gave freely with his movements. The breeches were much the same, stretching to mold to his calves and thighs as comfortably as a second skin. "Hae I yer husband to thank?"

Her eyes shifted, running down his length with something akin to despondency. "Well, we couldn't have you wearing those dirty clothes again, could we? I think they are beyond hope. We might have to just throw them away. Your necklace is on the counter though."

Unreasonably, Hugh's heart clenched at the thought of losing any of his few personal belongings, but he nodded tightly, turning away to retrieve his medallion. He fingered the cool metal, thinking of the father he had hardly known, whose only legacy now rested worlds apart from where he should be. Slipping the heavy chain over his head, Hugh felt the now familiar anxiety welling up in him once more. What would happen to his home? His people? Hugh needed to return as soon as possible.

If a return was even possible. Ruthlessly pushing the thought aside for a moment longer, he moved deeper into the room, taking time to study the effects in Sorcha's home he hadn't noticed before. He ran his hand along the fine velvety fabric of her cushioned settee, felt the smooth wooden floors beneath his feet. A knitted blanket was thrown over another chair near the fireplace.

Ignoring the horrifying device affixed to the wall above the fireplace, Hugh focused on the items on the mantle. A finely done portrait of a young man was propped there, leaning back against the wall. He was quite stern in appearance, clothed in what was obviously a military uniform of some sort. Other smaller portraits were propped nearby. Hugh picked up one of the man with Sorcha. The soldier was cradling her in his arms, and she was garbed in a white gown. She held a small bouquet of flowers in her hand. Both looked quite happy. Her wedding portrait, perhaps? Regardless, the detail in the paintings was extraordinary.

Other objects crowded the wooden mantle as well. A piece of cloth folded into a triangle. Medals, some framed and others hanging by wide ribbons, were plentiful. There were flat pieces of wood with gold surfaces printed with words Hugh didn't take the time to read except to make out a name.

Captain Matthew Manning.

Her husband. Where was he now? What would he think of his wife bringing a stranger into his home?

"Here." He turned to find her holding a steaming mug out to him.

"What is it?"

"If we're going to do this, you'll have to learn to trust me."

Hugh took a step forward to take the cup, noting that Sorcha stepped away as she extended it even farther. Did she fear him? It was difficult to tell. He'd frightened her at the lab, that much was certain, but their recent exchanges indicated that she was a bold and courageous lass. There were not many women who would dare argue with him when he was angry, and he admired her pluck. He only hoped it would not fail her now. He needed her assistance. At least for the time being. If she became a wilting lily, she would be of no use to him. Watching her, Hugh took a sip from the mug. It was coffee. Not the strongest he'd ever tasted, but it was welcome, nonetheless.

Sorcha sat down once again and leaned toward him with her elbows on her knees, cradling her own cup between her hands. "We need to talk."

He didn't argue. He needed answers as well. All he knew at this point was that she could not send him home again. That, as far as she knew, no one could. He knew nothing else, nothing at all. He didn't even know where he was. "Aye, we do. Tell me, what is this world I am doomed to inhabit? I ken that I am no' dead, so this cannae truly be hell."

However, she merely shook her head at his question, much to his annoyance. "Why don't you tell me how you got here first? Then maybe I can figure it out."

His hand fisted as he gritted his teeth, and her eyes widened in trepidation. Forcing himself to relax, to accept that the answers *would* come, he told her, "I was fighting wi' my clansmen against the Sassenach in a battle that was the gravest of mistakes." He sighed and sat as well as he recalled where he'd been weeks before. The blood. The battle. "Bonny Prince Charlie and his attempt to retake Scotland an' England for his own. He called on the Hielanders to aid him, and my uncle called me home to support him. Though I dinnae necessarily support the prince, I fought for my laird and my clan. Prince Charles called for an attack on the Sassenach though our troops were exhausted from travel and fighting. We had already seen many battles from York to Inverness. No one wanted the fight, ye ken? Even the French envoy begged the Prince on his knees not to continue. But the Prince was determined. He wouldnae even wi'draw to Inverness or take the higher ground at the river Nairn. 'Twas over almost before it was begun."

"Where was this battle?"

"On the Drumoisse Muir outside Culloden," he told her. "It dinnae last long but 'twas the bloodiest battle I'd ever seen. We were called to retreat but I was in the heat of battle, in pursuit of my enemy. I was running after him when the ground opened up before us, swallowing us whole."

XOXOXOX

"Culloden? The Battle of Culloden?" Claire asked, trying to place the vaguely familiar term in history. It sounded like something from *Braveheart*, and Hugh looked decidedly like the Scots portrayed in the movie, so it must have been in the Middle Ages somewhere, right? Shaking her head at her own ignorance, she thought about firing up her laptop and Googling for information.

"Ye've a name for it?"

"Yes." She nodded. "What year was that?"

"The year of our Lord seventeen hundred and forty-six," he answered. "So, yer turn, lass. Where am I now?"

Claire met his bright blue eyes. There was as much dread in them for her answer as she felt at being the one to deliver the bad news, which was why she'd been delaying the moment as long as she could even though she knew that her reluctance vexed him. "You are in the year two thousand and thirteen."

※※※※※

Hugh knew he was staring at her dumbly but he could not form any reasonable thought or response to her revelation. He'd known he was in a different world. Whatever witchcraft had torn him from his home had transported him far away—he'd known that. But, even with all the strange things he'd seen, for some reason he'd considered only distance. He'd never considered time until she'd asked him the year.

Two thousand and thirteen. More than 250 years into his future. He couldn't release the notion from his mind, and for several minutes he stood immobile, struggling with the knowledge and its implications. His family and his clan were all long gone. Nothing but dust in the sands of time. He felt numbed by the realization that he was alone. Alone in an alien land with no one but this single lass as his ally. "Am I even in Scotland?" he thought to ask.

"No," she told him with evident sympathy.

Reluctantly, his lips formed the question he was oddly the most afraid to ask. "Does it still exist?"

"Yes," she answered, then as if she could read his relief went on to reassure him, "Yes, yes, oh God, yes! I'm sorry. I didn't think."

Hugh felt the feeling return to his limbs. If nothing else, his homeland still existed. Rosebraugh, his home, was still out there somewhere. Perhaps, if he could find that then some sense might return to his existence. "Then I should like to go there," he said. "If I cannae hae my family and my life, I can at least have my homeland. Take me there."

"I can't just take you there, Hugh," she sighed. She crossed the room and waved him over to a large globe in the corner. "Never thought I'd use this tacky thing for anything useful," she muttered. It looked like other globes Hugh had seen before until she lifted the northern hemisphere, pointing to the glasses and bottles inside. "Matt's mother got this for us. Classy, huh? Finally, I can get some use out of it."

She bent over and pointed at the side, motioning to him to join her. "Humor me. This thing doesn't rotate. This is England and there's Scotland." She pointed out the easily recognizable landforms before straightening. "We are over here." She pointed to the top of the globe and across the ocean from the British Isles.

"Yer a colonist?" he asked in surprise as he recognized the general shape of the continent.

"American now," she corrected. "Our country is America, but I'm glad to know you've heard of us."

Hugh huffed with disgust. Did she truly think him so ignorant? Naturally, he'd heard of the colonies. He'd even once thought to travel there, to explore the wilderness. He turned his eyes about the room, seeing the many things there that he did not recognize. He recalled her "car, " the roads, and the prison where he'd been held. This was what the colonies had become. What perhaps even his beloved Scotland had become. Shaking away a tremor of trepidation—he refused to call it what he knew it really was—he fingered the globe instead, taking in the breadth of the nation marked in script as the United States of America. "Ye gained independence?"

"Yes, in 1776 or thereabout."

Hugh nodded, remembering the articles he'd read on the dissatisfaction some colonists had felt over the English rule and extrapolating them out over three decades past his time. It seemed few of England's subjects appreciated being ruled by English law and monarchs. "Did Scotland win its freedom as well?"

Sorcha frowned but remained silent and he felt some irritation that she wasn't providing him the answers he needed. "Do ye ken nothing of the world's history, lass?"

"About as much as you know about the future!" she retorted, pinching the bridge of her nose between her fingers. "Give me a minute, all right? I'm sure you're a regular Einstein. Geez!"

Hugh could feel the sarcasm in her words but he failed to grasp her innuendo. He would again have to ask for a reference, but in that moment he refused to give her the satisfaction.

At length, she dropped her hand and offered, "To answer your question, no, I don't think so."

"*Och* and how is that an answer at all?"

Sorcha scowled at him again. "Scotland is a part of Great Britain, so, no, I wouldn't think that Scotland is 'free' of England."

"Great Britain?"

"If you give me five minutes, I'll Google the whole history of it for you."

"Google?"

She rolled her eyes, clearly irritated now as well. "Listen, if we're going to get along, I think we both need to practice a little patience here. Obviously I've never met a time-traveler before, so please allow me some leeway when I say things you don't understand. Also, I am not a history teacher. The finer nuances of how Great Britain became so great were not a part of my education but I can and will find the answers you need. I will also try to explain things more clearly, okay? And first off, let me be as clear as possible in pointing out that America is way over here." She stabbed a finger down at the far western end of the North American continent. "There are a few thousand miles and an ocean between us and Scotland."

The number was a daunting one, Hugh had to admit as the chill of despair once again sent its icy fingers down his spine. But what was a journey of several months' time when his home—or as close as was available—awaited him at the end? "So?"

"What do you mean 'so'?" she asked in exasperation. "We can't just drive there."

It was Hugh's turn to feel some annoyance. Did she truly think him so dull that he couldn't comprehend that her vehicle could not cross over water? "We shall simply charter a ship for the next voyage."

"Charter a ship?" she repeated mockingly, setting his teeth on edge. "Take a voyage across international waters? Not after 9/11."

Hugh shook his head angrily, refusing to get lured into asking once again what Sorcha was talking about. "Perhaps ye should stop talking to me as if I am a simple-minded fool, lass, and explain the problem 'fore I lose my temper."

"Perhaps you should stop acting like an arrogant

barbarian before I call the police and turn you in!" she shot back with flames in her vivid eyes. The Scot had a propensity to thunder and roar, that fierce scowl clearly meant to subdue. She didn't know who was more surprised by her lack of intimidation—him or her.

A loud knock shook the door and echoed through the room, and they both froze, staring across the room at the door. "Mrs. Manning?" The pounding sounded again.

6

Claire met Hugh's wide eyes, her heart suddenly pounding with more fear than this Scot had yet to inspire. He might have showered, put on clean clothes, and much improved his smell, but he still looked savage and foreign in her living room. Those who were looking for him would know who he was in a heartbeat, and the thought chased through her mind that maybe she should just let them find him. Her conscience clashed with her good sense, winning out in the end. "Damn! You need to hide," she whispered.

"I willnae cower like some..."

"*Sh!*"

"Mrs. Manning?" a voice called insistently as the knocking continued.

"Just a minute, please," she called out lightly while glaring at Hugh and jerking her head toward the stairs. The obstinate man just crossed his beefy arms over his chest and glowered right back. "Oh for Pete's sake," Claire hissed, bodily pushing him toward the stairs. "Get up there. Get in

55

the closet and don't say a word."

"How do I know ye'll not …"

"You'll just have to trust me." She half pushed, half led him up the stairs and into her closet, quietly closing the door. Heart pounding, she raced back to the living room, hoping Hugh would remain hidden.

Taking a deep breath, she snatched up her phone on the way to the door and held it to her ear. Plastering on a smile, she opened the door and held up a finger with an exaggerated roll of her eyes. "I know I need to find a nice man, Mom, but can we talk about this later? There's someone here. Okay. Okay. I love you, too."

Claire lowered the phone and shook her head. "Sorry about that. Mothers, you know? Hey, you're Bryce, right? Bryce Muldoon?"

The words emerged cheerfully, and she was thankful for that because her insides were already twisting with fear. She recognized Muldoon right away, a security officer from the lab. The guards were always a step apart from the rest of the lab's employees. They didn't smile, gossip, or socialize. No one brought a cake in for their birthdays. How had they found her so quickly? Had someone seen them after all?

"Yes, ma'am. And this is Special Agent Phil Jameson with the NSA."

Claire was immediately able to assimilate and translate that particular acronym. "The National Security Agency?" she asked with wide eyes. The owlish expression was no act. She was truly surprised to have a federal agent standing at her door.

"Yes, ma'am," Muldoon answered. "Agent Jameson is the NSA liaison to INSCOM."

Agent Jameson added, "We've been called in regarding

the security breach at the lab today."

Fear snaked a path all the way down to her toes, and Claire was hard pressed to control the shudder that followed it. They'd called the Feds in? Already? "Wow," she breathed. "That was fast."

Bryce Muldoon apparently agreed with her. "I told Dr. Holmes that we could handle this internally," he said, referring to the director of the entire lab, "but it seems that there was some disagreement on that."

"It really must have been a big deal then. What happened? I heard the alarms and just figured it was a drill or something." She shouldered the doorjamb as casually as she could, then straightened again. "How rude of me. Did you guys want to come in? Can I get you something? Coffee, maybe?"

"No, no," Muldoon began, but Jameson boldly stepped inside and she studied him as he passed. Beyond the stereotypical dark suit, the agent was tall and lean. He was about forty with a receding hairline and deep furrows in his cheeks and brow that told her he didn't find much humor in life.

He probably wouldn't find any in this either.

"We'd like to ask you some questions, Mrs. Manning."

Claire felt as if she were going to be ill but plowed on. "Sure, come on in! But what can I do?"

"You were present today when the alarm was sounded?"

"Yes. Well, not in the offices. I was in the parking lot."

"Why did you leave the office early today?" Jameson asked.

"I wasn't feeling well," she answered honestly. "I cleared it with my supervisor before I left. You can ask Dr. Crandel if you like."

The agent sniffed in such a way that Claire had to assume they already had.

"Did you see anything unusual as you left?"

"No. I heard the alarm but, like I said, I thought it was just a fire drill or something."

Muldoon shrugged at the intelligence agent in what was clearly an "I told you so" gesture. Unfortunately the agent was not half so trusting in nature. Jameson drifted about the room, touching and lifting her things as he went. Though Hugh had done the same, the agent's intrusion delivered a sense of personal violation she'd never experienced. He wandered toward the stairs and Claire held her breath, but it was quickly evident that the agent was more idly observing her townhouse than executing a thorough search. Still, he lifted the Army sweatshirt she'd brought down for Hugh off the end of the staircase bannister and held it out by the shoulders curiously, making her breath catch. He carried the sweatshirt to the mantle and tapped on one of the framed photos. "Mrs. Manning, your personnel file says that your husband was in the Army, killed by an IED in Afghanistan."

Claire's lips tightened at the mention of her husband's death. "Yes, he was."

"How long ago was that?"

"Three years ago," she said tightly.

"Yet you still have his clothes out."

"You don't know women very well, do you?" she asked, countering his question with one of her own as she snatched the sweatshirt away from him.

"Do *you* wear them?"

She bristled at the question even as she hugged the shirt against her. "Is everyone being asked rude questions this afternoon or am I just the lucky one?"

"Sorry, Mrs. Manning," Muldoon cut in apologetically. "All the employees are being questioned. It's not just you."

"Well, we'll have to compare notes tomorrow then, won't we?"

"The lab is closing down until this issue is resolved," Muldoon told her. "You should be getting a call from Dr. Crandel this evening."

"An unexpected vacation. How wonderful," she said without enthusiasm. "Though it won't do much for the company's bottom line. Is that it, then?"

"No," Agent Jameson said, cutting off what might have been Muldoon's more affirmative answer. "I find it curious—given the way your husband died—that an up and coming engineer like yourself would choose to leave a promising career in materials engineering—saving the world, so to speak—to work in weapons development. Mark-Davis is the veritable antithesis of EnviroCom."

"You think I have a grudge against Mark-Davis and planted a bomb or something this afternoon to shut them down?" she snapped, resenting the agent's prodding into her life more and more with each passing moment.

"Did you?"

"Not that it's any of your business," Claire replied, her voice trembling now not in fear but in sick rage, "but I came to Mark-Davis because I thought that perhaps it might be a bit cleaner for widows in the future to have their husbands come back to them in one bag rather than in pieces. Now are we done here?"

The agent's eyes narrowed as he studied her, his expression carefully blank. "We are ... for now. But Mrs. Manning, be warned. We will be watching you."

"As we will all the staff," Muldoon put in.

"For what? You still haven't even said what happened."

"Some property of the lab was … stolen," Jameson said, watching her carefully. "Given the instability and potential danger of the item, our national security is at stake and the safety of the general public is at risk. We could offer protection and immunity to anyone who was coerced or forced into assisting in the robbery."

Claire glared at him stonily.

"However," he went on, "anyone who had a hand in the theft or aided and abetted anyone who did would be in violation of numerous federal laws and would be subject to the harshest punishment our government has to offer to those who threaten our country."

There had been enough news coverage over the years for Claire to know what he was saying. He was speaking of terrorists and federal indictments. Indecision lapped at the edges of her resolve but in the end she was too angry with Jameson to offer anything more than a shrug. "Well, I didn't take anything, so I have nothing to worry over, do I?"

"We'll be back if we have any more questions for you." Agent Jameson took a step toward the door before he turned back. "I would wager that I *will* have more questions."

7

Claire closed the door and leaned back against it, releasing a trembling breath as the burning fear that anger had pushed to the side rekindled within her. Closing her eyes, she tilted her head back and banged it softly against the door with a *thud*. What was she thinking? She'd just been given an out from prosecution and she hadn't taken it. All she'd had to do was point up the stairs and Hugh Urquhart and all his troubles, all of his cantankerous attitude, would've been swept out of her door. But her dislike of the agent had overridden her more manageable irritation with the lab's *stolen property* and she hadn't been able to do it. She hadn't wanted to give Phil Jameson the satisfaction of finding what he was looking for.

It had been the right choice, but eventually she knew she'd end up paying the price. This wasn't like freeing a dog destined to be put down from the pound. Evidently, this was a federal offense. She could go to prison. Or worse.

But what if she didn't help Hugh? What would happen

to *him*? His fate could be much worse than hers potentially was. He might be a massive, arrogant, ignorant bully but he was still a human being. Sighing, she opened her eyes to find the big Scot contemplating her solemnly from across the room. There were questions in his eyes that she didn't have the answers to.

"Ye dinnae tell them…"

"Yeah, yeah," she scoffed. "I've heard I have a soft heart."

"Sorcha…"

"We'll need to get out of here before they come back," Claire cut him off, pushing away from the door. Her mind was already spinning, thinking of what they could do. Where they could go. Clearly, Jameson hadn't believed her at all. Either that or he was naturally suspicious. Either way, she knew he'd be back, and next time a search of her townhouse wasn't something she'd have an option about.

She rushed up the stairs into her bedroom and to the closet, pulling down her biggest suitcase. Then she rejected it for a smaller version. "We can't take much. They'll know we're on the run for sure."

"Sorcha…"

"Cash! Damn, we'll need cash. The Feds can track you anywhere now with a credit card. I have some, but it won't last for long." Claire went to her dresser and opened the top drawer. She pulled a small box out from under her socks, grabbing some underwear and bras as well and throwing them into the bag before slamming that drawer shut and opening the small box to count the cash inside. "I can't go to my parents. If those guys notice I'm gone and connect the dots, that will be the first place they look. We need somewhere unconnected."

"Sorcha." Hugh's huge paw covered her hand and she looked up at him with wide eyes. She was panting, blood pumping with renewed fear and adrenaline.

"What?"

"This isnae yer fight."

"Really?" She raised a mocking brow, finding solace from the fear in the comforting arms of sarcasm. "You think you can go out there into the great wide open by yourself and come out a winner here? Do you have any idea what they will do to you if they catch you?"

He just shrugged as if it were of little matter. "More of what they've already done, I would wager."

"Wrong!" she shot back, infuriated by his nonchalant attitude. "If you go out there and more people find out what happened and where you're from, they won't be able to stick you back in that hole and pretend nothing's wrong! They're going to come after you with guns blazing, and after that—if you aren't dead by then—they're going to drag you back to the lab and make a science experiment out of you. They'll slice and dice you without mercy because you aren't a person to them. You're a *thing* to them. A mistake. And they'll have to cover it up. After that it'll get really bad."

"Are ye always so optimistic?"

"Always," she snapped. "Can't you tell from my charming, upbeat personality?"

"Sorcha, look at me."

"My name isn't Sorcha," she screeched.

Hugh only raised a brow and took her hands in his. He looked down at her, forcing her to meet his compelling gaze. "Ye're frightened. I ken that. I hae nae wish to burden you wi' my presence or the consequences of my escape."

"Which I'm already an accessory to," she added, but

Hugh only shook his head and brushed a tear Claire hadn't even noticed away from her cheek. As if his touch held a magical balm, her panic ebbed and her breath slowed, though her heart was still racing. "Forget it. There's no backing out now. I just need to figure out what to do about you."

"Yer a brave lass to be sure," he said softly, "but this isnae yer burden to bear. This is my war to be fought…and won."

Unconsciously, Claire tilted her head against his hand, feeling the rough texture of his palm against her cheek. The warmth of his skin against hers. He was alive. So very alive. She wanted him to stay that way. Call it pity. Call it a humanitarian effort to right a moral wrong. She knew that she couldn't just let Hugh Urquhart walk out that door and face the unknown dangers that awaited him in her time. The logical side of her knew he wouldn't last a minute out there. The dangers of this time were almost as bad as what awaited at the lab for a man so out of his element.

Out of his time.

Finally, she awed over what *science* had done. Dr. Fielding had somehow created a time machine. The ramifications were huge. There was no telling how the ability to travel through time and space might change the world as she knew it. It was a power that might be used for the benefit of all mankind. However, given the history of that selfsame mankind, Claire knew that it was more likely to be used for less than benevolent reasons. Business and national governments didn't normally have great track records when it came to altruism.

Releasing a deep breath, she smiled tightly up at Hugh. Her voice calmed. "I must say you're taking all of this incredibly well. Far better than I am."

"'Tis a surprise to ye, while I've had time to get used to it," he said. "I hae been in that prison for weeks, mayhap months, wi' time aplenty to consider the horror of what awaited me. I ken that it is a wee bit worse than I imagined, but I can make my own way now. I can make my own way now."

Claire shook her head. "No, Hugh. I'm afraid you're stuck with me ... for now, anyway."

Still Hugh did not relent. "It isnae a burden for a lady to bear."

Claire's brows shot up. How utterly primeval he was! "Are you saying that I shouldn't help you because I'm a woman or that you think I can't at all because I'm a woman?"

Looking puzzled, he grimaced at her tone. "The art of strategy and combat is historically a man's domain."

There wasn't much of a feminist in Claire, but his words were enough to rouse what little there was. "Well, I think now I have to save you just to prove you wrong. I know you don't want to hear this, but you wouldn't last a day out there on your own."

Hugh visibly stiffened, and she was quick to put a Band-Aid on his male pride by adding, "No, that is not a challenge. It is a simple truth and one you'll just have to accept. You have no money, no mode of transportation ... no clothes! You could walk through the NSA's front door without even knowing it. You need help, and I'm willing to give it to you."

"I dinnae need yer charity," he ground out stiffly, prompting a wave of impatience to wash over Claire, keying her up all over again.

What was it about him that was so irritating? Was it the masculine refusal to acknowledge that he was lacking in some way or the implication that, as a woman, she was? "Really?"

she drawled with a touch of mockery. "'Cause from here it looks like you could. I'm just saying."

The Scot drew away, crossing his arms over his thick chest as he glared down at her.

Claire would have none of his He-Man BS though. She shook out her hands as if the motion could wave off her growing frustration with his archaic ways. "I know, I know! You Tarzan. Me Jane. Well, welcome to the twenty-first century, pal. To America! Land of equal rights for everyone, the ACLU, ERA and Rosie the Riveter!"

"Yer a most bewildering woman."

"Is that a 'yes' then?"

"Aye to what?" he asked. "I dinnae ken a word ye just said."

A surprised huff of what might have been laughter escaped Claire and finally, the tension truly deflated. "How about my friendship then, Hugh? Instead of charity? Could you use some of that?"

The question hung in the air for a moment, and she held her breath until his shoulders dropped a notch. "Friendship is always welcome."

Claire grinned inwardly at his gracious acceptance as she turned back to her packing. "That I will take for a 'yes.'"

He responded with a snort but his blue eyes held a hint of bewilderment. "Why are ye helping me, lass? Is it for naught but the pity ye expressed before? Am I truly so pathetic?"

"No, it's not that," she answered without turning away from the suitcase. Pathetic, she scoffed inwardly. Hugh might inspire many things but pity wasn't truly one of them, so then why was she doing all this? Benevolence? Sympathy for a kindred soul? "I don't know, really. I guess at this point I would just have to call it a random act of kindness."

The momentary silence behind her told Claire that Hugh was either wondering at her response or doubting its veracity, but when he spoke, his gruff voice held a hint of softness and even warmth that it had been absent before. "Whatever yer reasons, tis gratifying to know wi' all that has changed, that human decency has no' entirely disappeared from the earth as I feared."

She jumped at the heat of his hand as it surrounded hers and stared up at him wide-eyed as he lifted it, pressing a gallant kiss against the back of her fingers. "Ye hae my gratitude, Sorcha."

Her mouth opened and closed of its own accord, but no words emerged. Jerking her hand away, she turned back to the packing, resisting the urge to rub away the unexpected and unwelcome tingling his lips had left behind. "So, we need a plan," she said briskly, pushing aside the awkward moment. "I'd ask you if you had any ideas, but ..."

"I'd be nae help," he finished wryly. "I am forced by circumstance to gi' my fate over to ye ..."

"A woman," she interjected.

"Aye, *a woman*," he relented, drawing out the concession. "But only because I ken nothing of this time and this America of yers. Bluidy hell, such ignorance goes against my nature."

She paused and looked at him skeptically. How could he even say such a thing? Look at him, she thought. He'd come to her dirty, mangy, and unkempt. His hair looked as if he hadn't cut it in a year, and given the length of his beard, he hadn't shaved in almost as long. Of course, appearances weren't everything, but how much could a man from the Highlands of Scotland in the eighteenth century really know?

Pushing the thought aside, Claire resumed packing, but her mind was already plotting her strategy for escape. Where to go, she wondered again, more calmly this time. It did need to be somewhere unexpected, somewhere unrelated to her. If even a portion of what was portrayed on TV was true, the Feds were pretty handy at tracking people. They could probably figure out each purchase and call she'd made during the past week with just a few strokes of the keyboard.

So, she'd need more cash and a prepaid cell phone if she planned on calling anyone for help. Which took her back again to what to do and where to go. Barring Scotland, was there someplace Hugh might like? Some place to remind him of home?

Claire paused, remembering a college friend of hers who was from Iceland once telling her that Seattle had a huge population of Icelanders. They had settled there because the terrain and climate were similar to theirs. Mentally she drew a longitudinal line around the Earth, thinking that Seattle lined up pretty evenly with Scotland and that the pictures of Scotland she'd seen over the years were comparable if not exact. Perhaps Hugh would find it comforting as well.

Unfortunately, she'd grown up outside Seattle, and as she had thought before, her parents' house would probably be the first place they would look. Then other family and friends. So she couldn't take Hugh to her brothers'. But …

"My Uncle Robert owns a nice place out on Bainbridge Island … it's an island in Puget Sound," she started to clarify, then shook her head. "Never mind. Point being, it should be a good place to hide out. I've got an open invitation to visit anytime, and this seems like a good one."

"A family member might be the first person contacted by those searching for us," Hugh said, employing her own logic against her.

"Yes, but Uncle Robert isn't really my 'uncle,'" Claire said using her fingers to make air quotes around the word. "He and Aunt Sue are my godparents. Lifelong friends. Maybe too close, but I happen to know that the house isn't titled under Uncle Robert's name but rather some big umbrella corporation of his. I heard him talking about it to Dad years ago. Anyway, it's secluded and fairly disconnected from anyone I can be linked to. I would think it would take them a while to find us there, so it might be our best shot."

"They will nae doubt question my presence."

"I'm hoping they won't be there," she said. "They're retired and travel a lot."

"I shall concede to yer greater knowledge of the possibilities."

"Why, thank you!" She cast an amused glance at him over her shoulder as she went into the bathroom to retrieve some toiletries. "It'll be getting there without being noticed that's going to be tricky."

"Getting there?" he asked, his voice carrying easily between the rooms. "Is this Seattle not local?"

"No, it's a couple hundred miles from here."

A pause. "How are we to travel there?"

"We'll drive there. It's only about four and a half hours away," she told him as she toyed with her toothbrush thoughtfully before dropping it back in the holder. Missing toothbrushes and toothpaste would be an easy giveaway that she'd packed up and gone. It would be easy enough to buy another along the way. And one for Hugh as well.

Lifting her head, Claire realized that Hugh had fallen silent, and for a moment she worried that he'd snuck away while her back was turned, determined to make his own way after all. Rushing to the doorway, she breathed a sigh of relief to find him where she'd left him. However, there was an expression on his face she couldn't quite make out under the beard. "What is it?"

"That *car*," the word rolled roughly in his deep brogue, "'tis a wicked fast thing."

The implication registered and she smiled sympathetically. "Don't like it much, do you?"

"I've never experienced anything moving so quickly," he justified.

She'd been in quite a hurry before. Of course, she'd been panicked and scared…not that she wasn't now. "I'd like to tell you that I could take it slower, but if we ever want to get there, we'll probably have to go even faster."

Hugh's throat worked visibly beneath his heavy beard.

"I'm sure you'll get used to it," she offered kindly.

A strangled sound escaped him and Claire bit back another grin.

8

Agreeing that a hasty departure might be noticed straight away—or perhaps Hugh was delaying the inevitable—they decided to wait until the next day to depart. Claire thought that surely if her house was being watched, the lack of activity within would lull Jameson's suspicions. Tomorrow she could leave, presumably under the auspices of making the most of her unexpected 'vacation.'

But was she even being watched, she wondered? Special Agent Jameson had seemed suspicious, but that might only have been his normal condition. She chewed on her lip as she paced restlessly and peeked out through the blinds, searching the streets for unmarked cargo vans.

Looking out rather than watching her back. Was it strange that she was more wary of Jameson than she was of her unexpected guest?

"And this?"

"That's the thermostat," she said, glancing over her shoulder. The afternoon had progressed smoothly with

71

mutual patience becoming their new unspoken standard after another brief but hot debate over the insanity of assaulting Dr. Fielding in his home and forcing the scientist to explain the *hows* and *whys* of Hugh's presence in the twenty-first century. Claire could understand the Scotsman's need for answers—she was curious herself—but was certain attacking the responsible party would only shorten rather than prolong Hugh's freedom. "It adjusts the temperature in here and automatically turns on either the heat or the air…the cooling system…to keep a constant temperature."

Hugh nodded with some appreciation and continued his examination of the room. Having gotten over his aversion to asking questions, he'd been filling the time with questions about nearly every object in her home while she divided her time between pacing and working the bloodstains out of his kilt and shirt. The thought of losing his clothing had visibly upset the Scot, and since she had time on her hands, she was determined to give her guest something to smile about.

But he hadn't as yet.

The questioning had begun reluctantly, as if he was loathe to ask anything more of her, but he'd gained momentum as the hours passed, though he'd quickly discontinued questions regarding how things worked when the engineer in her had given him a highly technical explanation of the ignition switch on the gas fireplace. He'd walked around each room, picking up or pointing to any unfamiliar object while she explained its purpose, from the water heater to the thermostat. Light bulbs intrigued him, and the automatic gas fireplace fascinated him so much that he spent almost five minutes flipping the switch to start and stop the flames.

He bounced on her couch and bed, complimenting the

comfort of both.

"What happened after you fell through the hole that brought you here?" she suddenly thought to ask as Hugh began to explore the kitchen.

"The man I was chasing died soon after we arrived. There was a woman there who argued for my freedom but then… *Och*, I cannae recall it clearly. All I ken is that I was taken into custody wi' nae explanation. They confiscated my jacket, belt, and sporran…and obviously my weapons," he told her and held up a whisk.

"It's to whip things like eggs," she told him. "Didn't you ask Dr. Fielding what had happened?"

"Naturally," he said, then scowled. "However, in retrospect, amid the confusion and disorientation, I might have represented myself as rather threatening."

Claire could clearly picture a bloody and heavily armed Hugh grabbing the much smaller Fielding by the throat, trying to shake the truth from him. "So they told you nothing?"

"Nothing whatsoever," he confirmed. "I couldnae communicate wi' the Indian… I hae to say, I dinnae imagine that he is what a man from India might look like."

"Oh, that. I should have been more PC and said Native American."

"*Ah*, the red savage." He nodded with sudden understanding. "I should hae known. I have seen some drawings done when a group of them were brought to London long ago, but this one was quite beyond any resemblance to the others. This?"

"It's a can opener." Claire moved into the kitchen to demonstrate the tool, giving Hugh a chance to repeat the process when she finished. "What did the hole look like? The one you fell through?"

"In truth, it happened so quickly I can hardly recall," he said, employing the opener on another can. "I tried to jink aboot it but was too late. Is there truly nae way to discover how I traveled here?"

"There might be a way," she said, voicing an idea she'd been toying with since their argument earlier about pressing Fielding for more information. "My brother is a bit of a hacker…he has some talent prying into things people like to keep secret. He might be able to find out what Dr. Fielding was working on. I don't know what good it would do to know, though. I know it's hard to hear, Hugh, but I can't even begin to promise that I can find a way to get you back home."

A shadow of sadness dimmed his features at her softly spoken words. "Aye, Sorcha, I ken what ye're saying. Still, I should like to know if only for my own edification."

Edification? Claire studied her unexpected guest curiously. He was so full of startling contrasts that she didn't know what to think of him. Savage yet gentle. Ignorant yet inquisitive. Unintelligible yet eloquent. She could see that beneath his analytical exterior Hugh was more deeply troubled by his current circumstances than he cared to let on. How could he not be? God only knew how she would react in similar circumstances. She supposed that she was lucky he was speaking at all and not still hiding in the closet, refusing to face reality.

Of course, Hugh—Highland warrior that he was—would never hide. His reaction to her offers of help told her that he was a proud man. He would face his fears head-on, and Claire found that she had to admire his courage.

On the other hand, what she perceived as courage might

have been nothing more a state of denial over the whole thing. He'd asked questions aplenty but strangely had not asked any further questions to test her knowledge of world history. Uncertain what emotions might be holding him back, she'd so far refrained from bringing up the subject herself, sure that he would ask when he was ready.

"What are our plans once we leave here?"

"Get you to safety."

"And then?"

"I haven't thought that far," Claire admitted. "Out of the country, at least. Out of reach. Do you have any thoughts?"

Hugh shook his head. "None beyond returning to my homeland as yet."

"Do you have family?"

He stiffened at the question. On the few previous occasions she had questioned his personal history, he'd merely held up another item for her to identify. This time, he only looked over her head at the mantel. "I overheard that agent say that yer husband had been killed. Was he a soldier?"

Claire looked at the array of photos as well, at Matt's smiling face. Tit for tat. Her prying questions answered with the same. Well, that was one way to shut her up, wasn't it? "I'm getting hungry. How about you?"

Taking over the kitchen, she cooked a simple dinner of fish, rice, and vegetables, demonstrating the gas range and microwave in light cheerful tones as she went along. While the veggies were steaming, she offered to get Hugh a drink. He rejected water briskly with a blink of disbelief but accepted a beer when she offered that instead. God knew she needed a drink as well.

Claire retrieved a bottle from the fridge and showed him how to twist the cap off. Hugh lifted it to his lips and took a drink but lowered it quickly with a grimace. "What?"

"'Tis cold and tastes like water," he explained, setting the bottle aside.

She considered him thoughtfully and went into her pantry to find the remnants of the six-pack of Guinness her dad had left behind the last time her parents had come to visit. Remembering that Guinness didn't twist off, she went through the motions of prying off the cap and watched as Hugh sipped more tentatively. His grimace wasn't nearly as exaggerated, and he took another, longer pull, which she considered a good sign.

She finished cooking and they ate in silence. After discovering that the fish and veggies weren't merely a first course but the only course, Hugh explored the contents of the refrigerator while Claire sipped a fortifying glass of wine and studied him.

That heavy beard still covered most of his face, so it was hard to tell what he actually looked like underneath, but on the surface, he still looked like some hulking backwoods lumberjack. The bloodied kilt was gone, of course, but since Hugh was several sizes larger than her husband had been, the only clothes she'd had that would stretch to fit him had been a pair of Matt's old Army sweatpants and a T-shirt. Matt had been six feet tall and a muscular 195 pounds. Given that his clothes fit him like a second skin hugging his huge body, Claire would wager that the Scot was at least four inches taller and thirty pounds heavier.

Through the thin cotton, every bulging muscle was evident, and Claire could see that there wasn't an ounce of fat on him. While part of her wondered what he did for a living—she imagined a soldier since he said he'd been fighting a war, or perhaps a blacksmith—there was another part of her that wondered if she shouldn't be more concerned for her own personal safety.

A man that size could kill her in an instant, snap her like a twig. That much was patently obvious. His vow to refrain from doing do so notwithstanding, her mother would call her a fool for letting any strange man into her home. Was she in danger? Hugh had insisted that he wouldn't hurt her, but wasn't that what all the best psychopaths said just before snapping their victim's neck?

Plus, what she knew of Scotland's history—and she acknowledged that it wasn't much—portrayed a fairly violent people. Their past was filled with wars and people who painted their faces blue. He might be waiting to murder her in her sleep for all she knew.

But even knowing that, she couldn't find it in herself to be afraid of him. For all that he was a warrior of sorts, she couldn't see him killing in cold blood. Besides, Hugh had already had opportunity aplenty to hurt her. If he'd been planning on killing her, she thought logically, surely he would've done it already.

Still, he was a stranger, and if there was one thing life in the twenty-first century taught a woman it was that she should always be cautious around them. So she watched the Scot, studying him as he rambled on and on of everything he'd seen, and his rough brogue became easier to understand with each passing hour. After a while it became clear that, while Hugh wasn't likely to hide in a closet to avoid conflict, he would rather wallow in mundane conversation or simple silence than speak of his own fears and worries. There was nothing Claire could say to sway him from his more inane dialogue. When she tried his only response was to turn the probing back at her.

Still, she'd seen his expression when he realized that his home was lost to him forever. That had to affect a man, any man. "I know this is the last thing you want to hear again tonight ..."

"Then I beg ye, dinnae say it."

"... but I really think you should talk about your family and what you're feeling about all of this. They say it's good sometimes to just ..."

"Nae more!" Hugh stood abruptly, pulling off the t-shirt in a sweeping motion, and Claire froze in uncertainty, not cowering away but tensing. He was incredibly large, and that massive chest was bulging with muscle and covered in recent scabs and scars. She'd already acknowledged and dismissed the idea that he could kill her without much effort but Claire realized only in that moment that—without expending much energy at all—there were other things a man could do to a woman that were just as bad.

And, in that moment, she was afraid of him as she hadn't been before. Afraid of what he was capable of. She eyed his bared chest warily. "Wh-what are you doing?"

"I've had enough of this natter," he said brusquely, balling the shirt in his meaty fists with a twist and she swallowed back the lump forming in her throat with an audible gulp. "I am going to make use of yer shower once again. Having hot water poured constantly over one's head is far more satisfying than buckets of cold ... or this conversation."

"Oh, okay." Claire released the breath she hadn't even known she was holding, but suddenly the thought of being in the same space with a naked Hugh was more than she had bargained for. "I think while you're doing that I'll just run out to the store and get some more groceries. You've emptied the fridge entirely."

She pulled on her cardigan, aware he paused at the foot of the stairs. Picking up her purse, she fiddled nervously with her keys while he studied her so gravely that she had to wonder what he was thinking. "Is—is there anything in particular you'd like?"

"A heel of bread and crowdie are more than any simple traveler should expect from those who gi' him shelter," Hugh said, his brogue soft now as if he regretted his harsh words. "But perhaps some bannocks to break our fast in the morn would be welcome."

Nodding stiffly, Claire exited into the garage and got into her car. Sitting there in the dark, she thought through her choices for what seemed to be the hundredth time, awash with doubts if not regrets. Doubts that she'd done the right thing, that she was *doing* the right thing. Yet she couldn't think of anything she would have done differently. Perhaps if she hadn't seen him in his prison cell she might feel differently. But ...

With a self-deprecating growl, she pushed Hugh, her doubts, and her fears aside as she drove away. She would not second-guess herself again. She might come to regret it one day when she was either brutally murdered or wallowing in a prison cell, but she wouldn't renege on her promise to help him. Ground rules were all they needed between them. He needed her, not the other way around. Surely he wouldn't risk her aid by doing something stupid.

No. We can leave stupid all to me because surely today I've completely lost my marbles. She was helping a savage, time-traveling Scotsman escape the federal government ... voluntarily. It just didn't get any dumber than that. Though, in truth, she probably had more to fear from the Feds than from Hugh.

9

Not knowing whether to laugh or cry, Claire instead occupied herself by watching her rearview mirror as she drove along, wondering if she were being followed or if her nerves were making her more paranoid than she needed to be.

She went to a nearby Safeway and slowly browsed the personal care aisles first, adding the toiletries they would need to her basket, including a toothbrush, toothpaste, deodorant, and a razor and shaving cream for Hugh and wondering if he would comprehend the function and importance of them. Clearly he enjoyed the shower, so cleanliness itself wasn't an issue, but how much emphasis had been placed on other areas of hygiene in his time?

Recalling some mention in one of her history classes that perfume was often used to cover body odor, she backed up the aisle and added a second stick of deodorant to the cart.

On the way to the grocery area, she Googled *crowdie* and

bannocks on her smart phone and bought the closest interpretation the grocery store had of both, adding some sausage to the cart as well to accompany the buckwheat pancakes she would make as a substitute for the bannocks for breakfast. Unable to think of anything else they would need, she checked out using her debit card to pay and employed their maximum cash back option. After stowing the food in her trunk, she went back into the store, using some of the cash to buy a prepaid cellphone.

Whether she was being clever or not, Claire wasn't certain. Whether it was necessary or not, she wasn't any more confident. Assumptions and spy thrillers aside, she simply had no idea just how much the government could track or discover. Of if they would even bother.

Picturing Agent Jameson's stern face, her brow furrowed again. Yes, there was a man who would bother.

Back in her car, Claire plugged the phone in to power it up and activated it. She wanted to call her parents, friends … anyone to talk about what had happened and perhaps get some advice, but she knew she couldn't do so just yet. A move like that would be just as incriminating as updating her Twitter status with something like *"Rescued a time-traveling Scotsman today and it turns out that it might end up being a federal offense. #CraziestThingIveEverDone."*

Who would believe it besides Jameson?

With a wry grin, she instead dialed another number by heart and waited while it rang.

"Hello?"

"Hey, Uncle Robert!" she said with forced cheer. "It's Claire."

"Well, hey there, sweetheart!" Robert Mitchell responded happily. "I didn't recognize the number."

Claire winced and improvised, "I'm on a temporary phone. Mine sort of died. *Um*, I was wondering if you would mind if I stayed on Bainbridge this week. I have some vacation time and I thought ..."

"We're still down in Florida, you know," he told her. "We'd love to see you but we weren't planning to be back for a couple more weeks."

"I know." She paused. "I just thought I might go there alone ... by myself ... for a little quiet time."

Silence followed the request. "Don't you think you get enough quiet time, sweetheart? You know your parents worry about you. I don't think they'd like it if I encouraged such solitude."

Claire mentally groaned. Yes, she knew how everyone worried for her. They never hesitated to say so, or to try to set her up on blind dates or have one of her brothers bring over a single friend when she visited. God, she loved them all but sometimes their overprotectiveness was hard to bear.

Robert took her silence to mean something entirely different, however. "Unless you weren't planning on going alone?"

Flexing her jaw indecisively, she decided it wouldn't hurt anyone to let that assumption play in her favor. "Do you mind?"

"No, no! Not at all! Not at all! I'm just glad to see you ... well, you know," he said effusively. "Would you like me to have the maid come in for you or would you rather be...well, *alone* alone?"

Heat crept up her cheeks at his innuendo. "I'll be fine alone, Uncle Robert. Thank you so much. Uh, would you please, please not say anything to Dad, though? I wouldn't want him calling or just dropping by at an inopportune moment."

"My lips are sealed," he promised, though Claire had few doubts that he would be telling Aunt Sue the moment they hung up. She could only hope that her hideaway would be a secret one for more than a few days.

After offering her thanks and promising to call again soon, she hung up and headed back to her townhouse, stopping for a Diet Coke Big Gulp at the 7-Eleven, and sipped on it while she filled up her gas tank. Cast in the glow of a street lamp, a policeman sat in his car across the street, a radar gun in his hand as he targeted the oncoming traffic. Thoughtfully she watched him as the pump was running, thinking about how easy it would be to cross over and tell him her tale. Agent Jameson could pick up Hugh at her house without her being there to watch. Just like that, all her troubles would be gone.

No lying to her family, no risk of imprisonment.

No half-naked Scotsman in her house.

And maybe that was at the root of her sudden unease. It wasn't that Hugh was in her house. It was that he'd taken off his shirt and bared that massive chest to her. It wasn't that she was afraid of what he might make her do. It was…

Driving the unwelcome thought away, Claire drove home and parked in the garage once again before gathering up her grocery bags and taking them inside. Half hoping for and half dreading an empty house, she found Hugh on the sofa, thumbing through a fitness magazine. Thankfully, he was fully dressed once more, his long dark hair curling damply around his ears. His eyes followed her from amid his hairy face as she put away the food. Clearly he was expecting some words from her, but Claire was suddenly tired, drained by the emotional toll of the day's roller coaster of emotion.

Yes, there was much to say, much to do, but it would have to wait until she had a good night's sleep behind her. Without a word, she gathered bedding and waved Hugh off the sofa to make him a bed there since her extra bedroom was filled with office equipment. That done, she went to her room, closing the door behind her. Her hand hesitated on the lock only briefly before she twisted it.

It was a pointless gesture. That little lock wouldn't stop him if he wanted to come in, and Claire was certain he wouldn't even try.

So why bother? To keep her in? Changing into her pajamas and washing her face, she climbed into bed, grateful to put the day behind her, but sleep would not come. Roller coaster of emotion? More like a merry-go-round! The heartbreaking pity of the morning. The fear of Hugh grabbing her in the parking lot. The arguments and back to pity and then sympathy before he challenged her once again. Up and down, round and round, again and again.

But oddly thrilling nonetheless. He'd loomed above her, scowling angrily, practically yelling at her and yet she hadn't been afraid. Instead she'd felt alive in those moments. Her heart had pumped wildly while adrenaline had surged through her veins. If she hadn't known better, Claire might have thought she'd enjoyed the confrontation.

Even knowing that caution was the better part of valor,

she had hardly felt any trepidation at all over having a warrior Scot in her living room.

Until Hugh had pulled off that damned shirt.

Of course, now she realized that he'd done it only carelessly. An abrupt escape from her prying questions. Well, it had certainly shut her up, hadn't it? She hadn't known what to say or where to look. As it was, the image of that vast, muscled chest was burned into her mind. Hugh wasn't just a project anymore or a benevolent mission. He was a man.

She rolled onto her side and hugged her pillow against her chest, staring out at the empty expanse of bed next to her. Reaching out, she ran a hand over the cold sheet. As a military wife, she'd spent many nights alone. She was used to it, but that didn't mean she enjoyed the solitude or didn't miss having a big warm body next to her. Claire blinked into the darkness at the thought, one she had never admitted before, even in the dark silence of her thoughts.

Maybe that's all it was. After all, it had been three years since she'd had close contact with an unrelated male, and she'd been taken off guard by a reluctant and unexpected appreciation for Hugh's magnificent physique … and by the shocking urge to reach out and touch him. Those feelings had been reserved for Matt. Only for him and never another.

She'd made her choices to remain alone after his death and was content with them. A little reminder that she was still a young woman who could appreciate a man's body wasn't so bad. It was natural, human even.

But that little reminder left her feeling lonelier than she had in a long while.

As the clock strained toward midnight and sleep

continued to elude her, Claire flung back the covers and crept to her bedroom door. Silently, she opened it and tiptoed to the top of the stairs, peeking into the living room. Hugh's bulky form was outlined on the couch.

Quietly, she inched down the steps and started when a deep voice broke the silence of the night.

"Once again ye dinnae call upon the authorities to come to yer aid."

He was watching her, she saw. His arms were folded behind his head and his eyes glittered in the dark room.

"You're awake."

"As I said, ye make as much noise as a startled stag," he said lightly. "Why do ye no' just rid yerself of me, Sorcha? Why dinnae ye turn me in, as ye threatened before?"

"Did you think I would?" she whispered.

)O(O(O(

Her eyes, though Hugh could not see her expression, were surely filled with uncertainty. An uncertainty he'd felt through the long evening as he awaited her return. Or the arrival of the authorities. "I must confess that the thought did cross my mind."

"Then why didn't you stop me from leaving?"

"'Tis no' my place to do so," he answered simply. There would be many moments in the days to come when his rescuer would have opportunity to rethink her decisions. Stopping her once would not change that. The decision had to be hers.

Sorcha had said that he must trust her in that matter, and oddly enough, he did. He didn't think that she'd the same faith in him, however. Her reaction after dinner when he'd rashly pulled off his shirt to escape her probing questions had spoken volumes. Her silence after her return had been equally troubling.

Pushing aside the blanket covering him, Hugh rose and walked slowly toward her. It was like approaching a young fawn one wished not to startle, for Sorcha stared at him with rounded eyes, tensed to flee. Still, she did not, once again gaining his admiration as she stood her ground, giving him time to study her.

Even with nothing more than a shaft of moonlight upon her, she was a bonny lass of classic beauty with her high cheekbones, straight nose, and smooth jaw. Her lips were full and rosy and her skin creamy smooth as well but her most prominent feature was her eyes. They were wide and so dark that under the delicate arch of her brow they looked almost black now.

They were eyes that expressed every drop of emotion she felt. There had been fear and panic showing in them that day. Curiosity and wonderment as well. Sorcha was brimming with questions about him that Hugh wasn't certain how to answer. And he was curious about her too. Curious as to why she hadn't turned him over to the authorities, why she wanted to help him. Curious why he'd entrusted his future to her, when he had always been the one entrusted.

And curious how, at such a crossroads of his life, he could be distracted for even a moment from his worries to look at Sorcha as a woman and feel such bewitching desire for her.

His eyes drifted down her length, absorbing her shocking night apparel. She was dressed even more immodestly than she had been before. The sweater and blue blouse with the open collar and trousers she'd worn earlier had been so provocative—once his worries had eased sufficiently for him to notice—that he'd been hard put to set the attraction aside. Yet focusing on her allure was far more pleasant than wallowing in his misery. Only constant conversation had kept him from fixating too intently on either one. Now Sorcha wore nothing more than a short, dark purple shift and a pair of short, baggy, plaid breeches without even a robe to cover her. Her shiny auburn hair that had been clipped at her nape earlier now hung loose about her shoulders.

In his time, such a display in a man's presence would be an unspoken invitation, one Hugh wanted to accept. And she was a widow to boot, after all.

Yet even with the entirety of her well-turned ankles exposed, he could sense nothing promiscuous about her nature. Nothing welcoming in her demeanor. Acting on his impulse to take her in his arms would serve only to cut short his welcome ... and would likely earn him a slap to his cheek as well.

"Are ye afraid, Sorcha?"

"Of you?"

"Aye." He held his breath, curious for her answer. He had no desire for her to fear him.

"No," she whispered finally, and Hugh breathed a soft sigh of relief, but she wasn't finished. "Of all the rest, though? Yes. Yes, I am."

"Justifiably so." She rubbed her arms as if she were suddenly chilled. He set his big hands there as well and chafed her arms lightly. He kept the contact light but her body tensed anyway, a shiver shaking her from head to toe. "Sorcha," he whispered, waiting until she lifted her head and met his gaze. "For what ye hae done for me, ye will forever hae my earnest and heartfelt thanks. Ye hae nothing' to fear from me, lass, I promise ye."

"Do you swear?"

"Often and wi' inspiring éclat," he responded solemnly.

Sorcha just shook her head, as she tended to, but Hugh saw humor lighten her eyes if only briefly before she continued, "Still, maybe we should set some ground rules."

"Such as?"

She didn't respond immediately, and he sensed she had a great many rules warring in her mind and was merely trying to prioritize them. The realization sent a shaft of humor through him, and he stifled a smile. She was a prickly thing but a good sport nonetheless.

"No more removing clothing in my presence," she said finally. "And no touching."

"Done." He agreed immediately, dropping his hands. "I promise I willnae touch ye again wi'out yer express permission."

"I told you before, I am offering … my help. Only my help." She stepped back out of his reach. "Get some sleep. We have a long day ahead of us tomorrow."

Hugh felt a reluctant grin tug at the corner of his mouth. She'd certainly put him in his place, but little did she know, for so many reasons, sleep would not be gracing him this night.

"And ye get back to yer warm bed 'fore ye catch a chill."

In her room, Claire leaned against her closed door, rubbing the goose bumps that covered her arms and refusing to acknowledge that they had nothing to do with being cold.

10

The day after the escape

The sofa was empty and the blankets folded in a neat stack when Claire crept down the stairs the following morning. Hugh was nowhere to be seen, but as she descended, muffled grunts and thumps became audible, and crossing the kitchen, she cracked open the door to the garage. There she found him beating on the punching bag she kept hanging from the rafters for her kickboxing as if he were battling an army of men. He hit it again and again, his muscular torso covered with sweat and glistening in the dim light of the overhead lamp.

Her hand tightened on the doorframe as she watched him move. The muscles in his back worked with the effort, and as he circled she could see the huge span of his biceps, the bulge of his pecs…and the stark despondency written on his face.

Pain. Aggravation. Desperation. Claire closed the door

before he saw her. Caveman type that he was, Hugh would probably resent being seen in such an emotional state, and better than many, she understood the need to lash out at something when in a hopeless situation. Venting the frustration and rage he must be feeling for the world at that point seemed natural. She supposed, in the big picture, she should be glad he wasn't venting it on her.

Still… She hesitated only a moment before opening the door again, aware that Hugh had stopped to watch her, his chest heaving. Silently, she went to the back of the garage and dug into a plastic storage bin before turning and holding out an old pair of her husband's boxing gloves. Not the huge ones used professionally, but rather fingerless gloves with heavily padded knuckles and wrist supports. She waited until Hugh pulled them on over his already bruised hands before wrapping the long strap around his wrist and fastening the Velcro.

Patting it down, she gave him a tight smile and a nod. He nodded as well, and she left him alone to thrash his demons, hoping for his sake that he was far more successful than she had ever been in driving them away.

The thump and grunt of his efforts resumed while Claire turned on the news and pulled out her laptop to Google the history of Scotland and Britain in the years before Hugh's departure, hoping to learn enough to answer his questions, should the subject come up again. With time to spare, she also looked up INSCOM, looking into the scope of their reach and finding that they worked hand in hand with both the Army and the NSA in all areas of counterintelligence, electronic warfare, and information warfare, which helped to explain nothing of what their project with Dr. Fielding might be about. The morning news ended with nothing about the situation at Mark-Davis on the local stations, and she decided that the director and INSCOM weren't going to go public with the incident.

No, all the better to do away with the problem quietly when they caught up with Hugh, she decided. No watchful public eye. No muss, no fuss. Just quietly dispose of the problem. Claire could only hope they would be more democratic than that with her after all this was over.

After a long while, silence fell in the garage. Picturing Hugh as she'd been so many times before—forehead resting against the bag, with energy, if not will, exhausted—Claire turned off the TV and took some orange juice out of the fridge. She was holding a glassful when Hugh came in, covered now by a T-shirt that clung to his sweaty body. Wordless, she held it out, and Hugh took it, drinking without hesitation. His eyes widened in surprise but he finished it. His first Florida OJ, no doubt.

"Get a shower," she whispered tightly. "Breakfast will be ready soon."

)()()()(

"Just in time," his hostess said as Hugh came back downstairs dressed in another of her husband's soft shirts and knit breeches. She handed him a plate with two dark brown discs stacked one on the other. "I'm sure they're nothing like your bannocks but I hope they'll do."

"I'm certain they will be delicious," he said seriously, noting that Sorcha still seemed as tense as she had when he'd looked up to find her watching him earlier. Whether it was wariness or her discontent at having him break one of her two simple 'ground rules' by having no shirt on, he was uncertain.

Joining her at one of the high stools on the opposite side

of the freestanding kitchen worktop she'd called an 'island,' he followed her lead, covering the bannock substitutions with butter and syrup, though he usually had his with jam. There were sausage links and more of the orange juice set out as well as coffee. Cutting off a section, Hugh met her solemn amethyst gaze with his as he ate. "Ye dinnae ask why."

Sorcha shook her head but remained silent.

"Because ye dinnae need to." It wasn't a question so much as a confirmation on his part. For whatever reason, unlike the women he was used to, she understood a man's urge to expel his frustration and anger, and had even encouraged it with her silent offering of gloves to protect his knuckles from further injury. He'd seen the understanding in her eyes when she'd come into the garage, had seen the empathy, and would be willing to wager that she'd done the same on more than one occasion, as odd as that might seem. Rarely had he seen a woman driven to violence, at least not the sort that wasn't dispensed justly or unjustly upon the nearest male. It was yet another thing that made Sorcha so unique.

"No, I didn't," was all she said before lowering her eyes to his plate. "How did you know what the punching bag was for?"

"I dinnae ken what it was when we first arrived yesterday, but I saw in yer periodicals an article on boxing," he explained. "There were portraits of the bag in use."

She considered that with a nod and changed the subject. "How are the pancakes?"

Hugh mouthed the foreign word to himself as his gaze returned to his plate as well. "Tasty. Thank ye again for all that ye hae done." The pair of pancakes were consumed within a few more bites, hardly putting a dent in his hunger, but Sorcha surprised him by bringing over another covered plate, raising the lid to reveal a pile of a half dozen more.

Lifting his eyes back to hers, he found the jeweled tones dancing with laughter even if her expression remained as solemn as ever. "After dinner last night, I anticipated that your appetite might be more akin to an elephant's, so…"

The words trailed off with a shrug but that bit of humor brought the color back to her cheeks, until she was once again radiating the life and energy that had seemed barely contained the previous day. Contained until he had subdued that energy with his own idiocy.

Hugh found he didn't want to see that light die in her eyes again. "Elephant?" he scoffed good-naturedly. "My aunt always likened me to a small herd of cattle or a wolf, though everyone knows that the last wolf in Scotland was shot by a Mackintosh in Invernesshire nae more than a decade past." Hugh paused, his humor fading, as did Sorcha's when they both realized what he had said. A wry smile twisted his lips. "A decade, a few centuries. 'Tis all the same now, is that no' true?"

She offered a tight, sympathetic smile. "Time is what we make it, Hugh. Some quantum physicist said that kind of tongue in cheek, but more than anyone, I think it applies to you now." She took her plate to the sink while he continued to eat and rinsed the platter before setting it aside. "I took the opportunity this morning while you were … uh, out exercising to do a little research on the history of Scotland so I could answer your questions better than I did yesterday."

Raising a brow, he did his best to look interested though his stomach knotted with dread when she hesitated. It wasn't a good sign. "Go ahead. Ye can tell me now what I would hae seen wi' my own eyes if I had stayed. We lost the battle, aye?"

"Yes," she told him. "King George stayed on the English throne, but the government was pretty shaken by what had happened. I read on one site that the forces in Scotland made up of Highlanders, who most in England considered a backward people—their words, not mine—had 'an ill-equipped, ill-prepared, and often ill-led army' but that it was one that had won many battles. It seemed to be something of a surprise to them."

"For hundreds of years they underestimated the determination of the Hielanders," Hugh said in answer to her unspoken question. "And then what happened? Go on."

Still, she bit her lip hesitantly before continuing. "The government wanted to punish those responsible for the rebellion. I guess that meant the lairds, because they took away all their power, trying to do away with the clan system. The Highland lairds forfeited their lands and legal rights …"

Hugh straightened at that. "*Bah*, a laird isnae a laird because of his wealth and land! Ye cannae just take the title away and make it so!"

She nodded in agreement. "One historian noted that a laird was something more personal to the people than a title alone, but the government fought pretty hard to make the clans disappear. They passed a law making it so the Highlanders could not carry weapons. They outlawed the broadsword, the playing of the bagpipes, and the wearing of Highland clothes or plaid for everyone except soldiers serving the Crown."

Anger curdled in his belly for his people, for Highlanders like himself who had been suppressed by the Sassenach. Appetite gone, he pushed his plate away. "Dinnae tell me there were nae executions," he said bitterly. "The Sassenach love a good execution."

"There were some," Sorcha admitted hesitantly.

"The Earl of Cairn?" he asked. "Was he one of them?"

"Not that I saw," she answered, and Hugh released a sigh of relief. "On the bright side, forty or fifty years later, most of the restrictions on the suppression of the Scots culture were lifted, giving back the right to wear the kilt and all that. Most of the lairds got their land back, as well."

"Then what?" he asked. "Do the Sassenach repress us still?"

"No, not really. Scotland is its own country," she said, inexplicably twitching the index and middle finger of each hand in the air as she said the word "country." "Scotland and Wales regained some control of their countries about twenty years ago but are still technically a part of the Union. They are part of Great Britain along with England and Ireland. A hundred years after Culloden, Scotland boomed during the Industrial Revolution. There was shipbuilding, mining, I think it said, and they were major exporters of linen. The Queen has a castle at Balmoral. There has even been a prime minister or two from Scotland."

Hugh grunted at that. The advancement of politicians from his land was nothing to brag over. It was heartening to know that his country had prospered over time, though he knew that the years immediately following the revolution would have been the worst of his life if he'd still been there. He didn't know whether to be saddened or cheered that he had missed them.

)O(O(O(

"Are you all right?" Claire asked softly when Hugh continued to wallow in silence. He must be miserable after what she told him. Certainly it was not what he would have liked to hear.

"Aye, Sorcha," he murmured. "I was just thinking about what was lost to us. I wish I could see my home once more."

He looked so homesick that when the idea sprang to her mind, she didn't think twice. "Well, you can!"

"How?" he asked suspiciously. "How might I do so when ye say it is impossible for us to travel from this country?"

"Two words: Google Earth," she answered enthusiastically. "We can just look it up."

"Look it up?" he repeated curiously, but she was already pulling her laptop in front of her. "What is that?"

She explained the basic operation of the computer as her laptop was booting up. Using the simplest terms, she gave him a base description of the Internet and finally answered his questions about Google. "Where is it?"

"Rosebraugh?"

"Yes. How do you spell it?" Hugh spelled out the name while Claire typed it in and hit enter expectantly. Nothing. "Is that a town? It's not coming up."

Hugh glowered suspiciously at the screen. There was a dislike between man and machinery that Claire was certain would take more than a few days to overcome. Of course, a more unnerved time traveler might have beaten the computer with a stick until it lay in bits. Shooting her guest a suspicious glance, she scooted the laptop out of his reach... just in case. "Nae, 'tis a castle."

"You have a castle?" she asked in surprise, eyeing him up and down as if she were trying to see more than she previously had. A castle said something more than blacksmith or soldier. "A castle? An actual castle?"

"I know of none that are less than authentic."

"Hilarious," she said, wrinkling her nose. "So you have a

castle?"

"Rosebraugh. It sits at the easternmost end of the South Sutor Cromarty wi' the Moray Firth on one side and the Cromarty Firth on the other. 'Tis the first place that the sun blesses each morning and the grandest place in all the world," he said with feeling.

"I'm sure you think so," she said not unkindly. "But it's a pretty big world, you know."

"You think me simple, Sorcha?" He shook his head at her reproach. "I hae seen sights to delight the senses, but there is nae place that stirs my soul as Rosebraugh does."

"I wasn't trying to pick a fight," Claire said apologetically at his defensive retort. Who could blame him? If she'd just lost her home, she doubted she would take kindly to anyone's attempt to dismiss her memories of it. In truth, she'd found his words poignantly poetic.

She retyped the word, adding castle to the end but still there was nothing. "Are you sure that's how you spell it? Maybe there's a variation or something?"

Hugh raised a disdainful brow and Claire sighed. "Fine, but it's not coming up that way."

"What do ye mean 'coming up'?"

Claire gestured for him to sit next to her, spent a few minutes explaining the program to him, how it worked, and what she expected it to find. As an example, she typed in Spokane to demonstrate. The image of the planet rotated and zoomed in on the city, making Hugh's eyes widen with surprise. He tensed as if ready to pounce and she shielded her laptop protectively until his posture eased once more.

"This is a map of this town?"

"It's a picture of Spokane," she clarified. "We have machines in outer space that we call satellites that have cameras that can take pictures of us down here."

"Camera?"

"A machine that captures an image to save."

Hugh nodded. "Like the roving eye at the prison?"

He was clever. Claire had to give him that. "Laboratory, but yes, like that."

"Fascinating." He fell into silence for a few moments, clearly thinking of all the implications of what she'd said. Or simply not absorbing them, she wasn't sure. He ran a finger over the monitor as if examining the texture then paused. "Hold. How did the machine get put into the skies above the earth?"

"We sent them there. We shot it up there in a rocket."

"Machines that go into the skies? People?" She nodded, and Hugh started to laugh. For a moment, she wasn't sure he believed her, but then he slapped his knee and barked out a harsh laugh. "I knew it! I told my cousin, Keir, that one day man would travel to the stars, and he believed me no'. 'Tis pleasing to know that I was right aboot that."

His unexpected laughter almost prompted the same in Claire. It was nice to see him happy, if even for a minute. Nice to see the flash of his white teeth against his dark beard as his eyes danced merrily. Under all that hair, she wagered he had a pretty nice smile. "Well, aren't you a regular Nostradamus? I can't wait to hear what else you predicted."

"Many things," he said with a chuckle. "But first, show me my home."

She typed in 'Scotland' and Google Earth zoomed out to planet view and back into the country as a whole.

"Where do I begin?" She tilted the laptop in his direction once more, and Hugh pointed to an inlet of the North Sea in the northern third of Scotland. Claire double-clicked and the image zoomed in.

"All right, here is the Moray Firth and here is the Cromarty Firth." The mouse hovered over each body of water in turn.

"Then here is Cromarty." Hugh pointed to the peninsula between the two. "My home is here, at the point overlooking the sea."

Double-clicking again on the area and zooming in some more, Claire waited for more instruction.

"What are all these different colored areas?" he asked, sidetracked by the image. "It looks much like a quilt my aunt might make."

"Fields," she said, thinking of similar views she'd seen from airplanes. "And here you can see the trees. Over here there are trees along the shore and here is the beach."

"And these?" He pointed.

Clicking on one of the little blue squares, she smiled. "Pictures." Selecting one, Claire pulled up a picture entitled the South Sutor of Cromarty. "Wow, that's beautiful!" She sighed with admiration as the sloping land rose from the sea against a gorgeous sunrise.

"I've seen such a sight most days of my life. Here, then." He pointed to another square. "This one should show my home."

But it didn't, and neither did the half dozen they tried after that. Claire zoomed in farther, trying to find evidence of a building anywhere in the region that Hugh insisted was his home. There was nothing. No buildings, no ruins. "Maybe we're just looking in the wrong place."

"Ye think I dinnae ken where my home is, lass?" he grumbled. "I assure ye, I do. It's gone. Gone the same as my family, wi'out a trace. As if we never were."

He turned away, raking his fingers through his hair with an aggravated groan that might have been the byproduct of a suppressed shout of rage. "Those Sassenach bastards undoubtedly burned it to the ground."

Considering the screen again, she double-clicked again and again until she was zoomed in almost to the ground on the spot where Hugh claimed with such certainty that his castle should sit. Even if it had been destroyed centuries before, surely there would be some indication of a ruin. Even Hadrian's Wall left a mark after hundreds of years. Roman roads were still evident after a thousand. But there was no scar on the land where Hugh's Rosebraugh should have been. Nothing. Not a stone or indention. Was that even possible? "I'm sorry, Hugh. I should have looked first. I just thought…"

"Ye've done nothing wrong, Sorcha." His harsh brogue so thick with emotion that he was once again almost beyond comprehension "I am no' angry wi' ye."

No, he wasn't angry with her.

Only with the entire world, and who could blame him? Claire wished she could somehow comfort him and had even turned to do so when an awful thought struck her and she scrambled for her new cellphone, dialing her brother Danny's number.

"Danny, I need a favor…" she said a little desperately. It hadn't occurred to her the night before. She could always call Danny. He was about as untraceable as an American could get these days … and smart enough to beat even the federal government at their own games. "How do I wipe the search history from my laptop, permanently? So no one could ever find it?"

"Well, Sis," her younger brother drawled. "Here's what

you do. You put it in a car and drive west…"

Claire rolled her eyes at his unsurprising sarcasm. Well, she was going that way anyway, wasn't she?

ANGELINE FORTIN

11

"Cannae ye lower the volume of that noise?"

Claire rolled her eyes. It wasn't the first time he'd asked, but there didn't seem to be anything she'd said or done in the past few hours that could turn the bear he had become back into a rational human being. "Music, Hugh, its called music."

"I've heard music beautiful enough to make angels weep," he said crossly. "That isnae it."

With a soft snort, she bobbed her head from side to side to the drumbeat of White Lion's "Radar Love." She had an entire playlist of songs on her iPod specifically chosen for their ability to shorten a long drive. Queen's "Fat-Bottomed Girls," Train's "50 Ways to Say Goodbye," the Black-Eyed Peas' "The Time (Dirty Bit)"... She'd had some scornful laughs over that one in that past but had always argued the "don't knock it until you've tried it" philosophy. It was the best pick-me-up song when fatigue started to roll in.

The drive between Spokane and Seattle wasn't excessively long, but it was too long to drive in complete silence with a man who had redefined the term *angry Scot*. "A long drive without music to pass the time is hell."

"*Listening* to it is hell."

Ha, Claire thought with an inward smirk, if he didn't like this she couldn't wait to see his expression when Toby Keith's "Red Solo Cup" came on. "Well, that's gratitude for you. You might as well get used to it, Hugh. I'm not about to drive hundreds of miles to the dulcet tones of brooding silence, so there is no escaping it."

"I would be happy enough to escape this car."

She sighed sympathetically. "Aren't you doing any better? Waiting until after noon to leave might have been a mistake. It's given you too long to think about it." They had waited until early afternoon to leave town on the I-90 heading west with Hugh hunkered down in the backseat until she'd felt certain—after watching the rearview mirror more than the road—that they weren't being followed. The retreat in broad daylight had been his idea, and she agreed it was a good one. They had to assume Jameson and his crew would expect their prey to run under cover of darkness. She also hoped Jameson would assume that any assistance given to his "national threat" would be forced, not voluntary. Hopefully they'd be on the lookout for an escape strategy more akin to a kidnapping than to collusion. For those reasons, Claire also ditched her first instinct to take the back roads and minor highways and opted instead for taking the interstate highway all the way to Seattle.

It was a bold move she hoped would be unexpected. Besides, another part of her wanted to get away from Spokane and Phil Jameson as quickly as possible. And she was moving pretty fast, exceeding the posted speed limits until she was cruising at a steady seventy-two miles per hour.

"It *is* wicked fast." Hugh repeated his sentiment from the previous day but she thought his death grip on the door handle might have relaxed a bit as they ate up the miles. "Might ye at least allow me to hear my thoughts and misgivings in silence? I assure ye, they gi' me nae greater pleasure."

There was enough self-deprecating humor in the request for Claire to acquiesce, and she turned the volume down but not off. "Compromise?"

He nodded, deliberately releasing his grip on the armrest and on his lingering resentment. "I suppose it *is* rather fascinating that we will travel in hours a journey that would take days on horseback, even at a steady canter."

She couldn't imagine facing such an ordeal, and told him so, gaining a new appreciation for the pioneers who had once made this trip in covered wagons. Running a hand around her steering wheel, she gave it an appreciative squeeze and sent up a prayer of thanks.

Hugh continued, "Aye, 'tis easy to see the appeal of this mode of transportation, but also I wonder why yer conveyance is so much smaller than many of the others I've seen?"

"Small?" She frowned. It wasn't as if she drove a Bug. Her Toyota Prius was fairly roomy on the inside, and the backseat was large enough to perform its primary function without breaking any kneecaps. "It's just a matter of preference, I suppose, but Goose and I get along fine, don't we Goose?" She patted the dashboard affectionately.

His eyes widened. "Ye named yer car?"

"You name your horse, don't you?"

"Aye, but my horse comes when I call."

"Yes, well, my car talks to me," Claire told him, pointing

to the navigation screen on the dashboard, a device Hugh had so far steadily refused to acknowledge or comment upon, much as he'd ignored the television when she'd watched the news again after lunch.

He didn't break that trend by acknowledging the device now.

"My carriage is much larger and far more comfortable, and many of the other vehicles look quite roomy," he reverted to their prior discussion and pointed out the window at the passing traffic. "This one is too small inside. I should think that one of the larger ones might hae more room for the comfort of a braw man such as myself."

"Well, unfortunately, I didn't buy this one thinking that I would be carting a braw Scottish fugitive across the state. Sorry," she added sarcastically before wincing and offering a more sincere apology for her flippant tone. "I'm sorry. I tend to get a little snarky when I'm stressed. So, tell me then, what would you have me drive?"

)О(О(О(

Hugh considered the road around them, glad to have something more to think about than the bitter revelations regarding his country and his home he'd received that morning. There were many types of cars in the lanes around them. Some small, others large. Some hugging the ground and others perched high off the ground like a fancy phaeton. Finally, he saw one that intrigued him more than the others and he pointed it out to her. "That one. I'd have one of those."

She shook her head with a laugh as he pointed out a huge black Ford F-150 pickup with an extended cab and big twenty-four-inch wheels. "An F-150? Really? Only moments in the twenty-first century and you're already such a guy."

"A guy?"

"Let's just say I shouldn't have been surprised," Claire chuckled. "It is an extremely manly truck after all."

"Truck?"

"That's what we call the vehicles that have that area in the back to load and carry things around," she clarified, naming the generic terms for other types of cars as she pointed them out.

"And the guy?"

"Only that the majority of people who drive those are men. Guys. Men. Pretty much the same thing."

"'Tis more of those colloquialisms ye spoke of?"

"Yes," Claire said. "Just like bloke or chap or whatever you would use."

"Ye used the word to the agents who came looking for me," Hugh told her.

"I did?"

"Ye said, 'ye guys want to come in.' I had thought it a term for a law-enforcement official." He stared out the window for a moment, but she could see the reflection of his sorrowful countenance in the window. "This time is confounding."

Reaching out, Claire squeezed his arm sympathetically before hastily withdrawing her hand. "You'll get used to it. Just give it time."

"I dinnae want to get used to it," he retorted sharply, but like her, regretted snapping the moment the words emerged. "My apologies for my rudeness, Sorcha. While I am prepared to forgi' such a rebuke from ye wi'out malice in return for all that ye hae done for me, I know I should no' bring such grief upon my host."

"A little temper is understandable. I get that you're

scared."

"I am not *scared*," Hugh ground out, clearly offended. "What a horrid word."

)O(O(O(

Claire raised her brows but didn't look away from the road ahead. The word had popped out of her mouth without thought and she wasn't anxious to pick another fight with him. Was it a Scot's thing or a generational thing that prevented Hugh from admitting to any weakness? Trepidation was reasonable and justifiable given the situation he found himself in, and beyond a doubt, he had to be feeling some level of fear. Was it really so bad to say so?

He was a pretty brave guy, and she admired him for it, but she would easily have forgiven him the admission.

"I merely want to go home," he added after a muted minute.

"I know you do." She offered a kind smile.

The silence stretched between them for so long even the lower volume of the speakers seemed to fill the car. "Why Goose?" He broke the quiet at last with his question.

A slight grin lifted the corner of her lips. "It's so when I get turned around or lost I can say 'Talk to me, Goose.' I know you won't understand the reference, but it's from a movie…before you ask, I'd rather show than explain that one."

"I can wait," he said hastily. "Explain to me instead, what is this 9/11 ye mentioned that prevents me from returning to Scotland?"

Claire explained the events of that tragic day in September to him and how the terrorists had hijacked planes—taking a slight detour to explain them as well—before concluding with a brief synopsis of the tougher travel restrictions. "There's just no way you're going anywhere without a passport," she concluded as gently as possible.

"Then we shall just hae to acquire one."

"You can't just 'acquire one,'" she said. "You have to show proof of who you are, citizenship, the whole nine yards."

"Nine yards?"

She bit her lip thoughtfully and shook her head. "I couldn't begin to tell you. The point is, we can't get you one."

He waved a hand dismissively. "Surely ye know someone wi' the right connections."

"I'm sorry I'm not as familiar with the seedy underground of society as you might like me to be," she quipped sardonically but immediately regretted sniping at him once again. The situation was enough to make anyone touchy and she was feeling entirely too prickly. They would both have to work on containing their outbursts if they were to get along. "I apologize for my endless sarcasm. It's a terrible epidemic these days. I know I keep saying it, but just give it some time, Hugh. We'll figure something out."

Silence fell again for a long while before he sighed and said with forced joviality. "Perhaps we might determine where we might find a fair meal. I am famished."

"You ate just an hour ago!"

"Yer pan-cakes this morning were verra good," he assured her, sounding out the word carefully. "And the salad at luncheon as well, but I am a man with a man's appetite. I need greater sustenance than yer puny meals provide."

Torn once again between amusement and irritation—though thankfully the former was growing stronger than the latter—Claire looked at the navigation screen. "There is a town up ahead where we could stop ... but only because I was thinking of doing so anyway," she added quickly, lest he think that she would always capitulate so easily to his demands. "We need to have you blend in better before we hit the city. Right now you might as well have a flashing arrow pointing at you, and the less conspicuous you are, the better chance we'll have of getting by unnoticed."

"What do ye hae in mind?" he asked suspiciously.

"Some better clothes and a haircut and shave."

"Shave?" Hugh stroked his beard protectively. "Is that necessary?"

"Absolutely," she insisted, taking a bit of devilish satisfaction in saying so. "The only men who wear a full beard these days are mountain men, Alabama football players, and eccentric San Francisco Giants baseball players. If you want to blend, it has to go."

For a moment, Claire thought she saw humor dancing in his eyes but then he just shook his head mournfully. "If we must."

Pushing aside the thought he was either hiding something or laughing at her, Claire took an exit into Moses Lake and slowed at the next stoplight, gauging the town's services. It wasn't a populous place, and she knew they weren't going to be able to be choosy. Finally, she pulled into a JCPenney parking lot and turned off the ignition. For a moment, she considered leaving Hugh in the car but knew it would be impossible to guess his size, especially in shoes. His feet were far larger than Matt's reducing him to wearing a pair of flip-flops that had his toes overhanging the edge. "I just hope they don't have security cameras," she muttered as they entered the store.

He looked at her curiously and she clarified. "More roving eyes."

Understanding hit, and to his surprise, he assessed the store's security within moments of their entry and led her around the perimeter of the department store, weaving through the racks until they reached the men's department.

"Remember, we don't have time to be choosy, so just pick something and be quick about it."

But Hugh wasn't to be coerced into a pair of jeans and another t-shirt. "In truth, I'm no' certain I care for yer clothing. 'Tis verra plain and thin. I might well be naked."

Claire looked Hugh up and down at the thought and felt a little shiver race through her. In the tight t-shirt and sweatpants, it wasn't that difficult to picture what he would look like in the nude, and she resented the fact that he had even prompted the imagination. "This coming from a man who had only a kilt and shirt when he arrived. At least your legs aren't bare anymore."

"Nor is my arse," he added. "But that wisnae my norm at all. I would wager I typically wore far more layers than ye, and heavier fabrics as well." He continued to browse the options slowly, fingering the fabrics thoughtfully, complaining about the lack of adornment or embroidery, and blatantly ignoring her pointed looks.

"Please remember, we have limited funds," she said when he finally gathered up a large bundle of clothing to take to the dressing room.

"I will need more of yer clothing if I am to 'blend,'" he reminded.

"We'll have to work on a complete wardrobe later, so seriously, be thrifty."

Claire didn't think there would be much trouble with that after Hugh saw the first price tag. His astonishment at the cost of a dress shirt had been evident. It was a good thing she hadn't taken him to a Macy's instead.

While he tried on the clothes, she held the coat she'd lent him while she gathered some socks and underwear for him, opting for boxers instead of briefs. At least Matt's old wool coat had fit Hugh, so they wouldn't have the added expense of outerwear for chilly evenings.

Claire hugged the coat tightly to her, smoothing it down with a gentle hand. It had hurt to see Hugh in Matt's coat. Matt had bought it long before he met her, before he joined the Army. He'd been bigger before, becoming leaner through his years in the military, but still he hung on to that old coat, wearing it even after it no longer fit him.

Like him, she hadn't been able to let it go either, since his death. As she hadn't been able to let go of a lot of things … and she wasn't thinking only of his clothes. Her past was like that old coat, familiar and comforting, and she didn't want to give it up. She'd never been able to let go of Matt. Of the memory of him, of them together. Everyone told her it was wrong for her to live in the past, to spend her life looking back instead of to the future. But Claire had hung on to it like Matt had hung on to that coat, thinking a new one would never be like the old.

"I'm ready," Hugh said, interrupting her thoughts. "I found a pair of shoes as well. I hae to confess, though some of the clothing in this time seems inferior, the comfort of the footwear is enviable."

"Says the man with the bloody, linen shirt," she muttered as she led him to the nearest register and paid for the clothes with some of her precious cash. He watched the transaction keenly, taking a special interest in the register, but she cut off any potential questions by announcing the store had an in-store salon that took walk-ins.

She led the way to the rear of the building. One of the two stylists present took one look at Hugh and announced that it was time for her break, but the other, male stylist shot Hugh a longer, more appreciative look and waved them in. She explained briefly what she wanted.

"It's a lot of work," the man who introduced himself as William said critically as he eyed Hugh up and down. "And I mean *a lot* of work."

Claire just nodded. Anyone could see that and, in truth, she didn't have the highest hopes for the end result. "Do what you can," she said and turned to Hugh, who was now frowning fiercely at her. "I'm going to gas up and get you some food. I'll be back."

"I guess she's the boss of you, isn't she?" she heard William say as she walked away.

She didn't hear Hugh's response, but seconds later the stylist's merry laughter rang out behind her, leaving her to wonder what witty comeback Hugh had offered.

)O(O(O(

A half an hour later, Claire had shaken off her doldrums and run her errands. She hadn't really needed more gas in her hybrid, but topped it off anyway. Returning to the salon expecting to find Hugh waiting impatiently for her, she was instead met by the sight of the lone stylist sweeping a large pile of dark hair from the floor. Hugh was nowhere to be seen.

"Where is he?" she asked, trying to keep the panic from her voice.

"In the back, changing," he told her with a broad smile. "You're going to love this, honey. He looks *amazing*!"

This last word was drawn out musically and Claire's brows rose in surprise before she offered tentatively, "Well, he couldn't get much worse, could he?"

The stylist made a sound in the back of his throat and his gaze shifted beyond her. "Decide for yourself."

She turned and her breath literally caught. She exhaled a soft sigh but her next attempt to inhale also hitched, her throat tightening around the effort. Sweet baby Jesus, she thought as her eyes drifted downward and back up again.

"I dinnae ken, William," Hugh was saying, "are ye certain I should leave these buttons open?"

He fingered the buttons of the blue striped dress shirt he was wearing over a t-shirt and under a charcoal grey, wool sport coat.

"Yes, yes," the stylist exclaimed, rushing over to fiddle with the buttons, fastening just one near Hugh's waist before smoothing the shirt down over his chest. "Leave the rest open! You look fabulous!"

"Are ye quite certain?"

If William wasn't, Claire was. With the heavy beard gone and his shaggy hair trimmed into a short, fashionable style, Hugh was … stunning. She hadn't been able to see anything but his eyes before, and under that beard, she might have imagined him chubby-cheeked and slack jawed but his now clean-shaven face revealed high cheekbones that turned to sharp planes before meeting his strong square jaw. Under his dark, thick brows, his vivid blue eyes now twinkled merrily as he glanced up to find her staring at him. A wide grin flashed white against his dark skin and…oh, Lord! Were those dimples?

To her everlasting shame, Claire's head swam deliriously and dark spots danced across her vision. She wasn't actually going to swoon at the sight of him, was she?

"How do I look, Sorcha?" he asked innocently, putting a

roguish purr behind his thick brogue.

Fabulous. Glorious. And he knew it, too. In retrospect, his reaction in the car spoke clearly of his expectations, and she felt oddly deceived. Still, as he neared, she swayed toward him as if he had a magnetic pull. "*Ah*, William!" He chuckled. "I told ye she would fall in love wi' me when she saw me thus."

Claire straightened abruptly and gave a careless laugh, still trying to tear her eyes away. "*Ha*! Don't flatter yourself."

Hugh only grinned down at her, flashing that deep, provocative dimple. "'Tis all right. All the lasses do."

What conceit! Claire sniffed and turned away. "Don't worry, Hugh. I've already had love. I've had my moment. It won't happen again."

Hugh just winked and turned to thank the stylist once again, adding, "My secretary will see to yer fee. I shall await ye in the car," he added to her before he left.

She watched him go, noting the tight fit of the jacket across his broad shoulders, remembering how the athletic cut of the shirt hugged the long V of his torso and how the jeans followed the muscular line of his thighs. Her breath left her in a shudder that was echoed by William's soft sigh.

"Yummy, isn't he? I never would've imagined he was so good-looking under all that hair," the stylist said. "And that body!"

Yummy, delicious. Yes, Hugh was that and more. She couldn't remember having ever been so taken aback by the sight of a man. He was perfect. The epitome of the clichéd tall, dark, and handsome. Even Matt ...

Claire bit back the thought but the betrayal in her mind was already flooding her with guilt and anger.

William wasn't finished, though. "You lucky girl, have

you worked for him long?"

"Actually, I've been thinking of giving my notice," she ground out. "How much do I owe you?"

12

Hugh looked at her expectantly when she got into the car. Waiting, she knew, for some comment on his transformation. Well, she wouldn't give him the satisfaction and wasn't in the mood for any of his nonsensical banter. She was too angry with him. Angry that he'd played her so well. Angry that he made her make a comparison between him and her Matthew.

Angry that Hugh looked so damned good.

"Hae ye nothing to say?"

"Secretary?"

He shrugged in that irritating way he had, making Claire grit her teeth even more. "I had to say something to explain why ye took charge, why I dinnae carry any funds on my person."

"If you had asked, I'm sure I could have come up with something better than that. I'm a pretty smart person," she said, shifting Goose into reverse.

"Most women think they are."

"Like most men think they're funny?" she asked snappishly. "I could tell you got a kick out of that."

It took Hugh a few moments to work through her words. "Do ye no' like the way I look?"

It wasn't so much a question as a tease. He was fishing for the compliments that Claire was certain had followed him throughout his life. "You'll do," she said shortly, refusing to give him the satisfaction of something more. "I doubt anyone would recognize you now."

But they would remember him. She was beginning to think that if they wanted to get by unnoticed, shaving off all that hair was the worst thing they could have done. Looking as he did now, any red-blooded woman they crossed paths with would be able to describe him thoroughly, right down to those slashing dimples. *Ugh.* Claire mentally slapped herself.

"I'll do?"

"You look fine," she allowed. "Good, even, and I'm sure you know it. But don't worry that I'll fall in love with you like all the other lasses. You're not my type."

"Yer type?"

"You know, like Matt. My husband, Matthew. You saw his picture. You're, like, his polar opposite." Claire pictured her husband in her mind, clinging to the image. Indeed, Matt was completely different. He'd been blond, god-like. Always laughing. He was nothing like this dark, brooding Scot except that they were both tall and fit. "You might think you're all that, Hugh, but times have changed. William seemed to like you though," she added, hoping to shock him. To regain the upper ground. "The way he was petting you, I think he wanted to take you home and keep you forever."

Hugh shrugged dismissively, denying her the moment. "He was much like any man's valet."

Claire rolled her eyes irritably and shoved a white, fast-food bag at him. "Just eat your food."

If he was disgruntled by her lack of fawning, he didn't show it as he looked in the bag and pulled out a paper-wrapped item. Opening it, he sniffed it tentatively and took a bite, chewing a couple of times with a grimace. "What is this?"

"A hamburger. Eat it."

"It has nae flavor at all. Terrible. Get me something else."

"You do realize that we are supposed to be on the run here, right?" she sniped crossly. "We can't afford to waste time stopping for a sit-down meal. We'll find something later."

"I hunger now."

"Hugh, just stop."

But he wouldn't. Even the near desperation of their situation couldn't stave off his hunger, and finally she pulled into a gas station with a mini mart and parked, commanding him to wait. Moments later, she emerged with an armload of candy bars and chips, dumping them in his lap. "There! Bon appetite."

"What is all this?"

"Food. Junk food," she said sharply as she got them back on the road. "You said you were hungry, so eat."

Hugh picked through the colorful pile, finally settling on the bright orange wrapper of a KitKat bar. He fumbled with the wrapper for a few moments—Claire was inwardly smiling at his efforts, not volunteering the knowledge that the new plastic wrappers could be torn from only one direction—before finally he got it opened.

Picking up the candy bar, he studied it for a moment

before intuitively snapping off one section. Looking over her shoulder before she made a lane change, she caught him taking that first bite. He chewed once and stopped, his eyes wide. He chewed again and once more paused.

Puzzled, Claire frowned. "What is it?"

"'Tis cocoa."

"Yeah? Well, most of that is. What about it?"

Hugh looked down at the pile in his lap. "But 'tis sweet and …" He shook his head, clearly puzzled.

"Of course, it is. It's chocolate." Claire drove for a minute while he took another bit, slowly chewing as if he were savoring each moment. "Okay, give. How is that so different from what you've had?"

"Our chocolate is liquid. We drink it," he said distractedly, his focus remaining on the bar as he broke off another section. "'Tis exceedingly bitter, and though we add cane sugar or honey to it, I ne'er tasted it like this. What is it?"

"A candy bar. A KitKat, specifically. Smooth creamy milk chocolate and crisp wafers," Claire said. "Everything a growing boy needs."

"And this one?" he asked, holding up one of the others.

"A Twix. Cookie covered with caramel and chocolate."

"And this?"

"Almond Joy. My personal favorite," she added. "Coconut, almond, and chocolate."

One by one, she told him what they were, and one by one, Hugh worked his way through the pile. He unabashedly gloried in each bite, savoring each one with greater groans of delight until he was moaning with exaggeration as he bit into a Milky Way.

The amusement bubbled up in Claire until she was

laughing aloud. Her anger gone, she shared in his joy. It was like watching a child experience Christmas for the first time.

"I already hae so much obligation to ye," he teased as he finished off the last of the candy. "But for this I owe ye my greatest debt of gratitude. 'Twas most delicious. Thank ye, Sorcha."

Hugh lifted her hand to his lips and her laughter faded away. His lips pressed lightly to the back of her hand before he turned it, pressing a kiss to her palm. Claire glanced at him, seeing the humor mixed with true sincerity in his blue eyes. He was just trying to be nice, she knew that, but at the same time the feel of his hand against her, the feel of his lips tracing a tingling path across her hand was anything but friendly.

Pulling her hand away from him, she curled her nails into her palm and turned back to the road. "I didn't expect you to eat all of it. All that sugar will probably give you a stomachache," she warned. "I suppose I should have explained that beforehand because…"

"Because I hae no' the intelligence to deduce that for myself?" His jaw tightened, a muscle jumping irritably in his jaw. "Please hold. I fear I cannae tolerate yet another slight upon my intelligence from ye. What hae I done to make ye think me dull and unlearned?"

Claire gaped at him for a moment. "Well, you…I…"

"Ye hae made assumptions," he said tersely. "Ye maun hae some basis for them. Are my countrymen known for their weak minds in this time?"

"No, but…well, Hugh, you have to admit then when you first got here…"

"Ye judged me by my appearance alone then."

She flushed. Hadn't she told herself that she was

stereotyping him even as she was doing it? "In my defense, you weren't exactly the picture of refinement when I met you. The hair, the beard, the kilt. The *blood*," she drew out the word with emphasis. "You looked and kind of acted like a big brutish Neanderthal with rocks in his head." He hadn't really, Claire thought, looking back on the events of the previous day. In fact, other than some flashes of irrational—if somewhat justified—behavior, she thought he'd handled himself fairly well, even to the point of reasoning out some of the same nuances of their situation as she. "So I take it that 1746 wasn't exactly the Middle Ages?"

"Nae at all. Sophistication was a hallmark of my generation. I hae had occasion to join the courts of Germany, France, and Venice," he said haughtily.

"You've been to Venice?" she sighed out enviously. "I would love to go there. Is it as beautiful in person as it is in pictures?"

"Ye've ne'er seen the world for yerself and ye think me the barbarian?"

Shrugging apologetically, Claire tried for some justification. "I know about the Age of Enlightenment in the eighteenth century and all that, but when you talked of war and clans, I guess it was easy to lump you in with the stereotype. To be fair, history might have tilted against you more than is justifiable."

Hugh just shook his head in disgust. "And yet I hae sat amongst and was welcomed by the greatest thinkers in Europe."

"Like Joe the Blacksmith?"

"Yer attempt at humor willnae soften my ire," he responded, staring stonily out the window with his arms crossed over his chest.

"Who, then?"

"I doubt ye would know of them." He leaned against the door with a yawn. "Though one of my friends, Francois-Marie Arouet, did write voraciously about everything. He dabbled in politics and philosophy. He even wrote a few plays, but I doubt any of that flummery stood the test of time. Mayhap ye hae heard of Frederick. He was a king, after all."

"King of what? The hill?"

"Prussia."

"Prussia?" She gaped at him until a horn sounded, recalling her attention to the road ahead of her. "You knew the king of Prussia?"

"I dinnae sleep much last night. I believe I will try to nap now."

Claire knew he was toying with her now. That he was dangling bait before her to lure her curiosity. Well, it had worked. It seemed there was much more to Hugh Urquhart than met the eye. She thought about how he'd avoided answering her questions the previous day, and now wondered at what amazing tales he could have told.

"You can't sleep now! Not with a lead-in like that!" she said. "I have to know, how does a braw Scottish man like yourself become a world traveler?"

"Another time," he denied, closing his eyes.

"That is so not fair," she grumbled as she stared at the road ahead of her, the sun setting against the mountains at the horizon. How had she so completely misjudged Hugh, she wondered? How could she have not, another part of her brain argued? Given the way he'd been dressed, the blood and grime, and his practically unintelligible use of the English language, what other conclusion should she have come to? In her fear, should she have taken the time to ask after his education and experience beforehand? Should she have asked for a resume of his lifetime accomplishments?

Yes, she had jumped to conclusions, but who wouldn't have done the same? Given the events of the past two days, with each moment being more unbelievable and fantastic than the next, she thought that overall she was handling everything fairly well. Really, she was sitting in a car with a man who had been born almost three hundred years ago and she wasn't freaking out at all!

Claire decided that, in the big picture, she deserved a gold star.

A big, shiny, twenty-four-carat-gold star.

13

"Hugh? Hugh?"

He blinked and yawned, looking around in confusion. "Did I sleep?"

"Yes. Sugar coma, I think."

"I willnae ask what that means," he replied, ignoring her grin as he looked around. He was still in the car but they were stopped, packed tightly amidst other conveyances in a structure of some sort. Long lamps on the ceiling overhead lit the space, shedding light on the iron walls and the openings in them, and Hugh could see that night had fallen. Beyond the open windows, there was water shimmering in the moonlight. Were they at sea?

"Where are we?"

"On the ferry," Sorcha answered, gathering her purse and coat. "I thought we could get out and stretch a bit. The ride will be about half an hour."

"Ferry? To where?" he asked confusedly.

"Come on, sleepyhead," she teased. "Shake off the

cobwebs. I told you we were going to an island."

"My apologies. I'm no' my best when I first awaken." He got out of the car. Cool air immediately surrounded him, prickling a refreshing path over his skin and clearing his mind.

"Don't forget your coat," Sorcha said, but he just raised an arrogant brow at the reminder. He'd been born on the fringes of the North Sea. Such a mild chill as this only served to invigorate.

They climbed narrow metal stairs to the large passenger cabin of the vessel. It was bigger than he'd imagined, perhaps four hundred or more feet in length and almost a hundred across. It was easily twice the size of any ship Hugh had ever been aboard. The main cabin was walled in incredible sheets of glass and spanned the entire length of the ferry. People were everywhere. Young, old, tall, short, fat, and thin. Some were dressed more formally and others in jeans like the ones he and Sorcha wore. Many faces seemed unfamiliar to Hugh, hinting at ethnicities and places he had never seen, yet they melded together here. More than that, the crowd was loud, and noticing a door at the far end of the cabin, he suggested they step out onto the deck.

She nodded and followed him out onto the stern deck, where the cool breeze licked at their cheeks. With a sigh, she leaned against the railing and stared down at the wake trailing the ferry.

Hugh, however, could not look down when the sight elsewhere was something quite beyond his experience, perhaps more astonishing than anything he'd seen in this century thus far. A mass of lights lit the shore like a cluster of stars hugging the ground. But, like the stars, many ascended toward the heavens and formed shapes against the night sky.

"What is that?" There was enough awe and curiosity in his voice to draw Sorcha's attention away from the water below.

"That? It's Seattle."

He'd never heard the word before, so it did nothing to fulfill his curiosity. "But what *is* it?"

"A city."

Those huge rectangles were buildings, he realized, lit against the night sky. How could that be? It looked like no city Hugh had ever seen, and he wasn't naïve. He'd seen much of the world and what it had to offer. He'd seen the soaring spires of the greatest castles in Europe, but none of them had reached such heights as this. And the tallest one of all seemed to be held up by nothing more than thin legs. These buildings touched the heavens and were lit with a thousand colorful lights. Blue lights flashing against the sky. Red ones. How?

A tremor snaked its icy chill through his chest.

What a fool he'd been to think that one world was much like next. To think that he was equipped to face what lay before him. To think that he might even do it all alone. It had all seemed so simple in Sorcha's home, with walls blocking out the horrible reality of his situation, when there was some joy to be found for an inquiring mind.

But this?

When faced with such a harsh reality, Hugh realized he had about as much influence over his own life as an ant did beneath a man's boot.

"How am I to survive this, Sorcha? I'd thought I might…" he whispered into the brisk night air, shaking his head. "But, nae. This place is foreign. No' even that. I might hae become accustomed to a foreign land, but this is alien to me. 'Twas a simple thing yesterday and today during our journey to hide beneath bravado and humor. To ignore what I knew deep in my soul and cast aside my … fear." He swallowed as he finally said the word, which was almost as alien to him as this land. He had never truly felt its power before. Never understood how it could seize a man's soul. Not even in the heat of battle had he felt such terror.

"Hugh," she whispered, breaking her own rule to reach out and squeeze his shoulder sympathetically.

Hugh did not pull away as he normally would have in the face of such compassion. Indeed, he longed to give in to a childish impulse to lay his head against her soft bosom and be cradled like a bairn in need. "I ken nothing of this world, Sorcha. Nothing at all, and it is that verra ignorance that frightens me more than anything else."

"The one good thing about ignorance, Hugh, is that it can be cured," she told him. "I can teach you what you need to know."

Hugh raised a haughty brow, and she answered it with a sheepish grin, adding, "And what I can't teach you, books and the power of the Internet can. You'll be fine. We'll get through this together."

He envied Sorcha her conviction on the matter. "I wish I had such faith."

"I thought you medieval men were all about faith and religious quests."

"I hae told ye before, I…" Hugh started irritably but halted at the sight of her mischievous grin. "Ye think to solve all our woes wi' humor."

"Great minds think alike. It worked for you, right?" Sorcha drew her jacket more tightly around her, hugging her arms tightly over her chest. "Now, let's go inside. It's cold out here."

Hugh took off his sport coat and threw it around her shoulders. Sorcha was a study in contradiction. Bold enough to brave the authorities of her own country but not the cold. Wary but trusting. Solemn but humorous. Her words of wit had often been biting in their humor, but when Sorcha had lost herself to laughter that afternoon in the car, her bonny face had lost all traces of the sadness that seemed to always linger there, replacing it with unmitigated joy.

That laughter had lit her eyes and softened her features, her winsome smile blinding white and radiant. The sight of it had filled his heart with the same light. He'd never seen anything so enchanting. He wanted to frame her face in his hands and kiss her thoroughly, sharing in that joy. Their agreement kept him from doing so, but the sight had inspired more desire in him than her scant nightwear of the previous evening.

Now, she burrowed deep into the warmth of his jacket and smiled up at him freely, as if their shared laughter had demolished any barriers between them. As if somewhere along their journey she'd crossed over the line between benefactor and friend. "Won't you be cold?"

The cold wind could hardly cool the desire warming his veins. Hugh could only scoff. "Ye would ne'er hae survived in my time."

"Let's get you through mine first, then maybe we'll test that."

A smile tugged at the corner of his mouth and he bent in a courtly bow. "I will expect ye to honor yer challenge."

)(○)(○)(

"Mrs. Manning," Phil Jameson called as he pounded on the door to the townhouse one last time before stepping back and nodding to the nervous man at his side. "If you could, please."

"I have to tell you that I can't imagine Mrs. Manning being in any kind of trouble," Rogers, the townhouse's landlord, said as he shakily inserted his master key into the lock.

Jameson didn't deign to respond. While it was true that he didn't have any evidence against Claire Manning, he was certain she was aiding the anomaly in some way. Only three people had left the campus before the lockdown. But of the three, only Claire and one other had been seen near Fielding's office. After hours of watching the video surveillance, he'd pulled the feed on her as she'd driven past the security gate. There had been something in her expression—not fear but enough of *something*—to make her the likely culprit. None of the others leaving the lab had looked even mildly suspicious.

Only her.

She'd been forced into helping in the escape, he knew it. Now all he needed was the proof.

The only thing that didn't make sense was her behavior when he had come to this townhouse before. She'd been breezy then, deliberately so. When compared to the expression captured on the video camera just hours before, the change between them was primarily what had caught and held his mistrust.

"Search every room," Jameson ordered the fistful of men under his command, a combination of NSA and INSCOM personnel charged with the suppression and containment of the lab breach. The men fanned out through the townhouse, leaving Rogers lingering nervously at the door. "Bring me something."

"I can't imagine why you would think that this Manning woman helped at all," Agent Nichols, his INSCOM counterpart who was in joint command of their task force, said. "There is nothing to link her to the experiment."

"Call it a gut instinct," Jameson said, though the question plagued him as well. Why? He'd seen the footage from the cellblock that Fielding's office had become. The escapee was a brute of a thing, capable of killing Claire Manning without effort. Clearly, it had forced her aid to escape. So why hadn't she confessed when she had the chance? What could it have threatened her with?

Jameson looked around the townhouse. Everything was tidy and neat. The sink was empty, and the dishes in the dishwasher were clean. There were no signs of either an unwanted guest or a forced departure.

"Jameson, sir," one of Nichols' junior INSCOM agents called out.

"What do you have?"

"Not much, sir. No purse or keys, but that doesn't mean much. Nothing else looks to be missing, though it would be hard to tell from a woman's closet if she took anything from it," the junior agent, Majors, said.

"Come on, people!" Jameson barked irritably. "There must be something!"

"Sir, I think I have something!"

Jameson turned to find one of his own agents standing at the head of the stairs. "What is it, Marshall?"

"We've found what look to be traces of blood in the shower drain, sir."

Was it Claire Manning's or the anomaly's, Jameson wondered? It didn't matter. The blood was enough. For him at least. "That's it! Let's get a BOLO out on Mrs. Manning's car. I want to know where they are and where they're going!"

Nichols raised a brow. "On what grounds? A little

blood? Gut or not, in my opinion, you're barking up the wrong tree here, Jameson."

"And when I find Claire Manning harboring our anomaly you will be proven wrong."

14

Claire punched the four-digit code into the garage door opener mounted on the wooden frame of the door and was rewarded by the whine of the small engine as the door began to rise. Rushing back to the car, she pulled Goose into the empty bay next to her Uncle Robert's bulky Chevy Tahoe before turning off the engine.

"Well, here it is. Our hideaway until we can figure out how to get away."

"Again, I cannot thank ye enough, Sorcha."

"You can thank me by hauling in the groceries," she responded cheerfully, determined to keep the atmosphere as light as possible following Hugh's heart-rending confessions aboard the ferry. That sudden vulnerability had torn at her heart and she'd nearly given in to the impulse to hug him, to soothe away his fears. For the remainder of the trip, they had stood side by side at the rail with their backs to the city skyline while he'd ruminated on his troubles. All she'd been able to do was absorb the warmth of his blazer and fight the urge to bury her face in the collar, breathe in the manly scent, and bask in the warmth in his eyes.

Now, she got out of the car and went to the interior door, hitting the button to lower the garage door, effectively hiding the car from plain sight. "I'll go turn on some lights and then, before you even need to ask, I'll cook you some dinner."

Hugh's dazzling smile flashed in the dim light provided by the garage door opener. "It pleases me that we are getting to know one another so well."

Claire shook her head with a chuckle, glad that he was retaining his sense of humor through all this. "I hate to disappoint you, but you're really not that much of a mystery."

The Scot merely grunted humorously at that and went to the back of the Prius to retrieve their meager luggage and the groceries they had stopped to buy at a market not far from the ferry depot before she'd guided her car through the winding, wooded roads that led to the north end of Bainbridge Island.

'Uncle Robert's' home was just north of Fay Bainbridge State Park, looking out over Puget Sound to the east and Port Madison to the north. The style of the house itself was a little modern meets Cape Town chic. The exterior that wasn't covered in plate glass was sided with cedar shakes. That was about as traditional as it got.

The inside was pure modern luxury, with an expansive kitchen of dark walnut, granite, and stainless steel that would make any chef weep with joy. It had all the best toys, from the sixty-inch Wolf range and seventy-two-inch Sub-Zero refrigerator to the built-in cappuccino maker. Claire fanned her fingers over the cool granite of the enormous center island and looked out the huge bank of plate glass windows that faced Puget Sound. The windows were black against the night beyond, with not a streetlight to pierce the darkness, but they did reflect her image as clearly as a mirror and she stared at herself in wonder.

She was alone in the veritable wilderness with a man she'd met—she used the term loosely—just thirty-six hours before, a hugely powerful, yet oddly gentle Scotsman from another time. She'd basically ordered Robert to make sure no one else knew about it and was entirely comfortable with that.

Wowzah, how her life had changed.

"Are ye well, Sorcha?" Hugh asked as he dropped the grocery bags on the counter.

"Fine. Fine. I'm fine." She waved her hands dismissively, moving around the island to put the perishable groceries into the fridge and simply arranging the others off to the side. She didn't want to infringe on Aunt Sue's kitchen more than necessary. "Just tired, I guess. It was a long drive."

"If ye'd care to instruct me, I could assume that duty in the future," he offered.

"Ha! Don't hold your breath," she sallied as she searched for a cutting board and knives to start slicing the zucchini and squash she planned to grill along with some mushrooms and cherry tomatoes. "I imagine you have a hell of a speed demon buried deep in you. There's a wine fridge over there." She pointed with her knife. "Why don't you pick us out something? I know I could use a drink." She'd have to remember to reimburse Robert later, she thought, making a mental reminder. "Or there might be some beer in the fridge in the garage."

Hugh shook his head. "Yer beer tastes like piss."

Claire choked on a bubble of laughter. "Don't hold back, tell me how you really feel."

With a broad grin, he turned as directed toward the wine bar but paused and asked with blatant curiosity, "What is this?"

The question was so common between them by that point that Claire barely looked up. "It's a jigsaw puzzle. Uncle Robert loves them and always keeps one out on the table to work on. He usually picks the hardest ones and never finishes them. I think he bronzed the only one he ever completed as some kind of trophy."

Silence prevailed, drawing her attention more fully than the question, and she looked up to find Hugh thoughtfully studying the puzzle before he picked up a piece, setting it neatly—and accurately—in place. Claire's brows rose, but her jaw sagged when he immediately placed another. "Are you kidding me?" she said, then snapped her mouth shut. "How the hell are you doing that?"

He just shrugged. "I've always been good wi' puzzles of all sorts. Wi' seeing patterns in things." He picked up another and then another, putting them in place.

"Remind me after dinner to have you watch a little movie called *Rain Man*. Somehow I think it's right up your alley."

"It troubles ye, this skill?" he asked, tilting his head inquiringly at her tone.

"Nope, it just puzzles me," she quipped, then smiled at her own pun before turning to flip on the infrared grill at the center of the Wolf cooktop. She tossed the vegetables in olive oil and sprinkled them with salt and pepper before dumping them on the grill.

Hugh returned to the kitchen with a bottle of wine and a relaxed grin, searching the drawers in companionable silence for a corkscrew, and the cupboards for glasses. Moments later he was handing her a glass. "It says it's an Oregon Pinot Noir. I've ne'er heard of the region so I thought to be adventurous and try something new."

She clinked her glass to his and raised a teasing brow. "Trying something new? How shocking! I'm sure you've never before had a chance to do that."

"Nae, ne'er," he rejoined with equally playful facetiousness as they drank.

Claire felt those smiles, his and her own, all the way down to her soul. The banter was nice, lighthearted. Enjoyable. Hugh Urquhart, for all fate had dealt him, was turning out to be a pretty likeable guy. There was nothing like a road trip for a bonding experience, and she felt that somewhere between the KitKat and the Whatchamacallit, she and Hugh had become friends. The tension born of wariness and uncertainty was definitely gone, even if another sort of tension had taken its place. She decided that continued denial in that area would serve her well. "Give me five minutes for your steak and we'll be ready to eat."

He nodded and looked around the room before opening one of the glass-paned French doors and stepping out onto the huge deck that ran the length of the house. Puget Sound was just feet away, however though the moon reflected of the smooth waters, it was too dark to have much to look at. A moment later he returned. "'Tis a charming cottage, quite—what was the word ye used? High-tech?"

"Uncle Robert does like his toys," Claire said by way of agreement. "Feel free to look around. There's a pretty nice library past the living room. Robert and Sue are both big readers."

Hugh nodded and wandered that way, looking this way and that as she poked a meat thermometer into the filet mignon she'd put on the grill with the veggies. The steak had been expensive and certainly they wouldn't be eating this way every night, but she was sure that Hugh would appreciate some red meat.

A short while later, she heard him call from the other room, "I found one of Arouet's books. I can scarcely credit it, though it is a work I'm no' familiar wi'. How can I tell when was it written?"

"The date should be behind the title page," she called from the kitchen. She flipped the big steak with the tongs and tested the top of it with her finger for doneness. Satisfied, she filled two plates with the grilled vegetables and turned to retrieve the steak. "Come and get it."

Hugh emerged from the library with the book open in his hands. "It wisnae written until after I left Europe. Many years after, in fact."

"I'm more surprised there is even a book in there by this Arouet guy. What is it called?" He snapped the book shut and held it out to her, but Claire didn't need to take it from him. The tongs holding his steak were forgotten in her hand as she stared agog at the title clearly visible on the cover. "That's *Candide*," she said in disbelief. "I thought you said your friend's name was Francois something."

"Aye, Francois-Marie Arouet," Hugh nodded, flipping the book open once again. "He wrote some of his work under this nom de plume Voltaire. I confess I ne'er thought it would last."

"You knew *Voltaire?*" she asked dumbly, punctuating the words with a wave of the steak.

"Aye, I met him in Frederick's court in Berlin and stayed wi' him at Chateau de Cirey for many months, though his mistress dinnae appreciate my presence," he said offhandedly as he perused the first several pages of the book. "They had a wondrous library of over twenty thousand books."

"You *knew* Voltaire?"

"Aye, Sorcha, did I no' just say so?" Hugh raised a brow, cautiously eyeing the meat she was waving around. "Perhaps ye should put that down while it is still edible. *Voltaire*, as ye call him, had some interesting notions on politics and religion as well. I always thought it would be interesting to witness an exchange between him and Hume on the subject. I daresay that would hae been quite a remarkable debate."

Claire groaned, finally laying the steak to rest on the plate. "Not David Hume?"

"Aye, we went to University in Edinburgh together. Hae ye heard of him?" he asked, still engrossed in the book. "I know many of his first writings were no' well received."

Claire carried the plates and silverware to table and set them on the end opposite the half-done puzzle. Retrieving her wine glass, she took a long, fortifying sip as she slipped into the chair Hugh was holding out for her. "I might've heard of him once or twice," she answered by way of understatement.

Hugh knew David Hume. More than anything she had been subjected to over the past couple of days *that* blew her mind so completely Claire could only poke absently at a piece of zucchini with her fork. She'd had a fascination with religious philosophy as an undergraduate, filling her electives hours with Hume and Kant.

"Are ye no' going to hae any meat?" he asked, nodding at her plate of vegetables as he sat and began to cut into his filet.

"No, I can't eat that," she responded absently, still awed over his revelation. "Seriously, why…"

"Cannae eat it? Why ever nae?"

"I'm a vegetarian." When he looked at her blankly, she added, "Basically, it means I don't eat meat."

"Ye dinnae eat meat," he repeated slowly, watching her as he chewed. "Ye *dinnae* eat meat?"

Her breath released with a laugh. "That just doesn't compute for you, does it?"

"Why would ye no' eat meat?"

"Why didn't you tell me that you knew Voltaire?"

"I dinnae think it of import."

"There you go," she nodded practically, pointing her fork at him. "But what is of importance is who else did you know?"

Hugh shrugged at the question. "How am I to ken who would hae been important? We were simply men sharing ideas, challenging one another to deeper thought. What puzzles me is that ye find it strange that a man might travel in his youth, or take a Grand Tour. How else is a man to learn of the world if he disnae see it wi' his own eyes?" He took another bite of his steak, chewing thoughtfully. "I am also puzzled by what benefit could come from avoiding meat."

"We can have that talk later. Seriously, tell me about your life, and no more avoiding the subject. Now I just have to know. Tell me about your family, your parents."

"I had two," he said unhelpfully. "A mother and a father."

Claire rolled her eyes. "Hugh!"

"Verra well," he sighed, raising his glass. "Since it is inescapably clear that ye willnae let the matter rest, I will tell ye. I hae three sisters, all older than I. We were raised by our uncle, who was mother's brother, as my parents are both deceased."

"I'm so sorry."

He waved his hand dismissively. "I dinnae remember them. I was verra young when they died."

"Was your uncle famous, too?"

"He is the Earl of Cairn."

"Of course," she nodded, remembering that he'd mentioned the name before and thinking just how greatly she'd underestimated Hugh Urquhart. "Did he live at Rosebraugh as well?"

"Nay, he had estates of his own west of Dingwall but he schooled me in my responsibilities wi' his own sons. I was fostered to the MacDonnell at Glengarry when I was eight, and at fourteen attended the University of Edinburgh, as was expected in our family. Afterwards, my grandmother insisted that I hae a Grand Tour in the tradition of her family. She was English," he added at Claire's inquiring glance.

Fostered at eight, she thought in surprise. Grand tour? "I thought you hated the English."

"No' the English so much as their politics and their incessant need to dominate all around them," he amended. "Surely as a descendant of the colonists, ye ken that."

Maybe not the Americans of today, but surely the founding fathers had. "I suppose I do. So what was this Grand Tour?"

"An extended journey to the Continent…to Europe," he clarified, still eating heartily. "I traveled wi' my cousin, Keir, though he was far more interested in the ladies than in anything else. Your Voltaire was a fine source of that sort of knowledge as well. He had an eye to be sure. As I said, we traveled to Venice, Austria, and Paris. We returned home to assume our responsibilities. I ran my estates and saw my sisters well wed, but after some years, the lure of further knowledge drew me back to Paris, where I joined the Academy of Science. In recent years, I spent time in France and Berlin, where I was invited to Frederick's court. The king was an interesting man. Eminently knowledgeable on many subjects, though ye might know as much. Did ye know he composed hundreds of pieces for the flute? Or that he wrote nearly as much as Arouet? There were some trifling rumors of his sexual preferences, as he neglected women, including his wife. Some say his lifelong friend, Hans Hermann von Katte, was actually his lover, but many at court argued that the king merely had greater things to contemplate than women."

※※※※

"From there I returned home at my uncle's insistence to take up arms in support of the Jacobites," Hugh ended, dropping his knife and fork on the plate and leaning back with a satisfied sigh. "Thank ye for the meal, Sorcha. It was most delightful."

Claire nodded, swirling her wine around in her glass. She'd finished her own small portion some time ago, and had just sat in wonder as he told his tale. Frederick was none other than Frederick the Great. And not only had he known Voltaire and David Hume, he'd met Johann Sebastian Bach as well. She felt mortified for ever having thought him little more than a country bumpkin, and told him so.

He only laughed her apology away. "I accept yer apology and wi' it will grant ye this one wee concession: I wisnae inclined to say so before but yer impression of my people as a whole was no' far from the truth. The circumstances and education of men of my ranking are far removed from those of the average man. There are many—too many—of my countrymen who lack education of any sort. There are some who would like to mandate schooling for all, but who is to say to a father that he maun lose his strong sons at harvest time to a schoolroom?"

"What about the girls?"

"What of them?" he challenged provocatively, crossing his arms over his chest.

"Don't you think they should have been educated, too?"

"A highly provocative question, which I shall abstain from answering," he said with a mischievous grin.

"Come on," she dared. "Tell me what you really think."

"I believe my thoughts and philosophies are obviously better suited to another era, and that is all I will offer on the subject." Hugh pushed away from the island and stood. "Now shall I assist wi' the washing?"

"That's a rather cowardly change of subject," she said, expecting him to bristle as he always did when his manhood was challenged, but Hugh surprised her with a wink and a broad smile that deepened his dimples as he gathered the plates and carried them to the sink.

"If there is one thing I hae learned in all my life that I adhere to more than any other, it is that one should ne'er argue wi' a lass in a righteous temper."

"Humph! Where did you learn that?"

"From my grandmother."

They laughed comfortably together as Claire joined him at the sink. "Smart woman," she quipped, laughing up at him, and he glanced down at her, his smile slowly slipping away.

Only then did she realize how close she stood to him, how she could feel the heat of his body warming her arm. How wonderfully handsome he was. His eyes were deep blue beneath his heavy dark brows. The planes of his cheeks were smoothly sculpted but for that devastating dimple that was slowly disappearing. Despite his afternoon shave, there was already a beard shadowing his jaw, but for the first time she could see the tendons of his lean neck and his Adam's apple move as he swallowed. It was so tempting, that urge to reach out and touch him. Touch him not to comfort or soothe but to simply feel the warmth of his skin beneath her fingers.

Hugh shifted slightly, his chest suddenly at eye level, drawing Claire's gaze to the V of the T-shirt and to the rise and fall of his chest. She could lay her head there … or press her lips there. Would he embrace her, she wondered? What would it feel like to be held in those strong arms? To have that massive body surround hers?

Did she really want to know?

Did she dare deny it?

"Sorcha," he whispered huskily.

She looked up to find his head bent, his lips just inches away. He was warm, oh so warm. Life radiated from him until she was engulfed in it. She breathed in deeply, swaying unconsciously toward him as if he were a magnet, her chest almost touching his. Hugh bent his head, his cheek inches from hers. "Release me from my vow, lass." His breath brushed her neck and she shivered.

How could she release him when she couldn't release herself? Regretfully, Claire stepped away with a long sigh that was echoed by Hugh's and changed the subject with forced gaiety. "Since your uncle was an earl, I suppose that you always had servants to wash dishes for you, huh? Why don't you just let me do these and you can take our luggage upstairs?"

"I am capable of assisting," he said, his hand covering hers as she reached to turn on the water. His rough hand set her skin tingling instantly, and she jerked away from his touch. "Sorcha, I…"

"No touching, Hugh, remember?" she whispered, almost inaudibly.

"Aye. How could I forget?" His voice was tight, disappointed in her, but perhaps no more disappointed than she was in herself. "Where should I take the bags?"

Claire gave him brief directions to two of the guestrooms above that her family had used before, adding brightly, "I'm sure your uncle would have a fit if I let his nephew do the dishes anyway."

"No' at all," Hugh said, his suddenly arrogant voice making her look up. "I am the Duke of Ross and I hae always done as I bluidy well please."

Stunned, she could do nothing but watch him turn and stalk angrily away. A duke? Good Lord, could it get any worse?

15

The third day of freedom

Daylight streaming in through the huge plate glass windows that served as the walls of Robert Mitchell's waterfront home woke Claire early the next morning, and she rolled over to look at the bedside clock. With a sigh, she flopped onto her back, rubbing her eyes tiredly.

The windows had been too dark the night before for her to appreciate the views the house offered, and she did that now as she climbed out of bed, sighing over the beauty of the sound. The day was overcast—no surprise there—but it wasn't raining. The sun was even bravely trying to pierce the cloudy barrier that separated them. Dressing, she left the guest room she'd assigned herself and peeked into the one she'd given Hugh, only to find him gone and the bed neatly made.

She wouldn't blame him if he left her now. And perhaps it would be better for them both if he did. Clearly there was a mutual physical attraction between them, but under the circumstances it would be foolish—insane, even!—to throw caution to the wind and…well, let nature take its course. It wasn't something she wanted, she told herself firmly. She told herself she wouldn't second-guess her decision, but it was fear for her personal wellbeing that prompted her to do so now. It was the fear of something much deeper. Something infinitely more dangerous.

Something that had kept her tossing and turning all night.

On top of that, he was a duke. To borrow an exclamation from Hugh, a *bloody* duke. No doubt he was used to bowing, scraping, and complete obedience. If he thought to expect as much from her, Claire knew she was the wrong girl for him, hands down.

So, he would just have to accept that theirs was purely a business relationship. Her business was to keep him safe and then get on with her life. Period.

Going downstairs, she called his name but received no response. She moved into the kitchen. Her voice rang hollowly in the empty house. The kitchen looked untouched.

A frown furrowing her brow, she took the empty pot from a small countertop coffee maker and went to the sink to fill it. Through the window, she could see Hugh sitting on a large driftwood log near the shoreline. While the pot filled, she watched him as he sat motionless, staring out at the water.

Turning away, she filled the coffee maker, setting the filter in place and measuring out the coffee, all the while mentally scolding herself, trying to talk herself out of doing what she knew she was going to do. Trying to remember that it was all just business.

With a sigh, Claire knew she was doomed to failure. Her resolution was undone within minutes of its conception.

Because underneath all of his bravado and teasing, Hugh was hurting. She could see the signs in his body posture as easily as she'd heard them in his words on the ferry the previous night. Under all the swagger he'd put on, under all the arrogance, he was just frightened ... as much as he hated to confess such a thing. He might hide it beneath humor, but it was there and her heart ached for him. That pain was what had softened her to him in the first place. She knew what it was like to be suddenly alone and scared. At least she'd had her parents to run to, someone to find some comfort in if she needed it. Who did he have? Just her. And every fiber in her being was urging her to give solace where she could.

)O(O(O(

It was gray and dismal, Hugh thought as he stared out over the waters. The desolate beach was strewn with driftwood and rock, one thrown onto the sand by the rough waters, another smoothed flat as a result of the same. The water of this Puget Sound was vast and turbulent, with shades of blue turning to gray as the waves peaked and dropped. In the distance, he could see the dark shadow of land at the horizon and closer another band of land jutted into view. The whole of it was bathed in rugged beauty.

It wasn't home but it was a good imitation. Just sitting there staring out over the waters as the sun had risen over them had put a balm on the aggravation of another sleepless night. Another sleepless night wondering what he would do. What he *could* do. So far, his only thought had been to assure his continued freedom and return to his homeland.

But what then?

Hugh felt for the medallion lying beneath his shirt over a

heart aching with loss. Even glossing over his life the night before had been difficult, though in the end he had felt all the better for it. What would his sisters think of his disappearance? Would they think him taken in battle? A prisoner of war? With his rank, it might have been a likely consequence if he'd been captured. They might have negotiated for his return. Would the Sassenach's denial of his capture lead to only more distrust and further hatred?

A gravelly crunch sounded behind him, and he turned to find Sorcha solemnly watching him. Taking the mug she held out to him, he shifted to the side in a silent invitation for her to join him. She did, and for a long while they simply sat in companionable silence, sipping their coffee. Hugh knew why she was there and her silent support was just one more thing to be thankful for. "This place reminds me of home."

"I was hoping it would."

"One could look out the windows of Rosebraugh and see a comparable view." Sorcha offered no response, and that restraint somehow prompted him to continue. "As I said, my home lies east of Cromarty, where the Moray Firth meets the Cromarty Firth. Beyond ye would see the North Sea." He swept his hand before them. "Across the south sutor, I could see land beyond. More of Scotland, just as ye see that land from here. Thank ye for bringing me here."

"You're welcome." She fell into silence once more before asking, "So should I be calling you 'your Highness' or 'your Grace' or something like that now?"

"Nay," Hugh said softly. "I hae many regrets for those words. My sense was overcome by my… " He let the thought fade away. He had many regrets in general. There was little need to point them out one by one or he might inadvertently voice his regret that he hadn't been able to take her in his arms as he wanted. Her rule had manifested itself as something of a challenge to his manhood. Even now he could feel the warmth of her body next to him, and the rekindled desire called for him to gather her close and feel that heat pressed against him.

He thrust away the temptation, forcing himself to remember that she didn't want him or at least wouldn't welcome him in that way. "Regardless, everything that made me a duke vanished long ago."

Years of training and aristocratic hauteur clearly were not enough to mask the pain in his voice when it came to speaking of his loss, because Sorcha hesitantly asked, "Are you doing all right?"

"As well as can be expected," Hugh responded with a dismissive shrug. "My decisions plague me. I hae put ye in serious jeopardy, and that cannae be forgiven. If they determine that yer helping me, they will come after ye, will they not? There will be nowhere left to run."

She shrugged as well, though her veil of nonchalance was not as practiced as his. It was an easy thing to see that she had her worries as well. "Let's worry about that later."

"I ken now that there is little I might accomplish on my own," he reluctantly admitted. "But to protect ye, we should devise some strategy, for they will unquestionably outnumber us."

"They'll have to find us first." Her small hand covered his. Her flesh, pale against his own. Her protective caring warmed his heart and he enveloped her hand between his, but as if she'd just realized what she'd done, Sorcha drew her hand away and wrapped it around her mug. She looked blankly out over the water, again changing the subject, as was her wont. "They will have underestimated us on some level,

Hugh. They'll assume, as I did, that you are nothing but a savage. They'll expect some rash, illogical behavior from you. Added to that, they will have to think—at least initially—that you are forcing me to help you. It gives us an advantage…two great minds on our side."

"Ye have been a great comfort to me these past days."

"Anyone would have done the same."

"I dinnae believe so. Sorcha…" Hugh said her name as a request, and after a palpable internal struggle, she turned to look at him. Her fair skin was dewy in the dense morning air, the brisk air drawing becoming color to her cheeks. Her eyes were wide and fringed by dark lashes stripped of the artifice that had covered them in recent days. Still she was lovely. Reaching out, He ran his fingers through the loose strands of her auburn hair, admiring how it shone so vividly red in the dim sunlight. There was so much to admire about her, her courage, her mind, and her beauty. She was like no woman he had ever known.

Having learned nothing the evening before, he caught her chin and gently guided her mouth to his.

The kiss was light and undemanding, but still he could feel her lips tremble beneath his. Stroking her chin with his thumb, Hugh parted his lips just enough to sample hers. She tasted delectably of salt, sweet coffee and cream.

Their lips clung a moment before she drew away and stared down into her coffee cup with a shaking exhale. He could see her chest rise and fall rapidly. What was she afraid of, he wondered? Sorcha had shown no fear of his person before, only understandable wariness. She was not afraid of their situation, as she should be; yet she feared this untapped passion between them.

The one thing that worried him the least.

"Perhaps it would be best after all if I left ye." He held up a hand to stall her interruption. "That way ye could turn yourself in, plead coercion, and get yer life back."

"I won't let you do that," she said with a sigh. "I just ... can't for some reason. You deserve to get your life back as well."

"What life do I have to regain, Sorcha?" he asked. "What is waiting out there for me to replace the life I hae lost? I miss my home. My family. But they are long gone."

She tensed by his side, and Hugh had to wonder what she was thinking. It took a long while before his curiosity was appeased.

"A-are you married, Hugh?"

There was something in her voice that made him look at her, but she refused to meet his eye. He wondered what had prompted such a question. Would it please her to know that he was unattached as much as it pleased him that she was widowed? Not that he didn't regret her loss, but he was inordinately glad she did not have a husband about. "I am no'."

"Engaged?"

"Nay, I always found myself emphatically disengaged." Glancing at him from the corner of her eye, her mouth softened into a slight smile to acknowledge his quip. "Would it trouble ye if I were wed, Sorcha?"

"No, I ... No, of course not," she stuttered. "I was just wondering, the way you said that about your family."

"Yet, ye were wed." She shot him another inscrutable look, her lips pressed firmly together, but Hugh continued doggedly on. "He was killed."

Her eyes closed and she mouthed the word silently but did not respond. He recalled the tiny portraits of the man on the mantle of her home. The ribbons and medals. And the folded flag. "He was a soldier, aye? A warrior?"

Sorcha's lips parted at that and she turned to look at him, her amethyst eyes glassy... and surprised. The shadow of satisfaction lit them then. "I like that. Matt would have liked that. A warrior." She paused, and he feared that was all she would say on the subject, but after a moment she continued, her words whispered on the morning breeze. "Yes, Matt was in the Army. It was all he ever wanted to do, to serve his country..."

She drifted off into silence, staring out over the water beyond until he was certain she wouldn't reveal any more and he found that he sincerely wanted to know. To know her better. She was his only ally in this time. She was his only friend, and he knew he couldn't have asked for a better one. And as he began to know her better, it was easy to see that it wasn't merely sympathy in her eyes when she looked at him. It was empathy. She understood loss.

"I met him my senior year of high school," she continued softly. Though Hugh wasn't acquainted with the terms, he didn't interrupt to ask. "His family moved here from Denver for his dad's job. And that was it. We dated through that year and we both went to UW...the University of Washington. Matt was in the NROTC and was commissioned after we graduated. We went to Fort Carson for a while and a couple other bases before Matt was first sent overseas. I hated it, but it was what he wanted. So I came home and he went overseas, first to Iraq and then Afghanistan..."

Again Sorcha trailed off. It wasn't difficult to know what came next but he was surprised when she continued, her voice laced with bitterness. "There wasn't even enough of him left to fill the body bag. I-I never even got to look at him again." Those last words were choked as her throat tightened around them. "Everyone wonders why I do what I do now. That's why. No one should have to lose someone like that and not even have one last moment."

A single tear trickled down her cheek, and Hugh gently wiped it away. His heart ached for her, for the loss of a man she'd clearly loved, and loved still. "I am truly sorry for yer loss," he offered. "How long has it been?"

"Three years," she answered with a sniff, and he straightened in surprise.

Given her profound grief, he might have thought it a matter of months, perhaps a year. Three years? It was a lifetime to grieve, even for one so loved. Death and loss were a matter of rote in his time. People lived and died, often young and unexpectedly. They were mourned but life went on. Had things changed so much since then? Did everyone in this time wallow in grief and misery when there was life and living to be embraced? Hugh wanted to ask but struggled with the words lest he offend her.

"Is three years or more a common period of mourning in this time?" he asked as gently as possible.

"No, apparently not," she answered with that same bitterness, swiping her hand across her eyes. "You'd think I'm the biggest aberration on the planet, the way everyone fusses about it. Everyone is on me about it, even Matt's parents. I should get out more, meet more men, date, remarry, live a little, let it go, move on!" The list went on until the anger in her voice rose in pitch.

"Why hae ye no'?" He couldn't help but ask. It was something he simply couldn't comprehend, but perhaps people in his time were more prosaic about life and death.

"Nae one expects ye to mourn forever, I'm sure."

"Because I don't want to!" she bit out, turning to glare at him. "I was happy! I loved him! Do you think something like that comes along every day?"

Ah. He met her angry gaze. Her ire had darkened the amethyst to vivid violet. Now they were getting down to the bones of the matter. "I ken what it is," he said softly. "Ye're afraid to lose again and mayhap to love again, aye? Ye're afraid that that was the best life had to offer ye."

"Excuse me?" Sorcha blinked up at him, shifting away from him on the log.

"Ye're family is right," he continued. "Ye cannae hang on to a ghostie forever. Dinnae be afeared of moving forward wi' yer own life. I doubt yer Matt would have wanted ye to wallow in misery for the rest of yer days either."

She shook her head in disbelief. "I'm sure I must have misinterpreted something in that nearly unintelligible brogue of yours."

"I'm sure ye dinnae misunderstand. Ye're afraid, lass, 'tis nothing to be ashamed of."

"Really? This coming from the master of denial?" she nearly sneered the words.

"Ye're going to turn this back on me?" he asked incredulously. "I was only trying to help."

"I don't need your help. I don't want it," she shouted, jumping to her feet, her hands fisted at her sides as she glared down at him. "I can't believe you of all people have the balls to try to lecture me about fear."

Hugh ground his teeth, feeling his own temper flare at her scathing words. "Calm down now, lass."

"Don't tell me what to do," she yelled. "I'm sick of people telling me what to do, and who are you to think you have the right anyway? You can hardly admit that traveling through time hasn't scared the shit out of you, and you're going to lecture me on the subject of fear?"

His jaw clenched and worked as Hugh fought to keep his notorious Scots temper from erupting. "Sorcha..." he warned in low growl.

"Claire!" she corrected, shooting a finger toward him. "And you have no right. No right at all, after all I have done for you, to judge me."

"I dinnae judge," he denied the accusation, but by this time his patience was nearly at an end. He rose to his feet as well, towering over her, but she was either too brave or too angry to be intimidated by him. Bloody hell, but it all made sense now, and Hugh couldn't stop the words from rolling off his tongue. "Nay, lass, it disnae take a genius to figure ye out. Any fool can see it."

"Go to hell, Hugh!"

"Verra likely," he shot back. "But yer godly Matt willnae be there, will he? He's a saint now, aye? That's why there's to be nae touching, nae kissing. Ye dinnae want anything to mar the purity of his memory."

"How dare you." Her body trembled with rage. "I loved him."

"Aye," he shot back, looming over her. "And ye've got yer shrine to him to prove it to everyone, hae ye no'? The pictures, the medals... Tell me, *Sorcha*, do ye pray to him as well?"

Sorcha froze in shock for only a split second before her hand shot out and she slapped him across the face. Hugh's head turned with the force of the blow and while at any other point in his life such a bashing would only have served to stoke his own anger more, for some reason her fair wallop seemed to knock the sense back into him.

Cheeks aflame with the sting of her blow, Hugh felt only remorse for his harsh words. "Sorcha…Claire," he corrected, "forgi' my words. I dinnae…"

"Don't, Hugh," she whispered shakily, holding up a hand to halt his words. "Just don't."

16

Claire turned away and walked dazedly up the beach, her footsteps carrying her quickly away from Hugh. She clutched her sweater tightly around her middle, as if her own embrace could protect her from the world at large. Her fingers curled around the burning sting of her hand as she replayed that moment, that eruptive anger, which had fled the instant she'd lashed out at Hugh, leaving her feeling hollow and spent.

Defeated.

And a little horrified. Well, perhaps more than a little. She couldn't believe she'd ranted at him like that—*hit him*—especially when he was only saying the same thing she'd heard again and again over the years. It was nothing new, nothing different than the homilies her Mom and Dad, her brothers, and her friends had plied her with over the years.

The temper, however, was new, and Claire couldn't quite figure out where it came from. She had never lost it like that before in her life. My God but she'd screeched like a harpy at him!

Well, she inwardly justified, Hugh had crossed the line with that last bit. Good Lord, that had hurt. A shrine? Is that what she'd done? Did everyone see her that way?

Looking back over the past few years, she'd wager they did. She could remember once after her brother, Ryan, had brought one of his friends unexpectedly to dinner at their parents' house, she'd left early. Earlier than was polite. "So what are you going to do now?" he'd taunted as she left. "Go home and drown your misery in a pint with your old friends Ben and Jerry?"

"No," she'd shot back sarcastically, "this is my night out with Jack and Daniel." But she *had* gone home and curled up on the couch with a tub of cookie dough, watched *My Life*, and cried like leaky faucet.

Another time when she'd shown up to dinner, her brother Danny had welcomed her with a jovial, "I see you got out of your PJ's today, Sis. What's the special occasion?"

"Very funny, Danny," she'd said.

"Who's joking?" Danny had responded—she thought—teasingly.

Had he been teasing at all, Claire wondered now? Had any of them been joking?

Was Hugh actually right in saying that she was afraid?

For years she'd evaded intimacy of any sort. First out of love for Matt, out of respect. Then… She bit her lip, seeing her life more clearly than ever before. Since moving to Spokane, away from her parents and brothers, the previous year, she'd become something of a hermit. She had friends, like Darcy, at work and had once or twice gone out for "Girl's Night," but those nights revolved around bars and men and left a bad taste in her mouth.

Sure, she'd been lonely. Who wouldn't be? But as lonely

as she might get, Claire had always gone to bed at night knowing that Matt would be there. Alone she could replay happy memories, recalling the sound of his laughter. She could keep a part of him alive.

But a lazy chuckle couldn't warm a cold bed, and hadn't she just days ago admitted—at least inwardly—that she missed a warm body by her side? And look how it had spiraled out of control! She'd thought herself content with her choices, but now Claire realized that memories alone weren't enough any longer. How long had it been since she even had a nice long hug? Suddenly she longed for the comforting contact of human flesh, specifically for the feel of Hugh's strong embrace.

Her mind spun and she dropped down on a large log that slanted across the beach, stunned. Where had that bit of brutal honesty come from? Had the bitter vitriol she'd just spewed all over Hugh stripped her down to a bared soul, leaving nothing but the naked truth? That astonishing eruption of rage had resulted in feelings and anger she'd never verbalized to anyone. She had never lashed out so cruelly at her parents, but now somehow she felt better for having voiced it all. She couldn't remember ever being so angry.

Rubbing her hands over her face, Claire splayed her fingers and looked between them out over the choppy waters of the sound. Seagulls soared overhead, boats crept by in the distance, but she didn't truly see any of it, for she'd just had the most startling epiphany of all.

In truth, she couldn't really remember a time when she hadn't been angry.

She *was* angry, and had been for a long while. Angry at the world for taking Matt from her too quickly, angry at the

Afghans who had planted that bomb, angry at the government for allowing such a war to begin with, angry with her family for pushing her too hard. Angry with Matt.

With a heavy sigh, Claire shook her head. Damn, that snooping Jameson had been right. She'd left a good, fulfilling job developing environmentally clean ultrasonic propulsion to make weapons worse than the one that had taken her husband from her, and she'd done it just because she was angry about the way Matt had died.

God, what an ugly, nauseating realization.

As for the fear...*ugh*, she really hated it when someone else was right.

)()()()(

"Hugh?"

Hugh lowered the book he'd been reading and exhaled a sigh of relief at the sound of Sorcha's voice. She'd been gone for hours. Hours where he'd awaited her return on the beach and had finally given up his post, sure that his harsh outburst had been enough to drive her away forever. Her absence had provided plenty of time for him to evaluate his position and the unanticipated friendship that had blossomed between them. Though he needed her more desperately than he cared to admit, he'd also quickly begun to care for her as well. She was courageous, resourceful, intelligent, and witty. There was much about her to admire and little to scorn.

And she'd been right. He held no position in her life that allowed for such personal observations of how she led her life.

Glancing up, he found her looking, not at him, but at the wooden bookshelves that covered the interior wall of the library. Her arms were still crossed tightly, a posture he'd come to recognize as protective, defensive. She'd employed it often over the past days as a means to maintaining distance between them. Initially, distance between herself and a stranger who might potentially harm her, and now between herself and a man who had done so in the very worst way.

Hugh had never been one to readily tolerate insult or injury from anyone. For all the refinement of Frederick's court, such things were commonplace, but swift and scathing rebuttal had quickly silenced any of the courtiers' gossip concerning Hugh or his friends. He could charm with a raised brow and censure just as easily. If any other woman had dared berate him so, his rebuke would have been just as sharp and quick. From a man such an insult might have been, in some cases, even deadly.

No, it wasn't unusual for him to make a weapon of words in such instances, words carefully considered and chosen for the sting they might inflict. However, it was unusual for him to lash out so thoughtlessly, and he regretted the rash temper that had prompted him to do so. Hugh wasn't certain if it was the situation or Sorcha herself who had roused his emotions so. She did have a way of getting under his skin, irritating as a gnat.

She also had a way of lightening a man's heart to the point where he forgot all his troubles and saw only her. That alone was worth making amends for.

"Sor…Claire." He pushed out of the chair, determined to atone for his insensitive taunting.

But Sorcha turned to face him with a smile—aye, it might have been tight and perhaps a wee tad forced, but it was there—and said brightly, "I thought we might go into the city in the morning and see if my brother can help us find out what brought you here."

And with that, he knew she'd miraculously forgiven him

his thoughtless words. How or why, he hadn't an inkling. After all she'd given, he certainly didn't deserve it. "Claire..."

She shook her head, holding up her hand in that way that would have seemed excessively rude in his own time but was delivered as a matter of course in this one. "I'm sorry for what I said. There are a million excuses I could give you for getting on you like that, a million justifications. I try hard not to follow 'I'm sorry' with a 'but.' There are circumstances here neither of us are used to. We both know it. I deserve what I got in return, but I'm hoping we can both figure out how to deal with our worries in more constructive ways than taking it out on one another."

He nodded gravely. "Ye hae my apology as well. My words were thoughtless and cruel. Ye hae my word as a gentleman that such ill-considered words willnae pass my lips again." Nay, they would not, Hugh inwardly vowed. Sorcha clearly had enough pain and conflict in her life without him adding to it. If she was still willing to help him, he had nothing more within his power with which to repay her than kindness and courtesy. The good Lord knew that he was perfectly capable of both.

Her arms loosened, though she did push her hands deep into the pockets of her sweater, and her pinched features relaxed. "You must be hungry. Did you get any breakfast at all?" she asked as she started toward the kitchen, and he followed, wishing there was more he could do to right the wrong his temper had wrought. Despite the cheer in her voice, he'd quickly come to realize she conquered worry and fear with sarcasm, and uncertainty with subjects changed.

"I found enough to satisfy me." In truth, he hadn't been able to eat at all as he wondered at her absence. "I can prepare our meal if you like."

Her arched brow told him clearly what she thought of that, and Hugh couldn't help but grin. "Even a duke can turn a rabbit on a spit, if need be."

"Next time I want to put Thumper on a skewer, I'll know who to call," she retorted, pulling meats and cheese out of the refrigerator. "For now, a sandwich or five will have to do."

Silence fell around them as Sorcha pulled out a bag with a fascinating loaf of sliced bread and began to assemble a tower of sandwiches as she explained to him the origin of the term, about the Earl of Sandwich and his penchant for eating while he played at cards. It was a story meant for his amusement and Hugh took it as such, along with a plateful of the objects, with his thanks. She made another for herself with tomato, lettuce, and cheese, her focus on her work as she assembled it.

"Just so you know," she said more to the cutting board before her than to him, "you were right. About everything."

Chewing thoughtfully on his meal, he tipped his head gallantly and offered a rueful smile. "As were ye, lass. As were ye."

The confession brought her gaze to his for the first time since her return to the house. For a moment she gripped her knife tightly and stared at him in surprise before a more honest smile lit her bonny face. "Life's a bitch, isn't it?"

Hugh snorted at the unusual quip and straightened, releasing a rumble of laughter that started deep within his chest. "Aye, lass, 'tis indeed."

"It's given us both a hell of a ride, but I suppose we just need to suck it up and get over it, right?" she rambled on, going to the refrigerator for drinks. "Just like everyone said ... though since you've had it way worse—yes, you heard me, way worse—I'll give you…say, another week to get over it and move on."

He raised a brow at that. She'd mourned for three years over the loss of a husband and expected him to "get over" the loss of his entire life in a week? Sorcha snuck a glance at him and winked and Hugh had to laugh. By God, but she was teasing him! She certainly wasn't one to hang on to her anger for long, was she?

She set a bottle down in front of him labeled Diet Coke, something she'd been drinking almost continuously since they had met while he'd only beer, wine, and the bottled water Sorcha had assured him was far safer and tastier than the water in his day. Trustingly, he took a swallow and felt the liquid burn its way down his throat. Gasping, Hugh glared at the bottle and then at her, only to find her eyes dancing. "Good stuff, huh?" she asked, taking a long pull on her own drink and swallowing with a smack of her lips. "*Ah!*"

"Yer a devious witch," he accused but they were both smiling at that point.

"Are we good then?"

Hugh nodded. "We are, Claire."

She just shook her head, rolling her eyes exaggeratedly. "Oh, just call me Sorcha if you like. Claire somehow sounds wrong coming from you."

17

"Now hold it like this. Just wrap your hand around it...No, not so tight. Loosely. You want to have a good grip on it, not strangle it."

"I am doing it exactly as ye said I should, lass."

"I think you're just not trying hard enough," Claire chided. "Come on, we did your thing, now we get to do mine. We have to do something to pass the time."

"When I said I was restless, I meant that mayhap we could just take a walk on the beach. I dinnae mean anything like this."

"Well, it's raining," she replied. "So this will have to do."

"Of all the things ye hae shown me of this time, this is my least favorite thus far."

"Would you like some cheese with that whine?" His brow shot up, and she smiled smugly. "Come on, what are you afraid of? That a *wee lass* like me might kick your butt?"

Hugh pressed his lips together grimly. "Challenge accepted."

"Good, now you just have to put your hips into it a little more." Claire moved behind him and put her hands on his hips, pushing them to the side. "See?"

"I ken how to do this," he grouched. "I've been doing so since I was a lad."

"Really?" she asked. "How old were you the first time? Because I've been doing this since I was eight."

"'Twas invented by a Scotsman, lass," he huffed. "I'm sure I ken how to do it better than ye. This just disnae feel right."

She laughed. "You'll get used to it. Come on, try again."

"Verra well." Hugh lowered his hands and wrapped them, loosely this time, around the base of the long object. Drawing them back, he swung them forward once more. "How was that?"

"Better." She nodded, looking at the television screen. "Three hundred yards. You're certainly better at this than you were at the bowling."

"As I said, 'twas invented by a Scotsman," he grumbled before taking another swing. His virtual Wii golf ball flew into the sky, through a tree, and landed on the edge of the green. "My countrymen would be appalled at what has become of the game. I cannae see that there is truly any skill involved with this."

Claire took her turn, swinging her controller and sending her own ball after his. Unlike Hugh, she was enjoying the rainy afternoon. After lunch, he'd taught her a card game from his time called whist before she'd insisted on showing him a more modern entertainment by way of Wii Sports, which along with Let's Dance 1–4 and Zumba, comprised sum of Robert and Sue's video game complement.

Generally speaking, Hugh hadn't completely gotten over

his initial shocking dislike of the TV. He'd hemmed and hawed over learning the games from the start, but she was determined to give him a little immersion into the twenty-first century and to show him some of what books could not. She'd offered fencing initially, but he'd chosen bowling, a game Claire was surprised to learn that he was somewhat familiar with in theory, though the game had changed drastically over the years.

They had played only a few frames before switching over to golf. She suspected her wicked curve on the bowling ball might have had something to do with Hugh's change of mind. Clearly he'd a competitive nature and didn't like the idea of losing.

But he was good at golf, or at least this version of it. She frowned as he putted successfully from twenty yards out and the cyber-crowd cheered. Even as unaccustomed as he was to the Wii controller and the awkward swing, he soon got the hang of them and was handily beating her by two strokes after the second hole. Playing as a child with her father, Ryan, and Danny—before Danny had forsaken physical activity for all things electronic—Claire had been the only female playing among men, a middle sister who had hated to lose.

She wasn't much better about it now than she'd been as a child.

She beat Hugh on the next two holes and was surprised to find that the Scot was also an awfully good sport. He praised her efforts, but the competition did become more heated. She played like a twenty-first-century woman. She flung her arms up with a loud *Woo-hoo* when she did well and cursed soundly when she did not.

"'Tis meant to be a gentlemanly game, but yer a verra vocal player," he admonished.

"My dad is a pretty mild-mannered guy but he used to say that he thought golf caused Tourette's Syndrome because he would always start cursing uncontrollably whenever he played." She grinned sheepishly before explaining what the illness was and how the symptoms sometimes manifested. "I guess I get it from him."

Hugh's lips tilted at the corners, but it was that sad smile that told her there was just another thing about being here that upset him. "I suppose the game itself has changed in many ways."

"I'm sure you'll find that most things you knew have changed in some ways," she said practically. "But at least it's still here, right?"

"If yer going to look at it that way, I suppose I should be thankful that some of the human race still eats meat wi' their meals and that everyone isnae a vegetarian now."

"See? Now you're looking on the bright side." Claire grinned at Hugh's chagrin as they returned to the game.

Again the question was asked about why she didn't eat meat, and as they played, she launched into a long explanation of why people became vegetarian; some for their health, others who protested the exploitation of animals, and others who, like her, were generally suspicious of the hormones used to increase production of those products. That was why she would eat wild-caught fish but not farm-raised, why she would eat venison but not beef or chicken, and why she avoided eggs and milk unless they were hormone free.

Hugh accepted her explanation with a nod but stated that there was not a reason on earth that would compel him to forgo meat with his meals, and Claire was fine with that. Her beliefs were her own and she didn't try to push them on others.

"Besides," she added wickedly, "your fine countrymen also came up with haggis. I'm sure once you've eaten that, nothing is offensive anymore."

"An innovation counterbalanced by the gentlemanly game of golf," he pointed out.

"*Ah*, yes, the gentlemanly game of golf," she teased in a haughty, British accent. "When one drunk Scotsman knocked a ball into a gopher hole and decided to call it a game?"

"That is no' how the game started!" he protested. "Is that what people really think?"

Claire wondered what it was about Hugh that made her want to needle him so, but she couldn't help herself. A humorous recollection tickled deep within her and she pulled him into Robert's office and turned on his computer. Oh, it was mean, she inwardly chided. She shouldn't do it. She shouldn't.

But she was going to anyway.

Going into YouTube, she pulled up Robin Williams's comedy routine where he poked fun at Scotsmen and the origins of golf only to laugh more at Hugh's outrage over the comedian's impersonation of a Scotsman than at his ire at the skit itself.

"I dinnae talk like that!" he argued, to which Claire could only raise a mocking brow before collapsing against him with laughter. Hands clasped around his arm, she sagged against him with her forehead against his bicep as she surrendered to the hilarity.

But that humor faded quickly when she realized what she'd done. That she'd forgotten so thoroughly her own rule and the argument and insult of the morning, to relax so completely with Hugh once more! To find comfortable companionship only to have it ebb into undeniable discomfort as the sexual tension that had ensnared them the previous night once more spun its web.

Releasing his arm, she glanced up at him, only to find his blue eyes dark and intense as he stared down at her. When had she softened toward him so completely? When had he gone from being a savage to a man? From a charity case to a point of distraction? When he made her laugh? When he called her out? In just days, Hugh had overwhelmed her every defense, defenses that had been in place for years. He wasn't a project anymore, and he wasn't just business. He was an unanticipated friend…and an unexpectedly virile man who tempted her with each passing hour to tread where she knew she shouldn't.

Hugh made no move to touch her, but neither did he pull away. He wanted to kiss her just as he had the night before, she could see it in his eyes, and Claire couldn't help but recall that brief but tender kiss on the beach.

She chewed the inside of her lip as she looked away. Damn, that kiss! It might have been what had set off the heated exchange that morning. She had enjoyed it, as light and innocent as it had been. She had enjoyed it…and felt guilty for it. Deeply, darkly guilty.

And that had put her emotionally on edge, to the point that one minute she was comforting him, and then she was crying, only to burst out like some madwoman seconds later. She knew it would be nice to blame it all on the stress of their situation, but in retrospect she knew that the guilt was the hands-down culprit.

Why? Why should she feel guilty for enjoying a kiss? For finding a man attractive? Hugh was right about more than her being afraid of discovering that another relationship might not live up to the first or being afraid of loving and losing once more. He was right in saying that Matt wouldn't have wanted her to become a martyr to his memory. Knowing Matt, he was probably looking down at her with a frown of disappointment.

Before he'd first been sent overseas, her husband had wanted to talk about what would happen if he didn't come back, but Claire wouldn't listen then, so Matt had put it in a letter that one of his fellow officers had given to her at the funeral.

Find happiness, he'd said. Find love. Have the family they had never found the time to make together. Everyone said the same thing. Even Matt's parents.

But she hadn't, for the very same reason Hugh had indicated. Fear. A fear she needed to conquer if she ever wanted to move on with her life and find happiness once again, fulfilling her husband's final wish for her.

Claire wasn't saying that a fling with Hugh was necessarily what Matt or her family had been suggesting with their urging, but if she did decide to play a little, would it be so wrong?

XOXOXOX

"'Eighteen fucking times!'" Robin Williams bellowed from the computer and Hugh drew in a deep breath and finally took a step back, putting what was to Claire's mind some much-needed distance between them.

"'...dinnae use a 'wee fooked up stick.'"

"What?" she asked confusedly before recalling herself to the moment. "What did you use?"

He proceeded to give her a history lesson, for a change, on the sport of golf. Grateful for the distraction, she asked more questions about the equipment they had used in the past and the courses they had played on. Soon she was leading him out to the garage to examine Robert's clubs so that he could see the difference between then and now.

Technology had had its hand in golf, as it had in so many other things over the years, and she explained to him about shaft flexibility, the different club head angles, and how just about any golf store could do a swing analysis to tell him exactly what sort of clubs he could use. Back inside, she used Robert's computer again, this time to pull up pictures of different golf courses from around the world for Hugh to see. He was suitably impressed, and slowly confessed that perhaps it would be something that he might try to pick up again in the years to come.

It was the first time he'd mentioned his probable future, Claire realized. The first time he'd vocalized the inevitable, but from his closed expression, he didn't want to pursue the topic. She let it go, though she wanted to assure him that everything would be fine, that she admired how well he was handling himself so far. All things being equal, as she'd thought back in Spokane, it was surprising that Hugh wasn't locking himself in a dark closet shrouded in denial.

A lesser man would have been, but he was dealing with the shocking transformation Earth had undergone since the mid-1700s remarkably well, which was encouraging since Claire was ninety-nine percent certain that, no matter what little tidbits of information her brother Danny might be able to hack into for them, Hugh was destined to live the remainder of his life in the twenty-first century.

There were serious doubts in Claire's mind that she would've fared half so well in Hugh's time. Even knowing—at least conceptually—the history of the world, could she have coped with the changes any better? She couldn't even light a fire without matches or cook a decent meal over one. And if she appeared there in her clothes of this time, would she have been taken as a witch? Probably a prostitute, she thought wryly. Hugh had generalized women's fashion as "beyond the pale," which certainly sounded negative, and the way he studied every outfit she wore, it was blatantly obvious that he wasn't used to women in pants, especially ones as tight as a pair of skinny jeans.

But when he looked at her, there was interest there. Appreciation.

And that kiss…

Shaking away the thought, Claire forced her attention back him. If they managed to escape the authorities and secure his freedom, he'd have to build a life for himself here or in Scotland. Sure, he could play golf, but she wanted to make sure he was more prepared for her time than that. Hugh would have to find some way to support himself. He might even get married someday.

Claire bit her lip at the thought. Damn.

"Sorcha? Are ye well?"

Not even a little.

She went to the library, pulled out a voluminous tome she had seen there earlier, and turned to him, who had followed her in. "Here," she said, handing the book off. It was Roberts's nearly one-thousand-page book, *The History of the World*. "This should keep you occupied while I make dinner."

ANGELINE FORTIN

18

The Fourth Day of Freedom

"I could travel in such a way each day wi'out tiring of it," Hugh said as they stepped onto the deck at the bow of the ferry the next morning after leaving Claire's car in the hold below. "'Tis more akin to the travel of my time than yer car might ever be."

"We'd have to compromise on that because I'm not sure I was made to ride in a carriage or a wagon. Too slow." The May morning was cool, the brisk breeze snapping at her cheeks and nose, but Hugh seemed oblivious to the chill, turning his face into the wind with visible pleasure as his keen gaze absorbed the sights that had been lost to the darkness on their previous trip. The buildings of Seattle, Mount Rainier, the people.

And she was absorbed in him. Watching his reactions and expressions as he took it all in.

"Of course, with the ferry, you might get a relaxing

commute but you have to be willing to work within the schedule," she sighed, knowing she wouldn't mind it at all with a travel companion like him.

She didn't know if it was the Scot in him, the courtier, or just the fact that he was from another time with a different set of rules, but Hugh wasn't one to allow an awkward moment to taint the hours following. He was charming and entertaining and had kept their conversation at the dinner table flowing smoothly. Afterward, they had taken a walk down the beach while Hugh had told her more about his time, his family and what he'd read about the years following his departure in the book she'd provided.

When the temperature dipped and Claire had shivered in the cold breeze from the sound, Hugh had once again gallantly offered his coat, gently teasing that one day she must learn to bring her own.

He was so damn likeable, she thought. Interesting and intelligent. Was it going to be the end of the world if she admitted—if only to herself—that she found him attractive? Or wonderfully handsome?

Or sexy?

There was no denying that Hugh was just that. Claire slanted him a covert look up and down. The wind at his face tousled his hair as he stood tall, broad shoulders thrown back. His thin, V-neck sweater molded to him with the breeze, showing the definition of his pecs and those rippling abs. He was breathtaking, drawing the eyes of every woman aboard, and every one of them, right down to the last octogenarian eyeballing him, was clearly tempted to run her hands over that chest.

Sexy, in a word, didn't say enough. It stood to reason that any woman would want him. From his own conceited comments, many had. But he wasn't the only hot guy in the world. After the swooning endorsements of her friends, Claire had rented the movie *Magic Mike*. Hot bodies had abounded. Muscles had rippled. And she'd felt nothing more than detached appreciation. Not one of them physically compared to Hugh...well, perhaps Joe Manganiello did. Wasn't that why so many women loved *True Blood*?

Years of nothing, not a spark. Now there was definitely something. An earth-shattering something that flared between them each time the distraction of entertainment and humor waned. Why Hugh? Why now?

"Sorcha?"

Claire jumped and felt a blush creeping up her neck as she turned to look at Hugh, taking in the bemusement that told her he must have called her name more than once. Exhaling heavily, she fought the urge to fan the flaming of her cheeks that couldn't be cooled by the wind alone. "Sorry, I must have zoned out there for a minute. What did you say?"

"I was asking about that." He pointed up at the sky, and she identified the airplane for him, referring back to her conversation about 9/11 and the hijacked planes. Hugh propped a hip against the rail and crossed his arms with a scowl. "Ye maun think me a veritable simpleton for asking so many questions, especially when ye need to repeat yerself."

"Ignorance is a far cry from idiocy." Setting aside her surprisingly lustful musings, she squeezed his hand consolingly. Usually her explanations were met with an impossibly attractive sheepish grin but today Hugh seemed more disgruntled by his lack of knowledge. "A description is much different than actually seeing something."

So far that day, he'd asked only a few questions, but she

knew that he had many more that spoke not to the wonderment but to his trepidation about his place in this time. After speaking of his fears initially on the ferry into Bainbridge two nights before and on the beach the previous morning, she knew Hugh disliked vocalizing his reservations, not wanting to appear weak or unmanly. That was something that had probably been driven into him since birth. She doubted that men of his time and heritage were even allowed to consider having a feminine side.

But how strange it all must seem to him! Alien, he'd said that night on the ferry. How must it look in broad daylight? Claire tried to put herself in his shoes, and looked around as well, contemplating how drastically the world had changed since his time. Buildings of today had made even the skyline of a city unrecognizable to him. Then to fill that city with the billions of innovations that had emerged in the past three centuries!

Aware that he was still stewing in his upset, she offered, "Don't be so hard on yourself. I would bet there's a thing or two you could teach me and everyone else in this century. Dozens of things, probably."

Hugh snorted. "Such as how to assemble some puir wee sowel's toy?"

She rolled her eyes at the harsh retort. Boy, he made her do that a lot. He was just so frustrating. Challenging. Invigorating. *Whoa, girl, back on topic*, she chided herself. "Or how to get that perfect shine on your suit of armor," she teased, trying to draw him away from his dark thoughts. "Come on, Hugh. What did you do for a living? I can't believe I didn't ask."

"I was a duke, a gentleman," he said almost sullenly, turning away to look at the cityscape once again. "I had nae occupation."

"Hugh," she gasped. "If I didn't know better, I'd swear you're being deliberately obstinate."

"Dare I insult ye wi' another history lesson?"

Claire gaped at his surly tone. "Is there anything I can do to stop you?"

"Gentlemen of my time and station were raised by nannies and governesses before we were shipped off to school and then university," he told her in arch tones. "After which we embarked on our Grand Tour, which was meant only to fill our time and allow us to sow our oats until we inherited our father's wealth."

"Poor, poor, Duke Hugh," she drawled, her patience tested, "leading a life of luxury and privilege. Now I do feel bad for you."

"Yer sarcasm is unwelcome."

"And so is this woe is me bullshit," she shot back, enjoying his wide-eyed stare at her words. "Yes, you heard me. You have met some of the greatest men in history. Most people in this time would envy you that. *I* envy you! Any historian would grovel at your feet for just one tiny morsel of what you know about how your time really was, and you worry about holding the can opener backwards? Hugh, you could write a book about Voltaire filled with things you consider insignificant that would fascinate millions of people and probably win you a Pulitzer, and you think that you have nothing to offer?"

Claire drew in a deep breath, her mind buzzing with the truth of her words. Hugh was amazing. Incredible! He'd seen the world, befriended some of the most remarkable men in history, and he thought he had little to recommend himself? The truth of the matter was that there was little she could

185

offer him, once he found his stride in this century. How ridiculous to think that she could match such a worldly man. How humbling that eighteen years of education and her hopes of completing her doctorate one day left her feeling intellectually inferior.

But whatever Hugh had been in the past, humble might not have been one of them. "In my years in Europe, I wrote as well. If my works were no' brilliant enough to stand the test of time once, I doubt this time would be any different."

"Is that what this is all about?" she asked more compassionately. "You didn't find your book in Robert's library so you believe you failed? Millions, billions of books have been written since the Bible, Hugh. They can't all be in one of the two places you've been since you've been here."

That haughty brow went up again. "Hae ye ever heard of me? Did my name survive through history alongside those I collaborated wi'? Nay, it dinnae. I lost my life and left no legacy that I even lived at all. My family, my home, my work. Gone! All of it."

It ate at him, she knew, and why wouldn't it? Despite the flashes of humor, the consequences of his predicament had not faded. He'd had little time to mourn, nothing compared to the three years she'd taken. But she couldn't let him wallow in it until it was all he saw. If she had to bully him out of his doldrums, she would. "You know what your friend Arouet would have to say about this pity party you've got going on?" She didn't pause to give him an opportunity to answer. "I'll tell you what he'd say because he's already said it. He said, 'Each player must accept the cards life deals him or her; but once they are in hand, he or she alone must decide how to play the cards in order to win the game.'"

"Who are ye to lecture me?" he said, throwing her words

from the morning before back at her.

The rebuke did sting, but Claire continued, lecturing firmly. "Yes, I know you could throw that same bit of wisdom back at me, but this isn't about me. This is about you and your moment to step up to the plate and take your swing at what's being thrown at you. So, you need some education on the way the world works today. A crash course on how to survive. A handbook, so to speak ..."

"*Ah*, like those ones I saw among others on the shelves," Hugh said flippantly. "We could entitle it *The Twenty-First Century for Dummies*."

Argh! Claire's mind screamed with frustration and she simply couldn't contain it. Instead, she pushed hard at his shoulder, which gave about as much as a brick wall might, which only compounded her frustration, and before she knew it, she was retorting loudly, "I was kidding about the damned week. Jesus, have a little patience. You're not a freakin' idiot, for crying out loud."

Panting after that outburst, she looked around at the curious faces turned toward her and wondered at herself. Twice she'd lost her temper. Twice now? What was wrong with her? "I don't know what's gotten into me lately."

The words were met by Hugh's deep chuckle, and she turned to look at him in surprise. "You think this is funny?" Still he laughed, his blue eyes twinkling with merriment, and then Claire knew. "You did that on purpose."

"But ye're so bonny when ye're in a rage," he teased, tweaking a lock of her hair.

"You made me shriek like a banshee for the second time," she accused, staring at him as if he'd suddenly grown two heads.

But Hugh seemed inordinately pleased by her words,

crossing his arms with a toss of his head and a chuckle. "Ha! I understood that reference. Finally." Grinning with self-satisfaction, he added, "As for yer temper, I wouldnae let it trouble ye unduly. Ye're a woman. Shrieking like a banshee is—how would ye say it?—yer thing."

Make that three heads. He might have been smiling but he said it as if he actually believed it. And maybe he did. He probably wouldn't recognize equal rights if she smacked him across the face with a copy of the Nineteenth Amendment.

"Oh my God, I can't believe you just said that."

He raised a mocking brow. "Are we going to argue again?"

"God, I hope not," Claire murmured sincerely, then after a moment, offered a slight smile. "You fight dirty." She paused hesitantly. "I guess I should apologize ... again."

"No need," Hugh said, his dimple deepening. "I understood nary a word of what ye said anyway."

"And with that I feel as if I've been firmly put in my place," she sniffed, though she knew he was teasing her now. "Should I go through it one more time? Cliffs Notes version?"

"Not necessary," Hugh smiled as well. "In truth, I did grasp the gist of yer lecture and I, too, ken when I hae been put in my place."

A huff of laughter escaped her with that. "Ha! I bet no woman in your time would ever yell at a man like that."

"Nonsense. My aunt reacts more harshly to a muddy boot on her carpets," he said with an engaging grin.

19

While Hugh watched, Sorcha shook her head yet again. At this rate, he might keep her head bobbing constantly for the duration of their acquaintance, though in all honesty, he knew he'd displayed such a reaction more than a few times in the past few days. It was the product of an odd combination of humor and incredulity. Both of which Sorcha inspired handily.

She was quite droll, really. Her dry sense of humor was finely tuned enough to keep him on his toes. Her words of wisdom, such as they were, had been spot on, and he was determined not to take part in a "pity party" again. Week or not, what was done was done, the past was past. As she said, using Voltaire's words, the cards had been dealt and were his to play.

As for her fits of temper—his absurd observation about the female gender aside—well, perhaps they were more easily forgiven from Sorcha than they might be from any other woman of his acquaintance simply because of her valued assistance and because she was even more lovely when roused by anger—and he'd provoked her purposefully this time, if not the last, for that very reason. Or maybe his reaction had been tempered by the knowledge that in rising to the challenge of her anger once, he had inadvertently caused her great pain.

In any case, it now was blatantly obvious with this last outburst that Sorcha was far more startled by them than he. She'd been appalled by a common reaction to provocation. Clearly such a temper wasn't her norm, and Hugh could only assume from her reaction that the strain of their association had begun to take its toll on her.

For that he was now deeply remorseful since it was becoming more and more obvious she wasn't normally one to be so expressive in her emotions. He'd wager she was the sort to cradle her hurt and anger to her bosom.

Nay, he had no desire to cause her pain despite the fact that he seemed to bring out the worst in her. What he did desire had been tactically barred from him by her "ground rules." Bloody hell but she was tantalizing, even when in a temper when her eyes darkened to violet and glowed with the fire of her rage. When her chest heaved and her pulse throbbed visibly along her neck. She had a passionate nature that wasn't the result of her red hair alone, but obviously she'd suppressed it for a long while.

He doubted that Sorcha had taken a single lover since her husband had died. After so long her passions were likely to be buried deep within her, and curiosity about how fiercely they would burn had haunted his dreams and tempted him to stoke them.

The attraction was mutual, the desire shared, though he knew she would never admit it. He'd seen it in the hair salon.

She'd looked at him as if seeing him for the first time and perhaps that was indeed the case, but ever since then it had been there, smoldering in her eyes when she looked at him. Simmering in that brief moment when her dewy lips had clung to his.

The voice over the speakers announced that it was time to return to their vehicles, and Hugh followed a still-stunned Sorcha through the cabin and down the metal stairs to her car. When they were both seated, she turned and looked at him expectantly. "I truly am sorry for yelling at you, Hugh."

"The fault is mine for deliberately provoking ye."

"Why did you? To shut me up?"

"Nay. Yer point had been taken. My quip was meant only to lighten the mood," he said. "Clearly, it failed in its purpose, but it was no' my intent to anger you so. I feel certain there has to be a bit of Scot in ye, lass."

"Maybe," she sighed. "Or maybe I just overreacted. This whole thing has just been so ... Well, let me just say that I'm usually not this difficult to get along with."

Hugh looked into her amethyst eyes, taken by the depths. They were so expressive, every emotion was there for him to see. The worry, the dread, the caring. He lifted a hand, letting it hover a hair's breadth over her cheek. The heat of her skin warmed his fingers, inviting his caress, but no matter how she provoked him, he wouldn't release himself to the temptation to take her lips with his again. Not merely because of their agreement or even because he needed her aid, but because the respect he had developed for her demanded that he cause her no more upset than he already had. He dropped his hand and heard her sigh—With relief? Or disappointment?—and her parted lips drew his gaze. Plump and moist, begging to be kissed.

When her tongue darted out to wet them, Hugh almost groaned aloud in frustration…his impulses urging him to turn aside his honor. He lifted his gaze back to hers as she caught her bottom lip between her teeth. Sorcha had no idea how alluring she was, how just the thought of her could lure him from his doldrums, how the sight of her in her preposterously snug clothing enflamed his senses. "Nonsense," he murmured, his brogue thick with burgeoning desire that he could not disguise. "I feel as if we *get along* verra well."

Her eyes widened in recognition of the inadvertent suggestion in his voice, and her breath released in a slow exhale. He could see her pulse quickening along her slim throat and liked to think that perhaps she was wavering in her resolve not to be touched, but the moment was lost when the cars in front of them began to move.

Sorcha quickly started her car and shifted into drive to follow.

"Then I'm glad my unusual temper hasn't made things awkward between us," she said. "I'd like for us to be friends."

"I cannae imagine why," he said, with a trace of humor to cushion the truth of the words. "I've been nothing but weak, irritable, dishonorable, and now unpleasantly provoking as well. In my time, such weakness is disgraceful."

"These days we call it being human," she countered as they pulled away from the ferry depot. "Just so you know, from my point of view you've been intelligent, humorous, and inspiring in the fortitude you have shown in facing an unimaginable situation. Maybe it's the softer side of the twenty-first century, but we don't generally expect…or necessarily appreciate…strutting and chest beating in our men."

"Might I no' beat my chest, if only a wee bit?" he jested.

"I am a duke, after all."

Sorcha laughed at that, the last remnants of her tension slipping away and her shoulders dropping as they drove into the city. "That might fly overseas, but while you're here you'll get along fine as long as you're nice to people. It's usually so unexpected that people don't know how to react."

He laughed as well, but couldn't help but add playfully, "That might be difficult. As a rule, I find the general populous to be intolerable."

"So what you're basically saying is that you don't play well with others," she said with a twist of her lips.

"Just so," he responded agreeably.

"Then I'm doubly honored that you tolerate me so well," she said before falling into thoughtful silence. A few moments later, she spoke again, this time volunteering answers to the questions he hadn't even asked, pointing out the stadiums side by side where the Seahawks and Mariners played and providing a brief rundown of football and baseball. Hugh took it all in, not realizing that his own head was almost constantly shaking in disbelief or consternation.

Soon Sorcha took a sharp left and parked in front of a shabby red brick building with large windows dominating the façade. She turned off the ignition and turned to him with a wicked grin that told Hugh he should dread what was coming next. "I know you haven't had a chance to meet many people here, yet, and in all likelihood, this is not the one I would've chosen to start with, either. My brother is ... well, he's unlike anyone you've ever met, and if there ever was a time to play nice with someone, if you want his help, this is it."

That she said such a thing, knowing the extent of his travels, worried him. "Sounds ominous. Should I worry?"

Her lips quirked. "I would."

))()()((

Laptop tucked under her arm, Claire led Hugh through a pair of heavy wooden doors at the front of the converted warehouse in SoDo, the aptly named area south of downtown Seattle where her younger brother lived. In an up and coming bohemian area where warehouses like these were being converted into art studios and lofts, Danny had managed to find a home in the grungiest building around. If there was anyone else living in the building, she'd never seen them.

The long hallways they navigated were flanked in walls of unrelieved, prison grey punctuated periodically by equally nondescript doors. For such an artsy neighborhood, there wasn't a spec of culture or decoration in sight. Reaching the end, she jabbed the up button for the elevator and turned to find Hugh eyeing the glowing circle with more than a little suspicion.

Damn, but that look was becoming absolutely adorable.

Funny, since she'd experienced more conflict with him in three days than she had with Matt in their six years together.

"You're not going to ask, are you?" she asked with a broad grin.

He shook his head. "I doubt I would be pleased wi' the answer."

The doors chimed and parted, leaving Hugh to struggle to contain his astonishment. Claire stepped in and turned to face him. "You're probably right. Come on. Let's go."

"Where?" he asked, gesturing to the compact container as if the lack of other doors spoke volumes.

"Up. You'll love it," she insisted, catching his hand and tugging him forward. Hugh grit his teeth and stepped in just before the doors slid closed behind him. Claire pushed the button for her brother's floor and the elevator ground into motion.

He closed his eyes, a prayer on his lips and she couldn't swallow the giggle that escaped her, drawing Hugh's apprehensive stare. "*Och*, I see it now," he grouched. "For every wrong I hae done ye, there will be a thousand opportunities for retribution found for ye in moments such as these. Do ye enjoy this? My discomfort? Or do all women in this time relish a man displaying such appalling uncertainty?"

Claire softened at the hurt underlying his words. "Of course not... No, I take that back. I guess I do enjoy it, but only for the joy it brings to introduce you to new things. I like your amazement, your awe for things I consider commonplace. It's like witnessing the face of discovery. And I personally believe that you are extremely brave for taking such leaps into the abyss, so to speak. I cannot think of anyone I know who would face the unknown with such aplomb. Including myself."

While the ancient elevator continued its laborious ascension, she squeezed Hugh's bicep before rubbing her hand up and down. The action was meant to comfort and reassure but the feel of that muscle tensing beneath her hand reminded her of the tension that had ensnared them on the ferry. She could have sworn for a split second that Hugh had been going to kiss her, and in that moment she'd wanted him to. Her earlier resolutions had even prodded at her to lean in and take it for herself, but indecision had won out and the moment had passed with the ferry's disembarkment.

Or had she only delayed what was starting to feel like the inevitable? Right or wrong, guilt or not, she did find him incredibly alluring.

She watched Hugh now beneath lowered lashes, sure

that he wasn't contemplating the slow grind of their ascension any longer. He was watching her, his brilliant eyes raking along her length and sending her nerves into a quaking frenzy. He wanted her. Surely it hadn't been so long since she'd seen that look in a man's eye that she couldn't recognize it now.

He looked down at her hand and then into her eyes, his blue gaze blazing with shared awareness. "Brave, am I?" he asked huskily, bending his head closer to hers. "Even after I confessed my fear of said abyss?"

"Incredibly." The words was whispered breathlessly, her eyes shifting to his lips. Even his lips were beautiful. Well-sculpted lips that had been firm against hers yet conversely soft. What would it hurt? One more kiss like the one on the beach, she thought. One more kiss that, this time, she could let herself enjoy.

She took a hesitant step closer and he stiffened beneath her touch as her hand slipped from his arm to his chest. It was as solid with muscle as she'd imagined it would be. She could feel the heat of his skin through the lightweight knit of his sweater, feel the heavy thud of his heart beating against her palm. Inhaling deeply, Claire breathed in the warmth of him, the musk of the outdoors and the sea. "Hugh," she whispered helplessly, willing him to do what she couldn't find the courage to do for herself.

Hugh groaned, or was it the heavy doors of the elevator as they slid apart? She wasn't sure, but he looked incredibly relieved as he stepped back from her hastily and turned on his heel to escape the elevator. Or escape her?

"Thank God," she thought she heard him mutter as he walked away.

For what? That the ride was over?

20

Stopping at an unremarkable metal door, Claire raised her hand to knock slowly three times and then twice again more rapidly. The pain in her knuckles was nothing compared to the sting of disappointment she'd experienced when the elevator doors opened before that profoundly desired kiss could be obtained. Why hadn't he kissed her? She couldn't have been more plain, could she? Hadn't he wanted to kiss her again?

She thought he did, but...

The door cracked open and a face appeared. Blue eyes similar to Claire's widened. "Sis, nice to see you. Who's he?" he added suspiciously, looking Hugh up and down. She couldn't blame her brother for his caution. With his height and size and those meaty arms crossed over his chest, Hugh demanded wariness.

"A friend," she answered. "Can we come in? I need a favor."

"Twice in one week? Unprecedented," the young man

drawled and opened the door wider to let them in. "Come in."

Claire motioned to Hugh and they followed Danny inside his renovated loft. Though Hugh probably outweighed her younger brother by close to a hundred pounds, he was eyeing Danny with equal caution, as if taking her warning to heart. Studying her brother as Hugh might, Claire tried to see him from an eighteenth-century point of view. There was nothing in her brother's appearance to threaten or to indicate the brilliance lurking beneath that unkempt exterior. "Danny, this is my friend, Hugh Urquhart. Hugh this is my younger brother, Danny O'Bierne."

The two men shook hands briefly. "My pleasure," Hugh said with what she understood now was ingrained ducal courtesy, but her brother just grinned lazily.

"A pleasure indeed," he drawled out before turning to Claire. "So what can I help you with, my favorite sister?"

"Only sister," she countered by rote.

"That's why you're my favorite." Danny turned and led them deeper into the wide-open space of his loft. It was a standard renovation. The kitchen, dining, and living area open with two bedrooms and a bath walled away, but unlike many others, her brother had packed his small dining area with a couch and huge television, with the console holding every conceivable gaming system and game, while the "living area" presently housed no less than a dozen tall racks filled with internet servers, fans blowing from every side to keep them cooled. Nearly a dozen workstations were set up on tables along the perimeter of the room, most of them manned by young men who turned to look at Claire as if she were some rare, exotic specimen.

The examination was par for the course when she came

to visit her brother. She was a woman in a room full of computer geeks. Danny himself had equated the phenomenon to them seeing a copy of Marvel Comics No. 1 at Comic-Con. It was rare and beautiful, but they didn't dare touch it or believe it was real. She waved at them merrily, seeing new young faces in with those she recognized. To a one, they blushed and turned away without a word.

"Did you bring your laptop for me?" Her brother dropped into his well-worn office chair.

She handed her laptop to him. It had been stupid of her to use it to search for Hugh's history. If Jameson got ahold of it, she might as well have written a confession of her collusion.

"Don't bother with that just yet, Danny," she said, glancing up at Hugh, who was looking around the room as she might look at Mars. "There is something else I'd like you to do."

Danny rocked back in his chair, scooping up a slice of pizza from an open box next to his keyboard as he did so. "*Ah*, yes, favor number two. I am intrigued."

Knowing there was little that could actually shock this particular brother, Claire laid her request out in no uncertain terms. "I'd like you to hack into Mark-Davis and find out what you can about a project being run by Dr. Roy Fielding."

"Is that all?" He wrinkled his nose and sniffed with some disdain as he took a bite of the pizza. "I thought it might be something more interesting."

"Oh, it should be interesting," she promised and scrunched her nose as well. "Don't you ever eat anything besides pizza?"

"Why bother when the four basic food groups are so brilliantly combined in one handheld delight?" he responded ridiculously before spinning his chair and dropping the pizza back into the box. "Do you want to wait?"

"Claire blinked. "Can you do it that fast?"

"More than likely." Danny rolled his chair to a table with three large monitors arranged around the keyboard. Pushing another empty pizza box aside, he began to type faster than she thought him capable of moving. "These high-tech guys think they're all that, but ..." he shrugged as if the rest of the sentence were an obvious one and applied himself to the keyboard. For a few moments only the hum of the numerous servers and fans and the tapping of keys broke the silence of the room.

Danny grumbled incoherently and Claire felt her hopes plummet. "Are you not going to be able to get in?"

"Your company is so untrusting," he complained. "Even the government doesn't try this hard to hide things." He typed again, the screens bringing up page after page of what looked like gibberish to her. "*Aha*, there we are. Oh, that's interesting," he mumbled more to himself than to her. "Might have to go back and look at that. Fielding, you said? There are five projects he's head of."

"Five?" She frowned. "Is there one that shows any connection to INSCOM?"

Danny's brows rose but he said nothing and went back to work. He snorted a few times, humphed once or twice, and rifled through a box with several labeled USBs before picking one and inserting it into the portal. "Really? Man, they don't want you in there, do they? These military types..."

Still, less than twenty minutes after they walked in the door, he pushed away from the desk, rolling back several feet as he gestured toward the monitor with a broad sweep of his arm. "Ta-da."

"Danny, you are a genius!" Claire announced, bending to kiss his cheek.

"Don't I know it? Well, pull up a chair and let's take a look. With all that encryption, it must be something good." She turned to Hugh with a winning smile. "You ready?"

)O(O(O(

Hugh nodded in the face of her enthusiasm, though he wasn't at all certain on the matter. Sorcha had been right. What good would it do to know how he'd gotten here? The knowledge would not give him power. It would not give him understanding. It would give him nothing if the key to his return were not there as well. Given hers previous comments on the matter, it sounded to him as if this Dr. Fielding had no control in the matter.

It was not for him, the fantasy of home.

He watched Sorcha, her head close to her brother's as they explored together. "There," he heard her say as she pointed at the screen. "Try that." Danny complied and another screen appeared.

Danny O'Bierne was an interesting specimen of a man, Hugh thought, studying the young man in turn. Sorcha had called him her younger brother but he could scarcely credit it given the man's appearance. He was tall, but long and lean with scraggly ginger hair and sparse beard. He was incredibly pale as well, more so than Hugh was after his recent incarceration. Danny had the look of a man who hadn't seen the sun in many a year, and Hugh had to wonder if he'd been imprisoned until recently. In any case, he looked years older than Sorcha.

"Let me try this one, my sister," Danny said in slow, drawn out words. His manner of speaking puzzled Hugh as well. He'd never met a man who had seemed so vague yet held stark intelligence in his eyes. He was more unusual than Sorcha had hinted.

Leaving them to their reading, Hugh turned his back on the alien room and went to the windows, noting the heights the moving compartment had allowed them to reach. How long would it take before nothing surprised him anymore? How long before he didn't take absurd satisfaction in knowing a simple colloquialism when it fell from another's lips?

How long would it be before the esteem in her eyes faded into disgust?

It was a game to her now, this thing she referred to as the joy of watching discovery, but surely the novelty would erode over time and her frustration with his inadequate knowledge would grow. He would become an annoyance to her while to him she was an ever-expanding source of fascination. Sorcha was incredibly complex, and he longed to explore each and every facet of her. Perhaps all women of this time were equally complex, but he doubted there was another who possessed such an intriguing combination of intelligence, pointed wit, vulnerability, and veiled passion.

And such beauty. She had glorious hair, fiery and full as it fell around her shoulders. Hugh wasn't accustomed to a woman wearing her hair so outside the bedchamber, though he knew she didn't wear it so all the time. The previous day it had been twisted untidily at the back of her head and secured with a large clawed comb. Nor did she dress provocatively as a rule, though she did favor the surprisingly comfortable of snug jeans. The tight blouse of the first day of their acquaintance and the snug cardigan were juxtaposed by the much larger cardigan she wore over a t-shirt today. This sweater hung to her hips but couldn't entirely disguise the luscious curve of her bottom.

Everything about her begged to be desired.

Hugh thought of that moment on their upward journey when she looked up at him with such beguiling wonder, when they had been caught together in Eros's web of mutual desire. Of course, it was cruel of Sorcha to entice him so when she was the one who had extracted his vow not to lay his hands on her. How she tempted him to break that vow as he had on the beach! She'd tempted him a dozen times since then to take her in his arms and strip away her reservations, revealing a passion sure to match his own.

Only the opening of those doors had precipitously stopped him from throwing his honor to the wind once more.

"Tell me, are you INSCOM?"

He turned to find Sorcha's brother at his shoulder and thrust his lustful thoughts aside. "Nay."

"Did you meet Claire at work, then?"

"After a fashion." Hugh felt bedeviled enough to add, "Ye could say I'm a part of Fielding's project."

"Some righteous stuff there, man," he nodded with some appreciation, taking a bite of the odd food—"pizza," Sorcha had called it— he carried with him. "I can't wait to read through it when Claire's done with it. But she didn't say why you needed it."

It was a prompt for information Hugh chose to ignore, but Danny wasn't finished.

"Normally, I wouldn't care, but it worries me that Claire would stick her neck out for just any random guy." Another pointed statement.

"As she said, we are friends," he responded.

Danny raised a doubtful brow at that. "My sister hasn't talked to a man in years, much less brought one home to meet the family. The only pictures she posts on Facebook are ones of our nephew. The only thing she Pins are recipes and cleaning gimmicks and she's never even clicked on a dating site. Not once. No secret life, no porn. Nothing. She's got the tamest cyber-life of anyone I've ever known."

"What's a cyber-life?"

"What? Did you just crawl out from under a rock, man?" Danny asked. "My point is, you look at her like these guys look at Princess Leia in a gold bikini, so I'm warning you, don't screw with her or I'll have to kill you."

It was Hugh's turn to raise a brow of disbelief as he examined the man from head to toe. There was no chance that he could come to harm at the hand of such a scrawny man, and Hugh leveled the young man with a baleful glare that told him so. But since he had no intention of "screwing" with Claire—whatever that was—he merely nodded. "Verra well."

"Well, all right then," Danny drawled amicably and nodded with a smirk as he took another bite of the pizza. If he ate like that all the time, Hugh couldn't imagine how Danny remained so thin.

"Danny," Sorcha called out, her voice filled with something akin to awe. That tone was enough to have both men turning to find her sitting back in the chair with wide eyes glued to the monitor, which now displayed some sort of schematic. "Come here. You have to watch this."

Hugh followed on Danny's heels as they returned to her side. As they neared, she clicked a button and a colorful image filled one of the screens. "Cool," Danny said. "Simulations."

Of what, Hugh wondered? To him it looked like a tornado he'd once seen, a funnel of sorts, but where the one he'd witnessed rotated, this one seemed to continually grow while the open end collapsed on itself.

Naturally, he had no idea what the image truly represented, but since Danny merely blinked at the screen, a piece of pizza hovering at his lips, Hugh felt that the astonishment wasn't only his own. "What is that? Is that what I think it is?"

"I think it is," Sorcha replied. "Incredible."

"Oh, the guys are going to love this," Danny said, dropping back into his chair and spinning around gleefully. Love what? Hugh frowned at them both, waiting for information, but Sorcha was too busy scolding her brother in a low hiss to notice.

"Danny, you can't tell anyone about this."

"Why not? It's classic sci-fi!" her brother protested. "You know what it reminds me of? That old TV show, *Sliders*."

By Sorcha's reluctant nod, Hugh could see that she agreed with him, but she remained stern in her whispered warning. "Not a word, Danny. I don't want to see this all over the Internet tomorrow. Swear it!"

Danny sat back mulishly. "You are where excitement goes to die, Sis."

It was a response that only earned him a blacker scowl. "Swear it!"

With one finger, Danny drew an X over his chest. "Cross my heart and hope to die…for as long as is deemed absolutely necessary by whatever secret you are keeping from me."

As this didn't seem like much of a promise to Hugh, he

was surprised when Sorcha sat back with a humph of satisfaction.

"Fine," she conceded. "Will you print it for me and save a copy?"

Her brother waved his hand beneath his nose. "I smell the mouth-watering aroma of blackmail in the air."

That had Sorcha smiling. "No, but it's not a bad idea. Make a few."

"As long as I get to keep one for my own personal amusement," he negotiated.

"Sure, whatever. As a matter of fact, make as many as you like."

21

As Danny went to work, Sorcha turned to smile up at Hugh with the devil dancing in her eyes. Rising, she grasped his arm, leading him back toward the windows and out of earshot of her brother. "What do you think?"

"That I hae no' yet a clue to yer discovery," he admitted reluctantly. "Ye seem pleased, however."

"I am," she said, her eyes still sparkling in a way that made him want to join in her excitement. "Well, not so much about what I found out—I'll tell you about that later—but Danny just gave me a great idea."

Hugh sifted through their conversation once again. He hadn't heard much that might inspire an idea of any sort other than... "Blackmail?"

"Yes!" She squeezed his arm enthusiastically, bouncing on her toes. "This might be just what we need to keep you safe from Jameson. Don't you see? They covered up the breakout, right? They don't want exposure. Not only would the public be outraged by the billions of dollars in wasteful spending with the economy as bad as it is, but the backlash from our allies and enemies around the world for keeping the nature of the project itself under wraps would be crippling."

Hugh looked doubtfully at the screen. "Is it truly something of such a controversial nature that they would worry so?"

"I think so," she answered slowly. "And we can use it as a bargaining chip in your favor, to keep you safe."

"To keep *ye* safe," he amended, knowing that beyond his own personal safety, he needed to know that Sorcha would emerge from all of this unscathed. The billions—he could hardly fathom the amount—wasted in this "project" and the risk of exposure and retaliation, with him standing at the center as not only proof of whatever it was they were doing but also a symbol of their failure, made the entire situation far more precarious than he'd originally imagined.

The logical move of any government would certainly be to immediately subdue or kill him and anyone who knew the truth about him outright. That was how it had been in his time and Hugh doubted that much had changed in that area at least throughout the past two hundred and fifty years. He explained his suspicions to Sorcha in no uncertain terms.

"Then we'll just have to make sure that the risk to them is greater than the reward in doing so," Sorcha said boldly.

Her brother called for her then, and she left Hugh at the windows to mull over her words.

He did not share her confidence that blackmail would assure their safety. The courts of Europe were filled with intrigue. Blackmail was a common tool to gain compliance and power. But he knew that, when backed into a corner, people were often far from predictable. There were those who would take a chance at exposure to exact deadly retribution.

To face an entire government head-on was a hazard to be wary of, but he vowed he would bring them to their very knees to insure Sorcha's safety. Exposure would be the least of their worries if she were harmed in any way.

※※※※※

"Minions are printing for you," Danny told Claire when she rejoined him. "Don't worry, they won't look. And here are your copies." He held out a pair of utilitarian thumb drives in one hand but lifted the other with a little object swaying hypnotically from one finger. "It's a USB hidden in a keychain of a little Tokidoki Thor. Isn't it cute?" He sent it swaying again.

"It's adorable," she said, taking them from him.

"I know Thor is your favorite superhero," Danny went on, then shot a glance across the room at Hugh. "Your boyfriend has that whole Thor thing going on, doesn't he? Except for the dark hair, of course. Kind of Old World Shakespeare meets Rob Roy."

"He's not my boyfriend," she insisted, ignoring the heat creeping up her cheeks.

"Of course not," he readily agreed. "That would be insane, wouldn't it?"

Claire leveled her brother with a glare that told him she knew he was trying to provoke her. Normally such a jab about what Danny had once referred to as her 'nunhood' would have angered her but now looking at Hugh standing proudly in the light cast through the windows, she acknowledged that there were worse things she could be likened to than Hugh's girlfriend.

She considered him silently for a moment, wondering where this latest discovery would take them, before turning thoughtfully back to her brother.

"Danny? How hard would it be to forge a passport?"

Danny barely raised a brow at the unusual question. "Are you in some sort of trouble?"

"No, it's not for me. It's for Hugh." Danny raised both brows at that, and Claire rushed to improvise. "He's being watched by the NSA…"

"What for?"

"What do they watch you for?" she shot back, not wanting to spill the entire truth just yet.

"Many things, but I doubt it's the same stuff they'd be watching him for," he admitted without shame. "Is he a terrorist?"

"No. Does he look like one?"

"No, but neither did Gertrude Moynihan and look how that turned out."

Claire didn't know what to say to that, as she had no idea who Gertrude Moynihan was. "He's not a terrorist, just sort of…undocumented. I'd like to help him get out of the country as soon as possible," she said, then added, "Before he's unjustly detained, you see. Do you know anyone who could do that?"

"A forged passport alone wouldn't get you onto a bus these days," he said as if she were an idiot. "I mean, you can get some good paperwork done, but if you're not in the system you're screwed."

"Then can you put him in the system?" she asked patiently. "If he's in there, maybe he can just go to the embassy, swear he's been robbed, get a new passport, and that's that."

"Nearest British consulate is in San Francisco."

As with any conversation with her brother, there was a

moment that astonished. "I'm not even going to ask how you know that off the top of your head."

"I always said you were the smartest of us all," he said sagely. "Are you smart enough to understand the inherent danger in what you're thinking?"

Claire nodded and her brother sighed. "Well, then, to answer your question, I could put him in the system but it wouldn't do any good."

"Please enlighten me."

"Well, first of all, if it's the NSA following him, they can follow him anywhere. A little international border won't stop them."

"They couldn't find him if they didn't know who he was."

"Which leads to point number two. Say you do get him a passport with a faked identity, he might still not be able to get out of the country anyway," Danny began, swinging his chair from side to side. "If the Feds are after him and have any idea where he might be going or even leaving from, they'll just watch customs and do a background check on anyone who goes through and catch him on the other side."

She frowned. She hadn't thought of that. "Shit."

"Shit is right," Danny agreed with a nod. "What he needs to do is get over there with one identity and have another new identity waiting for him so that he can start all over again. Then poof, he's a ghost."

"Which he can't do without a passport," Claire reminded him.

"Right," he said. "Why not just make him an American? Start small. Birth certificate, driver's license. Then slowly graduate up to a passport? He could stay right here, right under their noses."

She exhaled slowly at the thought. What would it be like to have Hugh stay? To help him along in small steps rather than cramming it all down his throat? To build on their friendship and maybe...one day... "I doubt he would have that much time."

Her brother raised a curious brow but thankfully refrained from further probing. "If you need to get him out that quick, then I can't see how ... But maybe..." Danny's words trailed off until he was still as a statue, pizza inches from his mouth and eyes far away.

"Maybe what?"

He held up a finger, putting her on hold. She could see the wheels turning in his mind. "Uno momento, my sister." He took a bite of the pizza, washing it down with a swig of Red Bull. "I've got an idea that might work."

"Might? What is it?"

"Let me brainstorm on it awhile and I'll get back to you."

Claire rolled her eyes with a sigh. She knew that Danny's brainstorming could last anywhere from an hour to a month. "You can hack into a high-security server in minutes but *this* takes time?"

"I might be a freakin' genius, but defrauding the federal government does take time," he informed her, grinning wickedly. "As I'm sure you already know."

Since she wasn't about to go so far as to call it that, she only said, "Fine. Call me when you figure it out." She wrote her new number on a piece of paper and handed it to him.

"This just keeps getting better and better. Someday I'll demand details."

"Someday I might just give them to you," she teased. "In the meantime, I wouldn't boot up my laptop unless you want some company of the type I know you don't prefer."

"Better and better." Tossing the pizza aside, he swiveled back to the computer and began typing madly. "Oh, wait!" He swung back again just as quickly. Danny pulled his phone from his pocket as he went to Hugh and physically pulled him to a blank interior wall of the loft. "Smile. No, don't," he corrected. "No one ever smiles on these things." A light flashed as he took a picture and then waved an impatient hand. "Okay, now go."

)O)O)O)(

Gathering up the printout, which had been contained in a large binder delivered by one of Danny's "minions," and the USBs, Claire gestured for Hugh to join her as she headed for the door. "Are we finished, then?" he asked, courteously taking the heavy binder from her hands as he blinked away the light flash.

"Thank you. Yes, we're done for now."

"Yer brother is most unique."

"My brother is an unemployed college dropout," she told him as they left the loft and headed back down the long hall toward the elevators. "He's also so damned smart he could probably head up his own think tank and invent world peace. I've always wondered what he does to make money. I mean, those servers didn't buy themselves. I probably don't want to know." No, probably not, she thought. She might have been joking when she asked what the NSA monitored him for, but Danny's response had been remarkably blasé.

"Why does he call those other lads 'minions'?"

Claire grinned. "I think it makes him feel as if he's some sort of mastermind…either that or he watches too many cartoons."

Hugh took her words in stride without asking for

clarification. Whatever the world at large might think about her brother, Danny O'Bierne was definitely far more canny than his shabby appearance might lead a person to believe. He also cared deeply for his sister and was protective of her. That alone had earned his approval. "I believe he might be 'hacking' into yer life. He knows what ye do." *And what you don't*, Hugh thought.

She only laughed, swinging a small object around her finger. "I've suspected as much for a long time. I'm pretty sure he knows me right down to my Netflix history. Sometimes I'm tempted to go to lesbian chat rooms just to see if he'll say anything."

Eight languages, Hugh thought with some exasperation. He spoke eight languages fluently and still he could not glean the meaning of her words. Often when she was excited or angry, she seemed to forget that some of her words were beyond his ken. He closed his eyes against her garble now, sure that one day he would look back on it all and be able to appreciate what amused her so.

"Aren't you coming?"

Hugh opened his eyes to find her waiting just inside that infernal box once again.

Never mind that the very mechanics of the thing sounded as trustworthy as King George's promises, the real difficulty would be in being enclosed within its confines with Sorcha for the duration of their return to the ground. Could he withstand the temptation when she seemed to be deliberately provoking him? He shook his head. He was a man of flesh and blood, not a Grecian marble. Honor aside, there was only so much a man could be expected to bear.

Looking around for an escape, Hugh spied a placard above a nearby door depicting an easily recognizable staircase.

"I'd rather take the stairs. That…"

"Elevator," she supplied.

"Aye," he nodded, adding with complete honesty, "It isnae to my liking."

Sorcha blinked not once but twice at him. "Oh, okay then. No big deal. We can walk."

"Ye needn't join me if ye'd rather ride," he offered, though the courtesy only served to deepen her frown.

"I can walk."

She led the way, bursting through the steel door and tripping lightly down the first series of steps. Hugh didn't need to be awash in the heat of her wake to know that Sorcha was disappointed in him. The question was why?

He'd asked, two nights past, to be released from his vow, and had broken it the previous morning, only to upset her. Clearly she was determined to deny the attraction that simmered between them, but ever since that argument, it seemed that she'd gone out of her way to lure him to the brink of breaking his promise again after he had only just redoubled his conviction not to do so in order to spare her upset. Now, she teased with her proximity only to pull away. Incited desire only to deny.

Never had he met a more maddening woman. It was almost as if she didn't have any idea of what she truly wanted.

22

"Tell me, lass, what's got yer feathers in a bunch now?" Hugh asked as they descended the final flight of stairs.

"Are you hungry? I know I am, and if I am, I know you must be," she responded pertly, ignoring the question as if it had never been spoken.

She was good at evasion, even if she was not terribly subtle about it. He'd noticed before that if a conversation wasn't to her liking or heading in her preferred direction, Sorcha simply plucked a new topic from the air and carried on as if nothing were amiss. She had done so that evening while standing at the sink, the previous morning when she'd overridden his attempts to apologize, and again last night after their walk on the beach, drawing close to him only to pull quickly away with an announcement that she was off to bed.

It was perhaps her most irritating quality.

Grinding his teeth with frustration, he fought the urge to take her by the shoulders and shake an answer from her. It wasn't in his nature to cater so to another's whims. He was a duke, after all. He'd been raised to command and lead with the expectation of being followed. He wasn't one to bow down to another, and he'd done so with Sorcha only out of appreciation for her aid and because he had yet to find his footing in this world, but at some point she would need to know that he wasn't going to be ridden roughshod over forever.

And now the point had been reached.

When they were once again ensconced in her small car, she started it with the key and reached for the gearshift between them but Hugh laid his hand over hers to stop her. "Hold, lass," he commanded. "I hae something to say."

She looked from their hands to his face, but this time Hugh refused to comply with the implied request. "I try verra hard, lass, to be an accommodating guest to ye," he told her. "I stayed wi' ye when I know I should hae left, and now I cannae leave, knowing that ye would be left unprotected and at our foe's mercy. I hae given my own will over to yer wishes because I ken that ye know best in this world, but I am nae fool, Sorcha. Nae lapdog to sit and stay on yer command. Nae flea to be brushed away like a minor annoyance. When I ask ye a question, I expect an answer as a matter of common courtesy and if I've done something ye hae issue wi' I expect ye to tell me so. I dinnae like this evasion, and it has to stop."

Sorcha looked away and drew in a deep breath, her lips parted...

"Nay," Hugh said firmly, foreseeing what was to come. "Dinnae even try to change the subject. There will be nae more of that."

Her shoulders dropped and she bowed her head. "I know. I do that, and it drives people nuts. It's like a nervous habit or something. When things get uncomfortable…"

"Ye maun be uncomfortable often then," Hugh grumbled.

"Pretty much since the moment I met you," she said honestly, slanting him a sidelong look.

"Tell me, then, what hae I done now?"

With a sigh, Sorcha shook her head. "You haven't done anything. It's just this damned muddled up brain of mine!" Her hand slid out from beneath his, but before he could say anything, she took his hand between her own, squeezing gently. "Hugh, you have to know that you have almost literally turned my world upside down in the past few days. I might have looked calm, cool, and collected but I was a mess inside. You have no idea how many times I wavered in my decision to help you."

"'Tis a good defense for yer actions," he allowed but added, "in the beginning."

"I'm still a mess inside," she confessed, her eyes begging for something he couldn't define. "It's like I'm riding an awful roller coaster and the carny just won't let me off."

Silence.

"Like I'm on a ship at sea during a storm."

"I see." Of course, he'd known that she was struggling with her emotions. They both were. "Then why did ye no' let me go my own way?"

She sighed, shaking her head as if asking herself that same question—one he had asked many times but had never received a satisfying answer to. "I guess it's because the ride can be just as thrilling as it is terrifying. These last three days have been more exciting for me than the last three years put together. Ups and downs until your head spins, but you know, sometimes all that commotion makes you want to…hang your head over the leeward side of the ship, so to speak."

Hugh almost had to laugh at her analogy, the anger slipping away…but then his anger with her never lingered for long. "So yer saying I make ye want to cast up yer accounts?"

"Sometimes," she nodded with a playful grimace, releasing his hand and shifting to look out the windshield rather than at him. "But sometimes you make me want to…oh, find a bigger storm. Like it could be even more thrilling but at the same time the thought is even more terrifying. Do you understand what I'm saying?"

He did. For all the doubt and chaos his appearance had brought, Sorcha was enjoying their time together and their burgeoning friendship. He, too, enjoyed their unusual camaraderie, their lively exchanges, and even their more vexing ones. Despite the brevity of their acquaintance, their relationship was already familiar beyond what might be expected. The days ahead were filled with uncertainty but borne by the knowledge that she would be there with him. And he welcomed them because of that.

But that wasn't all that Sorcha was saying.

There was another storm brewing. One that could be far more thrilling than any other. Her own reservations notwithstanding, she was alluding to something far more enticing than their evasion of the federal agents.

She was saying that she was tempted.

By him.

The realization sent a shaft of sudden lust through Hugh's veins, a primal urge to plunder, knowing the ravishment was mutually desired, but Hugh tamped back the arousal. He was coming to know Sorcha well enough to realize that an admission was not an invitation.

Forcing a calm he didn't feel into his voice, he asked gruffly, "So what do ye want from me, lass?"

"And that's where I'm still a mess," she said with a sigh, tracing a finger around the steering wheel. "I want… I want… And then I want something else."

Cryptic words to say the least, but somehow he understood her implication. What Sorcha was struggling with wasn't Hugh himself but her loneliness. After three years, it was more likely that she missed a man in her bed than that she carried any particular attraction to Hugh himself. She didn't want him. She wanted her husband back, a husband she loved still.

"Dinnae fash yerself, lass," he said, hiding his regret behind an exaggerated blustering brogue. "I told ye already that I wouldnae touch ye again wi'out yer permission. I might hae slipped yester morn but it willnae happen again."

She stared at him with some surprise. "Oh, is that why you didn't…? Oh, God, what a mess."

"I will keep my distance and respect yer wishes," he clarified, unsure of what the mess she was referring to was.

"That's not what I'm saying, Hugh."

He just shook his head. "I ken what ye mean, Sorcha. It all goes back to our argument, aye? Ye mourn yer husband still, but I can see yer lonely."

"I did… I mean, I do, but you were right. Everyone was right."

She was so flustered he couldn't help but tease. "Are ye saying ye want me in yer bed, lass? Nay, even if ye said so, I wouldnae believe ye. If the time comes, I'd be pleased to accommodate ye, for ye are a bonny, desirable woman, but I'll no' hae another man's ghost in my bed. If ye ever come to me, ye had best make sure ye come alone."

It might not have bothered Hugh before, but if he were to make love to this bewitching woman, he suddenly knew that he needed to be assured that it was he she saw, his name that was on her lips. He wanted to know that she was with him not only in body but in heart and mind. He would not have her any other way, and she was not likely to have him any other.

But even that knowledge could not stop his blood from boiling at the sight of her.

)O)O)O)(

Claire twisted her hands around the steering wheel, fighting back the incongruously girlish embarrassment that had been building throughout Hugh's speech. It was humiliating to know that she'd been so obvious in her attraction to him, but in a way, it was nice to know that the feeling was mutual, that he thought that she was beautiful—at least she thought that was what bonny meant.

That he intended to never act on that attraction, not only because of the promise she had wrenched out of him in a moment of self-flagellation but also because of her continued mourning for her husband, was disappointing. But given his reasoning, how could she be disappointed? She wouldn't want to sleep with a man who was in love with another woman, so why would a man want a woman who was in love with another man?

The problem was that she would always love Matt. He would forever hold a piece of her heart. Surely even with their temporal differences Hugh could understand that? That didn't necessarily mean that she would picture Matt when she kissed another man or be wishing that he was Matt instead. That certainly hadn't been the case when he'd kissed her on the beach. She'd drawn away for only the reason he'd identified afterward.

Fear. Claire's introspective time on the beach had provided a long list of things she was afraid of. Maybe the biggest of them all was that she would someday be content to put Matt in her past.

Which led to the reason Hugh hadn't listed. Guilt.

Indecision had set her nerves jangling. Take the leap. Cower back. Tease. Retreat. No wonder she was driving him crazy. She was a jumble of mixed signals! Like a teen with her first crush rather than a woman approaching thirty years. Perhaps it was a matter of experience in flirtation… she'd never had much of it. Had never needed or wanted it.

So she wasn't ready for a running leap into his bed—he was right about that—but she didn't want to take the option completely off the table, either. How was she to tell him that now, after what he'd said?

"I guess I've been put in my place for the second time today," Claire said at length, uncertain how to approach the true subject once more. "Or is it the third?"

"I am no' counting." Hugh's brogue had gentled again, the sting of his rebuke left behind.

"A very gentlemanly thing to do." She angled at look at him from the corner of her eye to find him waiting patiently, though she'd gotten the impression before that he wasn't a particularly patient man. Of course, what else could he do after delivering such a set down? "I'm not normally like this. You must think I'm some sort of tease."

"Nay, I believe nothing more than that ye are plagued by yer past and by yer indecision," he told her with remarkable insight. "Now, the courts of Europe are filled wi' women who lure and tease, who seduce wi' nae intention of giving a man relief. 'Tis a game to be played and enjoyed on both sides, one at which I hae much practice."

Claire couldn't help but smile at that. It seemed for a man of his years, Hugh had all he experience she lacked. "Are you saying that you are an experienced flirt?"

"I hae learned from the best. If ye are looking to wet yer feet in the pool of light romance, I would be pleased to be the object of yer flirtation."

"You're telling me that you're willing to be teased without expectation?"

"Aye, I willnae take it seriously."

Ah, but she might. Hence the guilt. Yet, the temptation he presented was still there, and he was neatly providing what she'd been afraid to ask for. Flirtation was a nice start. After all, how was she ever to know if she could move forward with her life if she never tried? "Verbal flirtation?"

"I am highly skilled."

Claire shook her head in amazement at his ego but carried on. "Touching?"

"Has been strictly forbidden," he said quickly.

"What if it wasn't?" she dared to ask and was rewarded by the heat that darkened his eyes and the flaring of his nostrils.

"Then it could play a valuable part in said flirtation."

Drawing in a shaky breath, she tried to calm her racing heart, which had been startled into a gallop by the banked desire in his gaze. Words and touching aside, he played a pretty good game with a single look.

Definitely a jumble.

"Kissing?" she whispered almost inaudibly.

His gaze shifted to her lips, and Claire could practically feel the pressure as they warmed and tingled beneath that scorching look until she couldn't help but catch her lower lip between her teeth to stop it. Hugh almost groaned as she did so, showing as no words could that flirtation was truly a two-way street.

"At yer discretion and instigation only," he said gruffly, finally looking away.

"Okay," she whispered, more to herself than to him, wondering what she was getting herself into. Right now it seemed more perilous than taking on the whole of the U.S. government.

Claire held a hand out, and ever so slowly Hugh engulfed it with his large one. His rough palm slid across hers, inciting the same riot of feeling that had surprised them both when they had first shaken hands just four days past.

God! Was that all it had been? Already it seemed like a lifetime.

"Ye mentioned being hungry," he began, leaving her to consider all sorts of hunger. But obviously he would never cease to surprise her. "It's long past luncheon and I find myself hungry as well. Can we return to the house for some food ere I wither away?"

The tension between them—of a more pleasurable sort, this time—faded, and Claire marveled at how handy Hugh was at driving a person's moods. That he could censure, humiliate, and soothe in a matter of minutes was astounding, but somehow he'd set them back to rights again.

"You're right," she replied, "we should get something to eat, and I know just the place."

23

Parking her car in a lot beneath the elevated highway near the ferry terminal, Claire turned off the motor and got out, joining Hugh on the opposite side of the car, where he stood staring up at the buildings surrounding them. "What do you think?"

"It is quite...loud."

She had to smile at that. With everything he had seen, noise was the greatest impression downtown Seattle had made on him. "Just loud?"

"'Twas one of the first things I noticed here. There is always some noise, a hum that lingers in the air, but there is surprising solitude as well. I am far more accustomed to having people aboot."

"What do you mean?"

"At Rosebraugh, there were at least fifty people within its walls at all times," he explained. "Family, retainers, servants. My home was open to my clan at all times. Court was even worse. There was nae privacy, even in the bedchamber, which often felt as if it were my valet's domain rather than my own. I hadnae dined wi' just one person in many years. The privacy is unexpectedly agreeable."

While she was conversely enjoying company where she'd been alone for years, Claire couldn't imagine sharing her house with so many people. It would be like attending a family reunion each day, and she shuddered at the thought. Every day with Danny again? Eighteen years had been enough of that!

"So we're noisy yet restful?" she teased. "Is that all?"

"Ye might no' be pleased wi' my other observations," he prevaricated. "Where is this place ye spoke of where we might find a meal?"

"It's just up the street a ways." She pointed to the north. "A restaurant called the Crab Pot. It's a little touristy, but the food is good."

"That sounds appetizing," he said, with a hint of facetiousness lacing the words.

"It's good. You'll like it." Hugh only grunted but offered his arm courteously to her. With only a heartbeat of hesitation, she took it, tucking her hand in the crook of his strong arm before leading him across Alaskan Way and up the boardwalk. As they walked, Claire relished the warmth of having a masculine arm beneath her hand once again, and he silently absorbed the sights and sounds around them, much as he had from the car earlier. The crush of people and tourists on the waterfront. The cars, buses, and cyclists to their right. The boats, birds, and shops to their left.

"What other observations?"

"Simply that ye live in a world of incredible luxury," he began, pausing to look over a table covered with small trinkets all marked with the city's name and an image of the

Space Needle. "For days now, I hae marveled again and again for what the future has wrought, marveled that the simplest object"—he lifted a souvenir pen from a cup—"such as this pen filled with ink is taken for granted." He rolled the pen between his fingers for a moment before dropping it back in the cup. "For ye, they are naught but novelties, but to me, they are nothing short of phenomenal. Yer people use wi'out care what I once saw as unimaginable. Ye hae machines to do everything for ye. To carry ye places, to cook for ye, to clean and to do yer laundry. Everywhere there are machines. It hae spoiled ye and made ye—no' just ye but all these people—lazy, I daresay. Ye cannae even walk the stairs any longer or take pride in the craftsmanship of yer buildings and furniture. There is nae adornment, nae real style. Nothing seems to be built to stand the test of time. Yer people take all that ye hae for granted."

"You're right. We are spoiled," she agreed as he guided her back into the flow of bodies moving along the sidewalk. There was no way to deny it the truth of his words. "But weren't you once spoiled as well? You had money, servants to do everything for you. By your own admission, you had no job."

"In my frustration, I was less than truthful in saying I had nae occupation."

"I can imagine as a duke you had responsibilities." She'd seen enough of the British royals to know that having a high rank didn't free a person from burden. "But then and now, that is the one constant. You work hard and you get rewarded. Only the reward has changed a little over time."

"And what will be my reward in this time?"

"That depends. What do you want badly enough to work for?"

Silence met her question and Claire looked up at Hugh to find him looking at her now instead of the city around them. His blue eyes were deep and penetrating as they met hers, telling her without words what he wanted and a bolt of excitement zipped through her veins. "Oh, well…um," she stammered with a blush, uncertain what to say, given their recent conversation on the subject. "We're here."

She nudged him toward a crowded doorway, pushing the moment aside.

"This is a restaurant?" he asked, pronouncing the new word slowly, and she cast him a bright, if somewhat forced smile.

"Like it?"

"'Tis even more deafening than the city beyond."

Another fine point that Claire could not deny. The Crab Pot was housed in the Waterfront Arcade, a building that also housed a couple tourist gift shops as well as an actual arcade. The entry hall was exceedingly loud and bursting with people. Some were shopping while others were sitting on benches that lined the way. It was Saturday afternoon on the waterfront, she realized with a grimace. Surely, there would be a wait to get in.

Grabbing Hugh's arm, she pulled him to a halt before he could just saunter pass the hostess podium into the restaurant and take any table. "Wait."

"Why? Ye cannae expect me to wait in queue."

"Sure I can. You just can't walk right in there like you own the place."

He raised a brow. "I can do anything I please."

"Really? Anything?" she scoffed. "You couldn't just walk in there naked."

"I probably could, if only just the once," he said with a

straight face.

She studied the harried hostess as she took the name of another among the waiting patrons. A half-hour wait, at least. Slanting a speculative look at Hugh, she said, "Care to prove it? Prove that you can do what you want? That you are the greatest flirt ever to come out of Scotland?"

"A wager?"

"Call it substantiation."

Hugh turned to the hostess thoughtfully but didn't move.

"Here, I'll even get you started." Approaching the hostess station, Claire cleared her throat. "We'd like a table please."

"How many?" she asked without looking up.

"Two," she answered as the girl dragged her finger down a list of names on the sheet in front of her before stopping at a blank space. "Name?"

With a sweep of her arm, Claire invited Hugh to take over, whispering "Impress me" as he passed.

With a grin, he leaned against the podium and drawled in a seductively deep brogue, "I'm called Hugh Urquhart, my bonnie lass. What is yer name?"

The hostess's head shot up so quickly Claire was certain the girl would feel the strain of it later. She was a pretty, petite girl of about twenty, but in that moment she might have been a pre-teen with her favorite teen idol in her sights, and what happened next so astonished Claire that later she would be certain she had imagined it all. The beleaguered hostess straightened, a blush spreading across her pale cheeks as she stuttered out, "I'm J-Jessica."

"Jessica, lass, ye see before ye a famished man. Might I beg ye for a table?"

"Oh, sure," she sighed and tore her eyes away to look at the list before looking up at him once again. "I just love your accent. Are you Scottish?"

Hugh leaned in and smiled an amazing, roguish grin that Claire had never seen him display, and the hostess all but melted on the spot. "Aye, lass, I am. A verra hungry Scot aboot to waste away to skin and bone."

"Oh! We can't have that, can we?" Jessica gushed with a flirtatious smile of her own.

"God, no," Claire drawled under her breath. "We can't have that."

Hugh shot Claire a wicked glance and a wink before he turned back to the hostess with a flash of white teeth and a definite smolder in his eye. "Can ye secure us a table, lass? If it wouldnae be too much of a bother?"

"Oh, no bother at all," Jessica replied without hesitation as she shuffled out a pair of menus. "Will you follow me?"

"Anywhere ye lead, lass," he said with a gallant sweep of his arm, indicating that the hostess should lead the way. She did. As she led them around the main floor and up the stairs, Jessica flirted with Hugh over her shoulder, asking questions that required answers, which he gave in thick teasing tones, exaggerating his brogue.

"I just love your accent," the girl cooed again as they arrived at a prime table near the windows.

Claire rolled her eyes. "Oh, brother."

"Will this do?" Jessica asked.

"Verra nice. Thank ye, Jessica," Hugh said, shifting to walk around the hostess just as the girl turned. The pair collided and he reached out to steady her.

"Oh! I'm so sorry!"

"No' at all," Hugh said smoothly. "*Mea culpa.*"

Jessica giggled uncertainly and Claire translated drily. "That's kind of like 'my bad.'"

"Oh!" the hostess said brightly, setting the menus on the table while Hugh held out Claire's chair and moved around the table to the other side to sit. "Well, anyway, here's your menus"—she was inwardly surprised that the girl remembered that there were two people present, since she'd hadn't torn her gaze away from Hugh the entire time—"and Becky will be your server. She should be right with you."

"Yes, I'm sure she will," she said under her breath once again, gaining another devilish grin from Hugh. A split second later, her eyes were rolling once again as he took the girl's hand and kissed it gallantly. "My thanks, Jessica, for yer kind assistance."

The hostess giggled with another blush. "Just let me know if I can get you anything else."

XOXOXOX

Claire could almost see the hostess's knees wobble as she walked unsteadily away. "Well, you proved me wrong, didn't you? You really can do whatever you like. And your powers of flirtation are truly unparalleled. Are you always such a charmer with the ladies?"

The grin turned from roguish to amused, his eyes lighting with real humor. "It is a skill required at court, and if it gets me what I want, why shouldn't I employ my many gifts where they benefit me the most?"

"Those gifts being good looks and charm?"

"'Tis my curse."

"My, you are cocky."

"But another burden to bear."

She had to laugh out loud at that and rolled her eyes yet again as the waitress eagerly approached, bearing a wooden cutting board with a loaf of bread on it. "Hi, I'm Becky. I'll be your server this afternoon. Can I get you something to drink?"

The waitress was of similar age to the hostess, Jessica, and like her co-worker, directed all of this to Hugh with an alluring smile and even batting eyelashes. It was so incredibly amusing and insulting to her gender Claire was tempted to wave a hand in front of the girl's eyes to force her attention away.

"I'll have a pint of Sam's," Claire said loudly in an attempt to draw her attention. "And he'll have the darkest, thickest, nastiest thing you have on tap. The liter."

"We have a Black Butte Porter," the waitress suggested, eagerly. "Looks like mud."

"Perfect," Claire said, expecting the waitress to wander off, but Becky lingered, gazing at Hugh with adoration. With a long-suffering sigh, Claire motioned for her to leave. "Incredible," she said to Hugh as she buttered a piece of the bread. "I would bet that she's back with those drinks in record time."

"Jealous?"

"Hardly," she denied quickly. "If your 'many gifts' benefit me as well, employ away."

He drew in his breath to respond, but as she'd predicted, Becky was back with the beers and a smile in a matter of moments. The flirting ensued, as the waitress bent farther over the table than was necessary to put Hugh's huge mug of porter down in front of him. Naturally he flashed his dimples, spoke husky compliments, and generally made the girl feel as if she were the most amazing person on the face of the planet.

It *was* a gift, she decided as she watched the show. She'd

never seen anyone who could so easily make everyone like him as Hugh did. Well, the fairer sex, anyway ... and men like his hairstylist. How would normal, heterosexual men respond to Hugh, she wondered? Would they be like some women who grew nasty in the company of women prettier than they were, or would they fall as quickly under his spell?

No, they would love him, too, she decided. He was a ladies' man but he was also a man's man. He'd probably never met a stranger in his life and was the epitome of jovial grace.

She studied him as he spoke to the waitress. His big body lounged back in the wooden chair, his arm hooked over the back, drawing his sweater tight to show off his muscular physique and washboard abs. The blue knit brought his eyes out vividly, framed by his dark lashes. His dazzling smile flashed again as he ran a hand through his hair, and Claire thought Becky might pool right there at his feet.

And she wasn't the only one. Hugh simply being Hugh was like a magnet to the room at large. Most of the diners and staff were watching him, either covertly or openly. Did it come naturally to him or was it ingrained as part of his ducal training? Could that kind of charisma be taught?

If it could, he'd had a great teacher, because he was fascinating.

Even to her. How could she deny it when there was so very much to like about him that none of these people could see? What was it about her that drew him, she wondered?

Becky paused to take a breath and Claire leapt at the opportunity to place their order, asking for "The Pacific Clambake" from the Seafest menu. This item was ordered by the person, so she requested a bucket for three, then changed it to four, knowing Hugh's appetite was often insatiable.

Lifting her mug to her lips, she considered him over the top as the waitress finally left them once more. Hugh drank as well, smacking his lips in appreciation as he downed half the liter in one swallow. "Fairly satisfying."

"High praise," Claire said as they shared a grin. "Maybe you should forgo becoming a professional golfer and open a brewery in your new life." She was biting her lip before the last word was complete, regretting the reference to that mysterious something that awaited him in the months and years to come. She could only imagine how the uncertainty of the unknown rubbed him raw and was sorry to have brought up the painful subject again. "I'm sorry. I shouldn't have said that."

"Ye needn't watch yer tongue wi' me, lass," he said softly, but there was a new, firm resolve in his eyes that hadn't been there before. "'Tis nothing I hae no' already considered. I hae determined that I need to accept my fate such as it is wi'out mourning for the past. For now, my goal is to secure my freedom and yer safety. When those things are assured, I will consider how to best pass the remainder of my years."

All of that without a trace of self-pity. he could certainly teach her a thing or two about how to move forward from tragedy.

Stretching across the table, she covered his hand with hers and gave it a squeeze. Hugh turned his over and clasped her hand in his, tracing his thumb over the back of her hand. "You are an amazing man, Hugh," she said sincerely, but he just shrugged off the compliment.

"Nothing I hae done as yet would make my ancestors proud," he said. "I intend to remedy that. But until I do, I am going to apply myself to yer uncle's library and try to find out everything that has happened in the world between my time and yers."

"That could take awhile."

"Dinnae worry, lass," he said with a wink. "I am equally resolved to begin enjoying life here as well and I will certainly enjoy the chance to engage in an innocent flirtation wi' ye." His thumb slipped between her fingers and slid across the center of her palm. The calloused pad chafed lightly, leaving a tingling warmth trailing behind the caress, and Claire suppressed a shiver, pulling her hand away.

"I think your definition of 'innocent' and mine might be vastly different."

"Indeed? Innocent words can describe yer beauty. Like how I wonder if yer skin is as soft and silky as it looks and how I long to touch ye, how I love to see yer blush creeping up yer cheeks and I wonder at the thoughts that prompt yer pulse to quiver just here." As if having the full force of Hugh's husky brogue turned on her hadn't been enough, he traced a line down the side of her neck, sending that pulse skyrocketing and Claire's head spinning. "*Ah*, 'tis as soft as I imagined," he whispered, his eyes dark with desire.

She fell back in her chair and grasped the handle of her beer mug once more, eager to cool the fire that was building inside of her. "God, you're good. I'd hate to see what you can do when you have a vested interest."

"Who says I dinnae?" he asked, and her gaze clashed with his, wondering at his words and what she read in his eyes.

It was the same look he'd given her on the street. It wasn't playful flirtation there but compelling seduction that enticed her to cast her caution and fears aside. Their attraction was a mutual one, she knew that, but she'd thought it to be a casual one, at least from Hugh's perspective. Just a this-leads-to-that sort of thing that he had downplayed as anything more powerful with his invitation for light flirtation. But unless she truly was verging on nunhood, that wasn't simply wanton desire she saw in his eyes. It was hunger. The kind that demanded total, soul-baring surrender.

It was thrilling and terrifying at the same time, and Claire was once again aboard her proverbial ship at sea, tossing and tipping. A part of her wanted to ride out the storm, while the other part demanded that she abandon ship *immediately*.

An image flashed through her mind from an old movie she'd seen once where the people aboard a ship lashed themselves to the masts during a storm to avoid being swept overboard, and Claire mentally did the same. In laying out the terms of their flirtation, she'd committed to taking a leap into the unknown, not the leap overboard. She needed this challenge if for no other reason than to force a change in her life, and she was going to brave it even if she had to mentally tie herself down for it.

24

Thankfully, their food arrived—again with unusual speed—to break the thoughtful mood, and Becky, accompanied by a pair of helpers—each one predictably female—set cutting boards and mallets in front of Claire and Hugh and arranged a plate of skewered salmon and halibut and another of little cups of melted butter and lemon slices at one end of the table before dumping out a large bowl of Dungeness crab, snow crab, clams, mussels, oysters, shrimp, Andouille sausage, corn on the cob, and red potatoes onto the thick white paper that served as their tablecloth. The bowl and a roll of paper towels found a home on the other end of the table.

The delicious scent of the hot seafood filled the air, and, eyes closed, Claire leaned forward to sniff appreciatively. Her stomach grumbled in anticipation of the carnage that was about to take place. Fingers curling around the mallet, she opened her eyes to find Hugh staring at her, aghast.

"What is this?"

She frowned, looking to the food and back at him. "Dinner." She pointed with the mallet here and there, listing, "Clams, oysters, mussels …"

"I know what they are," he said with some exasperation. "But to simply *shovel* it upon the table so. And do ye truly expect me to use this?" He picked up the wooden mallet as if it were something foreign.

"And these." She lifted her hands, spreading them wide and wiggling her fingers. His expression went from shocked to appalled, and she couldn't help the laughter that bubbled up and spilled over. "Oh, come on, Hugh! It's fun. I wouldn't think you'd mind."

"Ye think yers is the only culture to employ a fork?" He eyed the feast apprehensively. "It does smell most appetizing, though."

"It is." She smiled. "Wait. We're forgetting something." Taking a small, plastic-wrapped package off the table, she rose and walked around behind Hugh. Within seconds, his expression was beyond priceless as he stared up at her in horror.

"I willnae!" Claire burst out laughing as he tore the plastic bib she'd just tied around his neck off and crumbled it in his hand. "I am no' some wee bairn to be needing such a thing."

Forcing her lungs to draw in air, she fought for breath as she continued to laugh. Eyes dancing, she opened her own bib and tied it on, smoothing the red and white printed plastic over her chest before picking up a snow crab leg and expertly cracking it on first one side and then the other. Pulling it apart, she popped the long piece of crabmeat into her mouth and smiled brightly.

"I thought ye dinnae eat meat."

She shrugged. "I should've said pescetarian. I'll eat seafood. The sausage is all yours though." She lifted another piece of crab and he followed suit. "You'll ruin your sweater."

"I might rather do so than look so foolish," he said, taking up the skewered salmon and pulling a piece of fish off the wooden stick carefully before putting it in his mouth.

Eyes still dancing merrily, Claire signaled to Becky, who was still lingering nearby, and the waitress approached instantly. "Becky, you forgot our forks. Could you bring us a couple?"

The waitress nodded and dashed off, and Hugh stared at Claire incredulously. "Ye knew there were to be utensils?"

"Of course, you silly thing," she said cheerfully as she squeezed a few lemon wedges over the pile of food. "You can't eat potatoes or get the clams out of their shells without a fork, you know."

※※※※

Hugh scowled at Sorcha, whose attention was firmly focused on shelling the shrimp in her hands, an amused smile still playing at her lips. The angry expression was merely for show, and he suspected she knew that. But he did so enjoy her propensity to tease and provoke.

Unless she was provoking him in far more stimulating ways.

"Another of those moments I spoke of?"

Sorcha blinked blankly.

"Retribution?"

She grinned knowingly but offered a helpless shrug. "Maybe just a little. I can't seem to help it. You just make it so easy."

Joining her in her laughter, he applied himself to the feast before him. Though he truly had been shocked when the meal had been presented, he'd been more than pleased to exaggerate his outrage to entertain her and to encourage her playfulness.

She was lovely when she smiled. Breathtaking when she laughed, her unusual amethyst eyes bright and shining with humor, a blush coloring her cheeks. Hugh felt the desire he'd been fighting against stir once again. Her 'innocent' flirtation might well be the end of him.

Unaware of the thoughts in his mind, Sorcha continued on after Becky returned with the forks and they began working their way through the pile of food before them. She pushed all the sausage toward him but feasted heartily on the shellfish and vegetables. "Does this really bug you?" she asked, and then added for clarification, "Bother you? You're not actually going to tell me that an eighteenth-century Scot has never eaten with his fingers before?"

"Nay, I cannae say that I hae ne'er done so," he conceded. "Even as recently as the battle at Culloden it was so, as a soldier has few options when in the field. But I again remind ye that I hae also dined wi' kings. The appropriate silver was always wielded wi' each course."

"How many courses?" she asked curiously, catching a drop of butter off her chin with a fingertip before licking it away in a manner that once again sent Hugh's thoughts skewing. She thought she was the only one affected by their flirtation? The lass could set his blood on fire with an innocent gesture!

"What? *Och*, upwards of a dozen at times," he answered, and her brows rose.

"I can't even imagine," she said, dabbing at her mouth with a paper towel, much to Hugh's regret. "What was it like? King Frederick's palace?"

So, they ate on while Hugh regaled her with stories of court, comparing the simplicity of traditional Scottish meals with the rich French cuisine that was all the rage on the Continent. From there he began recalling some more ridiculous moments, such as the pageants and plays that would be performed, often with a man or two heavily rouged and dressed as women, as well as some more cultural ones, such as the orchestras assembled to perform the King's work.

It was astonishing to him to discover that his descriptions of the clothing worn at court were of equal amusement to her. Oh, she punctuated his accounts of the ladies' garb, silks and satins crusted with gemstones and dripping with lace, with *oohs* and *ahs*, but describing a gentlemen in the same seemed to tickle her immensely. Though he'd powdered his hair as a concession to fashion on occasion, he found himself glad he could honestly deny ever having worn a wig or jeweled heels.

With such a reaction, Hugh felt he might have cried like a bairn in her arms and maintained more respect as a man in her eyes than the fashionable wearing of lace and satin allowed him. It was yet another aspect of this strange time to puzzle over.

Eventually, she sat back in her chair, wiped her fingers, and removed her bib, leaving him to conquer the remaining mountain of seafood alone. She nursed her second mug while Becky solicitously brought one porter after another for him. Just as Hugh would reach the bottom of one, another would appear at his elbow.

When the last shell had been shucked and the last bit of fish consumed, he sat back with a sigh of contentment and raised his mug to his lips once again. "Most satisfactory."

"Sorry I can't feed you so well all the time."

"Ye hae done verra well, lass. Ye a far more skilled cook than I in any case."

"I think we both know how much of a compliment that truly is," she said drily, and he chuckled. "We already determined that as a duke you have no practical skill in the kitchen."

The sound of his laughter seemed to draw the waitress like a magnet, for within seconds Becky was there once more. She watched him from beneath her lashes as she cleared away the leftover bits and the bowl of shells. "Can I get you anything else?" she asked. "Another beer? Or dessert maybe?"

Sorcha shook her head at the eager girl and asked with a raised brow, "Anything else, Hugh? Dessert?" The last was drawled out with a touch of humor.

Hugh gave his denial to the waitress and asked for the check as he'd seen Sorcha do before. As Becky walked away, Sorcha gave a little laugh as she finished her second beer. The alcohol had softened her through the course of the meal. He'd not yet seen her so relaxed. "She would've served herself up for dessert if you'd asked her to, Hugh."

Glancing after the retreating waitress, he knew her teasing words were true enough. If he dared to say so aloud, she would no doubt laugh and call him conceited or some such but truth was truth. With his looks, position, and wealth, he'd never lacked for female company. Offers for affairs or single nights were common enough, and Becky was a bonny young lass. Doubtlessly, she would make a satisfying bedmate.

But she wasn't what Hugh wanted. She wasn't *who* he wanted. He'd seen enough women in this time—whether on the television or in passing—to know that there were many attractive ones. The abundance of cosmetics saw to that, but none could compare to her ravishing beauty, her auburn locks, beautiful eyes, and beguiling smiles, or to the spirit of her soul or the caring in her heart that had saved his life.

Becky returned to the table, but he couldn't spare her even a look this time. His focus was on Sorcha as she counted out a large sum of money from their meager funds and tucked it into a black folder.

Not only had the time come to start thinking of the uncertain future that loomed before him but the time had also come to consider his path to a more equitable relationship with her. To offer recompense for more than she provided him, whether it be given in humor or funds. It was time to discover a way to truly pay her back for all she'd given.

"Ready?"

Hugh nodded and stood to pull her chair back. He followed her through the restaurant, watching her hair swing back and forth hypnotically as she walked.

)O(O(O(

The sun was beginning to dip behind the mountains to the west, a sign that the day was nearly done and it was time to return to their island hideaway, but he was hesitant to do so. Much had occurred between them in the hours since their departure that morning. They had moved from anger and wariness to friendship. They had gone from an arm's length to the warmth of Sorcha's body pressed against him as she held his arm. They had changed the rules for the behavior that guided them, allowing for flirtation, for touch, and his fingers already itched to do so.

It wasn't his habit to care so deeply for a woman, to like her so well. His past relationships had been distant and oddly professional. He'd kept an occasional mistress but had found ample company among the ladies at court; each had sought to gain something, whether it be wealth or notoriety, from him. There had never been a more serious flirtation, nor had he seriously courted a woman with intent of marriage. In his time and in his position, marriage was a business, not a romance, and at some point in his life, Hugh would have approached it as such.

Of course, that might have been why their mourning period was more unemotional and methodical as well. He knew men and women alike who might have declared love for their mistress or lover, but could think of none, including his uncle and aunt, who claimed it for their spouse.

He had not ever before experienced, nor could he think of another who had admitted to experiencing, anything like this overwhelming desire he felt for Sorcha. It was provocative and frustrating, fraught with both freedom and possessiveness. His arms ached to enfold her and his body yearned to be encompassed by hers. Never in all his days had he simply *wanted* so profoundly what could not truly be his.

How was he to go back to that quiet house with her, with nothing to think about but her? How he could bear wanting her so, flirting and teasing, knowing all the while that another man held her heart?

25

The Fifth Day of Freedom

"Wow. No wonder they want to keep this secret," Sorcha said, setting aside the binder filled with the information Danny had printed for them the previous day as Hugh looked up from the stack of old newspapers he'd been working his way through while she read through the technical report.

She rubbed her eyes with a sigh before lifting her head to stare out the window, but he wasn't certain if she was truly seeing the misting rain and rolling waters at all. She looked dazed and introspective, but since she'd spent the whole of the previous evening and most of the morning poring over the contents of the thick binder, Hugh couldn't blame her.

Nor did he rush to ask about what she'd discovered. A part of him wanted to know, but as he'd conceded the previous day, there was probably nothing in the report that would be able to change his circumstances. Perhaps the only good they might truly derive from it was the knowledge of what they were up against.

So, instead of asking, he went into the kitchen and poured her another cup of coffee, preparing it as he'd learned she preferred it, with little coffee and large amounts of sugar and flavored cream. Returning to the library, he pressed it into her hands and went to the fireplace, stoking the flames and adding more wood to fight the lingering morning chill. He loved the room with its huge stacked stone fireplace, clean white painted shelves, soft green walls, deep, comfortable furniture, and wealth of books.

With Sorcha there with him.

As she'd said, it was easy to become spoiled.

"Are you going to ask?"

She was hugging her mug in both hands, peering at him curiously over the brim as Hugh returned to the sofa they had been sharing and sat next to her. Not too close; he was finding that her permission to flirt had made her proximity an almost unbearable temptation. "I'm sure ye will tell me when yer prepared to do so."

"But you don't really want to know any more, do you?"

She was coming to know him so well. "I believe I *need* to know."

Sorcha nodded solemnly. "So do you want the gritty details or just the Cliffs Notes version?"

"One day ye might hae to tell me what these 'Cliffs Notes' are," he teased, reaching out to tweak her chin but pulling away before he made contact. A brief caress of that silky skin would not be enough now. "'Tis a rainy day with little else to do, so tell me all if it pleases ye to do so."

"What? Oh, right," she said, casting him a sidelong glance, as if the request was at odds with her thoughts. "Let me start with the basics then. Do you know what a wormhole is, Hugh?"

No, but he didn't ever want to admit such ignorance again. Instead, he only raised a brow. "Okay, how about a black hole?" she asked, then sighed. "Gravity?"

Hugh scowled at that. "As ye said, I am nae simpleton, Sorcha."

"Okay, imagine a body in space with a gravitational pull stronger than light," she said, prompting a vague recollection.

"Aye, there was a man, an Englishman, I cannae recall his name but he was a rotund, dark-faced man ... a member of the Royal Society, who experimented with gravity and magnetism. He theorized such a thing." He tapped a finger on his lips as he tried to remember the details of the brief discussion. "Something about a heavenly body so massive that light couldnae escape it. Is that what you are referring to?"

"Right. A black hole."

"He said ye cannae see it. 'Twas only a theory."

"That has become truth. The reason you can't see it is because it won't reflect light, but we know where they are because they pull on other objects around them." She paused, then asked, "With me so far?"

He nodded, and she continued. "Jump through history to the theory that a black hole is a region of space/time. A combination of the two, okay? A wormhole—and I am going to be incredibly simplistic here so don't beat me up over it after you read a textbook on the subject—would be like two black holes meeting in the middle, like a tunnel with each end in a different space/time, connecting two points even a million miles away from each other with a pathway between. They always use the example of a folded piece of paper where two ends that were far apart are suddenly right next to each other." Shea drew two dots on the back of one of the pages in the binder, representing them as black holes and bending the page so that the dots met as a demonstration.

He nodded again. He could visualize that. "Carry on."

"These wormholes aren't constant. Again, it's all theory—I mean, we don't know, because we haven't been there to see it—but we think they form and collapse pretty quickly and they exist at a Planck-scale level. I mean, it's far below subatomic levels…" She paused at his petulant scowl. "It's really, really, really small. So small that it is pointless to try to physically measure them. Anyway, at that level it's believed that space/time is unstable and chaotic. They call it quantum foam, and the wormholes form pretty easily in those conditions.

"Most of the quantum wormholes in the foam lead only a few Planck-lengths away. About this far," Sorcha said, pressing her thumb and forefinger together with no space between. "But sometimes they can span light-years or even across the universe. Well, one theory leads to another and someone gets the idea that you can cross through it. Then comes the idea of a transversible wormhole that says you should be able to go back and forth across it. But all in all it's a naturally occurring event."

"In space," he clarified.

"Yes, in space. That's what makes this whole thing so weird." She picked up the binder and idly flipping through the pages. "There's this organization called INSCOM—it's an acronym; the military is big on them. It stands for U.S. Army Intelligence and Security Command. Basically they are the covert sector of the Army tasked with counterintelligence, information warfare, and electronic warfare."

"They're spies?"

She waggled her hand back and forth. "It's a gray area. It's hard to be an Army wife without getting a feel for these kinds of things. I would say they are spies as much as they wage a little warfare electronically themselves. These days you can cripple a nation with just a few keystrokes."

He only raised his brow. "Verra well. Carry on."

"Okay, so this whole thing started when INSCOM contracted DARPA—another acronym that stands for Defense Advanced Research Project Agency. DARPA is a military think tank paid by the government agencies to just spout out new ideas. Mark-Davis works with them a lot, kind of like two brains in the same head. Apparently there are places already that can create a wormhole, but DARPA has been trying to develop a way to take one of those short-lived wormholes, stabilize it, and expand it for macroscopic use... Making it big enough to actually see. They want to trap one end and stabilize it using negative energy. Theoretically, negative energy is the stuff that caused the initial inflation of the early universe."

"The early universe?"

"Are you too early for the Big Bang Theory?" she asked, but read Hugh's closed expression well enough to know there would be no answer forthcoming. She rubbed her eyes again, tiredly. "Oh, I so don't want to argue creationism with you right now. Let's just leave it at the idea that with this negative energy, you could open one end of a wormhole and expand it, okay? Are you with me so far?"

Surprisingly enough, he was. Other than a few of her terms, Sorcha's explanation had been simple enough so far. "So how are they employing this power?"

"DARPA hooked up with Dr. Fielding to start

developing new surveillance technology for INSCOM using wormholes. Basically, they started out wanting to be able to open a tiny wormhole into a room or area where bad guys are meeting or whatever. From their end, they could open a large enough one to send through a small camera or a microphone so they could see and listen to conversations even in bunkers far underground. It would be virtually undetectable."

"Would they truly attempt something so far-fetched?" Hugh asked after a moment's thought. "It disnae sound like ye believe it either."

"I wouldn't normally but since INSCOM is part of the same organization that tried to develop parapsychologic methods in the seventies and eighties, I guess I can't be too surprised. They were trying for this thing called remote viewing, where a psychic or seer could look into the minds of people across the world and see what they were planning."

He snorted at that. "And ye think my time was filled with witchcraft and other such nonsense!"

"I agree with you on that point."

"But if a wormhole is a natural phenomenon, how are they controlling it?"

She shuffled through the pages once more, obviously not searching for an answer but occupying her hands. "An electrical charge—we've gone over electricity, right?—well, the charge steers the destination end of the wormhole, which stays on Earth rather than taking off across space because it is the nearest gravity well to the opening. I mean, it could go somewhere else but the tendency is for it to stay on Earth. But it requires vast amounts of power. We're talking a whole grid devoted to keeping this thing running for just a few minutes, so they can't keep it on all the time."

Hugh nodded as he processed the information she'd

provided. "So how did I get involved in all of this?"

"Well, now that's where Fielding really screwed up—or I guess found their moneymaker, depending on how you look at it. They found out through a little trial and a lot of error that if the power was shut off abruptly rather than slowly backing it down, the negative energy construct—the force that was holding the wormhole open—would just collapse. As the negative energy collapses, it momentarily enlarges the wormhole. Think of it as an implosion followed by a larger explosion. When this happened, the opening would enlarge and last for a second or two, leaving no trace once it was gone. Fielding stumbled onto a gold mine here, Hugh. That is why the NSA was called in on this whole thing. The government agencies are notorious about not wanting to share their toys, and INSCOM obviously doesn't want this ability to become common knowledge among the other agencies or our allies. Can you imagine the power in being able to get somewhere, knowing that there was no way for anyone to track your movements?" she asked. "I mean, they can't keep this thing open for long with their current energy source. It wouldn't be long enough to send troops through, for example, but it would probably stay open long enough to kidnap or assassinate someone. Or at least long enough to toss a bomb through."

"Or to have an innocent passerby fall into it."

"Yeah, that too," Sorcha said, her voice ripe with sympathy. He pushed off the sofa and went to the window, staring just as blankly as she had before. She continued softly, and he knew that the worst was yet to come. "I think that the trouble my friend Darcy was referring to is that Dr. Fielding hasn't been able to nail down the destination point at all, and if he can't do that, then what's the point, right?"

"What do ye mean, he cannae control the destination?"

She bit her lip hesitantly. "The other end just bounces all over the place…and time, apparently, each time they power it up. As far as I can see, the targeting software is showing that it opens up at different destinations with no discernible pattern."

"So I just walked into this wormhole when it 'bounced' into the Drumoisse Muir two hundred and fifty years ago?" he asked unnecessarily. He already knew the answer. By God but he had always thought he'd lived a fairly charmed life. How unlucky could a man be to happen upon such an occurrence with such incredible bad timing?

"And you and that Native American probably startled Fielding to death when he realized that his wormhole didn't travel through space alone," she told him. "I didn't see anything in there about anticipating time travel."

He grimaced at that. "And the reason he dinnae simply send us back through the hole is because he cannae duplicate the destination," he said dully. He'd been expecting that, of course, but it didn't make the truth any easier to hear.

"And the reason he kept you was because there was no way he was going to go public with such a huge mistake."

Lovely, Hugh thought. How terribly comforting to know that it was all nothing but an innocent mistake.

26

Hugh fell into a brooding silence, standing at the window with one hand braced against the pane. Unlike at his last such lapse, this time Claire was all sympathy. Lord only knew she had hated telling him the truth. It couldn't have been any more pleasant to hear it.

His attention had drifted to a cargo ship chugging by in the distance, but she wasn't certain if he was truly seeing it or if his thoughts were turned entirely inward at that point.

It was there again, that urge to comfort, but this time she didn't try to turn it away. She went quietly to his side and slipped her cold hand into his warm one, giving it a comforting squeeze. Finally, he looked down at her with the desolation that had been temporarily banished lurking once again in his eyes, but even when all must have seemed lost to him, Hugh was still chivalrous enough to recognize the chill that had come over her. He caught her hand between his and chafed it between his. "If we have the schematics for the machine, could we build it ourselves and find a way to send me home?"

"I'm not a quantum physicist, Hugh," she said regretfully, absently slipping her other hand between his for warmth as well. "And I don't know anyone who is. Time machines are as new a concept to me as they are to you. It's always been just science fiction."

"So we cannae just build our own then?"

"Not unless we can harness the 1.21 jigawatts of electricity it would take to work one," she quipped, then bit her lip. "Bad joke. But, no, there is no way we could find a power source even if we could build the machine itself."

He grunted but remained silent. Silent enough to renew her worry as he looked into the distance once more. She wondered what he was thinking but couldn't bring herself to ask. Instead, she slipped her arms around his waist and hugged him close, resting her cheek against his chest. The warmth of his embrace, the press of his body against hers was everything she'd imagined it would be. She could only hope that human contact provided him the comfort it gave her now when he needed it the most. "I'm sorry. So sorry that I can't give you the answers I know you want to hear."

His arms came around her, tenderly at first, but then he was clutching her so tightly it almost stole her breath. He buried his face in her hair, and she could feel his deep breaths caressing her neck. One hand crept up her back until his fingers tangled in the hair at her nape.

Her heart full of worry for him, she whispered into his shoulder, "Are you okay?"

Lifting his head, Hugh pressed a kiss against her temple and eased away, raising his other hand until he was cradling her head between them, the heels of his hands against her jaw and his fingers curling at the base of her skull.

Looking down at her, he seemed as fierce and hard as he had been that first day, but this time it was not trepidation that made Claire tremble.

"You can kiss me now if you like," she whispered helplessly, fully expecting that he would take advantage of the offer. But as he tended to, he surprised her again.

"Nay, lass, I do plan on kissing ye long and hard, but when I do, it willnae be in a moment of gratitude," he said, searching her eyes intently. His eyes were dark with growing desire but there was a question there as well. "I dinnae ken what it is about ye, Sorcha, but for some reason I cannae remain in a mood for long since I hae been in yer company. For as long as I was held in that prison, I was angry. Every day more so than the one before. I should be angrier than I am now for all that was done to me, for what was taken away. I should be angrier wi' ye for being so provoking, but I am no'. Why is that?"

"My charm is irresistible?" she jested, summoning the hint of a smile to the corner of his mouth.

"Is that what it is?" he asked with just a whisper of humor but it was enough for her to know that the worst had passed. "Either way, ye've been a balm to my soul."

"Gee, I've never been anyone's balm before," she whispered in an awed tone, hoping to banish the shadows lingering in his eyes. It seemed to work.

His blue eyes brightened at that, and the tension in his expression eased. She felt the pad of his thumb caressing her cheek tenderly. "And what am I?"

Temptation? Salvation? She shook her head. "You're a vacuum."

"A vacuum?"

"It's a..."

"I ken what a vacuum is, lass. I only wonder how it might apply to a person."

"Oh, well, that's easy," she said with a winsome smile. "You have sucked all the anger right out of me. I hadn't realized how angry I was with the world at large and everyone in it, but you've helped me to see that and send it all away. Admittedly, it lingered on the surface there for a while, but now I'm all cleaned out."

"Is that so?" He raised an arrogant brow. "I may provoke ye to anger again."

"Nope, I won't let you. This is now an anger-free zone."

Hugh released a dry chuckle. "I doubt that. Ye are easily roused."

Yes, I am, Claire thought, and he must have intuited her more lascivious thought in some way because his brow raised slightly. Suddenly she realized that she was still standing in the warmth of his embrace as naturally as if she belonged there. She was locked in his arms with his hard thighs pressed against hers, his broad chest against her breasts. With her head tilted back to look at him, she was arched against every inch of him. The desire that she'd fought against and denied assailed her once more, but this time Claire let it flow over her, savoring the feel of her heart fluttering in her chest, the shaky intake of breath, and even nerves that made her hands tremble as they slid up his muscular back.

Hugh's fingers tightened in her hair, forcing her head back even more until his lips were just inches from hers, but his body was taut, as if relaxing would allow his mouth to fall on hers against his bidding.

"I'm not feeling an ounce of gratitude, I swear it," she whispered. "Are you?"

"Nay," he murmured huskily. "Nary a bit."

But still he did not kiss her, and then Claire remembered their bargain. Bringing an arm between them, she skimmed her palm along his rough jaw and around the back of his neck before urging him down as she rose high on her toes. The soft brush of her lips against his set them tingling immediately, and a quiver followed, coursing down her body and answered by his. How could she have thought to deny this? Something so powerful was unusual, too rare to brush aside. It was meant to be seized, an opportunity meant to be taken.

"I'm instigating," she whispered against his lips. "Please kiss me, Hugh."

And there in the glow of the roaring fire, he bent her back over his arm with a low growl and lit a fire in them both. His lips moved across hers tenderly at first, as if testing her response, but she parted her lips and urged him to deepen the kiss, drawing in his lips as her tongue flicked against them. With a groan, he swept his tongue against hers, dueling skillfully, only to withdraw before his mouth covered hers once more.

He drew away slowly, his kiss softening until he brushed one last tender kiss across her lips and lifted his head. Brushing her hair back from her temples, he looked down at Claire with a warm smile that went all the way to his blue eyes, and she couldn't help but return the gesture, lifting her face for another kiss, but he eased back.

"Now that that is all settled, I believe it is time for luncheon," he said smoothly as he drew away, much to her disappointment. Who was changing the subject now?

Parted from his warm body, she felt a chill wash over her and waited for regrets to do the same. For guilt to take her in its own icy grip.

The only regret she had was that their kiss had ended too soon.

※※※※

Phil Jameson strode into the stark control room of mounted monitors with ill-concealed impatience. "Where are we? Talk to me people."

"All the animals have been retrieved and contained with minimal injury."

The agent waved an impatient hand. "And the others? What have you got?"

"We got a retrieval team setting up near the Canadian border north of Spokane."

"Which one?"

"Eyewitness reports identify it as Anomaly X20."

Jameson grunted. "ETA?"

"Twenty-four to forty-eight hours. Tops."

"And the other?"

There was palpable hesitation among all the junior agents at the question. "Nothing on Anomaly J42, sir. No eyewitness reports as yet. Blood tests were inconclusive."

"I found her, sir!" Marshall, parked in front of one bank of monitors, announced happily, tapping a series of buttons to bring up surveillance footage on one of the larger monitors and pausing it to freeze the image of a car in the frame. A sigh of relief exhaled simultaneously from the other underlings. "It's Claire Manning. We got her car off a traffic camera in Seattle north of the airport."

"Is J42 with her?" Jameson barked.

Nichols followed Jameson into the surveillance room and studied the monitors. "Are you still pursuing this, Jameson? I thought we decided that Claire Manning wasn't a suspect."

"*You* decided," Jameson told his INSCOM counterpart. "I have my own thoughts on the matter."

"Your gut," Nichols said dryly, sipping from his coffee as Jameson pinned him with a scowl. "I'm telling you, we should be out scouting the area instead of pursuing this bullshit. Your J42 is either hiding or dead."

Jameson ran a frustrated hand through his hair. He'd had an entire detail working night and day to track Claire Manning but still had no solid proof that she was even harboring the anomaly—Jameson could hardly think of him any other way. He'd seen the video from Fielding's lab, had seen the thing that had escaped. It was a beast, a terror. There was no reason at all to assume that Mrs. Manning had voluntarily aided its escape. No significant proof that she was being coerced.

But there was no proof she hadn't aided it, either, and his gut said she had, for whatever reason. There had been no sign of the escapee at all, despite Nichols's "scout the area" crap. No sightings. No reports, though his agents were at the point of exhaustion from hours spent in front of the monitors. They needed to find this Manning woman before more people were hurt, including Claire Manning herself.

"Show me what you got, Marshall." Jameson commanded, turning away from Nichols.

"Impossible to tell, sir." The enthusiasm in the agent's voice dimmed and faded after he had watched the interaction of the two senior agents. He backed up the video footage and played it forward slowly. "Camera shot every two seconds. We got one of the front, but the angle is too deep to see inside. We're lucky we could get enough of the license plate for someone to catch it."

Jameson grimaced as Nichols lifted a mocking brow.

Nichols pulled out a chair and sat next to Marshall.

"How goes it on the other escapee?"

"Much more promising, sir. He..." he cast a look up at Jameson and corrected himself. "I mean, X20 has been fairly resourceful but was easily noticed making its way out of Spokane. Simms and his men are currently tracking it through the mountains on infrared. They should have it soon."

"Any chance the other one is with him?" Nichols asked.

"It doesn't appear so, sir."

Jameson was disappointed with their progress. Finding one being's heat signature in the wilderness was easy, but how would they track another body through a crowd of millions if the anomaly had made it into Seattle? "Get men at the Seattle airport. I want every flight checked and Claire Manning found. Nothing on the family yet?"

Marshall shook his head, "No, sir, as far as we can see she hasn't attempted to contact her parents or call them. No emails, either. We've got their phones tapped and the older brother's. Tails on friends, just in case, as ordered."

Nichols shook his head for another reason. "You're wasting time on her, Jameson." The INSCOM agent raised a brow to the nervous Marshall. "Anything to connect her yet?"

Marshall swallowed tightly. "No, sir. Not yet."

"Anything solid on J42 at all?"

"Still attempting to track him down, sir."

With a grunt of aggravation, Jameson slapped his palm down on the desk. "Get me something!"

Nichols rocked back in his chair and considered Jameson levelly over his Styrofoam cup as he sipped his coffee once more. "Jameson, I mean no disrespect here," Nichols said softly, "but this is bullshit. You have no grounds to push to this extent. Watching her house, her family? Tapping her phones and email based on a hunch? Did you even bother with a warrant?"

"And what have you got, Nichols?"

"I've got confirmation that nothing leaked and nothing is missing from the lab. Anything so problematic that it might have been questioned has been rounded up or disposed of, besides those two men."

"They are not men."

Nichols snorted rudely. "Look who's talking. They are nothing in the big picture. We get them, fine. We don't, who cares? They will never last out there either way, and they know nothing that can threaten the project if they are exposed. We have done our job. You should relax."

"You should shut the fuck up," Jameson snarled.

"Going off half-cocked like this will only land you knee-deep in shit if Colonel Williams finds out you've been jacking with agency resources without cause," Nichols warned.

"I have cause," Jameson said. "She is helping him. I know it."

Nichols only laughed at that. "You don't know shit."

ANGELINE FORTIN

27

Three days later...

Claire mentally shook herself and forced her attention back to the book in front of her, only to realize that she had no idea what had been said on the page before her. Turning back a page, she scanned that one and then the one before it, only to realize that she hadn't absorbed a word of the book in almost a dozen pages. Closing her eyes with a groan, she opened them again in time to see Hugh crossing the deck outside the window with yet another load of firewood. His T-shirt was damp with sweat, clinging to his muscular body. She could see the bulge of his pecs, the movement of his lats as he walked. His biceps stretched the short sleeves tightly.

Had the definition of flirtation somehow changed in the past 250-plus years? Because this was beginning to feel more like payback.

Admittedly she hadn't finished that first kiss with the intention of slipping right into bed with him, and it was true that she was lacking recent experience in the whole arena of romance, but she'd expected something…more. That extra edge that transformed playful interaction into flirtation.

But ever since leaving the Crab Pot, nothing more significant than that single kiss had taken place. When they had returned to the house, the evening had followed the same theme as others before. They talked, ate and cleaned up together before retiring to the library, where he'd built up a fire to ward off the chill. Hugh had then taken up the monstrous *A History of the World* to read, but instead of ensconcing himself alone in the cocoon of the library's big armchair, had taken a space on the couch a few feet from where she'd curled up with the thick file Danny had printed for her.

The evening had been pleasant but not at all what she had expected after Hugh's confident assertion of his flirtatious skills and after his demonstration at the restaurant. He was close enough to tease her with his presence, for her to feel his body heat and to hear him breathe, but far enough away to deter any of the touching he'd been allowed by their new agreement. When the clock had struck midnight, he'd banked the fire and led her upstairs to her bedroom door. There he had bid her goodnight and turned away to his own room, leaving her to wonder when it would all begin. To her, their casual camaraderie had turned to intimacy. It was that shift when friends were not merely friends any longer, when awareness overrode friendly interaction. The attraction had been there before their departure that morning, but by that evening it had increased tenfold.

Surely, given license to proceed, he meant to act on it?

Still, the next day only delivered more of the same. After that single embrace and intoxicating kiss, he'd been nothing but courteous, charming, and humorous company as they were confined inside throughout the rainy May day. They'd played games and read with Robert's collection of classical music CD's streaming in the background, and through it all, Claire had laughed freely, worrying less about the world outside the haven they had created and liking him more with each minute that passed.

But it wasn't enough. Nothing was enough. Life wasn't enough for her any longer. She wanted more. More from life. More from herself. More from Hugh. But Hugh—self-acclaimed king of courtly flirtation—wasn't giving it to her at all.

That night, she'd lain in bed staring up at the ceiling, unable to find rest, but had realized somewhere between one and two in the morning that the anticipation of waiting for something to happen had only made her more attuned to his every move, more aware of him. The feel of his body next to hers, the restrained passion of his kiss ...

He was all she could think about. When would he touch her? How? Where?

God, he *was* good, wasn't he?

The following day, as if knowing she was onto him, he'd changed tactics and the casual touching had begun. He'd brushed his fingers over her hands while they were cooking, stroked her hair or cheek when passing by until she was tensing with delicious anticipation whenever he was within arm's length. It was as much a tease as his withholding of the same had been. That afternoon, as the rains had continued, Hugh had offered to read aloud to her and surprised her by lying on his back and putting his head in her lap.

He read aloud superbly, and the continuous soft purr of his brogue had made for a heavenly evening. It was surprising for her to realize that where she had barely understood him at all when they had first met, she no longer needed to concentrate on deciphering his words. Instead, she only listened to the words with half an ear as his rich brogue flowed through her, sending her senses quivering. She rested her head back against the couch and closed her eyes as he read, stroking her fingers through his hair, trailing them around his earlobe, and spreading a trembling hand over his shoulder and across his chest.

He'd looked up at her then, blue eyes on fire, and reached up to caress her cheek. She'd been sure that he was going to kiss her, but instead he'd pulled away and announced that the rain had stopped and he was taking a walk on the beach.

The tension between them was thick and heavy by that time. Claire waiting. Hugh restrained. She acutely aware of every move he made, every breath he took, every muscle that contracted, and in an attempt to provide a distraction—any distraction—had suggested a movie. A nice violent action movie to cool her shameless thoughts. Since he'd become more comfortable if not friendly with the TV, he'd agreed, and she'd put on one of her favorites, *Mr. and Mrs. Smith*. Settling comfortably next to him on the couch, she'd launched into a technical explanation of movies and their history that had calmed her nerves and mind until…

How she could have forgotten that scene when the fighting stopped and the sex began, Claire had no idea. But one minute, Brad Pitt was shooting at Angelina Jolie and the next he was throwing her up against a wall for reasons that had very little to do with violence.

Hugh, who up until that point had been brimming with questions about everything from the concept of a movie, to the reality of it all, to the weapons they used, fell silent as the sex scene played out. His warm, relaxed body was suddenly tense next to hers. "Stop this, please," he'd said quietly, and Claire had hit the pause button, looking at him curiously and waiting for him to say something.

"I am nae voyeur," he'd growled. Though she'd awkwardly tried to explain to him that it wasn't real, she couldn't argue with his point that it had looked real. With him in the room, pressed up next to her, it'd felt real. Arousing. Undeniable.

That's when the wood chopping had begun.

Why he had chosen to vent the tensions on the chopping block rather than on her, she had no idea, but she couldn't help but watch him move, always moving. Prowling. Flaunting that big, heavenly body before her until her thighs clenched together involuntarily. It had been so long. Too long.

Lust had never been a problem before. Claire reasoned that it must be the isolation that was driving her insanity. There was no one to talk to but Hugh. No one to look at but him. But that was a lame excuse for what she felt. Even if it hadn't been three years since a man had touched her, he was undeniably physically magnificent.

And he wasn't just a hunk of manly flesh. He wasn't defined by that twelve-pack of abs or by biceps so bulging that she couldn't wrap both hands around them. Or even by a dazzling smile that made his face so beautiful that the ancient gods would have been envious.

Hugh was intelligent, challenging. Confounding in his ability to complete puzzles of all kinds. After finishing *The History of the World*, he'd completed an entire book of Sudoku in just an hour after Claire had explained the objective, and

Robert's jigsaw puzzle in just a couple more, before destroying his effort and rebuilding it to the point where Robert had left it. On top of that, he was learning about the twenty-first century with amazing speed.

She'd gone full immersion on him, lecturing him on the importance of being technologically savvy and forcing him to become familiar with the online world…or at least more familiar than a fifth-grader's grandparents. She made him use the computer for his history lessons and to show him how the world worked today on a global scale. They focused on the economy of the United Kingdom, so that he would know what to expect when he got there, and he absorbed it all like a sponge, going so far as to read Robert's entire backlog of the *New York Times*.

And Hugh was funny and entertaining. He made her laugh as she hadn't in years. They walked for hours up and down the beach, with each minute filled with stories of his time or coaching on life in her world. He lightened her heart and her mind until Claire was able to forget her heartbreak and years of loneliness, and she thought she helped him to do the same. Though he went to great lengths to be constantly entertaining—a talent he claimed was a necessity at court—he sometimes fell into spells of pensive reserve, standing on the deck and staring blankly out at the sound.

The loss he'd suffered was an enormous one, but since Fielding's research had been uncovered, Hugh hadn't again broached the subject of his feelings and the world he clearly pined for. Since he steadfastly refused to speak of his feelings, she did everything she could to offer her silent support and lure him from the darkness where she'd dwelled for so long, back into the light.

He'd brought her spirit back to life…and apparently her

hormones as well.

Yet her hormones were much farther ahead in the game than her mind was. For all that she wanted and desired him with almost overwhelming urgency, her mind was still at war.

Denying her body's urges left her with energy of her own to expel, and so she had gone for a run the previous morning, a practice that had long been her habit but had been neglected since she'd met Hugh. In the misty dawn, she'd run for over an hour along the windy back roads of Bainbridge before returning to the house, pleasantly exhausted.

Concerned by her unexplained absence, he'd been pacing the kitchen when she returned, and she told him that she'd gone running. The humor that his bafflement had wrought had buoyed her mood considerably, and a lighthearted argument had begun.

Hugh stated that a man might run from an angry bull but not for sport. She pointed out that clearly he must exercise regularly. There was no way he could look like that without it. Oh, there was no chance he was a runner with that big body but clearly he did something to bulk up.

After finding out that he fenced, rode, and helped his tenants in their fields and in repairing buildings, she argued the finer points of cardio fitness, pointing out that it was good for heart health, and that good cardio would be essential when the zombie apocalypse came.

That'd led to an explanation of pop culture and an offer of a movie to explain the zombie phenomenon. Hugh quickly rejected the idea, now clearly wary of the medium.

But the balance had been restored between them...at least for a brief time.

Until last night.

The day had been fine and sunny, so he offered to build

a fire on the beach after dinner. She ran to the store and purchased the fixings for s'mores and showed Hugh how to toast the marshmallows and create the heavenly treat. As with all the sweets he'd availed himself of thus far, he loved it. The atmosphere had been playful, and the laughter plentiful as they talked and ate them all, right down to when Claire had held the last bit of chocolate and he the final marshmallow. She playfully tried to keep the chocolate bar out of his reach while he lunged for it. He caught her about the waist and thrown her down on the sand, laughing down at her.

He'd wrestled the candy away from her and popped it in his mouth before dropping down on the sand next to her with a grin. Relaxing back on the beach, she'd just been entranced by his joy and her own in the moment until Hugh bent his head and pressed a hard kiss against her lips. As unexpected as it was, she'd only a moment's impression of warmth and chocolate before he'd lifted his head, his eyes suddenly serious on hers. Resting on one forearm, he lifted a hand to twist a lock of her hair around his finger as he stared down at her.

She'd been sure he meant to say something or do something, but in the end, he'd only stretched out next to her and folded an arm beneath his head as a pillow. Wrapping an arm around her waist, he pulled her close against him with a satisfied grunt. "Sugar coma," he whispered in her ear, drawing another round of low chuckles as they relaxed against each other in the warmth of the fire under a canopy of stars.

It had been as disappointing as it was lovely. Claire hadn't wanted to let the moment end, and it hadn't. This morning she'd awoken with the dawn, still in his arms on the beach. Hugh's big body had been curled around hers, warding off the chill of the night after their fire had burned to embers. She'd relished the feel of his body against hers, gloried in the body contact she had been missing for so long. She'd felt exposed yet sheltered, free yet ensnared. Alive. Loved.

And as Hugh had started to awaken, his hands roaming over her body, desired. Aroused.

He nuzzled her neck, whispering husky words she couldn't understand as he pulled her tightly against him, against the length of his hard arousal. Her breath caught, her heart racing, as his hand crept up to cup her breast. Rolling her onto her back, he lifted himself over her but seemed to come fully awake then, staring down at her with some surprise.

As hot as his eyes had been, as fully aroused as his body had been, Hugh hadn't taken advantage of the moment. Instead, he levered himself away, muttering something about needing more firewood.

Now Claire was staring at those forgotten pages, not knowing what she'd read or even what book she held, wallowing in unrequited lust while he stacked wood. No, lust wasn't the problem. Hugh wasn't even the problem. She was.

There was no way she could continue to deny that she wanted him. She did. Desperately so.

So what was she to do? Give in? Seduce him into bed? Have a good, sweaty romp to relieve the tension? *Oh, yes*, her body cried, and she shivered at the thought of him looming over her.

Then what, her mind argued?

)O)O)O(

A door slammed and Claire jumped a foot off her chair as Hugh stomped into the room. "I hunger."

Don't we all?

"Well, then, by all means, your grace, it must be as you demand, mustn't it?"

He frowned, assessing her from head to toe. "Yer angry. I meant nae disrespect."

With a sigh, she shook her head. "I didn't mean to snap at you." Looking at the clock, she was surprised to see that the morning had quickly faded and it was well past noon. "What do you say we have a quick lunch and get out of here? I think maybe the cabin fever is making me a little edgy."

"Cabin fever?"

"You know? Like in the winter when you're stuck inside for days on end and just can't wait to get out again?" she explained. "Just too many days of the same thing. Don't you just want to get away from here?"

"Nay, no' at all." His brow furrowed more deeply.

"I think you're in denial."

"Denial?"

"You're hiding out here."

"Sorcha, lass, we *are* hiding out, remember?"

But her nerves were too taut to soften to his gentle ribbing. "You can't just read about the world; you need to see it for yourself. Get a feel for it. You're not going to be able to ignore it forever."

"I'm no' ignoring it," he argued. "In truth, I hadnae given it much thought. I find the wealth of books and amusements to be a verra satisfying way to pass the time. Barring a return to my home, I am more content in this place wi' ye than I have been in a long while, and I could spend many a day here wi'out feeling yer cabin fever."

"Well, I'm feeling it." And more. More than anything, she just needed to get out. As flattering as his words were, she needed to see something else. Someone else. "Let's go out and see a few sights."

"Sights?"

"Sights," she repeated with a definite nod. "Why don't you go clean up a little and we'll go into town?"

ANGELINE FORTIN

28

Leaving the island had brought color to Sorcha's cheeks and a light to her eyes. Hugh thought perhaps she'd been right about getting out for a wee bit, if it benefitted her so. In his time, many long days in winter were spent indoors. Time was occupied with estate business, games with the ladies of the household, and long hours reading books and newspapers as Hugh had done these past many days. With so much to learn and a future to plan for, he hadn't considered that this time would be any different. Though he wasn't familiar with the term 'cabin fever,' he had felt what she described before, but usually after weeks rather than days.

Although, mayhap it wasn't the isolation she was truly running from, but Hugh himself and the feelings they roused in one another. Though he knew exactly what he wanted from Sorcha and had contemplated a dozen ways to achieve it, he still wasn't certain that she was as confident in what she wanted from him. She wanted him physically, that much was evident. It made his blood roar each time she looked at him with desire in her eyes. However, the hesitance was still there as well, and it had become more and more vital to Hugh that her ghosts were banished before they came together.

He wanted her to come to him unreservedly, free of her past. He wanted her spirit, her heart. He wanted her love as well, he acknowledged to himself as he leaned his hips against the ferry's rail, watching not the city beyond but Sorcha as she closed her eyes and let the breeze caress her face as he longed to. The wind threaded through her vibrant hair as his fingers itched to do the same.

Aye, he wanted her love but he wanted it all for himself, and jealousy for a man long dead gnawed at his heart, the luckiest of men who had carried with him the love of this amazing woman when he left this earth. He longed for the ability to reach into the heavens and steal it back.

His body ached to possess her so, he hadn't even been able to actively partake of the liberties she had offered as a part of their new bargain. Their kiss had been tortuous to end. It might have been better to avoid bodily contact altogether, and Hugh had made a terrible misstep the previous night by sleeping with her on the beach and waking with her in his arms. Every fiber in his being had urged him to take, to plunder what she'd drowsily offered. Hauling a thousand cords of wood wouldn't be enough to tire him to the point where that lust was exhausted. He was certain that if another kiss was taken, it would not end there.

Sorcha released a deep breath, the tension in her shoulders visibly seeping away even as his constricted with self-restraint. Turning to him, she smiled brightly, clearly more relaxed than she'd been at the house. Aye, she had needed this excursion, and perhaps he had as well even if he hadn't thought so. The sexual tension between them, buried beneath humor and idle chatter, had been stretched nearly to a breaking point.

※※※※※

"You don't mind that we didn't bring the car, do you?" She asked as the ferry docked and the gangway was put in place to offload the passengers onto the pier. The day was so fine and the touristy places so close to the ferry terminal that it seemed a shame to drive when they could simply walk, so she'd left Goose parked back at the Bainbridge station.

"No' at all," Hugh replied as he guided her through the thick crowds with a gentle hand at the small of her back.

As enjoyable as the ferry ride was, it always seemed that everyone was anxious to be the first one off, and they were jostled from all sides as the passengers converged on the narrow walkway that led down to the street. "Do you mind if I run in here and grab a soda?" Claire indicated the McDonald's housed at the base of the station.

He shook his head. "I'll wait here for ye."

"Do you want anything? A Diet Coke?"

His eyes narrowed at the blatant mischief in her voice. "You get used to the burn," she added with a grin and strolled away, laughing, as he rolled his eyes.

Inside, she placed her order and waited for it to be filled. Through the plate glass windows she could see Hugh waiting patiently for her, his arms crossed over his chest as he leaned his hips back against an iron bike rack.

What a pleasure it was to simply watch him, the way he moved, the play of his muscles beneath the modern clothes and the shift of his thighs against his jeans. While it was certainly nice to be out among people once again, the trip hadn't done anything to curb her desires. He was simply too appealing for his own good. No one had the right to look so freaking hot in nothing grander than an untucked dress shirt and a pair of jeans.

Unpeeling the wrapper from her straw, Claire poked it through the plastic lid of her cup and turned for the door. He straightened with a broad smile that warmed her to the core and stepped forward to meet her…walking straight into the path of a pair of elderly women wearing Space Needle T-shirts and cropped floral pants.

The more rotund of the pair began to rail at him immediately as Hugh bent to retrieve the bags they had dropped. More than likely they were complaining about the rudeness of the locals toward the tourists or some typical nonsense, but as he stood, Hugh put a hand under his abuser's elbow and bent his head low, speaking.

From a distance, Claire couldn't hear what he was saying, but a moment later the woman who had been near to a stroke minutes before was patting his cheek and smiling up at him while the other beamed just as brightly.

He glanced at Claire from the corner of his eye and winked. She grinned back, shaking her head exaggeratedly, dumbfounded that he had soothed them so quickly but more flabbergasted to realize that his charm had manifested itself as some sort of inside joke between them. As if it had become an unspoken challenge to see how swiftly he could do it.

In her experience, things like inside jokes took time, sometimes years to develop. It bespoke a comfortable familiarity she wouldn't have thought could be cultivated so quickly.

What did it mean? Did it mean anything at all, other than demonstrate that they had spent too much time together?

"Are ye well, Sorcha?" he asked courteously as he waved the now-smiling women off, flashing his slashing dimples.

"Yes, I'm just standing in silent awe of your amazing skills. Raving harridan to cookie-baking grandma in less than ten seconds. That has to be a new record."

"It isnae as hard as ye might think." He shrugged modestly. "Sincere apology, genuine compliments. It is a skill cultivated and honed over the years to survive in the fickle courts of Europe."

"So you're saying anyone could be as charming as you with the right teacher?" she asked as he held out his arm gallantly with a slight bow and a raised brow. Claire slid her hand into the crook of his arm with a smile. "Yeah, I didn't think so."

He laughed, a deep infectious rumble that couldn't help but draw a like response, and she joined him, falling as yet another victim to his tireless charisma as they walked up the busy street. "So you're the tourist—the visitor from out of town like those ladies back there—what do you want to do first? We can take a harbor tour or take a ride up to the top of the Space Needle."

Hugh's eyes followed her finger as she pointed to the tall building that he'd recently described as little more than a disk on a tripod of legs.

With a shudder, he declined, "To the top? Nay, I hae nae desire to be so far off the ground."

She grinned. "That takes away most of our options but don't worry, I've got it covered."

29

They walked several blocks more arm in arm while Sorcha pointed this way and that, describing the city of her birth. The climb was steep in places, and when she stopped her fast-paced walk to point out a colorfully textured wall, Hugh was almost out of breath. His breath caught for other reasons when she explained that all the different colored blobs were actually chewing gum stuck to the wall, and she took transparent joy in his revulsion at it after she explained to him what chewing gum actually was. Then they were off once more, heading uphill through a narrow alleyway, and Hugh thought if he were to be in this harried time for long, he would do well to work on his 'cardio,' as she'd encouraged him to do.

It *was* a hurried time, with harried people anxious to get where they needed to be in all haste. Though he doubted that he would ever fully grasp the need for such alacrity, he couldn't deny that he'd never been one to fall behind, literally or figuratively. It would be yet another aspect of his new life to cultivate.

Bringing up the subject as they walked, he was astounded to learn of the advancements in medicine that had been made since his time. More incredible perhaps than anything else he'd learned thus far was how far the practice had changed from the bloodletting and superstition of his time, to the organ transplants and mechanical replacements of hers. It was truly a remarkable world, with much to appreciate, and Hugh regretted in many ways that he hadn't yet fully reconciled himself to the permanence of his situation.

They soon reached an area bustling with people, their voices tumbling one over the other. A sign brightly lit against the gathering dusk labeled it as a public market, and another just below further defined it as a farmer's market.

As busy as it was, for the first instance since coming to this time, he experienced something familiar. Perhaps not exactly the same, but the stalls of vegetables, meats, seafood, and flowers echoed the market days in Cromarty, and for a moment, he felt a wave of homesickness unlike any he'd yet experienced, made worse by the recently acknowledged certitude that he would never see it again.

It was a staggering thought, that "never." It was easier not to think on it, which was perhaps why he hadn't been successful in reconciling himself to his fate. It was easier to look forward instead of looking back, but when the thought did take hold, as it did then, it was sickening to his very gut. It brought to mind faces he would never see again. A family lost to him by a scientific accident. How many people could fathom mourning the loss of all their loved ones at once? How could he explain the soul-crushing pain to anyone who still had even a single loved one?

Sorcha paused at one stall, buying a few apples, but for

the most part was content to browse the shops and save their dwindling funds. She was as serene as he was turbulent.

Never. *Never.*

"Hugh?" She paused with a hand on his arm. "Are you all right?"

He met her concerned gaze and forced a smile. He would not burden her with his sorrow again. For all that she had done for him, she didn't need any guilt for her inability to return him to his proper place. Only her presence had softened the blow and was the balm he so desperately needed. Also, despite her assurances that the women of this time welcomed a man with a softer side, it was not his habit to show one. "I'm well. There is much to take in."

"It's good for you to get out," she said. "Good for both of us. You know what might be fun? Maybe when we're done here we could take a cab over to the Burke Museum. It would be educational for you, too."

"An art museum?"

"No, it's a natural history museum that has exhibits on the local Native American tribes, and there is an exhibit on the Kennewick Man that I haven't seen yet."

"Who is the Kennewick Man?" Hugh asked, thankful for any conversation that would draw him away from his bleak thoughts.

"They found this skeleton at the bottom of the Columbia River almost twenty years ago," she told him as they continued to browse the produce stalls. "They dated the remains at almost nine thousand years old, from around 7500 B.C., and they weren't Native American but something like Polynesian, I think. Which would be weird, right? It's become something of a mystery, where he came from and how he got here."

Several astonishing thoughts streamed through Hugh's mind. How did one "date" the age of bones? How did they know they were not "Native American" in origin? But the most profound was the age of the skeleton. Seventy-five hundred years *before Christ*? How was that even possible, when all theologians of his time agreed that the world had not even been created by then? Most dated the time of Abraham at 4000 B.C. "How is that possible?"

"Well, some think that there was a land bridge between Asia and North America at some point …"

He closed his eyes against a wave of exasperation, not for Sorcha's inability to grasp his true question but for the ignorance of his own people. The world had changed in many ways, far beyond the medical advances of which they had spoken. Invention had turned a manual world into a mechanized one. Those changes, those advancements through science, he could understand. But to consider that the theological foundations of mankind were no longer true was incomprehensible. "Nay, lass, study of the Bible has shown that God created the world but six thousand years ago. How can this skeleton be nine thousand years old?"

With wide eyes, she stopped midstride and blinked up at him. "Oh shit. When you read that *History of the World* book, didn't you start at the beginning?"

No, he hadn't. His interest had been in learning what had happened in the intervening years between his time and hers, not in reviewing what he knew—or thought he knew—of the past.

"Maybe it's better if you just stick with the more religious timeline of existence for now," she was saying in the wake of his silence. "There's nothing wrong with that. A lot of people still believe that way."

There had been so much to absorb these past days he hadn't even considered how far-reaching the changes had been. His concerns had been over whether Scotland and his home had endured. It had never occurred to him—a man of science!—to consider how the winds of change might have altered the broader scope of the world. "Tell me there is still an accepted God," he beseeched with feeling.

"Yes, there is still a God...I mean, most major cultures still follow a religious deity. Christianity is still the most widely practiced religion on Earth," she offered in what Hugh had to assume was meant to be reassurance, but he wasn't entirely comforted by her words. "Wasn't it a huge philosophical debate of your time to argue over the existence of God? You did have atheists."

"Aye," he allowed. "But debating and believing are no' the same. What led the world to show such falsehood in the Bible? More science?"

"Apparently some science you could have done without." She clasped his arm consolingly. "But most scientists generally agree that the universe is about four and a half billion years old."

While Hugh tried to absorb that inconceivable number, Sorcha went on to explain the expression he'd heard her use once before, the Big Bang Theory. There were other terms like evolution, creationism, Darwin, and survival of the fittest; descriptions of large reptiles called dinosaurs; and then something about monkeys that turned into men. Australopithecus and Neanderthal. "Hold," he commanded harshly. "Are ye saying that the populous genuinely believes that men were born of apes?"

"Evolution is a commonly accepted scientific fact," she said. "Most religions hold firm in the belief that God created the Earth and put man on it just as he is now, but there is evidence that humans evolved over the course of millions of years from an ape-like being into the man or *homo sapiens* we are today."

Something akin to nausea roiled in his gut. Of all the things he'd had to absorb since his arrival in this bizarre future, this had to be the most unpleasant to contemplate. "I dinnae like to think that my ancestors were apes."

"I don't think anyone does when they ponder the idea too deeply."

Hugh snorted at that. "And what do ye believe?"

"I do believe in God. As far as creationism, I like to think that the seven days God took to create the universe are a relative thing in the big cosmic picture and that maybe God was the one who initiated the Big Bang," she said, then shrugged. "Who knows? Either way, there are still fights about it and how or if to teach it. Just like in your time, wars are fought over religion every day."

"How is it that what a man would like to see changed through time never does, and that which he wishes to remain the same is all that does change?"

"Now that is a mystery, isn't it?" she said kindheartedly. "I'm sorry to always be the one to deliver upsetting news."

"There is nae one else I'd rather hear it from," he said with complete honesty. "Ye hae been an excellent tutor these past days on all I will need to know as well as those things I would rather not."

"I try," she shrugged modestly but hugged his arm to her breast with a pleased smile. "There is still a lot to catch up on."

"Which I shall do naught but anticipate wi' ye by my side." Thoughtless words, but Hugh had no desire to amend them even though they implied more than either of them had spoken of thus far. In the weeks, months, and perhaps even years ahead, he did want Sorcha with him. Picturing his continued discovery of the twenty-first century without her was nearly impossible, and not only because she was a fair teacher.

Clearly she hadn't given the future beyond gaining his freedom as much thought as he had, since she merely stared up at him with an owlish expression that rounded her lovely violet eyes, her lips parted in surprise. Hugh stroked a thumb across her lower lip before lifting her sagging jaw back into place. "I know in the face of our plight we hadnae spoken of it, lass, but I would like to hae ye wi' me when I see the Scotland of this time. Will ye come wi' me?"

Her mouth opened and closed again without even a whisper of denial or acceptance. Mayhap it had been a foolish thing to ask, but Hugh was becoming more certain about what he wanted from a life in this new world, and Sorcha was undoubtedly a part of it.

Shouts echoed through the building, catching their attention. "What is the matter?" he asked with some concern, looking around for the source of the commotion.

Though the distraction wasn't one of her own making, she was obviously eager to welcome it, as she slipped her hand down into his, tugging him through the crowd until they came to a throng of people forming a large ring about one of the stalls.

"*Ya-a-a-ah!*" He could hear the long shout that had initially drawn his attention, and with his height was able to see over the group as one man threw a large fish to another. The crowd cheered and laughed with delight as yet another fish was thrown across the space.

"What madness. Why do they do this?" he asked Sorcha. "This is a market. Not a carnival."

"It's like a show for the tourists," she explained. "Don't tell me your markets never had entertainment."

"The marketplace is always filled with those who entertain," he said defensively, though he inwardly embraced the distraction from his morose thoughts. "Jugglers, musicians, and the like. However, they do not play with the food."

She sighed, shaking her head. "You are a hard man to please. I can only assume you're hungry. Come on."

In truth, Hugh was an easy man to please, but he didn't dare to say so to Sorcha. Instead, he followed her out of the crowd and around the corner, where she motioned for him to wait while she went to a small vendor in the hallway. In moments, she was back with a small brown bag. She handed it to him with a smile, and he could immediately feel the warmth seeping through the bag. He raised a curious brow.

"Try it, but if you don't like this, I will know you're truly insane."

Shaking his head with an exasperated grin, he reached into the bag and withdrew a rounded piece of what looked like a bread of some sort that was covered in what a quick touch of his tongue told him was sugar and exotic cinnamon, which he had only rarely tasted. Encouraged, he bit into the warm treat and was moaning with delight when the sweet, crisp exterior gave way. "*Mmm.*" He couldn't help the childish expression of satisfaction as he finished the small pastry. A quick look into the bag showed him nearly a dozen more, and he took another with delight. "I promised myself I wouldnae ask this again but what is this?"

"It's a doughnut. Deep-fried dough covered in cinnamon

sugar. Are you going to share? Or will I lose my hand if I reach into the bag?"

"Perhaps," he said with a laugh and held out the bag for her to help herself.

"These are the best, aren't they?" Sorcha said around a mouthful of doughnut. "My favorite thing about this place."

Hugh bit into his pastry, casting an eye over the crowd around them and their ridiculous entertainment. He chewed once, then paused. The air around them seemed suddenly dense. "I dinnae like this."

"Are you kidding? How can you not ..."

"No' the donuts," he said with an impatient slash of his hand. "Something is wrong."

"What do you mean 'wrong'?"

He could feel her body tense at his side as if the danger he sensed had been passed on to her. "I dinnae," he said, his body tensed. "Just a feeling."

"A bad feeling," she clarified.

"Aye," he answered, still searching the crowds around them. A bad feeling that was usually accompanied by an unpleasant surprise. It was a precognition that had served him well in the past, in battle and at court. He'd learned to trust it. His gut twisted. He needed to get Sorcha to safety, to protect her at all costs. "I hate to say this ..."

She groaned. "Then please don't."

"I believe they are here."

XOXOXOX

Claire didn't need to ask who 'they' were. Damn, she should have known better than to come out. She should have never dragged him off the island. "Have they seen us?"

"Nay, I dinnae think so," he whispered brusquely. "It is probably incidental, coincidence that they are here. If no', they couldnae see ye through the crowd and I would think they dinnae ken what I look like now."

A swift sigh of relief escaped her. "Should we try to sneak away?"

"Nay, if we part from the crowd, we will be easier to spot. I dinnae want to take the risk and be seen together." Hugh shook his head as he considered their options.

"What should we do then?"

"Stay here."

She blinked up at him in disbelief. "What?"

He bent his head, slouching to meet the general height of the crowd. "*Ye* stay here," he clarified. "I'm going to circle aboot and see if I can spot them."

She grabbed his arm. "Maybe we should just try to sneak away."

Hugh laid his hand over hers, rubbing his thumb across the top of her hand. "I realize that this is yer time and yer land, lass, but please trust that I know what I'm aboot. Ye stay wi' these people. Dinnae go off by yerself, do ye ken?"

She nodded jerkily. "What if they see me? What if they try to take me away?"

"They willnae get the chance, I promise ye," he swore solemnly, his blue eyes intense on hers.

"Hugh, be careful," she whispered, catching his hand as he turned.

He grinned then, his white teeth flashing. "'Tis what I do, lass. I am the savage, remember? They'd be best to fear me, aye?"

She met his eyes and saw the humor and excitement reflected there. "Oh, God, you're going to enjoy this aren't you?"

"A wee tussle will be good for my heart health," he

teased, tweaking her chin.

Shaking her head, she squeezed his hand before dropping it. "You're such an ass."

"That's no' verra flattering, lass."

Her response was nothing short of a snort but it seemed to please him, as his grin grew even wider and he pressed a kiss to her forehead. "There's my bold lass again. Now stay."

"I'm ever obedient," she whispered, swallowing back her fear.

"*Och*," Hugh scoffed in turn as he melted into the crowd. "There is nothing obedient about ye."

Just like that, he was gone from her sight, and Claire felt the urge to stand on her toes to try to catch sight of him but refrained, knowing that in doing so she might give whoever was looking for her an easy target. And there was no doubt in her mind that they were out there. She trusted Hugh's instincts on the matter absolutely, so she tried to look casual, taking another doughnut from the bag and taking a bite. It was sawdust in her suddenly dry mouth.

"*Ya-a-a-ah!*" The shout came again and she eased further into the crowd as they pressed around the fish market. The fish flew back and forth as her eyes followed the action, but her mind was fogged with worry for Hugh, his safety rather than her own at the forefront of her mind. For all his bravado, these were modern times with modern weapons that he wouldn't be able to combat.

Bodies pressed in from all sides and a voice whispered close to her ear. "I hae them. Walk now. Leave the way we came. I will follow." She turned but Hugh was already gone.

Her feet began to move automatically and she thought with a touch of wonder that if he'd asked her in that particular moment to follow him to the moon, she would have complied without hesitation.

30

On shaky legs, Claire walked woodenly out to the street, along the sidewalk, and around the corner from Pike's Market. In less than a block, she was on an empty narrow lane heading toward a deserted alleyway. Traffic hummed from nearby streets, but all she could focus on was the footsteps echoing behind her, calling for her to look back. Clutching her purse, she fought the urge to do that or to run. Bold lass? Ha! This sickening anxiety was akin to being stalked by a mugger, knowing that they were there and knowing that trying to flee was the quickest way to provoke an attack.

"Mrs. Manning."

The voice was close behind, but she ignored it and walked faster. A car passed by and she resisted the impulse to call for help. Was it one agent or two, she wondered, fighting the panic welling up inside of her and trying to remember what she had learned about self-defense, but her mind was clouded. How had she put this danger aside all week? How had she forgotten about it? Where was Hugh? What did he mean *see* Scotland with him?

"Mrs. Manning?" A hand landed on her shoulder and, unnerved, she swung around to face her dark-suited pursuer just as Hugh emerged from between two buildings and slipped a brawny arm around the lone agent's neck. She stepped back with surprise, a hand to her throat, as the agent struggled against Hugh's unyielding grip and kicked out.

"This guy botherin' you, ma'am?" Hugh said in a brash Southern drawl, dragging Claire from her shocked stupor. "Do you know this guy?"

"I've never seen him before in my life," she answered honestly, raising a brow at his "good ole boy" accent.

The man tried to pull Hugh's arm away, to no avail. "I'm a Fed …"

Hugh tightened his arm around the man's neck, cutting off the words that would have been impossible to plausibly defend against. "A fiend? A thief? A molester of innocent women?" He looked at her. "Are you all right?"

"I'm okay," she said, not having to fake the quiver in her voice. It *was* an agent. And he would've had her if not for Hugh. Thank God for his instincts. "Thank you, he was really creeping me out." The agent's eyes bulged, his face turning red then purple before her eyes. She darted a look at Hugh's determined face and then back to the agent. "*Um*, maybe you should …"

The agent sagged and fell to the ground at Hugh's feet.

She gasped. "Oh, my God, is he …?"

"He'll be fine."

She threw herself into his arms, hugging him fiercely before pulling back with a frown. "Are you crazy? You could have killed him."

He lifted a brow and waited a moment for something further before asking, "Am I to assume by yer tone ye would consider that a bad thing?"

"Yes, it's a bad thing," she huffed, slapping ineffectually at his chest. "We don't need to give them more reason than they already have to hunt us down. Oh my God, how did they find us? Me? How did they know I'm here? What do we do now? And ma'am? *Ma'am?* Where did you get that accent?"

"Heard it from a man in the market." He brushed her hair back tenderly and pressed his lips against her forehead as he soothed away her fear and panic.

"Well, it was smart," she told him with a slight smile, his touch having worked its usual magic and her heartbeat returning to normal. "He never saw you and will hopefully assume that some tourist came to my 'rescue.'"

He shrugged off the compliment. "I hae my moments. Come, we need to away quickly. He wisnae alone in the market, and there may be others to follow."

"What about him?" she asked. "Would it be wrong to just leave him here?"

Hugh shook his head. "But it willnae be long before he awakes. We need more time."

"He might have some handcuffs," Claire suggested, then reconsidered. No, they couldn't leave any indication that they had known who he was or leave any fingerprints. A car passed them by then, the driver looking on curiously, and with a glance at her watch, she knew that they didn't have long before the street was filled with rush-hour traffic.

"Let's just leave him and go."

He pulled the unconscious agent into the gap between the two buildings, hiding him from view of passersby, and urged her into motion. She turned to walk away then but had an idea and hurried back to the agent. Pulling the large handheld radio from his belt and finding his cell phone in his jacket pocket, she used her shirt to wipe her prints away before dropping both into the sewer runoff drain.

Hugh took Claire by the hand, pulling her along as he strode briskly away from the scene.

"That should buy us some more time, since he'll have to find a phone before he can call it in," she said, almost at a run to keep up with Hugh's long strides.

"Good lass," he said but was frowning fiercely. She could tell that his mind was working on a solution. "Is there some place we can go?"

"My brother Ryan's office is not far from here." He nodded and released her hand.

"Go then, walk quickly," he said, giving her a nudge forward. "I will follow once I make certain the others are no' following."

"No," she protested. "Come with me."

He shook his head. "I will follow ye, lass, but I will nae walk wi' ye. I will no' give them proof that we are together where they mayhap hae none. Now, go!" He gave her a push and Claire went reluctantly. "Faster, lass," he urged. "This is nae time to dawdle."

Resisting the childish urge to stick her tongue out at him, she hitched her purse over her shoulder and began to walk with purpose to the south. It was four o'clock and the streets were filling with cars and pedestrians, a crowd that would only thicken in the next hour or more. It would be good for them to have bodies to lose themselves among, but would Hugh be able to track her movements through them?

Her weak estimate of 'not far' was closer to a mile, and

she reached her brother's office building twenty minutes later, worrying Hugh hadn't been able to follow and was even now wandering lost on the streets of Seattle, worrying over how close the agent had come to getting her, and worrying that they would find her again.

Time ticked slowly away as she paced the lobby restively.

When Hugh did walk in the door almost ten minutes later, Claire's relief knew no bounds. She ran to him, flinging her arms around his shoulders and hugging him tightly as he gathered her up in his powerful embrace. She kissed his cheek, nose, and mouth frantically before he caught her head in his big hand and took her lips in a more ardent kiss as he lifted her to her toes and then off her feet before they finally eased apart. "I should go away more often," he said with a grin.

"You should never leave me at all," she countered. "I just worry then worry some more. As long as you're with me, I don't worry at all."

His eyes were dark with concern at her words. Not for the danger they had faced or the unknown awaiting them together, but for her alone. "Surely ye can see that I can nae longer be wi' ye, lass," he paused with a sigh as he eased her back onto her own feet. "They hae nae way of identifying me, nae way to know for certain who I am. I can slip away, disappear, and I should do so now while they hae no evidence linking us together."

She shook her head vehemently in denial. "No, Hugh. I promised to help you get back to Scotland. You just asked me to go with you."

"That isnae my priority any longer. My priority is ye and yer safety. I thought I had to be at yer side to protect ye against the danger I wrought, but now I can see that I am jeopardizing yer safety every moment I am wi' ye. We need to part now before they hae proof that ye aided in my escape," he insisted.

"We don't know that they don't," she said stubbornly. "They could have a mountain of proof that we don't know about! It would be better if both of us got away, right?"

Hugh's nostrils flared and his brows drew together as they did when he was getting angry, but Claire just stared back until his head was shaking once again. "Nay, 'tis too much to ask of ye any longer. Too much risk and too much for ye to deal wi'."

Her eyes widened at that. "You think I can't handle it?"

"Lass, yer scared already," he pointed out, using—perhaps deliberately—the word that had offended him so when she'd used it days before.

She bristled. Perhaps she was a little *concerned*, but given the circumstances, she thought it was completely reasonable. And it wasn't like she was so lost to her nerves that she couldn't be helpful to him. "You were right. It is a horrid word. I am not scared, Hugh. I am rightly and justifiably concerned for your wellbeing."

"And I am concerned for yers."

The harsh bite of the words gave her pause. She looked up at him curiously, aware that his arms still bound her tightly against him. His expression was dark, uncompromising. It told her clearly that he wouldn't relent now if he thought he was doing what was best for her. Hugh would sacrifice any chance he had to escape the country to spare her. He would fight for her. Claire's heart skipped a beat, then warmed. Well, he might not believe it but there was a fighter in her as well.

"It is too dangerous, lass. Surely ye can see that now?"

"No, you need me."

"Cannae ye hae the faith that I might be able to make my own way?"

"I do believe you could," she said. "I just don't think you should."

"Well then, yer wrong aboot that."

With a nod and a bright smile, she stepped away and played the age-old game of pretending to hear only what one wanted to hear. "You're absolutely right. So we're agreed then? We stick together."

"That is no' what I said," he protested hoarsely. "We part ways now."

"Right, we stay together."

"Sorcha! Dinnae be mad."

She just smiled serenely and pecked him lightly on the cheek. "Together."

Hugh eased away and ran his hands through his hair until it was standing on end. "Why, lass? Why?"

Because I love you. Claire swallowed the astonishing thought back before the words made it to her lips but she couldn't deny the truth.

It had been an incredible whirlwind. Not a romance or even a seduction but rather a *charming* that had taken her completely by surprise. Yet it didn't truly come as one. There was so much about Hugh Urquhart that was worth loving and so much more worth risking herself for to save him. It was what called to her from the moment she'd first seen him, what had started all of this. She wasn't going to back down from it now.

"We should get moving before our agent friend has a chance to wake up and close the net on us," she said pertly, turning for the door, though she was aware that Hugh hadn't moved to follow.

"Sorcha!"

Claire blinked up at him innocently as his commanding voice echoed through the lobby. "Yes?"

"Yer doing it again," he growled.

It should have been terrifying, but she found the sound of his furious brogue to be oddly comforting.

"I know, and feel free to berate me soundly about that when we get back to the house," she said cheerfully. "Now, come on. We need to hurry."

"I told ye, I willnae endanger ye any longer."

But all his anger and frustration couldn't crack the calm surrounding her heart. "You're yelling at me," she said softly.

"I'm trying to make ye see reason, lass."

She nodded sagely. "How's that working out for you?"

"I'm aboot to strangle ye wi' my bare hands," he grumbled as she pushed open the glass doors and walked out onto the sidewalk, forcing him to follow.

"Again, feel free, once we're safely back at the house."

"I willnae …"

Her temporary phone rang, surprising them both, but she didn't hesitate to answer it since only one person had the number. The traffic had picked up as rush hour set in and she could hardly hear anything. She plugged one ear and yelled into the phone. "Danny?"

"Hey, Sis, I got what you need."

"You figured it out?" she asked in surprise, meeting Hugh's gaze with a smile.

"Did you ever doubt it?" he asked with his usual narcissism. "What's all that noise? Where are you?"

Frowning at her usually languid brother's suddenly urgent tone, she answered, "At Ryan's office."

"Holy crap, Claire," he cursed. "You're not in your car, are you?"

She looked at Hugh. "No, it's back at the terminal. Bainbridge side. Why?"

Danny was silent for a moment, and she had to wonder what was going on in his head. "That was pretty stupid."

"You don't know the half of it."

"Listen, I want you to come over here," her brother said. "But don't get in a cab. Just wait there and I'll come and get you."

Glancing around at the thickening traffic, Claire knew they couldn't stay put even in the crowds that would soon be filling the sidewalks. "I don't think that's a good idea."

Strangely, Danny didn't even question her, and that worried her more than anything else. "You're right. Start walking south and I'll get you along the way."

"Danny, what's going on?"

"Walk. I'll explain when I get there," was all he said.

"You don't have a car."

"Minions."

He hung up on her, and she turned to Hugh with a frown. "Danny's coming to pick us up. Let's go."

"What's going on?" he asked, falling into step beside her.

She chewed her lip. "I don't know. Maybe nothing."

"But ye dinnae think so," he said perceptively. "I told ye I should leave ye."

"You leave me now, you leave me to the wolves," she predicted grimly.

ANGELINE FORTIN

31

"Okay, spill it," Sorcha commanded her brother the moment they were seated in the backseat of one of the vehicles she had previously identified to Hugh as a van. Their walk of almost a mile in the shadows of the towering buildings had passed in silence between them but had been filled with the raucous noise of hundreds of cars driving by them. She'd clung to his hand, clearly apprehensive once more, but he didn't even consider reiterating the need for them to part.

She was the only thing he had a care for in this time, the only thing that made his life worth living each day. He had no other family, no home. In comparison, nothing else mattered, not even his own future. On and on she had gone these past days, preparing him for a life without her, when he was certain that he would've forsaken any life at all to protect her. He would've killed that agent to assure it, and he would take on a hundred more, if need be. All that truly mattered was her safety, and if it was better guaranteed now with him at her side then that was where he intended to be.

Safe for the moment in the speeding van that rattled and groaned in a manner quite unlike Sorcha's virtually inaudible vehicle, Hugh waited expectantly with her for Danny's explanation. But he should have known even from brief acquaintance with the young man that a simple answer would not be forthcoming.

"Maybe you are the one who should spill it, Claire," Danny retorted, his voice more direct than Hugh had thus far heard. The lazy drawl of days past had been replaced by crisp tones.

She shot Hugh a wary look and answered, "I don't know what you mean."

That earned her a snort of disbelief from her brother, which he thought was understandable. He wouldn't have believed her either. His Sorcha was a horrible liar. Hugh met Danny's gaze in the little mirror once more and saw the young man roll his eyes dramatically.

"She does know how to push a person's buttons, doesn't she?" Danny directed this at Hugh, who was able to comprehend the colloquialism well enough to quip in return, "Aye, a fellow might think such an ability to be her ..." he paused, searching his mind for the correct modern expression. "Special gift? Do I hae the right of it?"

"Dead on." Both men looked at Sorcha, who just crossed her arms irritably.

Och, she was adorable in a pique. He returned his attention to her brother. "What vexes ye, Danny?"

"You do, my friend. You do," Danny said, looking over his shoulder to cast an accusing glare at Hugh before looking at his sister. "Be glad you didn't drive into the city. There's a BOLO out on your car."

"A BOLO?" Hugh and Sorcha said at the same time, but for different reasons. Understanding his question, she looked at him worriedly, and explained. "It means that the police, the authorities, are looking for my car. How did you find that out, Danny?"

"Oh, I was doing a little light reading into that Fielding's project and found out any number of interesting facts, including exactly why the NSA is involved." Danny wove through the traffic, turning on to side street after side street to avoid the rush hour traffic with all the skill of a lifelong resident. "Got the name of one NSA Special Agent Phil Jameson and poked around in his files a little as well. Lo and behold, it is *you* the NSA is looking for. Not Hugh, as you said before. Why is that, do you suppose?"

"They're idiots?"

"Beside the point," he said but didn't push the issue. "Anyway, I saw a report that says they spotted you on a traffic cam not far from here last week."

Chewing on her lip, as she tended to when worried, Sorcha looked at Hugh steadily for several long moments. He could see her thinking, plotting, planning, but he was doing some thinking of his own. "Is it only yer sister they search for,?"

Danny met his eyes in the rearview mirror. "Who else would they be looking for? Hugh Urquhart, perhaps? Your name is nowhere in the files. But it wouldn't be, would it?"

"Nay, it wouldnae."

"Because they aren't looking for you at all, or they don't really know who they are looking for?" her brother asked perceptively.

"Danny," Sorcha protested, but Hugh took her hand and squeezed it comfortingly.

"Dinnae fash yerself, lass," he said calmly. "Yer brother isnae looking for an answer from ye. I would wager that he already knows all, perhaps more than we do."

Hugh met Danny's gaze once more and the young man nodded. "You are pretty smart for a 'bloody, unintelligible savage of unknown origins given to rage and violence at the smallest provocation.' I'm thinking they didn't mean bloody the way the Brits do. Had them fooled, didn't you?"

"No' really." He shrugged, for he was all that and more while imprisoned. He had tried to kill them, he had raged against his imprisonment, and he had threatened to dismember them limb by limb even if they hadn't understood his words. "When did ye figure it out?"

"Suspected something was amiss when you looked at my setup as if you'd never seen a computer before … or was it the pizza?" Danny said. "Knew for sure when I read the files."

Hugh nodded. He'd known from the moment he met Sorcha's brother that he was a sly one. Danny O'Bierne truly was a bit of a mastermind and might have made a troublesome adversary, but he would be an even greater asset if he were to assist them. "I appreciate yer silence on the matter."

"Oh, don't get too excited," the younger man cautioned. "I haven't decided if I trust you enough yet to keep that silence."

The warning didn't concern Hugh. There was no doubt in his mind that Danny would do anything to protect his sister, even if it meant extending his trust to Hugh by necessity.

"So what now?" Sorcha asked worriedly and slanted a glance at Hugh, whispering, "I knew I shouldn't have left him those reports."

"You sound like you'd be surprised if I offered my help," Danny said over his shoulder as he turned into the parking lot next to his warehouse. "Even knowing my feelings on government oversight. Shame on you. Besides, you're my favorite sister. Why wouldn't I help?"

She sighed and shook her head as if she would never understand this brother of hers. She accepted Hugh's assistance out of the van and went to her brother, giving him a soft peck on the cheek. "Only sister," she whispered. "Thank you, Danny."

"Don't thank me yet," he said and waved for them to follow him inside.

※※※※

"Okay, here we go." Danny rocked back in his chair and gestured to the bank of monitors. "May I present Mr. Rupert Waldroup. Environmental consultant. Resident of Inverness. Age thirty-four ... sorry if I overshot, man. I had to take a ballpark guess. Nothing personal."

"No offense taken. It was a good guess."

Sorcha looked at him in surprise. "I can't believe I never asked. How old are you?"

Hugh tilted his head toward the monitor and raised a brow. "And how old are ye?"

"Twenty-nine."

"So she says," Danny interjected. "Seems to me you've been stuck there for a while."

"Don't pay attention to him. I'm not one of those women who hit twenty-nine and stopped counting."

Sorcha was studying the information on the screen, and Hugh studied her in turn, trying to see something he might have missed. It was surprising to discover she was nearly thirty. She certainly did not appear so old to him. Her skin was fresh and unlined, her magnificent body firm and youthful. Naturally most women of his time did not "exercise," as she did, but all had used any means to retain their appearance of youth with not half her success. At Frederick's court, many would have pursued the young widowed beauty, begged her to become their lover.

A quick calculation told him she'd had been widowed at twenty-six, and he wondered how long she had been married. Had she married young? Given the many young, unescorted women he'd seen on his two excursions into Seattle, he didn't believe that was the case, but he was reluctant to raise any topic that referred to her lost husband again.

Her blatant elation when he'd arrived at her brother's office building had been all for him, her kiss his only. In that moment, she'd belonged to him, and he'd savored the moment. He wanted more, so much more. Even when he was sure he would have to let her go, he only wanted her more.

Hugh unconsciously reached out and placed a possessive hand at the small of her back. She looked up at the gentle pressure and smiled, leaning into him before turning back to her brother.

"So this is the temporary guy you made up for us?"

Danny snorted at that. "Even with my excellent imagination, I couldn't come up with a name like that. No, Rupert Waldroup—unlucky bastard, thought he doesn't know it yet—already exists in the records. Arrived in Vancouver from Glasgow last Thursday. His blog says he's there on business for the next two weeks or so, traveling all through British Columbia and Alberta."

"But that's Hugh's picture," Sorcha said, tapping Hugh's

image on the screen.

With a nod, Danny rocked back in his chair. "For the next couple days, yes it is."

"I don't get it," she said with a frown, but oddly enough Hugh did, and he offered a nod to her brother. Aye, he was a cunning lad.

"Yer brother has offered me an alias. A legitimate means of traveling incognito."

Danny nodded. "That's right. Hugh gets to go to Scotland as a real person with a personal history, Facebook page, and blog that would've taken me weeks to create. The bonus is that this guy has already come into Canada. I didn't even think about it before, you know? Getting him out without record of him ever having come in? That might have raised a few flags."

Sorcha pursed her lips as she glanced up at Hugh, and he had to wonder what she was thinking. "So, what now? If we have the guy, can't we just forge a passport?"

"Perhaps Danny isnae any more familiar wi' the seedy underbelly of yer country than ye are," Hugh offered with a smile.

"Oh, I'm sure he is."

"I am," Danny said agreeably. "I am getting to that. It is all part of the grand plan. Hugh will go home as Rupert Waldroup, nice and legal-ish, but when he gets there, he's going to become someone else entirely."

"Myself," Hugh said.

"Right," Danny said, nodding with approval. "Really not a savage, are you? Too bad. That might've been more interesting."

"Ye would hae done nae more than fear for yer sister if that were the case."

"Who says I'm not?" Danny shrugged and turned back to the screen. "So, you'll go to the British Consulate—thought you'd have to do San Francisco before. Linear thinking and all that. Forgot that there is one in Vancouver. You'll get some emergency travel documents as our guy and off you'll go. Poor old Rupert might have a hell of a time later explaining how he needs to leave Canada twice when he only arrived once, but, hey, that's the challenge of life, right?"

"And then?" Hugh asked.

"Soon as you are safely in Scotland, I can erase all trace of your photo from the system and voilà," Danny waved his hands in the air. "The journey is as if it never happened. You're a ghost, a vague image on bad airport security footage. Best part is, you never even have to pass through American customs, where the NSA is probably watching."

Hugh was impressed by the lad's skills, which clearly were abnormal even in this time of technological wonder. "Yer brilliant, Danny. Really, ye hae my thanks."

"No problemo," Danny said with a modest nod.

"No," Sorcha countered. "Big problemos. Mondo huge problemos. I could fill a supertanker with them."

Hugh looked curiously between Sorcha and her brother, to whom he said, "We speak the same language but sometimes I dinnae comprehend a word she says."

Danny grinned. "I have that same issue."

XXXXX

"Oh, ha ha," she said, slapping her brother on the back of his head. "You know what I'm talking about. There are holes everywhere in this. Hugh can't get into Canada without the passport he's going there to get. And how am I supposed to go there with him? If I flash my passport at the border, I might as well call up Jameson myself and tell him where I'm going."

Danny's eyes widened with mock surprise. "Kudos on the big brain, Sis. Is that all?"

Claire was still shaking her head. "No, that's not all. What does Hugh do in Scotland after he's there? He can't get a job or an apartment or even a bank account."

Her brother rifled through some papers on his desktop and came up with a slim envelope, from which he withdrew a passport. "Seeing as the only Hugh Urquhart in the entire UK is a four-year-old kid, I figured we're safe letting him use his own name." Claire thumbed through the small book before handing it to Hugh with a nod. She was impressed that Danny had accomplished so much in less than a week, but was even more so when he pulled out a birth certificate as well that looked suitably worn to Hugh's age. "You'll have to hide those well on the way over, in case he's searched. It would be hard to explain. I've started building records for Hugh Urquhart in all the normal UK databases and should have it done by the time he gets there. He'll have to pull his same story back home to replace his other 'lost' documents like his driver's license or NHS card, or maybe a tragic fire will have burned down his family home. I'll build him such a solid life that there will be nothing to link him to Rupert Waldroup or Mark-Davis's lost science experiment."

"Okay, fine. But what about Canada?" she asked, concerned on that one sticking point. "Surely, San Francisco would've been easier."

"That's a fourteen-hour drive," Danny pointed out.

"A fourteen-hour drive in the same country." She met Hugh's gaze and read the question there. "Vancouver is less than three hours from here but it is in Canada, and to get in there these days, you need a passport," she explained before turning back to her brother. "I told you we should have just made him American." Claire caught his incredulous look and shrugged. "Fine, *you* said make him an American, but why didn't you then? Since you decided to just replace some random guy with Hugh's picture, wouldn't it have been easier to get him a passport here instead?"

"Really? Think about what you just said."

Damn, she hated it when someone was smarter than she was, and there had been a lot of that going around lately. "Because in the U.S. you can't just get an emergency passport to fly out of the country. Fine, I got it. So how do you propose we get into Canada?"

"Isn't it obvious?"

Claire glared at her brother. Nothing was obvious any more, other than the fact that she had gotten in way over her head. She had no idea what Danny might be referring to.

Hugh must have sensed her impulse to tackle her obtuse brother to the ground, because he laid a calming hand on her shoulder and leveled one of his haughty, ducal glares at her brother. "Come now, lad, this is nae time to rile yer sister so. Tell us yer idea."

Danny sighed impatiently. "Claire, when was the last time your car was searched going over the border?"

"You want to sneak him into Canada?" she asked incredulously.

"What's the big deal? You're trying to sneak him out of here, aren't you?" her brother snapped back. "Or have you suddenly drawn some fine line between legal and illegal that I don't know about?"

"Enough." Hugh's calm command halted both the siblings, and they turned to him with identical expressions of surprise. "Arguing will accomplish nothing. Sorcha, yer brother has been naught but our ally thus far. Trust that he has a plan. Danny, lad, dinnae provoke yer sister unnecessarily. She's had much to deal wi' these past days."

"When did you become the peacemaker?" she asked.

"When I was eighteen and my uncle turned the dukedom's courts over to me," Hugh said.

"You're a duke?" Danny asked. "I suddenly feel so humble."

"That would be a miracle," Claire mumbled. "So, dear brother, what's your plan? I hope it doesn't involve the two of us in one trunk."

Danny grimaced. "It might have ... Well, I suppose we'll have to go with a boat then. Here's what I was thinking. One of the minions has a brother who works a small fishing boat out of Blaine. It's right on the Canadian border and he'll do anything for a buck. So if you can be at the marina there by five a.m. one morning, he'll take you up into Surrey. From there you'll just have to take the bus or something."

"Or something?" she taunted. "Nice plan. What's next? We grow wings?"

"Am I expected to do everything?" her brother asked. "You don't want the trunk, you get to use your imagination."

Hugh held up his hand once more, preempting another argument. "I imagine we're clever enough to make it the rest of the way. And then?"

"I'll book you a hotel room in Vancouver, prepaid but with your name on it. They'll need ID but won't run a card," Danny continued, turning to shuffle through some papers on his desk before handing one to Hugh. It was a copy of Waldroup's passport with Hugh's image from his database. "I've printed this for backup. You can say it's a photocopy of your passport that you carry with you or something. I hear they recommend that. I read the procedures for emergency travel, so when you get to Vancouver, the first thing you need to do is get robbed. Yes, your idea, Sis. Shouldn't be too hard. I recently read that Vancouver is the eighth most dangerous city in Canada."

Claire scoffed at that. "Yeah, in *Canada*. Not like it's L.A." She looked down at the copy in her hands. "Couldn't we just use this to get into Canada legally?"

"Wouldn't risk it," Danny shook his head. "You only want one use on that thing, if possible. God, Sis, you're worrying over the easiest part of the whole thing."

"I'd just hate to get caught before we even got started."

Danny rolled his eyes yet again and Hugh began to understand where Sorcha had developed the habit. "Anyway, I got a nice hotel already picked out in Gastown. Eastside downtown in an area heavily populated with vagrants and addicts looking for a handout or their next fix, so it shouldn't be too hard to get robbed there."

"Or killed," she said dryly. "Great. I'm loving this plan."

Hugh laughed. "In my time, ye hae a better chance of getting robbed than avoiding it in many cities but why need we risk such a thing at all? What we need is merely the appearance of a robbery."

Both siblings looked at him curiously, their rivalry forgotten. "What do you mean?" Danny asked.

"Might we not simply go to the constable's offices and report the 'crime,' as it were? I shall be this Waldroup fellow, in town on business. Sorcha shall be a mere witness to the robbery."

Claire nodded while her brother looked at Hugh with growing respect. "With your accent, it would be easy to assume that there is no connection between us."

Danny chimed in as well. "Our friend Rupert is staying downtown at the Hotel Georgia. So in case they ask, you can tell them that to support the lie."

"You know where he's staying?" Claire asked with raised brows.

"Sis, I could tell you where he ate breakfast this morning." Danny turned to Hugh. "But why would a guy from Scotland be hanging out alone in Gastown?"

"Doesn't that restaurant at the top of the Harbour Center attract a lot of upper-class businessmen?" Claire asked.

Danny nodded. "Yeah, he could say he was having dinner with clients there or something. It will get him close but not close enough. Why would he be walking alone?"

"To get somewhere no one else wanted to go." She leaned across her brother to call up GoogleMaps, searching for nightclubs in that area of Vancouver. She hovered over the pinpointed options one by one, but Hugh stopped her search, pointing at the list on the left.

"That one," he said decisively. "The Blarney Stone. There isnae a person I've met beyond Scotland's borders who could tell a Scotsman from an Irishman. I doubt there would be any question of a weary traveler longing for his homeland."

Claire beamed up at Hugh, impressed with his cleverness, but Danny said, "It's not in the worst of it."

"It's close enough."

"It willnae be too much of a blow to my pride to claim I was lost," Hugh said at the same time and he shrugged, his dimple deepening in response to Claire's raised brow.

Danny only shrugged. "You should probably agree on a description of the guy who robbed you, too, while you're at it.

Who do you want to admit robbed you?"

"A short, frail fellow of sallow complexion, perhaps?" Hugh suggested. "If I am comprehending your term 'addict' appropriately?"

"Not a new epidemic, I take it?" Danny asked curiously. "What was the poison in your day?"

"Opium, mostly."

Danny snorted at that. "Guess not much has changed. Heroin is made from the same stuff."

"Okay," Claire said. "So Hugh's got his police report saying that his passport was stolen. We just take that to the British Consulate? And then what? They issue a new one just like that? What if they question him?"

"You do worry too much, lass." Hugh's fingers entwined with hers.

"Planning, not worrying," she corrected.

"Dinnae fash yerself. I'm certain I can get what I need. I will just ask nicely."

"That's what you're going to go with? Your charm alone?"

"Haven't we already determined that I am the greatest flirt in Scotland?"

Or in the world. "What if it's a guy? What if they try to call someone or ..."

"Sorcha, please," Hugh cupped her cheek in his hand and forced her to look at him. "Trust me. How did you say it? I got this."

"I'm just scared they're going to figure out that it's a scam and detain you or something."

"I'm certain Danny will keep a weather eye on their computers and telephones. I hae every faith in his abilities to protect me from exposure."

Danny nodded, looking speculatively back and forth between them. "I'll be watching the surveillance feed, too."

"Then I shall feel doubly secure. Hugh clapped a hand on the young man's shoulder. "For what ye hae done for me, lad, I shall be forever in yer debt."

Danny shifted uncomfortably, and Hugh suspected, after hearing Sorcha's description of her brother, that the lad was more comfortable praising himself than receiving it from others. "Yeah, well, don't thank me yet. It might not work at all."

"I hae faith in yer abilities," Hugh repeated assuredly. "Ye dinnae need to go to such extremes after ye realized the truth of the matter."

"I did it for Claire."

"I know."

Danny looked up at Hugh then with a grin. "Someday, man, someday I'd like to sit down with you and hear your side of this whole thing, like where you're from and all that."

"And someday I'll be happy to oblige."

Hugh looked at his solemn face peering out from the computer monitor and thought about all that it represented. Safety for himself and Sorcha. Second chances. Freedom. Hugh thought of his homeland, waiting now within reach. As much as Rosebraugh would be missed, it was Scotland itself that his soul yearned for. The smell of the heather in the Highlands, the salty winds from the North Sea. In a matter of days it would all be his once more ... and Sorcha! How she would love it there.

"Good enough." Danny lifted another envelope out of the pile on his desk. "Claire?"

Lost in thought, she started and blinked at her brother,

taking the envelope he held out.

"Anticipating that this whole thing is alarmingly bigger than you first implied and since you haven't accessed your credit cards or bank accounts since last week, I assume you'll need this."

She peeked into it, finding a thick stack of twenties. She stared at him, dumbstruck. "Danny ..."

"It's nothing." He brushed away the thanks. "I'll also get one of the minions to book an emergency flight out of there when you're ready. Can't do it too early or it will look too planned for his emergency travel documents."

"Thank you, Danny."

"I already said ..."

"I know, don't thank you yet." Claire nodded, swallowing back the lump in her throat. Brothers were notoriously pesky things, always teasing and tweaking, but every once in a while they did something that forgave it all. She pulled her brother out of the chair and into her arms for an affectionate hug. "Can we at least get a ride back to the ferry?"

"You're a real nag, you know that?"

"I know." She blinked back the tears burning at her eyes. Danny really was the most impossible brother but damn, it was nice to know how much he really cared.

32

"Just pull over there," Claire pointed to the corner of the parking lot away from her car. Danny had insisted on carrying them the entire way, keeping her and Hugh safely hidden in the back of the van throughout the ferry ride in case the NSA was monitoring the security feed, now that they knew for certain that she was in Seattle. Her brother had been full of admonishment since learning of her near apprehension at Pike's Market that afternoon, washing away any lingering sentiment she'd been feeling for him.

She'd been called an idiot more than once in the past hour. Numbskull. Moron, nitwit, nincompoop—that was a nice throwback to their childhood, though it was an insult she had delivered more often than received.

Parking in an empty space, Danny shut off the van and turned in his seat. "Well, I guess this is it," he said. "Try not to do anything stupid, all right? Or in this case, stupider than you already have. Just stay off the grid. No buses, no public transportation. Be at the dock in Blaine by five in the morning the day after tomorrow."

"How are we to take the ferry then?"

"Just take Robert's car."

Claire rolled her eyes at his casual direction. "You want me to steal Uncle Robert's car?"

"Borrow," Danny emphasized. "It's not like you're not going to bring it back."

She looked at him expressionlessly while Hugh shook Danny's hand and thanked him one last time. Commanding Claire to stay put while he scouted the area, Hugh slid open the van door and disappeared.

Danny leveled a stern look at her the moment Hugh was out of sight. "I saw that frown when I said that about Robert's car, Claire?" He paused, running a hand through his hair. "Shit. You do know that you can't go to Scotland with him, don't you?"

Shaking her head, she stared at her brother in disbelief. "What are you talking about? Of course, I have to go with him."

He ran both hands through his hair then. "You cannot be this stupid. Not if this is going to work."

"We'll be fine," she insisted stubbornly.

"Damn it, Claire! Always, always got to have things your way, don't you?"

"You think I always get things my way?" she asked in disbelief. "I and my personal history beg to differ. Besides, I have to go with him. Hugh isn't ready to face the modern world alone yet. He hasn't even seen an ATM or the inside of a bank yet, much less knowing about anything like utility hookups or tax forms. He's going to need some help, and I plan to be the one to give it to him."

She started to scoot out of the van but Danny caught her

arm tightly and pulled her back to face him. "You get on that plane with him and the NSA will tear a hole through everyone that was on it," he told her bluntly. "When they can't get him on paper, they will start going through the airport and customs surveillance footage. Then they will have his picture and that will be that. You get him on that plane and get out of Vancouver before they know you were ever there and he *might* have a chance of making this thing work."

The truth of it all resounded in her, but her heart denied his words. She wouldn't let Hugh go. She couldn't. "He can't go alone."

Her brother laughed harshly. "Give him some credit, will you? I don't know who he is or was but Hugh is freakin' smart. He's a survivor. He'll be fine."

Clenching her teeth to stop a biting retort, Claire shook her head once more, but knew that all her reasons for going were just an excuse. Danny was right. Hugh would undoubtedly find his way without her help or anyone else's. He was brilliant and resourceful, and that charm of his would probably take him anywhere he wanted to go. "But—"

"No buts, Sis," he interrupted. "I get it, I really do. I never thought I'd see you look at a guy like that again, but you can't have him. Not now. Maybe not ever. As long as they think you know where he is, they'll follow you. They're tenacious like that. Believe me, I know."

She stared at him, her heart thudding heavily in her chest as his words echoed in her mind and heart. *Not now. Maybe not ever. No,* she thought, feeling the tears well once more. Not tears of gratitude this time but tears of loss. How could she let Hugh go? Let him walk away? He needed her.

No, that wasn't it at all, was it? It was her. She didn't want him to go. She didn't want Hugh to leave her alone once more, not when it seemed that life—which had long ago left her standing alone by the side of the road—had suddenly seen fit to pick her up once more.

"Good-bye, Danny," she said, getting out of the van.

"Claire," he pleaded. "Be realistic."

Claire pulled the door shut and walked numbly toward Goose, not caring if the entire NSA saw her do it. Getting in the car, she slammed the door and stared dully out the windshield. She had to let Hugh go. Truth that it might be, some part of her refused to digest it.

She couldn't go through that again.

With a sigh, she pulled her phone out of her purse and turned it on. Thumbing across the pictures, she pulled up a picture of her husband taken the last time he'd been home on leave. Matt was smiling that light, teasing smile he'd always worn. The smile she always thought of when she pictured him. Hugh had been right. She'd enshrined Matt in her memories, making him perfect in her mind. He'd been far from perfect. Claire forced herself to remember that. To remember that they had fought like normal couples. To remember that Matt had had bad habits. Done things that annoyed her from time to time.

But she'd loved him and he'd loved her. Claire stroked her thumb across the image tenderly. She'd been happy and in losing that happiness, had almost been destroyed.

Emptiness had filled her, lived within her for years. Hugh had been right. She had lived in fear of loving and losing once more. The anger over his loss and the subsequent fear of trying again had ruled her life. Now, somehow, she was filled again. Miraculously, amazingly filled. Filled with joy and anticipation and love because of Hugh. He wasn't perfect either, not by a long shot. Hugh was superior and occasionally condescending. That sense of entitlement had probably been ingrained in him from birth. But he was perfect for her. There was that laughter, that challenge—he would always call her out on her stubborn flaws and bad habits! And he challenged her mind as well.

How was she to give that up willingly? How was she supposed to, in essence, hold the door open for it as it walked away from her again?

)(()()()(

The car door opened and Hugh slid into the seat. "I told ye to wait."

"Sorry," she mumbled as she swiped the picture away before turning off the phone and throwing it in the backseat. "Can we go?"

"Aye. I dinnae see anything suspicious, so let's make haste."

Nodding, she started Goose up and backed out the parking space, heading through the twilight back to Robert's. She knew she should be making plans for their departure, needed to do so sooner rather than later, but she couldn't get Danny's warnings out of her head. She didn't want to lose Hugh, but really, what was more important? Her happiness or his freedom? If she didn't let him go there was ample chance that they'd have neither.

"Sorcha? Are ye all right?" Hugh asked, taking her free hand between his and chafing it lightly. His hand was rough, hard, and warm. The press of his skin against hers made her hand tingle. She'd have to remember that feeling.

"Sorcha?"

"I'm fine," she lied woodenly.

"We should pack our things tonight and be ready to leave tomorrow evening," he said, not recognizing—perhaps for the first time—the falsehood on her lips, as he was too busy making the plans she could not. "We dinnae want to cause undue troubles for yer uncle, so I believe it best if we dinnae leave yer car there to be found but somewhere else along the way before we leave the island. If we're to meet this boat by dawn and this Blaine is three hours away, as yer brother said, we will need to leave in the early morning hours. What time is the last ferry?"

"What? Oh, about one in the morning."

Hugh nodded thoughtfully. "We will have the day then to gather our things with plenty of time to rest if necessary before we leave. That would be best, do ye agree?"

"Yes," Claire agreed stiffly. "Whatever you think."

She could feel his eyes on her, wondering at her sudden capitulation no doubt, but she finished the drive in silence until the garage door fell protectively behind them.

"Sorcha?" Hugh lifted her chin until he was able to meet her eyes. "I will keep ye safe, I swear it. I willnae let any harm come to ye."

The warmth of his hand felt like fire against the flush of her cheeks. Hard and rough against the softness he must feel. Remember it, her heart cried. Memorize it because it is all you will have left.

But it wouldn't be enough.

Yes, even if it killed her to do it, she would let him go to ensure his freedom, but she needed more than the memory of a few gentle kisses, she decided. If she was truly going to let happiness walk away from her once more, then damn it, she was going have something more spectacular to remember.

33

"Sorcha? What troubles ye, lass?" Hugh asked, finding her alone on the balcony outside her bedchamber late that night.

She visibly started at his words, turning away from the rail but gripping it behind her back with both hands. "Nothing, Hugh. I'm fine."

The words were as transparently false as her habit of introducing a new topic when another was uncomfortable, and he had to wonder what had unsettled her so. She'd been abnormally withdrawn ever since their return to the island, which was to say she participated in their conversations, including another more in depth dissection of human evolution, but her thoughts were clearly elsewhere. Her eyes followed him unblinkingly as if she were studying every inch of his person. It might have been that her thoughts had returned to the offer he'd made back at the marketplace, and Hugh wondered if her considerations were leaning toward joining him or not.

Perhaps he'd asked too much, too soon.

Or perhaps she was simply not as confident of their success with the plan they had laid out as he was. It was certainly an easier topic to broach, and Hugh cursed himself for his sudden cowardice. "Do ye hae a concern over our strategy, lass? Is that what preoccupies ye?"

She was chewing her lip uncertainly. Her feet were bare, one on top of the other as if it might warm the one beneath it. She looked smaller and more nervous than Hugh had yet seen her. "I do worry about getting into Canada safely," she murmured.

There was some truth in the confession, but he could tell that wasn't the whole of it. Something more was bothering her. If it was not their strategic departure, there had to be something else that had changed her mood between their arrival on the island and their return to the beach house. "Did Danny say something to distress ye?"

She blinked and met his gaze, and Hugh knew that he had the right of it. "What is it? What did he say?"

"Nothing."

Also patently untrue.

"Come now, lass," he murmured as he approached her. "After our time together, I've become a fair hand at telling when yer lying. What is it?"

Tilting her head back to look at him, she said, "You said I was a terrible liar."

"Aye, that's why it is so easy to see it." He cupped her cheeks in his hands and bent his head, brushing a tender kiss across her lips. He meant for it to be only a kiss of affection but her dewy lips unexpectedly clung to his. Nostrils flaring, he inhaled the warm scent of her, citrus and floral. The heady desire of being so close to her when he'd endeavored to keep his distance set his heart pounding heavily, his body tensing with the need to pull her close.

Her soft lips parted with a sigh, encouraging him to deepen the kiss. Easing away, Hugh looked down at her in surprise. She looked soft and sweetly feminine with her hair loose around her shoulders, her lovely face pale in the muted glow of the moon, but her eyes shone like jewels as she caught her lip between her teeth once more as if she were suddenly nervous.

"There is nae need to worry so, my love," he said, hoping to reassure this unexpectedly vulnerable woman who up to this point had shown nothing but spit and fire. "I swear to ye, all will be well."

"I know it will," she said softly, looking up at him through her thick lashes. Hugh felt her hand against his waist and her fingers curling into the fabric of his t-shirt before her palm flattened against him and smoothed across his ribcage and over his chest. Skin met skin as her fingers tickled at his neck above his collar and curved around to tease the hair at his nape, and Hugh swallowed deeply. "Sorcha, what are ye about, lass?"

Lifting herself onto her toes, she kissed him once and then again, sighing against his lips. Hugh's fists clenched, fighting the urge to grab her, to pull her closer. All week he'd fought this. Even with permission to flirt as outrageously as he chose, Hugh had resisted the temptation to touch her, knowing that once he succumbed, he wouldn't be able stop. The theory had become truth, and soon he had been taking any opportunity to hold her hand or touch her. Each tiny caress was a torment. He'd wanted her too much; knowing that she wanted him as well, knowing that she was tempted and teetering on the edge of surrender had only inflamed that desire. He hadn't been able to touch her without longing for more, and didn't trust himself to kiss her lest he take so much more.

Now she was luring him into passion's dark fire, tempting and teasing, and he braced himself against the onslaught of lust that hardened his body, resisting his body's call to plunder her sweet depths. He had no wish to be faced with the guilt and remorse that would surely plague her if he did so. "Lass, ye hae to stop this."

"*Shh*," she blew against his ear, kissing his jaw and neck. Then her hands were beneath his shirt, her palms on his stomach, his chest, pushing it upward. "Lift your arms."

The request was so faint Hugh wasn't entirely sure if she voiced it or he imagined it, but he lifted his arms and helped her pull the shirt over his head. Then her hands were on his chest again, burning a path around him as she pressed a hot kiss there. She rubbed her cheek against him, purring like a kitten as she kissed her way upward once more. Her lips were hot, her tongue unbearably arousing as they grazed his neck and the underside of his chin. With a groan, he looked up at the ceiling, praying for help as her mouth closed over the base of his throat.

Then she was tugging at him again, forcing him to look down at her. Those purple eyes were dark and heated. Insistent. "This isnae what ye want, lass."

"Oh, but it is. It is what I've been waiting for all night," she whispered, stretching to kiss him once more. Then she took his hand and pressed his palm against her heart. It was beating erratically, matching her breathing. "I want you, Hugh. My heart is pounding like this for you."

By God, but he'd never wanted a woman as badly as he wanted his one. He wanted to possess her, become one with her, but he wanted to be completely alone with her. To have her be his fully. "I told ye, I cannae share ye, lass. I want ye too badly to hae ye hold back."

"I won't," Sorcha offered the softly spoken promise as her arms twined together behind his neck and she lifted herself, her lithe body pressed against the hard length of him. "I couldn't."

With a groan, he surrendered to the heady desire raging through his veins.

)()()()(

With a powerful arm around her waist, Hugh lifted her against his muscled chest as his lips took her with all the passion and desire that had building between them for the last several days. His mouth devoured hers as he carried her into the bedroom, his tongue plunging as a groan rumbled deep within his chest. Breathless, Claire clung to him in complete surrender, allowing him to plunder at his will. Her head was already swimming, but when he cupped her bottom and lifted her against his rigid length, her head fell back dizzily as her blood surged and roared in her ears.

Yes, this was exactly what she needed.

"Oh, God," the words escaped her with a moan as his mouth descended on her neck, nipping and licking at the side of her throat. She ran her fingers through his hair, knotting, pulling him closer. "I feel like I'm going to faint. It's so... so...*mmm*...oh, Hugh."

"I want ye, lass. I've ne'er wanted anything so badly in my life," he growled thickly. His hand was up the back of her shirt, his hot, rough palm searing her skin as he pushed her shirt up. He tugged then swore, easing back from her. "Ye hae too many clothes on."

Claire swayed unsteadily, her head spinning euphorically

when he set her back on her feet and began to pull her shirt up … then down. He swore. Then reached to unzip the North Face fleece vest she wore and she looked down, realizing what the difficulty was. She did have too many clothes on. In typical Seattle fashion, she'd dressed for the unpredictable May day in layers. The vest over a long-sleeve T-shirt with another short sleeve T under that. Helpfully, she shrugged out of the vest and pulled the first T-shirt over her head before Hugh helped with the second.

"My fumbling wi' yer masculine attire belies the fact that I was once skilled at undressing a lady," he murmured in a thickened brogue as it came off.

Claire smiled at that. "I bet you were."

He reached down to unbutton her jeans. "I ne'er tried to remove another's trousers before."

"I should hope not," she teased, pushing down the jeans and stepping out of them only to hear him release an anguished moan. "What is it?"

Hugh cupped her breasts through the lacy cups of her bra, squeezing gently before thumbing her bra straps off her shoulders. He bent his head, kissing her shoulders as he removed the straps. One hand skimmed over her bare ribcage, over her hip, and dipped into her panties to cup her bare bottom. "When I imagined ye without yer clothes on—and I hae a hundred times—I dinnae think ye'd be dressed like this. I would hae had ye naked in an instant if I had. Yer so bonny, Sorcha. Bewitching. *Och*, lass, ye've been driving me mad!"

His lips were on her neck once more, his hands everywhere, moving over her as if he couldn't get enough of the feel of her bare skin. Claire reached behind her to unclasp her bra and let it fall down her arms and then his hands were there as well, massaging and tweaking her swollen nipples. She gasped and clung to him once more as Hugh pushed down her panties and lifted her off the floor, inviting her to wrap her legs around him, and she did.

Never had she felt so beautiful, so light and fragile. In contrast to his big body, she felt wonderfully petite. "*I've* been driving *you* mad?" Claire said incredulously. "Really?"

With a growl, Hugh lowered himself down until he was looming over her, braced by a hand on either side of her. His head bent until their lips were inches apart, waiting, and she threw her arms around his neck and pulled him down to her. His lips took hers with none of the tenderness he'd displayed before. His mouth slanted across hers, kissing her passionately, deeply, until she was clinging to him, whimpering with need as she tried to raise her body to his or bring him down to her. But Hugh did not relent. He kissed again and again, nipping and sucking on her lips, sweeping his tongue across hers until his breathing was as labored as hers.

The denim of his jeans chafed against the inside of her sensitive thighs as he moved lower, his hands, mouth, and tongue exploring her entire body, licking and sucking until her body was on fire, tensing. Panting desperately, Claire tugged at his hair, lifting his head until his blazing blue eyes met hers. "Please."

Nostrils flaring with lust and desire, Hugh stood and reached for the button of his jeans, his eyes never leaving hers as he kicked them off. Then he was over her once more, pressing Claire into the bed and lifting her legs around him. His lips took hers fervently again as he pressed against her then thrust deeply, filling her, stretching her. "*Ah!*" she cried out, throwing her head back as she clutched him to her. Her thighs trembled with ecstasy as he withdrew and plunged hard. She clenched her thighs tightly around him but couldn't stop the release that came swiftly and unexpectedly, sending throbbing delight coursing through her. Sobbing with the intensity of her climax, she held his body close to her. "I'm sorry, I'm sorry. It's just ..."

Hugh shushed her, his lips tender against hers, as he began to move inside of her again. "Nay, lass, I'm no' done wi' ye yet," he murmured thickly as he thrust slowly. "*Ah*, my bonny lass." His hand slid up her bottom, lifting her hips higher against him. Desire rekindled into a flame, and Claire rose to meet him as his pace increased until she was at the precipice once again. This time she wasn't alone. Hugh's arms were shaking, his hands trembling as he took them over the edge together. His lips captured her cry of release only to join her with a low growl of pleasure as he came hard against her womb, flooding her with scorching heat as she throbbed around him.

Wrapping his arms tightly around her, Hugh rolled onto his back, carrying Claire with him until she was sprawled across his heaving chest. His lips skimmed down her throat lazily. "*Mé gráigh tú. Mé adhradh tú. Mé grá tú, mo Sorcha. I gcónaí,*" he murmured against her as his hands stroked down her back.

Claire nuzzled her cheek against his damp neck, inhaling the musky scent of his skin as she snuggled against him. "What does that mean?"

Hugh shook his head, his hand sliding down over her bottom once more. "It means, I am glad that we hae another day together before we must leave."

She didn't believe that but Claire wasn't in the mood to question him. The moment was too magical, too extraordinary to question. Instead, she sat up, straddling him and spreading her hands over his chest. Brushing her lips across his, she whispered with a smile, "For you, I would make all the time in the world."

※※※※※

Olson, one of that fool Nichols's junior agents, was hopping from one foot to the other in Jameson's doorway as if he needed to use the G.D. John, Jameson thought irritably as he slammed down the phone. He'd be damned if he was going to take on one more academy stripling after this fiasco. "What is it?"

"Sir! Well, shit, sir... I can't believe it, really," Olson stammered excitedly.

"Spit it out or you're fired."

"She turned on her phone. Claire Manning, that is," the junior agent said, bouncing on his toes. "Who would've thought..." Olson paused at the look on his superior's face. "We were able to trace her, sir. I mean, she didn't have it on long, but we've definitely narrowed it down."

"Who did she call?" Nichols asked, stepping into the office.

"N-no one, sir," Olson stuttered. "That's why I can't believe it. She just turned it on and then off again a few minutes later."

Jameson hid his surprise well. After days of nothing, he wouldn't have thought the woman would be stupid enough to get caught twice in one day. "Where is she?"

The junior agent was hopping again. "She wasn't on long enough to pinpoint her exact location but she's somewhere on Bainbridge Island."

Blood surging with satisfaction, Jameson pounded on his keyboard, looking up the location. "Get Marshall. I want men on that island now. Lock down the ferry. Do a door-to-door search of every building on the fucking island if you have to, but I want her found. Now!"

"Y-yes, sir," Olson piped and was gone.

"You don't have enough evidence to get a warrant to do a sweep like that," Nichols said, closing the office door behind him. "Might I remind you that all you have is the fact that she left work early one day and left Spokane when the lab closed."

"Probable cause excuses everything, Nichols. I thought you knew that by now."

"You have nothing. We should be focusing all our efforts in the Spokane area instead of going off on some wild goose chase."

"Dammit, Nichols, I understand you're hovering on the edge of retirement but some of us still have to do our jobs if we want to suck off the government tit for the rest of our days, too."

Nichols frowned. "You think I'm being complacent because I'm not jumping at shadows? Maybe I'm just as sure as you that this entire line of investigation is absolute bullshit."

Jameson pinned the INSCOM agent with a murderous glance that would have had young Olson fainting at his feet. "Then who attacked my agent this afternoon, Nichols? Huh?"

"Marshall said that he never saw the man who grabbed him and that the guy spoke with a Southern accent," Nichols reminded unnecessarily. "Hardly one of your savages. He was probably a tourist who thought Mrs. Manning was being mugged or something."

Given that his life was practically on the line, Nichols was proving to be surprisingly resolved in his need to follow the protocols, which demanded some evidence of culpability before such extreme measures were taken. Jameson didn't give a rat's ass about protocols. What the evidence said and what he knew were two different things, so to hell with it all. "Get her, Nichols," he growled. "If she gets off that island, Colonel Williams will be looking at you for answers."

"And if she comes out of this clean, it will be your balls in a sling."

Spreading his hands across his desktop as Nichols left the room, Jameson felt a surge of primal satisfaction, and a satisfied sneer curled his lip into some semblance of a smile. Soon, every one of his naysayers, like Nichols, would see that his gut had been right all along when he had Claire Manning, and by extension his missing anomaly, in his grasp.

Fuck the warrants. He'd burn down every building on the island if it meant proving himself right.

34

Hugh turned and spooned behind her, slipping his hand up to cup her breast comfortably as he pulled her snuggly against him. She'd forgotten how good that could feel. What a safe and warm place it was. How it made a woman feel sheltered and protected. Right then there was nowhere Claire would rather be.

She sighed with contentment, but misreading the exhalation, he shifted behind her, lifting his head to look down at her with his brow furrowed. "Are ye well, lass? Do ye hae regrets?"

She almost snorted at that. Her regrets were many, but none of them fell where she might have thought they would. Lying there in the bed with Hugh after they made love, she had waited for the guilt and regret to flood her over what a week before she would have considered a betrayal to Matt, but she'd known almost instantly that they weren't going to come. What was happening between her and Hugh felt right.

What she did regret was that she was going to lose him

and that she had no choice in the matter. Claire skimmed her fingers over Hugh's cheek and stretched up to kiss him softly. "No regrets. It was incredible."

"And it will be again. I told ye I am no' done wi' ye."

The husky words were possessively spoken, and Hugh settled in behind her once more, his hand at her hip, pulling her back against the arousal already hardening again against her bottom. Her wild Scotsman was proving insatiable, but after a week of simmering lust, Claire was happy to have as much of him as possible before they were forced to part. Wiggling against his groin, she was rewarded with the press of his hot lips against the nape of her neck as he murmured foreign words similar to those he'd whispered before into her ear in a thick, sensual brogue.

What did those words really mean, she wondered? His answer before hadn't felt honest. His hoarsely spoken words had been too tenderly voiced to be mere sex play. Was it possible that he was beginning to feel the same as she was? Had he come to care? While the thought thrilled, Claire conversely hoped that wasn't the case and did not ask him again about his words. One broken heart out of this mess was better than two. Especially when Hugh's heart had already been broken by too much loss recently.

"Yer mind is wandering," he whispered in her ear, enfolding her more tightly against his chest. "Are ye wearied of me already?"

A chuckle of incredulity escaped her and Claire hugged the burly arm wrapped around her waist against her tightly. "No, not at all. If it helps, I was thinking about you."

"A pleasing thought if it has kept ye from fretting over other things."

"Oh, I'll always do that," she confessed lightly, shifting

onto her back so that she could look up at him. No man should be so beautiful, but Hugh was. With his blue eyes lazy and warm, his often fierce expression softened, and his broad chest covered with nothing more than shadows, he was every woman's fantasy of an impassioned lover. Claire smoothed a hand over the bulge of his pectoral, feeling the rigid line of a long-healed scar there.

Hugh had fought a great many battles, but what might be the greatest of them all awaited him in the days and weeks to come. If only Hugh knew that there was so much more she worried about than their escape from Seattle. She worried more over how Hugh would proceed with life once he was safe with his new identity. Danny was right, of course. Hugh was smart and resourceful. He learned quickly and adapted even faster. No doubt he would thrive on his own, but Claire hated the thought of him returning to Scotland without her. The world was a hard place for people today to make their way in without a friend at their side. She felt like Moses's mom must have, putting Hugh out in a proverbial basket on the Nile to fend for himself.

"Have you given any thought to what you'd like to do when you get to Scotland?"

"Am I to assume ye are speaking of something more than my desire to set foot on the land where Rosebraugh once stood?"

"Yes. In the big picture, what do you think you might want to do? Go to school, maybe?" she asked. "Learn a trade?"

"Ye think me a tradesman?" Hugh asked in surprise. "I may nae longer be a duke but I was raised to lead no' to serve. Nay, my love, fret not. I hae already a verra excellent notion of how I might earn my living."

"Really?" she asked, surprised by the confidence in his voice. To her mind this was the one downfall of Hugh returning to Scotland and a major source of the anxiety she bore for his solitary return. "What is it?"

"I plan to trade in the commodities."

Claire blinked. That was not what she had expected at all. "What? How do you plan to do that?"

"In my own time, I invested heavily in the London Exchange and was always quite successful," he told her. "I've been reading yer uncle's books on the subject and his news sheets and I cannae see that the foundation has changed much. Do ye recall what I said about being good at puzzles and the like? Part of it is seeing patterns others cannae see. That is all this trading is. Applying variables to the rhythm of the market and extrapolating a course of action. Some of yer businesses today I dinnae hae any expertise wi' to predict such a thing, but the basic commodities hae changed verra little over time. I'm certain I can make a go of it once I learn the use of the proper technologies."

Impressive, she thought, feeling proud he was so self-assured in building a financial future for himself. It was an ambitious endeavor. "You'll need capital to begin, though."

"Aye." He leaned over the side of the bed and fished his medallion out of the pocket of his jeans. He held it above them, letting the dim light shine dully off it as it swayed. "'Tis solid gold. Wi' the current value so high, I should be able to gain a tidy sum from its sale."

"But you can't sell that, Hugh," Claire protested. "It's one of your only personal possessions, a family heirloom."

"I have my plaid to remind me of my family and my home, but this will be my future, Sorcha," he corrected, solemnly. "The foundation for a new life."

Her heart twisted with sorrow over the sacrifices he had already made. She couldn't bear to see him lose any more. "I hate to see you do that. I have a pretty good amount in my 401K that I could cash out for you ..."

"Nay, Sorcha, dinnae even suggest such a thing, for I willnae take any more from ye. I hae taken too much already and the time has come for a change. I will make my own way from now on."

"Of course." His own way. Without her. She knew that, planned on it even, but it sounded so dismissive coming from him.

As if he read the insult in her eyes, Hugh nudged up her chin, forcing her to meet his gaze. "I would share it wi' ye, Sorcha." Her heart skipped a beat at his softly spoken words. "I would like to share my future wi' ye, as uncertain as it is."

There it was again. An offer and a question, and every fiber of her being demanded that she accept his unspoken proposal, that she commit to a future with him. She wanted to. Wanted to be the one to share in the experience with him. Wanted to keep the thrill he had brought into her life. If two weeks in near seclusion with him was so exhilarating, how would it be to spend the rest of her life ... Oh, Lord, was she really thinking that? Now? When she knew it was impossible?

Just that morning, she'd thought this thing between them nothing but lust, her emergence out from under her shell of solitude only to be blinded by his radiance, to bask in the warmth of his desire. Desire for her body, her mind. It had taken first the threat of his loss that day and then the reality of it for Claire to realize just how deeply she'd come to love him.

But he wasn't meant to be hers. Danny was right about that as well. If she wanted Hugh to have the future he deserved, she'd have to let him go. She would drop him off at the airport in the days ahead and very likely never see him again.

He would go out into the world on his own and find that she was nothing special in the bigger picture. He would charm more women, and maybe one day one of them would charm him in return. Claire genuinely envied that imaginary woman, but at the same time hoped with all her heart that Hugh would find a life to make him happy in this time, to wash away his regrets, to soothe his longings for home. A woman to fill his heart and provide him with a family to comfort him against the loss of the one he had before could do that.

She wanted everything for him. She wanted the world for him, even if it meant leaving hers empty. She looked up, blinking rapidly to banish the tears in her eyes before he noticed, but he was nothing if not observant. "There it is once more. I see it in yer eyes, Sorcha. What is it?"

But her throat was too tight for words to escape, her hands trembling with the emotion that she fought to hide. She felt pinched, her head already throbbing from the effort of containing her feelings.

Claire slid her hands over his chest and around his neck, pulling him down to her until she felt first his heat and then his weight bear her down into the softness of the mattress. Wrapping her arms and legs around him, she urged him downward, nuzzling his warm neck encouragingly before running her tongue up along his rough, whiskered jaw. A shudder of lust shook him but Hugh braced himself resolutely above her, denying her efforts.

"Yer doing it again, lass," he growled brusquely in her ear though his lips caressed the sensitive flesh behind her ear with his next breath. His powerful arms tightened around her as he turned until she was lying on top of him. "Ye cannae avoid my question with such a diversion."

Trailing kisses across his chest, she scooted down farther, raking her teeth along the edge of his ribcage and swirling her tongue around his navel as her palms slid over the hard planes of his abdomen and down his rock hard thighs. With a harsh intake of breath, his body grew taut, and she lifted her head, her eyes dancing impishly as they met his shocked blue stare. "Oh, I bet I can," she whispered before bending her head once more.

Hugh's heartfelt groan was his only riposte.

35

Day Ten since the escape

"You keep that up and we're going to miss the ferry," Claire murmured as Hugh pinned her up against the Prius, engulfing her with his massive body, and took her now tender lips in another fiery kiss as his hands crept up under her shirt. He met no resistance. For all she cared just then, the last ferry could leave without them.

They had spent most of the day lost in a sensual haze as they made love again and again. The last twenty-four hours had been the most remarkable, most passionate she could remember. Hugh was an amorous lover, fervent without forsaking tenderness, erotic without being carnal, demonstrating effectively that past generations had made an art form of lovemaking while her own had probably invented the 'quickie'." Together they had reached unimaginable heights.

She hadn't been keen on giving up him before, but now

she thought she would risk discovery just to have a few minutes more with him.

"*Ah*, Sorcha," he whispered huskily, thrusting his hand into her hair to cup the back of her head and draw her lips back to his for another ardent kiss. "I dinnae want to be apart from ye even for as long as it takes to reach the depot."

Neither did she. Nor for longer than that. Pain lanced through her heart at the unsolicited thought. The fifteen minutes they would be parted for this short drive was nothing compared to what awaited them in the days to come. A raw sob rose in her throat but she choked it back. "But you get to drive, right? That will be fun."

He turned away, and she took the opportunity to dash a hand across her eyes as he finished loading their bags in the back of Robert Mitchell's Tahoe. "Hae we got everything?"

"Everything I could think of." Since all she'd really been able to think about was Hugh, Claire hoped the cleaning they had hurriedly completed to return the Mitchell beach house to its original state had been enough. At least she had remembered to wipe away possible fingerprints. "Are you sure you can drive this?"

"Sorcha," he said with some impatience.

"I'm a worrier, Hugh. I thought you had figured that out by now."

"Aye, lass, I've ne'er met anyone who could fret so."

"I know it's not my finest quality," she said. "Combined with my sarcasm, bad temper, and unequaled evasion tactics, it's a wonder you're not anxious to see the last of me."

He paused and turned to face her. "Is that why ye've avoiding answering me question? Ye think I am eager to leave ye behind?"

"I'm difficult and stubborn," she said lightly. "Everyone

says so, even you."

"Mayhap I like a lass who can keep me on my toes," he responded, reaching out to caress her cheek once more.

His blue eyes were dark with emotion she didn't dare guess at. He hadn't expressed any more tender feelings than friendship, nor had she, and she wanted to keep it that way. If there was any chance Hugh might feel for her as deeply as she cared for him, she knew it would make their parting even more difficult to bear. "So, the car?"

He shrugged with a disappointed sigh. "I watched ye well enough to hae the gist of it. I ken where to shift to go forward and to stop. Right pedal go, left pedal stop. Stay to the right of the line. No' too hard."

"What about the lights?" she reminded. "There will be some between here and town."

"Go on green. Stop if it's already red when ye get there."

Claire rolled her eyes at that but it was close enough for their short trip. "What about yellow?"

His brow furrowed once more as Hugh thought about it. "That's a good question. I cannae see that it made any difference to anyone along the way."

"It means get ready to stop."

That only deepened his frown. "Are ye certain? That's no' the impression I got at all."

Biting her lip to cut off a smile, she only said, "You'll just have to trust me on that one. Stay close behind me. If you lose me just pull over and I'll come back, okay?" He nodded and she handed him half of the money Danny had given her. "When we get to the depot, you pull in to the boarding lanes and load the car where they point. Don't forget to put it in park before you turn it off. I'll walk on and meet you on the front deck after I ditch poor Goose."

They left the house, and in the end, Hugh probably drove better than she, since she spent the entire journey watching him in the rearview mirror. They reached the ferry station without incident and Claire pulled along the left side of the parking lot to park Goose as far as she could from the station. She'd have to abandon her trusty vehicle there, far from Robert and Sue's. Hopefully it would be enough to save them and maybe even her when it was eventually found.

Or, maybe that wouldn't even happen and she would return to find it still there. She wasn't certain either way. Popping the catch on the hood, she got out and moved to the front of the Prius to lift the hood. It had occurred to her along the way that an excuse for leaving it was better than none at all. A breakdown was what she needed—just in case, of course—and she had learned enough from her dad and Matt what to look for in case she ever had car problems to create a few for herself.

Claire loosened the bolt off the battery cell and, satisfied with the damage she'd done, was just about to slam the hood shut when a deep voice uttered, "Hold it right there."

Heart in her throat, she turned to find a thickly built man standing next to a black suburban that had pulled in behind her car. Another taller but thinner man was getting out of the driver's side. Both wore the same government-issued black suit as the agent who had nearly caught her the preceding afternoon.

They had found her. Damn, how had that happened? Had they seen her pull in? Had they seen Hugh? Did they have him already?

Damn, damn, damn! Forcing back the rush of panic, Claire thought of Hugh, who seemed the embodiment of calm in a crisis. If he could do it, surely she could do the same.

"Either of you guys good with cars?" she asked with studied indifference. She leaned back over the engine and poked idiotically at the parts. "My car broke down."

The two men exchanged puzzled looks before one asked, "Claire Manning?"

Could they hear her heart pounding in her chest, she wondered? No doubt they could see it. She frowned and decided to play dumb...or dumber, as it were. "I'm sorry, do I know you? Riley Cooper, is that you?"

"We're federal agents, ma'am," the driver said as he came around the suburban to join the other agent. Together they moved slowly toward her. "Would you come with us, please?"

"Oh no," she said insipidly, coming around the side of the car, surreptitiously scanning the area and wondering if she should make a run for it. "I couldn't do that. I mean, I don't know either one of you, and a girl has to be careful these days, you know?"

Her dismissive response gave the men pause. "We're federal agents, ma'am," the driver repeated with clear frustration.

"Are you really?" she asked, trying to keep the desperation out of her voice as the pair came ever closer. In just a moment more they would be able to physically retain her despite her weak protests. She looked them up and down, trying to size them up. Years of kickboxing had given her the potential to defend herself, but could she take them both on?

One agent nudged the other and they reached into their jackets. "We have ID, ma'am." They held them up in unison.

"Not very impressive," Claire sniffed as she examined their badges. "They could be faked."

A blur of motion caught the corner of her eye and before she could even blink, Hugh swept in, taking the driver down with a hard hit behind his knees with what looked like a short tree limb. He wielded it like a sword, swinging it around to catch the second agent on the side of the head.

Down he went, but the first agent was struggling to his feet as he shot a flabbergasted look at Claire, who only shrugged. "See? Now that's impressive."

The broom handle caught the agent behind his knees again and the man hit the ground hard before Hugh brought the end of the branch down on his chest. If it had been a Scottish claymore, the agent would've been skewered to the ground but instead all four of the man's limbs bounced into the air before falling lifelessly to the ground.

Hugh looked at Claire, looking more wild and untamed than she'd ever seen him. His eyes were almost black with rage, his brow furrowed and his nostrils flaring as he looked down at the agent once more with a curl to his lip. Picturing him in his kilt, the wooden pole a sword, she couldn't imagine a more magnificent picture.

XXXXX

Hugh looked down at the man cowering at his feet with some disgust. These feeble men were the authorities they had feared encountering? They were no more threatening than a gnat, and put up about as much a fight. How had this time ever reached such amazing heights with men such as these to defend it? He spat on the ground and wiped his mouth with the back of his arm.

Pitiful.

He looked at Claire, finding her wide-eyed but unafraid. "Did they hurt you?"

"No…watch out," she cried, pointing behind him, and

he turned to find the agent he'd hit upside the head rolling to his side with a pistol in his hand. It was smaller than the flintlock pistols of his time but perhaps more deadly. Hugh whipped the piece of wood around once again, catching the man across the hand and sending the pistol skittering across the parking lot.

Disarmed, the man staggered to his feet, watching Hugh warily before glancing at his partner. "Don't worry, your friend ain't dead, but you will be if you don't leave this woman alone," he threatened in a flat, accentless voice. No southern boy this time, just an average Joe.

"This is none of your business, pal," the agent said, holding out a palm toward Hugh as if that could hold him off. "Listen, I don't want to hurt you but I am taking this woman with me."

Hugh's brow went up as he sized up his opponent. The fellow was large but likely more flab than muscle and he didn't seem to Hugh to be much of a threat. He tossed the stick to the side and beckoned his opponent forward with a wave of his hand. "You're welcome to try."

And despite the blood trickling down his temple, the agent apparently felt the need to.

"I'm gonna kick your ass, man."

He came at Hugh, turning his body along the way and swinging out a leg, which Hugh deflected easily, throwing the man off balance. The agent came at him again with more exaggerated kicks and arms swinging, and Hugh thought a child could see the punches coming. Spinning about, the agent tried to kick again, and Hugh caught his foot and twisted sharply, sending the man to the ground.

Panting, the agent leapt to his feet and came at Hugh more directly, this time swinging like a man, or at least a strapping youth, though his efforts were still laughable. Hugh's fist shot out, catching the man hard in the stomach and again under the jaw while deflecting a dozen wildly thrown punches easily. It was ridiculous, really. Sneering at the agent, Hugh asked, "Are you not even going to make it a challenge for me?"

With a mighty swing, Hugh caught the agent under the jaw and sent him down on one knee. "What are you, special ops?" the agent asked with a gasp of pain.

"SEAL," Hugh said, throwing himself forward to head-butt the agent and sending him sprawling to the ground, unconscious, before looking up at Sorcha, shaking his head in disgust. "The braggarts in this world. Is there nae one who can put up a worthy fight?"

"I don't know. Are you planning on testing them one by one?" she admonished, though she was anxiously scanning Hugh for injury as he backed away from the fallen agent. She denied the impulse to fling herself into his arms like a damsel saved from the dragon. "We are on the clock, you know."

"Thought I might let him get in a few punches before I put him down."

"He didn't need a feel-good moment, Hugh," she said, shaking her head with wonder. "But you're right, normally the bad guy does get in a couple good punches before the good guy knocks him out."

He grinned as well, pulling her into his embrace. "Am I the good guy?"

"*Mmm*, very good." Claire said, giving in to the urge to hug him tightly. "You're my hero."

Hugh snorted at that but looked pleased nonetheless. "Where did you learn to head-butt like that?"

He smiled. "Keir. Did ye think it was something new?"

"I guess I did," she said with a grin. "Did you have SEALs as well?"

"Nay, I read about them in the *TIME* magazine," he said, his heart warming under her praise and enchanting smile.

"What were you doing over here, anyway? You were supposed to be putting the car on the ferry," Claire said with a sudden frown. "What's wrong?"

"They're searching the cars," He told her, the humor slipping away.

"So? They usually have bomb dogs checking the cars."

"Nay, lass," he shook his head, looking suddenly grim as he studied the unconscious agents. "*They* are searching the cars."

Claire looked toward the far side of the lot, where past the fence, six lanes of cars waited to board the last ferry of the night. There was nothing to indicate that a search of any sort was going on, but she didn't doubt what Hugh had seen. Damn, that Jameson. All she wanted to do was get Hugh to safety but that damned Jameson wasn't going to make it easy, was he?

"We need to get back to the house. Where is the Tahoe?" Hugh pointed up the hill, and Claire worried her lower lip between her teeth.

He was at risk now and it was her fault, because they were looking for her. Only her.

The truth hit her hard. Not only could she not go with him to Scotland—though she hadn't told him that yet—she was a danger to him every step along the way. Before she had thought that it was better for Hugh to be with her, to have her help, and she'd fought against his previous attempts to separate based on that belief. But Hugh had been in the right all along. They *were* better off apart. Not because of the threat he posed to her but because of the one she presented to him.

They wouldn't know who he was if she wasn't with him. Even if he got caught speeding or without an ID, there would be nothing to link him to Mark-Davis. She did that, and as long as she was with him, Claire was a threat to his freedom. "You should take the car and go, Hugh," she urged. "I'm leading them to you. Without me, they'll never be able to find you."

"Nay," he said sternly. "'Tis as ye said, we are in this together. They hae no proof against ye. Now, come, we need to go before they wake."

"Damn it, Hugh, I'm saying you were right," she cried, standing firm. "I don't say it often, so please listen! If they find me, they find you. I'll take my chances that they don't have anything on me."

"Well, I willnae," he said, commanding as he reached for her, "Come now."

"No," she said, pulling away from his grasp. "You go."

"Bluidy hell, lass, we hae nae the time for this!"

"Hugh! Put me down," she shrieked, beating Hugh's back as he hauled her away over his shoulder.

36

With the ferry unavailable to them and Hugh refusing to drive away and leave her, Claire had no choice but to take the wheel and drive them away from the terminal, though she cursed his undignified handling of her person along the way. Taking the main highway north across the island, she mentally plotted an alternate course to Blaine, on the border of Canada, where they were scheduled to meet the boat. The trouble was that without getting to the mainland first, the only other option was an island-hopping adventure across most of Puget Sound. There were some bridges available, but in the end, another ferry would be required. If the NSA was watching one ferry, it stood to reason that they might be watching others as well. That would take the Bremerton and Fauntleroy ferries off their already short list of available options. The Port Townsend ferry on the most direct northern route required reservations as well. Even if they made it going north without incident, they would be at least an hour late in meeting their ride.

They might reschedule, but if Jameson already knew or suspected that she and Hugh were on Bainbridge Island, as the agent's presence hinted, would they even have another twenty-four-hour grace period to wait before they were found?

It was ridiculous, she thought as they crossed the first of many bridges, leaving Bainbridge behind. Or maybe she was. All week long, while sharing a solitary existence with Hugh, she had been fine with hiding away from their troubles. Even Hugh, who had originally abhorred the concept of such "cowardice," had seemed content with their voluntary seclusion.

So why did scurrying from the agents like a startled rabbit now suddenly seem like too much to bear? Especially when it looked like constant running would be a prominent fixture in her future?

If what Danny said was true, she could expect to see an unmarked black Suburban in her rearview mirror each time she left the house for months and maybe years to come. It would never end, and she would never again have that solitude with Hugh.

Claire hated Jameson for that, and she didn't plan to live out her life in fear.

So what options did she have? Option A: try to sneak into Canada, save Hugh, and save herself but remain a hunted woman. Option B: turn Hugh over to Jameson, plead coercion, and live in guilt and misery instead of fear for the rest of her days.

At the intersection of Highway 3, Claire stopped and considered her options. North for plan A, back the way she had come for plan B. Shit, she thought, tapping her fingers against the wheel. Neither one really worked for her.

Claire gunned the accelerator and turned to the left, heading south on Highway 3, down the Kitsap Peninsula. Screw all the cloak and dagger B.S., she was going to go with Option C, where she ended this thing once and for all.

)()()(*)(

"What are we doing here? I thought we were to go to this Canada," Hugh asked, yawning and stretching as they exited the SUV at Danny's SoDo warehouse almost two hours later, twisting and wincing at the pain in his back. For all that the seats in these modern vehicles were cushioned and well sprung, he would have opted for the comfort of his carriage without a second thought. Travel was always tiring and uncomfortable, but these last couple of hours trapped in the small seat had been physically exhausting.

"We couldn't get there in time without the ferries, so we need a new plan," Sorcha said somewhat evasively, gaining a look of disbelieving surprise. She'd hinted at nothing of the sort since leaving the ferry terminal, nothing at all to indicate that the plan wasn't to move forward as they had intended. Hugh had thought her silence nothing more than a female stewing for what she had termed his manhandling and stubborn refusal to drive on without her.

"Ye said nothing of this," he scolded. "No' even when ye had me drive us through the toll road."

"What difference does it make?" she grouched irritably, her ire still visibly festering. The drive had been a long one as they had gone south through Tacoma before circling back north to Seattle. The ferry truly was a blessing in comparison to that drive. She stretched her stiff limbs as well, lifting her arms over her head and distracting him from the subject in the process.

As fatigued as she might have been, she was still a

beauty. Their hours spent exploring the rapture to be found in one another's arms had been the most fulfilling of his life. He'd not only made love to her but had been made love to, as well. She'd shared in that passion fully. Just when Hugh had thought he would never see anything as lovely as she, the sight of Sorcha caught in ecstasy's snare had proven him wrong.

From side to side she leaned with a low moan and then bent over to touch the ground. Her shirt rode up in the back and her jeans stretched across her bottom, tempting him, and he didn't fight the impulse, reaching out and sliding a hand over those luscious curves.

She turned her head with a raised brow before levering herself back up. "What's with the hand? You think you can just sling me over your shoulder and haul me off like a sack of potatoes and still have the right to cop a feel?"

"We dinnae hae time to stop and argue the matter. Moreover, yer so verra bonny, I cannae help myself," he told her, his voice surprisingly rough, though he punctuated it with a leering grin. Reaching up to pull the band that held her hair back out, he spread his fingers through the auburn masses. She stiffened, stubbornly refusing to relinquish her anger, but she did not fight him as he brushed a tender kiss across her lips. He wrapped his arms around her and hugged her tightly with a sigh of contentment as the tension finally left her and she rested her cheek against his broad chest. She fit against him perfectly, and Hugh covered her bottom with one hand to pull her in for a tighter fit.

"Sure, now you get all flirtatious," Sorcha said with a frown, though her eyes were lit with a touch of humor as she looked up at him. "Days and days of nothing and now, when we're on the run, you get handsy."

Aye, he'd wasted those idyllic days.

Now such moments were lost, at least for the time being. As she said, they were fleeing their foe with little time for play, now that they knew how close the pursuit was. Once the threat was gone, there would be time for exploring how deeply their passions flowed, Hugh reminded himself. Even so, he knew he would risk much for a chance to hold her in his arms once more.

"I've done only what I thought best." The words encompassed his actions not only that night but for most of the week.

"Do you think that excuses you?"

"I think much can be excused if it is done for the right reasons."

"I'll remember you said that."

37

"What the fuck? It's one in the morning." Hugh's pounding on Danny's door was met with those irritable words as it swung open.

Claire pursed her lips impatiently. "Oh, give it a rest. It's not like you were asleep yet."

He might not have been sleeping but he did look like hell. "Claire? What are you doing here?" Danny scratched his head as he looked with confusion from his watch to the suitcases they carried. "You're supposed to meet Jake at the boat in like an hour."

"Obviously there's been a change of plans, lad," Hugh said pleasantly, his present mood clearly a far sight better than either of the siblings'. "Would ye hae us stand in the hallway for the remainder of the night or might we come in?"

Danny must have realized Hugh was asking in a far more amiable manner than Claire might have, given her fatigue and raw emotions, because he stepped back and waved them in without further comment.

"There were agents surveying the ferry," Hugh continued before Claire could say anything more. "We managed to evade them but our escape route was compromised."

Danny frowned at that. "Why come here? Why didn't you just call me? I'm sure they would have held the boat for you. You'll never make it now."

"I don't intend to," she said flatly but didn't offer anything further on her newly minted plan. Better not to alert either of them at this point and inadvertently compromise her next escape route as well. "We can work it out tomorrow, but right now I just want to sleep. Can we use your room?"

"What if I was sleeping there?" Danny asked.

Claire snorted at that, noting that though her brother was alone in the loft, a bank of active computer monitors cast the only light in the room. "Any sleep you get is probably done between eight and noon. Do you mind? Please?"

"Well since you used the magic word …" Danny shrugged and waved an arm toward one of the bedrooms and turned his back on them to wander into the kitchen. He pulled out a can of Red Bull before returning to his computer station, leaving them to make their own way.

XXXXX

They undressed in silence down to their undergarments and Hugh pulled Claire tightly into his embrace as they slipped under the tangled sheets. Absorbing the warmth of his presence, she set to memorizing the feel of his body next to hers while in the back of her mind she examined the variables of her plan. "Ye should sleep, lass."

"How did you know I'm not?"

"Because ye keep wriggling yer arse against me. What is on yer mind?"

"I keep wondering if the sheets are sanitary," she quipped in a whisper and felt the warm rush of his laughter against her hair.

"It looked clean enough," he said. "I would wager he disnae rest here often."

"You're probably right."

Silence reigned for a moment with only the hum of electronics to break the peace. "I'm going to ask Danny to take you to Canada," Claire said into the dark room, feeling Hugh's negative response in the tightening of his body behind hers before he even spoke.

"Nay, my love. We will go on together as planned."

The denial of her newly conceived Option C came as no surprise. In truth, she hadn't expected him to accept total abandonment as a possibility any easier now than he had at the ferry terminal. At least now she wasn't in a position to be forcibly bent to his will.

But she couldn't bend him to hers, either, which left them at an impasse of sorts. During the nearly two-hour drive it had taken to get to her brother's loft by swinging completely south of Puget Sound and traversing Tacoma, she'd weighed her options, hoping for inspiration. The term stubborn Scot was something she'd heard before, but with Hugh she now knew exactly what it meant. He was stalwart and implacable in the face of her pleas to drive on without him. Even if she refused to drive the car any further, there was nothing she could do to force him to drive it away from her. She was stuck with him, he said, and there was nothing she could do to change his mind.

But she had to try.

"A logical man, a man of *reason*," she drew out the word, "would see that you would've better success without me."

"I suppose that would depend on how ye define success," he whispered into her ear. "If success to me is having ye wi' me and that instinct is pursuant to my pleasure then reason argues that I hae the right of it."

Of course Hugh would pull out a classic argument of Voltaire's from the enlightenment period that a man's desire to pursue his personal happiness above all else was instinctive and therefore reasonable. Self-entitled duke or not, Claire thought it was awfully convenient that he would argue such a thing now, and told him so, adding as she rolled onto her back to look up at him, "That's a pretty liberal interpretation of the original philosophy. Voltaire didn't mean that just because you want something, that makes it all right."

"Betwixt the two of us, who can better say what he meant?" He pushed himself up onto one elbow, his free hand splayed across her midsection. "Personal freedoms are given to us by God and right."

"This is no time for a philosophical debate, Hugh," she said, though as with many conversations they'd had over the past week, a thrill of challenge shot through her at the thought of engaging in just that. That they would do it half-naked and in bed made it all the more interesting. There could be nothing sexier than Hugh arguing philosophy wearing nothing but his boxers, and nothing harder than making a logical argument due to the distraction offered by the same. "A statement like that can lead to all sorts of arguments, like the rights of governments and monarchs over those personal liberties you use so high-handedly. What do you do when their edicts and the law are at odds with your personal desires?"

"What did my countrymen do at Culloden? What hae *ye* done for the past sennight?" he countered, making a fine, irrefutable point, much to her consternation. Everything she had done for the past week had walked a fine line between what was right and what was legal. "A man's will is no' alone in driving his reason. Reason itself is often a slave to his passions."

"You're going to pull Hume into this? Your buddy Francois-Marie said that if a man did whatever his passions led him to do then he was putting morality at risk."

It was a springboard launching them into free will, and Hugh latched on to the topic happily; clearly it was a favorite of his, arguing against his old friend's well-documented philosophies and supporting individual freedoms and free will.

"So ye see, moral distinctions between good and evil are no' derived from reason," Hugh pointed out. "Besides, if we hae nae free will and our fate is already determined, why do we fight at all?"

"Hume again?" she sighed, wondering when her argument had been lost. Not defeated but rather misplaced amid what had been a remarkably enjoyable—if somewhat off-topic—debate. Damn, she wanted more of these mad, outrageous, wonderful moments with him. She reached up to caress his whisker-roughened cheek. "*Ah*, Hugh, I'm sure we could argue all this for days on end, but it's past two in the morning, we've got the NSA closing in on us, I'm too tired to think straight anymore, and we haven't even gotten to Kant yet."

"Kant?" he asked. "Immanuel Kant? That puppy?"

Claire stifled a laugh. "I'm not going there right now, and I want to be well rested before we get to Sartre."

"Who is that?"

"Later."

"Later?" he questioned with a smile, skimming his hand over her ribs and under the T-shirt she wore to cup her breast.

"Much later," she said, taking a deep breath to fill his palm more fully. It was no use. The time had come for truth. "Oh, Hugh, you do know that even if I did go with you to Canada, I can't come to Scotland with you."

His hand stilled on her breast. "I see."

"No, you don't. Danny was right." Claire clutched his hand to her breast, refusing to let him pull away, and explained to him all of the annoyingly logical points her brother had made. "I guess we both just thought that once we were out of the country it would all be over, but it won't. If I go with you, Jameson will follow."

"I will stay here then."

She shook her head, though her heart ached tenderly that he should even voice such a sacrifice. "Then what? Live out of a suitcase for the rest of your life? Survive off of three pairs of jeans, a few T-shirts, a couple dress shirts and a sport coat for the rest of your life? It's just like what I was saying before. I am the danger now. You will never be free to live your own life as long as I'm around."

"We will find another way."

"Do you want to live the rest of your life looking over your shoulder?" She smoothed his hair back from his forehead with a tender hand, meeting his gaze and reading there all the resolve she'd been trying to overcome still burning strong.

"I will, if need be."

He was never going to let it go. Ignoring the dangers, he would have an answer for everything. If she had it in her, she would truly do what was best for him. There were any number of things she could say to force his abandonment. Things that would have made him angry enough to leave. Things to make him hate her. She could convince him that she'd had enough of him and was ready for him to go. But she couldn't do it. Couldn't cheapen what they had shared together. Claire sighed heavily. "Another way it is, then."

"Does that mean ye've given up this mad notion of me leaving ye behind?"

"It means you've worn me down until I'm unwilling to fight with you anymore," she allowed.

Bending his head to nuzzle her neck, Hugh whispered, "Will ye ne'er admit defeat, lass?"

"I will if and when I'm truly defeated."

He laughed softly at that, his warm breath teasing at her hair. No, she thought again. Not defeated, only disappointed over his stubborn refusal to see what was from her point of view reasonable, but it wasn't unexpected and maybe inwardly she was a little thrilled that he didn't want to let her go any more than she wanted to be gotten rid of.

"Let me take care of ye for a change, lass," Hugh said, brushing his lips against her hair. "Gi' me a chance to find a way."

"I'll give you a chance to kiss me," she whispered in lieu of a promise she couldn't keep. "I mean, it's been at least a couple of hours."

"And that is too long?" he murmured as he nuzzled her neck, but she could hear the smile in his words.

Claire rolled toward him, sliding her hand over his back and downward over his taut backside. "Way too long."

Diving his fingers into the tangle of her hair, Hugh tipped her head back and brought his lips down on hers gently. They brushed and tugged playfully while his tongue stroked across her teeth and the sensitive inside of her lip. The scruff of his whiskers grazing lightly against her tickled and teased, and she moaned softly, parting her lips and urging him to explore more deeply as she slipped her tongue against his.

A husky groan echoed her impassioned sigh and he rolled her back, coming over her without breaking the kiss. Lean hips pressed between her thighs as he descended, letting every inch of his body surge across hers, letting her feel the weight and power of his body and the strength of his arousal as he thrust against her. His hard length ground against her core and Claire gasped, sharing the breath of astonishment with Hugh before their lips met once more.

Sweeping her hands down his back and buttocks, she lifted her legs high around his hips and urged him even closer as their passion ignited and flared. Rough hands skimmed over her shoulder, pushing her bra strap down until her breast was freed. Breaking the kiss, he dipped his head lower, capturing her nipple between his lips while his hand slipped beneath her to nimbly unclasp her bra. He dragged it away, and, freed from the garment, her eager hands resumed their exploration of the powerful body that had delivered such frustration over the past week and such fulfillment over the past days.

Over the defined ridges of his stomach her hands slipped, and around once more to dip into the indentation of his spine and down under the band of his boxers, over his sculpted backside and around, slipping her hands between them to rake her fingernails up his abdomen, just grazing his rigid length. Hugh growled against her breast, hooking the side of her panties with his thumb and forcing them down even while Claire nudged off his boxers.

Soon they were freed of barriers. He tossed her panties aside and caught her ankle, running his palm roughly up her calf and thigh before delving into the warmth between them. She panted harshly when his fingers found her, teasing and circling without mercy as he suckled at her breast. Cradling his head to her, Claire arched helplessly against his hand as heat pooled and clenched low in her belly.

Hugh had already proven he could deliver her into the arms of mind-numbing ecstasy in moments; indeed, it seemed as if he felt obligated to bring her to one soul-shattering release after another before finding his own pleasure. Even now her body was beginning to pulse as he drove her to the edge of rapture with the taunting thrust of his fingers, but Claire wanted more. She wanted to share that rapture with him, fall over that cliff together ... one last time.

Her fingers slid around his thick length, and Hugh hissed, drawing in a harsh breath that melted into an agonized groan as she stroked him, guiding him to her weeping center. Nipping at his neck and earlobe, she whispered, "Please, Hugh. Love me now."

Hugh lifted his head and looked down at her with blue eyes blazing with mesmeric fire. There were questions there, perhaps protests for the expediency of their lovemaking, but wordlessly he pressed forward, nudging against her before thrusting slowly into her silken depths. His eyes held her, sharing the wonder and rapture of his unhurried possession until he was buried deep within her.

Claire lifted her hands to his cheeks, overwhelmed by the unguarded moment, by the emotion in his gaze. "Hugh ..." She bit her lip, denying the words she longed to say. Her heart cried, yearning for confession, but she couldn't do it. She couldn't deliberately gift her love, knowing that it would only make worse what was to come.

Instead, she clenched her muscles around his erection, gripping him tightly with her thighs and his eyes closed as he helplessly arched his hips against her, tendons tightening in his neck as he fought for restraint. But she wouldn't have restraint. She wanted her wild, impassioned Highlander to lose control and yield to their uncontrollable desire. "Yes," she whispered, urging him deeper with her thighs once more and Hugh complied, gathering her tightly in his arms as he retreated and thrust. One arm slid beneath her hips, lifting her against him as he drove into her again and again, his harsh breaths matching hers until they were both panting desperately for the release neither of them wanted to surrender to yet.

His lips took hers ardently as his body grew taut, and Claire abandoned herself to the molten desire coursing through her, letting the mighty orgasm take her as Hugh erupted inside her with a hoarse cry against her lips. The full weight of his body covered hers but she only gloried in it, wrapping her arms and legs around him more fully as his mouth trailed down her cheek, jaw, and neck, murmuring those same foreign words as before against her skin: *"Mé grá tú gcónaí, mo Sorcha."*

Hugh's lips returned to hers for one last tender kiss before he rolled to his side, drawing her along with him until Claire was nestled against his side. His heaving chest was damp and hot against her cheek but no more so than the tears that began to spill from her eyes as she brushed her lips softly against his skin. Her fingers skimmed across his hard abdomen as the taut muscles relaxed beneath her hand. She hugged him against her as he slipped into Morpheus's embrace.

Damn, she thought as she suppressed the heaving sobs within her as best she could. Her chest burned with agonizing pain that warred with the joy Hugh had given her, and the base of her throat was raw and thick with misery. It shouldn't be like this. It shouldn't end like this. "Oh, God, Hugh," she whispered inaudibly, swiping uselessly at the tears as they continued to flow freely. She knew what those words meant now. They had resonated with emotion she shared. "I love you, too."

38

Day Eleven

As the black skies took on the darkest hue of blue, Claire dressed quickly and crept from the bedroom, leaving Hugh slumbering behind her. Danny was still awake, though he had abandoned his array of monitors in favor of the shabby leather sofa recliner that faced his monstrous television and worked the Xbox controller in his hands with nimble thumbs.

"We need to talk." She walked between her brother and the screen to get his attention but not lingering in his line of sight, knowing from years of doing so that it would only lead to a long and vocal fight. She sat on the sofa next to him. "Can you pause that, please?"

He sighed heavily but complied. "You're up early."

"I know. I guess that means it's almost your bedtime," she retorted but couldn't find the humor to support a smile. "Here's another unprecedented moment for you to savor. You were right in what you said the other day. Yes, take it for what it is. I don't plan on repeating it. I know I can't go with Hugh to Scotland but I've also realized that I shouldn't even be going with him to Canada."

"Glad to hear you've come around," he said, throwing his arms to the side as if the movement would have some effect on the video game soldier he controlled. "So what's the plan then?"

"You are going to do it for me."

"I am?"

"You are," she said in an inflexible tone, holding out the envelope containing Hugh's new passport and birth certificate. His new life. "You are going to take him to Canada and make sure he gets on that plane. Promise me."

Danny nodded with a shrug, one eye still on the frozen screen of his video game. "And what are you going to do?"

"I'm moving on to Option C."

"Option C?"

"I doubt you'll like it," she predicted, wringing her hands indecisively. It certainly wasn't what she wanted to do, but one infuriating Special Agent Phil Jameson had removed her own personal desires from the equation. "Let's just say that if you don't hear from me by Friday, send all that stuff we found to every major news agency in the country."

"Claire…" She had his full attention now. Those blue eyes, so like hers, were wide with astonishment. "Shit, you're going to do exactly what I told you not to, aren't you?"

There was no use denying it. "Yes, I am."

Danny cursed colorfully. "Does Hugh know what idiocy you're up to?"

"No, he doesn't." Reason and personal freedoms aside, sometimes a person had to accept that there were some things that just had to be done for their own good. "He'd never leave without me, Danny, and I can't convince him otherwise. He proved that tonight, and if he won't leave me, I need to leave him."

"Without even saying good-bye?" he asked with uncharacteristic sentimentality. "After what I've seen between yo—"

"Don't let him come after me, no matter what, okay?" Claire cut off any reminder of the undeniable bond between her and Hugh, and handed her brother her burner cell phone. "And give this to him to take with him. He can call you when he's back in Scotland if he needs any help or advice on getting his life started there." Scotland. It was so far away. Would he ask Danny about her from time to time? Would he miss her? Would he know how much she missed him? Claire banished the heartbreaking thoughts away, wishing the emotional squeeze of her chest could be shaken off as easily. "Your number is already in there."

"If he leaves me alive after finding out you're gone, that is."

A chuckle escaped her but ended in a watery sob. Her eyes burned with tears as hot as the fiery ache in her heart.

"Claire ..." He reached out hesitantly, wanting to comfort but unsure how to proceed.

She might have flung herself in his arms and sobbed pitifully on his shoulder but was afraid that giving in to the sorrow would only weaken her resolve in doing what she knew she had to do. Instead she prayed for strength. "Be a friend to him, Danny. He'll need one."

"And what am I supposed to tell him that will spare my life?"

Swallowing back the lump tightening her throat, she replied, "Tell him much can be excused if it's done for the right reasons. His own words used against him. How can he argue against that?"

"What kind of bullshit is that? Now you're sounding like that weird old Irishman or whatever he is who just moved in next door."

Grabbing up her small suitcase, she blindly fled the loft as the tears she had been fighting began to fall, casting a blur over her vision, ignoring her brother's protests as she went. She would rather face Jameson a thousand times than ever again experience the pain of leaving behind the man she loved. Claire raced desperately down the hall. Knowing that even the time it would take to wait for the elevator to arrive might be all that was necessary for her to surrender to her pleading heart, she took the stairs, with each step denying herself what she wanted most.

Go back, her heart cried. *Don't leave him. I can't*, her footfall answered. *I won't*. Being a warrior Scot, a Highlander, a duke, and not to mention a gentleman with more chivalry in his little finger than most men in her time possessed in their entire bodies, Hugh would insist on his own sacrifice before hers. He would want to slay the figurative dragon and save her, his damsel in distress. He would never appreciate that sometimes the damsel could be the one to save the knight in shining armor, and no doubt he would be angry with her for what she was about to do.

He would never admit that he had far more to lose than she did and how that was completely unacceptable to her … because he didn't know how much she loved him.

And now there would never be another chance to tell him.

There would never be another chance to hold his hand, to curl up at his side in front of a roaring fire, to tease him about his sweet tooth, or to watch in awe as he assembled a jigsaw puzzle as if he had an instruction manual. She would never see him again and she hated passionately the reason for it.

Twice love had been taken from her by the actions of her own government. The first time had nearly destroyed her. The second had the potential to do the same.

It was enough to make Claire consider becoming a Canadian.

She was shifting the Tahoe into park in the hold of the ferry at the Seattle terminus when she realized that she couldn't recall how she had even gotten there. Hers was one of the few vehicles traveling from Seattle to Bainbridge Island in the early morning rush, when most were on their way into the city, and there were no NSA agents aboard searching cars or passengers. Obviously Jameson had never dreamed that she would come to him.

Wearily, Claire climbed the iron stairs to the passenger cabin and dropped into a rear-facing seat, watching as the grind of the engines propelled the vessel away from the city. Through the rain-spattered glass, she could picture Hugh standing at the rail, glorying in the chilly nip of the wind while other travelers were bundled in their fleece, his skin warmed by the meager sun, his dark hair tossed and ruffled this way and that as he watched Seattle shrink in the distance.

She would stand sheltered in the circle of his embrace, warmed to her toes.

She stared up at the buildings that had awed him so, their faces dark with the rising sun at their backs and cast in gloom, much like her shadowed soul. Lost in thought, she let the trip slip by in silence until the blast of a horn announced their impending arrival. Struggling to her feet, Claire glanced one last time at their wake. "Good-bye, Hugh," she whispered into the air. "I wish I could kiss you good-bye one last time. I wish I could see your amazement the next time you try something new. I wish I could be there to love you forever."

Returning to the Tahoe, she disembarked, noting the agents who were searching the long lines of vehicles waiting to board but paying no mind to those arriving. Able to swing around and park the SUV without incident, she buttoned her coat, grabbed her purse, and walked purposefully back toward the terminal, where more agents were patrolling the mass of pedestrians waiting to walk onto the ferry for its next departure.

Ahead a dark suit and hardly discreet earpiece labeled one of the agents as he stood scanning the crowd. Approaching from behind, Claire tapped on his shoulder to gain his attention. He looked over his shoulder with some annoyance and nearly turned away before his eyes widened in surprise.

"Take me to your leader."

)()()()()(

"Wake up, Danny," Hugh grumbled, kicking at the young man's foot, which was dangling over the edge of the sofa he was sprawled out on, an arm flung over his eyes to block out the morning light streaming through the bank of windows.

"Go away," Danny muttered irritably, rolling onto his side away from Hugh.

"Danny," he barked more forcefully. "Wake up, lad. Where is Sorcha? Where is yer sister?"

"God, stop yelling, would you?"

Hugh paused at the barely intelligible words. There was "music" playing loud enough in the room to make it nearly impossible to think, much less sleep, and Danny thought he was loud? Reaching down to grab Danny by the arms, Hugh dragged him under protest to a vertical position. "Where is she?"

"That will probably bruise, you know," Sorcha's brother groused, loosing himself from Hugh's grip and bending to retrieve a can of soda from the floor next to the sofa. He swirled the contents of the half-empty container with a grunt before tipping it to his lips with a grimace. "She's gone, man."

"Gone where?"

"Where do you think?"

The explanation told Hugh nothing and everything, and he sat heavily on the sagging sofa, dropping his elbows onto his knees and running both hands through his hair, fighting the temptation to pull it out by the roots while the heavy beat of the music thrummed through his brain. He didn't know which made him more insane. The music or Sorcha.

All their arguing to separate hadn't turned the tables in her favor, so Sorcha had let him believe that the matter was settled and then bolted like a deer in his sights as soon as he slept. Anger, fury ... and something akin to pride for her resolve and determination swept through him. His fair lass did not like to lose.

But neither did he.

Hugh lifted his head and pierced her brother with a menacing glare. "Ye will take me to her," he directed with all his ducal command, but as he was quickly learning, the Americans of this bloody time had little respect for noble authority and not much sense for self-preservation.

"Nay, verily, I will not," Danny drawled, scratching his backside as ambled to the refrigerator and removed a bottle of water. Uncapping it, he tipped his head back, gulping down the contents and eyeing Hugh cautiously over the top as if he were expecting some physical application of force.

At least the lad had the good sense to be wary of him, Hugh thought with a grunt as he stood clenching his fists. He was nigh prepared to rip Danny limb from limb and most certainly it showed.

"I was already handed down my diktat this morning," Danny added, "and that was specifically *not* to take you to her. Sorry, dude."

"I could force ye."

"I know you could," Danny agreed readily, setting the bottle aside and pulling a carton of milk from the refrigerator. "Told her you probably would, too. My sister has no respect for my life." He gathered a bowl and spoon from the dishwasher and set them on the counter before shaking the contents of several boxes displayed on the counter. He chose one, poured the contents into the bowl, and covered the whole of it with the milk while Hugh waited impatiently with his arms crossed ominously over his broad chest. Danny shoved a spoonful of the stuff into his mouthed and chewed loudly, saying around it, "Make it quick, okay? I'm not much into pain."

The lad had unknowingly offered the perfect defense in not defending himself at all. It went against the grain for Hugh to attack those weaker than he. Bullying Danny into capitulation would be akin to forcing his page into the front lines of battle. Hugh grunted with vexation. "Verra well. Gi' me yer keys and I'll go myself."

"Dude, you know I don't own a car," Danny said around another mouthful. "We'd have to wait for one of the minions, and by then it would be too late anyway."

Hugh gnashed his teeth with tenuously leashed vexation

as he paced the room. Of course, Sorcha had known she was essentially marooning him here when she left. Indeed, she would have counted on it. Bugger it, she was a crafty lass, but what did she expect him to do? Sit on his hands while her life was torn in two? "Bluidy hell, what was she thinking?" he muttered aloud, more to himself than to Danny.

"I suppose she was thinking to make some kind of noble sacrifice or something," Danny answered anyway. "She wanted to clear the path for you to go to Scotland, to do what she promised. I'm supposed to take you to Canada and get the rest of it done as planned while she distracts the Feds."

"And I am to just leave her to the wolves and walk away wi'out a second thought for her and the consequences of this rash folly she's undertaking?" Hugh snapped back, longing for a neck to throttle.

Danny lifted his brows and shrugged in a way that told Hugh he agreed with him, but verbally Sorcha's brother remained her loyal compatriot. "That's about the sum of it. She also said to tell you ... let me see if I got it right. Much can be excused if it's done for the right reasons. Sound familiar?"

Hugh loosed an aggrieved grunt, knotting his fingers in his hair to stifle the urge to put his fist through a wall. Blast the woman. Had she completely lost her senses? Sorcha was by far the most infuriating woman he had ever met. Never had there been another who would defy him so. Who would chance his wrath. He couldn't believe that she would make such an ill-considered, perilous play. That she would risk everything for...

Bracing an arm against the window frame, Hugh looked up in astonishment at the fields of towering buildings that shrouded them more fully than any towering pine might dare.

She had done it for him. Sorcha had wagered her future against inconceivable odds. For him. And she had done it from the beginning when she had opened the door to her car and to her life for him back in Spokane. Not for the pity she had claimed she had for him. Not because it was the right thing to do.

She had done it for the one reason she had yet to voice.

Because she loved him.

Her sacrifice was born from love. The same love that burned within him and demanded that he sacrifice the same for her. That he give up all for the promise of her future. It was what had driven Hugh all this time. He loved her. Hugh rubbed at the poignant ache spreading across his chest. "Nay, I cannae go wi'out her."

Danny groaned loudly. "God, I never thought I'd ever meet anyone more stubborn than my sister. I cannot imagine how you two managed to get along at all."

For some reason, that summoned a ghost of a smile to Hugh's lips. Aye, it was what made things interesting, that constant battle between the swagger and chest beating of the past and the self-reliance and independence of the future. Still … "Would ye hae her ruin her life, Danny? For me?"

"Would you stop her from saving what life she has left?" Danny countered. "I'm not saying this is the smartest move on her part, but if this is the only possible way to stop them from hounding Claire for the rest of her life, would you take it away from her?"

Hugh's heart clenched at the lad's reasoning, turning what Hugh knew with certainty was an act of love into a selfish one, implying that Sorcha had acted in her own self-interest. That she had done it to save only herself.

No, Sorcha had taken on a role that few women he had

ever known would have considered in endeavoring to be the heroine of their particular story, and—though it wounded his male vanity not to act, though his inherent masculinity demanded that he hasten to her rescue—Hugh was unexpectedly proud of her bravado. "Nay, Danny. I'm no' so petty as to ruin her life for the sake of my pride."

"Then respect her decision. Don't make it a worthless effort."

Which Hugh knew translated to "let her go" and never see her again.

His heart slowed, thudding hard against his ribs as his blood roared in his ears, and a little of him died inside at the thought of yet another *never* to bear ... this never considerably more heartrending than the other.

The city outside the windows was a looming monstrosity of glass and metal draped in a dark haze that seemed to diffuse the rays of the sun. The whole of it was bleak and cold. Unwelcoming.

Was this what Edinburgh had become as well? Glasgow? Even Inverness? A metallic nightmare hung with a gray miasma of misery? Hugh had been anticipating a return to his homeland, picturing the lonely moors and deserted beaches. Would he not even have that to comfort him in the years to come? The very thought brought the bitter tang of bile to the back of his throat, and Hugh swallowed it back. It served no purpose to wish and hope and long for things to be different; that sour lesson had been grudgingly absorbed these past weeks and months. He might beat his chest and howl at the moon, cursing Fate and God, without expectation for this future to change once more. Regrets were naught but wasted time, but they stirred in him anyway, compounding the painful ache that lingered in his heart.

And then there was Sorcha. A balm to his soul, Hugh had called her and thanked God again for providing that one consolation to banish the gloom. When he had thought he would have her by his side in the days ahead, he hadn't dreaded the future so. Where Sorcha was, there would always be light, but he would dwell in darkness forever for one last kiss.

"I cannae do that."

"'Course you can," Danny said. "What is it the Brits always say? Keep calm and carry on?"

"Nay, Danny, I cannae leave her. Sacrifice or no', I cannae," Hugh said, for there suddenly seemed no sacrifice greater than leaving her behind. "Ye will take me to her."

But Danny was already shaking his head. "No way. Claire would kill me if I did."

"And I might if ye dinnae."

"Sorry, man, I'm more afraid of her than I am of you."

The response prompted an inward smile, but Hugh still glowered darkly at Danny. "Do ye think that's wise?"

"If you have to ask that, you must not have sisters," the lad said in a dire tone that did provoke a silent chuckle from Hugh. Aye, he did have sisters, more than enough of them—all older than he—to appreciate Danny's reluctance. "Death would be cleaner than getting on her bad side. Like when Matt came to pick her up for prom dressed in a tux—I mean, it was like their second date—and I kept asking if he was going to marry my sister. I ran for my life, man."

Hugh couldn't stifle a smile then. "Yet ye continually provoke her."

Danny shrugged. "I have to. She's my big sister. What a paradox, huh?"

"Aye, and another paradox would be my refusal to do

the one thing I know I hae to," Hugh rejoined. "I willnae leave until I hae assured myself that she is safe."

"Crazy, stupid, stubborn people," Danny muttered under his breath as he carried his cereal bowl over to his workstation. "This is exactly why I like computers better than humans. You're being completely irrational."

"Then I believe that is what it must mean to be in love," Hugh said softly, his brogue so thick with emotion that he wouldn't have been surprised if Danny didn't understand him at all.

But the lad must have, because he swore under his breath with great detail before falling silent, his brow furrowed. "How about a compromise, then?"

Never in all his years as Duke of Ross had Hugh ever forsaken his own will for that of another as often as he had so recently. There might have been a lesson there that nobility did not necessarily beget governance, and as much as Hugh loathed the insult of bowing to another's dictate, he was discovering that the legacy of manly dominion passed to him by his ancestors was better suited to another place and time. He considered Danny's serious countenance, the wickedly intelligent gleam in his eye, for a moment before answering. "I assume this involves more than ye lowering the volume of that wretched noise."

"Most assuredly," Danny nodded. "If you're going to try to go in there yourself, we're going to have to make it hurt them a little."

Hugh smiled at that. He might have considered himself a man of enlightenment and reason but he was also a Scotsman to his core. A man who ruled, who dominated, and who fought for what he thought was right in a sometimes brutal and savage manner if necessary. He could be everything they had accused him of.

It was past time the peoples of this century discovered what a true Highlander was capable of.

39

"You let her get away again?" Jameson yelled, the sound echoing through the small room of the mobile NSA surveillance unit that was serving as his temporary office while his team searched Bainbridge Island. He glowered at the two men who stood, eyes cast to the ground, before him. Well, they had better fear for their lives, if not their jobs, at this point. Enough was enough. "Who saved her this time? My ninety-year-old granny?" he sneered. "Did she hit you over the head with her purse?"

"He took us by surprise, sir," the more senior of the pair justified the failure. Simms might have been a lean man in his forties but he was by all reports an excellent fighter.

"He took *both* of you by surprise?" Jameson asked disbelievingly as he shuffled through the grainy surveillance photos taken from cameras at Pike's Market and the Bainbridge terminal. None of them provided a clean shot of Claire Manning or the assailant who had taken out three of his best men that day. "How is that possible?"

"He was fast, sir," Simms explained. "I was out before I even knew what happened. I barely even saw the guy."

Jameson snorted rudely at that and leveled a glare at the second agent. Jackson was built like a defensive lineman and had actually been one. By all accounts, no one in his class at Quantico had ever been able to take him down. "What about you, Jackson? Aren't you supposed to be a black belt in something or the other?"

"As Simms said, sir, he was pretty damn fast," Jackson defended lamely. "He fought like a pro. Said he was a SEAL."

"And you believed him?"

Jackson shrugged as if his defeat had offered the only answer.

To Jameson, the outcome was inexcusable. Two armed and trained agents defeated by a single individual equipped with nothing more than a stick. It was an embarrassment to his department. "Do you think it was J42?"

The two agents shared a look, and Simms responded with a shrug. "I don't see how it could have been. He didn't look anything like the man on the surveillance tapes and spoke with a local accent. I was given to understand our mark couldn't even speak English."

Jameson only grunted at that. He wasn't certain what his target was capable of any longer. The anomaly had evaded capture for eleven days. Eleven days! Obviously it was resourceful, perhaps more able than Fielding had thought. To Jameson's mind, there was no chance it had managed to elude them for so long without help, but he couldn't see it making intelligent conversation.

"Damn it, Jackson," Jameson cursed and dismissed the pair of agents. "Go get your fucking nose looked at. You're bleeding all over the place."

So, if Claire Manning hadn't been saved by their escapee, who had helped her? Did it even matter? Maybe she knew the guy, maybe she didn't. All that did matter was that the Manning woman's presence on the island had been confirmed, and if she was there, Jameson was certain that he was close to finding his prisoner.

He didn't know if she had been leaving or arriving at the island when Simms and Jackson had come across her in the parking lot, but he did know that she hadn't gotten on the ferry then, and her car was still under surveillance in the parking lot. She had to be somewhere nearby.

"Marshall, what have you got on the search?" Jameson said to his junior agent, who had been lingering silently in the corner of the makeshift office.

"Still waiting on a warrant for a door-to-door search, sir," Marshall said, prompting a round of vile cursing from Jameson.

"You're not going to get one, you know?" Nichols said from his position behind the desk with his feet up. "I told you, you have no grounds."

"Marshall, extend the BOLO to Claire Manning's person," Jameson said. "Get her picture out to every police station in the city. Tell them to use deadly force, if necessary."

Even Marshall's brows rose at that, and his nervous gaze shifted to Nichols, who shook his head at the junior agent. "Hold on that, Marshall. Please close the door and give Special Agent Jameson and I a moment."

Marshall fled the room and Nichols looked up at Jameson. "I cannot condone this, Jameson. Colonel Williams already feels that you're chasing a red herring here. What are you going to do with this woman if you find her? Torture her for information she doesn't have? Kill her and call it collateral damage?"

"What agency do you think we work for, Nichols? The Sunshine and Fucking Roses Agency?" Jameson sneered. "We need to get this thing closed out by whatever means it takes."

"There is no agency in this country that has the right or power to harm American citizens," Nichols pointed out. "It was one thing to threaten violence to your anomaly but I cannot let pass a threat to Mrs. Manning's person without cause."

"What do I need to do to convince you that I am right here, Nichols?" Jameson wanted to know. "A another tragedy like so many others this country has seen lately?"

"No one wants that, but how about showing me some actual proof?"

"She's somewhere on this damned island. Let me find her and you'll have it."

A knock on the doorjamb cut off any response Nichols might have made.

"What is it?" Jameson barked.

"Sir, Mrs. Manning is here," Marshall sputtered, and Jameson smiled grimly. His blood pumped in triumph.

"Where did they find her?"

"She, uh … well, she came to us, sir."

His brows shot up at that. Nichols's did as well. "Did she now? Well, don't keep her waiting. Show her in."

The agent skittered away as Jameson wrung his hands in malicious glee, looking at Nichols with victory in his eyes. He had her. Finally he had her. Hot damn.

"Jameson, I feel that I should remind you …"

The growl in Jameson's throat turned to a purr of triumph when Claire Manning was escorted through the narrow door. She looked tired, as if she hadn't slept. A quick look at the clock showed it to be seven in the morning, which might explain many things or nothing at all.

"Mrs. Manning, come in. Have a seat."

Jameson leaned against the desk, blocking Nichols's view and sipping lukewarm coffee from a paper cup as he savored his moment of triumph.

"Do you have any more of that?"

Jameson looked up to find the woman staring pointedly at his cup. "Of course. Where are my manners?"

"That is the million-dollar question, isn't it?"

Gritting his teeth, he stood and moved to the door. "Cream? Sugar?"

"Both."

Cracking the door, Jameson shouted for Marshall and put in a request for more coffee for both of them and waited, studying his elusive prey with all the pride of a hunter taking down his first big buck. For all her visible fatigue, Claire Manning was a lovely woman of slender build and vivid coloring. She would be eye-catching to any red-blooded man. Perhaps that was why the anomaly had latched on to her after seeing her in Fielding's lab.

Marshall returned with the coffee, and Jameson shooed him away once more before handing one of the cups to Claire. Leaning his hips against the desk, Jameson sipped from his cup, contemplating the best way to force the truth from her. He doubted Nichols would be game for anything more forceful than a moderately raised voice.

"Nice RV, Phil. Can I call you Phil?" she asked, looking around the small space as she sipped her coffee. "I have to say I'm surprised to find you here. I mean, if I had known you were looking for me, I might have come sooner."

Jameson gnashed his teeth, not believing a word of her innocent prattle. "I did mention in Spokane that I'd have more questions for you, didn't I?"

The woman had the gall to wave her hand dismissively. "I thought that was something you said to everyone. When Dr. Crandel called to confirm the lab closure, he didn't mention anything about staying, so I leapt at the chance to get away."

"And where did you get away to?" he asked as evenly as possible. "The lab reopened at the beginning of the week, and yet you did not report for work."

"Oh, well, that's your fault, really," she said, surprising him into silence with her words. His fault? The only blame he was due would be in hunting her to the point that she didn't feel safe to return.

"How is that?"

"What you said before when you were at my house? Do you remember? You were right. You were absolutely right. What an epiphany. But I suppose I should thank you. You made me see what a mistake I was making, so I've been trying to figure out what to do with my life."

Jameson tried to remember what he had said that would have garnered such a reaction. Something about trading one job for the next? Was that it? "You're going to try to tell me that the reason you've been missing for the past two weeks was because I said something that made you rethink your life?"

"That's exactly what I'm saying. I'm quitting my job at Mark-Davis because of you."

Nichols choked with laughter behind him, and Jameson frowned more deeply.

"If you've got nothing to hide then why have you been

evading my agents?" he wanted to know.

"How could I evade them when I didn't know you were looking for me?"

"Still, you didn't cooperate when they came for you. Why?"

"Well, a girl can never be too sure that ID's like that are real, you know? I wasn't going to hang around only to find out they were serial killers or something," she said. "Like I said, I wasn't expecting you."

That had to be a lie. There was no other possibility.

"They didn't identify themselves to the other man?" Nichols asked, and the woman leaned to the side to see him better.

"Actually, no, they didn't," she answered with a ring of truth. "That guy thought they were trying to kidnap me. Nice to know that there are still good people in the world who would stop to help a woman in need, huh?"

That inanity was so trite, Jameson could only snort humorlessly.

"He took out two of my most formidable agents."

"If you say so."

My God, Jameson thought. Did she really think this was funny? "And the man you were seen with at Pike's Market?"

"My brother."

"You have an answer for everything, don't you?" Jameson shoved a hand through his thinning hair with barely contained frustration. "If you didn't know that I was looking for you, then what are you doing here?"

"I came because they won't let me have my car back until I do," the woman said with a serene smile. "So can I go now?"

"No," Jameson ground out. "I want to know where

you've been for the last ten days. You haven't been to your parents' house or returned to your own. Where were you? On this island?"

"I came over to walk on the beach and reflect on life," Claire said, draining the last of her small Styrofoam cup of coffee and tossing it into a waste bin next to the desk. "As for the rest of it, I'd say it's none of your business."

"I say it is."

"Then I say show me your warrant, Phil," Claire said pleasantly, hazarding a guess, and was rewarded by Jameson's glower and a chuckle from the man behind him. "But you can't, because you don't have one, do you? Tell me, does Big Brother even know you're here? Whatever you've been after, you've been barking up the wrong tree."

"I told you," the other man said, and she leaned to the side to get a better view of the man at the desk. He was a pleasant-looking man in his mid-fifties or so who managed to somehow look both amused and completely bored with the entire situation.

"Who are you?"

"Jim Nichols with INSCOM, Mrs. Manning," he said pleasantly. "It's nice to meet you at last."

"Nice to meet you," she answered slowly, weighing his importance in comparison to Jameson's with the NSA. Given his relaxed posture behind the desk, Nichols must not be far down from Jameson, and he looked far more unconcerned with her presence than the NSA agent did. Was it her imagination or did he seem to be on her side? "Do you support this madness, Mr. Nichols?"

"Can you assure me that you aren't hiding a savage beast from us?"

Claire's brows rose but she nodded. "I can. Am I free to go then?"

"I don't see why not."

"She knows where it is and she's not leaving here until she tells us where it is!" A muscle jumped in Jameson's cheek as he ground his teeth. Clearly frustration was eating at him, but she wasn't about to give him what he wanted when he turned to her. "I don't know how you managed all this, but you're making a big mistake."

"As Charles Schulz once said, 'I've never made a mistake in my life. I thought I did once but I was wrong.'" Claire tilted her head to the side and smiled. She could almost hear Jameson's teeth grinding. It was an unexpected pleasure.

"It's dangerous, you know."

"Charles Schulz? I doubt Snoopy would agree."

Nichols bit back a bark of laughter, which only seemed to string Jameson's nerves even tighter.

"Mrs. Manning, you are walking on very thin ice here. Where is it?"

"I don't know what you're talking about."

"My conversation with your friend Darcy Washington tells me that you do," Jameson countered. "You felt sorry for it, right? You wanted to save it."

It took a lot of effort for Claire not to lash out as Jameson repeated those derisive words. *It?* Was that all they thought of Hugh? Was that all the consideration they had ever given him? "I told you, I don't know what..."

The agent slammed a palm down on the desktop, the smack echoing through the small office, and Claire jumped in her seat. "Where is my fucking science project?"

"Jameson ..." Nichols cautioned.

With one last frown, Jameson pointed to the door. "Out,

Nichols, and take your bleeding heart with you."

"I will not," Nichols said as he stood. "Someone in this room needs to remember that she does have some rights."

Fear and rage coiled inside of her, sending her heart racing, but when Claire spoke, her voice was arctic in its chill. "Why are you pushing this so hard? Leave me alone. Leave him alone."

Jameson smiled coolly in triumph, and even Nichols's brows rose. "So you do know it." He looked over his shoulder at the other agent. "Now who's to say I told you so?"

"*Him*, and I never said I didn't," Claire countered as calmly as possible. The anger roused by his objectification of Hugh had thrown her thoughts into chaos, and she had spoken without thought. "You don't need to do this. He's not dangerous. Leave him alone."

"I can't do that because it… he *is* dangerous, Mrs. Manning," he sneered. "Whether you'd like to admit it or not. He could bring disease into this world that you know nothing about."

Claire shook her head. "The only disease around here is you, Agent Jameson."

"Mrs. Manning," Nichols cut in, though there was a smile playing at his lips as if he was pleased with her icy retort. "Are you saying that you *did* assist in the security breach at Mark-Davis?"

"What? No. Of course not," she said honestly.

"But you lied when you said that you weren't hiding it from us," the INSCOM agent pressed.

"No, I wasn't," Claire insisted, trying to regain the upper hand. God, she was a miserable liar. All this was for naught if she didn't keep Hugh safe. "There can be one without the other, you know."

"Where is he, Mrs. Manning?" Jameson pressed once more.

Claire took a deep breath. "Honestly, Phil, what makes you think I know? He forced me to get him off the campus and he hid in my house for a while, but I left him on the highway between here and Spokane more than a week ago."

"I don't believe you, Mrs. Manning," Jameson said after studying her shrewdly for a moment, and Claire decided she needed to make a concerted effort to hone her skills at fabrication in the future.

"Mrs. Manning," Nichols broke in softly. A classic case of good cop/bad cop, she thought. "I do believe you were coerced into helping him escape. I do and Jameson does as well, whether he admits it or not. No one blames you for being strong-armed by a greater power, but you needn't protect him any longer. Just tell us where he is and we'll take care of the rest."

"You'd kill him?"

"No, we could send him home," the agent baited the hook with an undeniably potent lure and Claire's heart skipped a beat. "Do you know what that means? What it really means? You do, don't you? You want to save him? Give him up to me then, Mrs. Manning, and I promise to get him back where he belongs. To his real home," he offered silkily, proving that he was as dangerous as Jameson, perhaps even more so.

But was it possible? She mentally reviewed Fielding's reports. There was nothing in them that evenly remotely hinted that Fielding had overcome that setback and could control the destination of the wormhole. Nichols had to be lying.

But what if he wasn't? Hugh should have the choice.

But if Nichols *was* lying … Hugh would be at Jameson's mercy, and it was obvious to Claire that there wasn't much of that in the NSA agent. "You can't do that."

"I can if you tell me where he is."

Every fiber of her being urged her to negate the possibility that there was any truth to his words. "No, if you could do that, you would've done so before all this."

"Are you really going to make that choice for him?"

Indecision held her in its grasp for only a moment. Clearly both these agents would go to any length to find Hugh. Nichols was calm and composed, but Jameson's eyes were steely with determination, and lying would be only the tip of the iceberg to a man so obsessed. She could not risk Hugh's safety on the off chance that Nichols's benevolence would see him home once more. Though she might be condemning Hugh to a bleak future when his own life awaited him in the past, Claire shrugged with forced indifference. "I guess so, since I don't know where he is now. If there's nothing else, I think we're done here."

"Mrs. Manning, you have to tell us how to find him," Jameson cut in once more.

Ignoring him, Claire stood, hitching her purse over her shoulder, and turned to the door, but Jameson caught her wrist. "He's a killer, brutal, violent, and vicious."

She looked pointedly down at his hand. "I'm sure you would know the type."

"He is a savage, Mrs. Manning."

"You truly think that, don't you? And that's precisely why you'll never find him. You couldn't pick him out of a crowd to save your life." They were making the same mistake she once had. Looking for a primitive savage who grunted and pounded on the table for his food. She almost laughed because he had done that once ... almost. They would never believe Hugh read Michio Kaku much less understood his work. Not if she swore it on a stack of Bibles.

"God damn it, woman," Jameson ground out. "We'll follow you. We'll always be a step behind, and eventually you'll lead us right to him."

"No, Phil," Claire said, unable to fully banish the grief from her voice, knowing that in that one thing there was truth. "I won't."

She wrenched open the door and to her surprise, there was Hugh filling the small space. He looked from her to Jameson's hand on her arm and pierced the agent with a fierce scowl, a low growl rumbling from deep within his chest.

"Who the hell are...?" Jameson began before Hugh's fist shot out and caught him hard across the jaw. The agent spun, his eyes rolling back in his head as he fell to the ground.

40

Ten minutes earlier

"Did you find her?"

"Aye," Hugh answered slipping into the seat of the small sedan, a vehicle considered the "nicest" available to any of Danny's minions. If he had understood the dark-skinned Indian—this time a young man truly native to that country—correctly, it belonged to his mother. It wasn't as luxurious as Sorcha's 'Goose', but the nondescript vehicle had served its purpose in delivering them without incident past the Bainbridge terminus.

Sorcha's car remained undisturbed where they had left it the previous night, which meant either that she had been apprehended and taken away or that she was still in the area. It was Danny, with his knowledge of the twenty-first century, who had recognized the significance of the large black van parked on the street about a block away, and it had been Hugh who had directed Danny farther up the street as he scouted the area, determining the number and location of the guards assigned with its protection.

Danny's tense features relaxed into a smile as the nervous tapping of his fingers against the steering wheel subsided. "Thank God. I thought you'd been busted for sure, and I was sitting out here for so long I thought for sure that some cop would think I was the getaway driver for some bank robbery and haul me away. I don't think I'm cut out for fieldwork," he added. "My place is definitely at a keyboard, but at least it all worked out okay, right?"

Aye, Hugh had found out what he wanted to know with incredible ease. No doubt it had been far simpler than convincing an officer at a Vancouver Metropole station that a strung-out junkie hoping to finance his next high could successfully rob a man of Hugh's height and breadth might have been. "She's in a rear compartment of the van wi' two men," Hugh said. "I counted a half dozen more guarding the vehicle."

Danny swore. "How are we going to get her out, then?"

Hugh grinned. "As I said, there are only six of them. If their resistance proves to be as laughable as in every other confrontation I've had wi' them in the past day, there should be no difficulties." Jameson's underlings were skilled to an extent but they were not experienced in true combat. He doubted any of them had ever fought for their lives, for their homes, or for anything greater than their own self-interest.

"In broad daylight?" Danny asked. "Well, if you're sure."

"Aye," Hugh nodded. "I will retrieve yer sister and impress upon them the necessity of ceasing their pursuit in the future."

Danny laughed at that. "Well, don't impress them too much. It is a federal offense to assault a federal agent in this country."

"But this isnae my country, is it?" Hugh patted the pocket of his sport coat, where the new passport Danny had given them rested to confirm his identity if needed, just in case the agents were somehow able to recognize him as the escapee from Mark-Davis.

"Still, don't get too close," Danny warned. "I know I won't. Call me when you're done."

"Yer no' coming?"

"Oh, hell no. I like to keep my distance from the NSA."

"I daresay they feel the same."

Hugh pushed open the door and strode back down the street to where the van housing Sorcha was parked. The plan was a simple one, and he could only hope it worked.

)()()()(

The first agent standing sentry at the corner went down without a sound as Hugh took him out in a manner similar to the one he had employed near the market a few days past. Given that the attack was unexpected, the man went down without a struggle before Hugh tucked him safely among the hedgerow lining the street. The next one was far more aware of his surroundings and turned upon Hugh's approach. The fight was brief but served to get his blood pumping pleasantly.

He flexed his fingers as he approached the van. Here things would get thornier if he were not to simply kill the men, which would have been more expedient but would also certainly offend Sorcha's sensibilities. There were two agents remaining outside and pair more within before he would find her ensconced with the two older agents at the rear of the van. He needed to defeat the remaining quartet efficiently enough to silence them for a prolonged amount of time without rousing suspicion from within.

There was a challenge in that at least.

It was good to know that his Highlanders who lost at Culloden would have found victory in this time if the fight were in hand-to-hand combat. These men were not raised and bred to battle as his own were, and they did not have a cause worth shedding their blood.

They did have guns, though. One of the agents turned, pistol in hand, as Hugh neared and raised it defensively. Hugh spread his arms wide in supplication before lowering his shoulder and charging into the man's abdomen, driving him to the ground as he wrenched the weapon away while blocking his blows. He was just about to slam his fist against the agent's jaw when he felt the weight of another man on his back, pulling at his arm.

Hugh wrested his arm back, flinging the new opponent to the ground before driving his fist into the first agent's jaw once and again quickly until his head listed to the side. Leaping to his feet, he faced the man he had shaken off. It was his opponent from the previous night. The agent's nose was bloodied, perhaps broken, but he stood warily, awaiting his attack with far less cockiness than at their last confrontation. "You needn't do this," Hugh warned softly. "You know what I am capable of."

"I do," Jackson answered. "Unfortunately, I have a duty."

"All I want is the woman. Let me have her and I will leave you unharmed."

Jackson only shook his head. "I wish I could, man. I really do." He looked over his shoulder at the rear opening of the van a score of feet away. "Simms, get out here. We've got company."

The other agent from the previous night appeared and paused in surprise. "What the fuck?" Simms spared a nod for his partner and the pair charged Hugh in unison, determined to take him down by force. But Hugh was prepared for their attack and had even practiced what to do in such a scenario with his cousins. When they were lads, Keir and one of his brothers would often launch such a surprise offensive, much as Hugh had in turn. Lads would be lads after all. It had honed their responses, kept them agile.

Thankfully, it wasn't a skill lost to years in a more civilized court.

The fight was violent but thankfully brief. Hugh was able to use one man against the other, making one agent into a shield and the other into a weapon, deflecting blows until the agents were doing more harm to one another than they were to him. Finally, Hugh trapped Jackson's head beneath his arm, bracing himself against the struggle, and was fortunate enough to catch Simms across the cheekbone with a raised knee as he turned, rendering the man unconscious. Jackson followed him into oblivion a moment later.

Hugh cracked his neck to the side as he climbed the stairs into the back of the van, finding the remaining agent standing nervously to the side, wringing his hands. He was a young fellow, barely a man at all.

"Yo-you can't go in there," the lad boldly announced, stepping forward to impede his progress, but Hugh simply took the young man by the neck and slammed his head into the bank of monitors mounted across the inside wall of the van, and the lad slipped silently to the floor.

All that remained was behind that door. Two agents, one presumably the tenacious Special Agent Jameson, and Sorcha, his bold, defiant lass who would be in need of a sound scolding when he got her out of there.

The door opened like magic beneath his hand and she was there, haggard, surprised, and utterly bonny as she stared at him. Flames of joy licked at Hugh's but burned to a cinder when he noticed one of the agents had a tight grip on her arm. His eyes shot up hotly to meet the astonished gaze of her assailant.

"Who the hell are…?"

The low, protective growl came from deep within Hugh and served as the man's only warning before Hugh's rock hard fist lashed out and took him down with a single blow.

Sorcha sagged with relief almost indiscernibly before she straightened once more. "What is this? What are you doing here?"

"It is my turn to remind you that much can be excused if it's done for the right reasons," he said softly. "I am here to save ye."

"From what?"

A grin jerked at the corner of his mouth. "From yerself." Hugh caressed her cheek with the back of his fingers before he opened his hand and dangled the little Tokidoki Thor USB from one finger. "Ye forgot this."

41

"Who the hell are you?"

Hugh lifted his head to study the other agent standing behind the small desk that was the only furniture in the room besides a small chair in the cramped space. "Are ye Jameson?"

"Agent Nichols," the man corrected with some justifiable wariness. "INSCOM. And who the hell are you?"

With a nod, Hugh stepped forward, taking the agent's measure. There was none of the fanaticism in his eyes that had been so readily apparent in the other agent, even at a glance. Hopefully here was a man who could be reasoned with. "My name is Hugh Urquhart. I am a friend of Claire and her brother. I've come to ask ye to leave them alone in this matter."

"And how are you aware of the matter?" Nichols asked, clearly trying to visibly dissect Hugh, to determine *exactly* who he really was. Undoubtedly he was suspicious but Hugh bore almost no resemblance to the savage who had once been housed in a cell at the lab.

"I've done some light reading on yer project wi' Mark-Davis Laboratories," Hugh said.

Sorcha tensed by his side, no doubt wondering at his words, but Hugh had been well drilled by Danny in the past hour. He knew what he was about. "I've managed to unearth every last detail of Dr. Fielding's project and the entirely unethical uses INCSOM has planned for his discovery. Sneaking up on the enemy? Planting evidence where none existed? Espionage here? A bomb dropped there? The ability to assassinate anyone in their own bed and behind locked doors?" Hugh tsked with a shake of his head. "I doubt even your allies or my government and those of all the other UN nations would like that, considering that there was no intention of sharing with your friends. That's one way to rule the world, is it not?"

"I doubt the media would be able to keep quiet about it," Sorcha chimed in. "I doubt the president and the FBI would be too happy, either. A little interdepartmental tantrum over who has the best toys. Boy, that could get ugly for you."

Nichols stiffened but his tone remained as pleasant as ever. "Are you threatening the federal government, Mrs. Manning?"

"No, Agent Nichols, just you and Jameson. Because I bet it would look really bad on your record to have something of this magnitude leak."

"I could just take you out … both of you. That would solve the problem."

There was no doubt in Claire's mind that the implied threat of death wasn't an idle one. The tenacious Special

Agent Jameson was clearly capable of doing anything to protect his interests, and she was beginning to think that Nichols was no different, though his methods were certainly gentler. "There are other people who know."

Nichols waved an unconcerned hand. "A common threat."

Hugh held up the keychain USB. "Given the reputation of certain people in Mrs. Manning's family, I'm sure ye know it's not an unfounded fail-safe."

Claire could tell by the look on his face that Nichols was taking his words seriously, and she breathed an inward sigh of relief. Why hadn't she thought to begin with the threat rather than trying to find humanity and reason in people where there was none?

"There is a keystroke between ye and disaster, Agent Nichols," Hugh continued. "Astonishing really, to hae such an... outbreak at a facility – that despite the nature of its top-secret projects – had never experienced a threat greater than an occasional chemical leak. So many negative... side effects. It would be a shame if it all got out."

Eyes narrowed, Nichols refused comment, but Claire wasn't discouraged by his silence. She could see his mind spinning, calculating just how bad it would be for him. "If ye'll take a moment to look at a website called *whistleblower.com*?" Hugh suggested, nodding to the desktop monitor.

Nichols lifted a wary brow but moved to an open laptop and depressed a few keys. His eyes widened only slightly but it was enough for Claire to know that whatever Hugh and her brother had planned, it was proving affective.

"That is just a teaser," Hugh's brogue wrapped awkwardly around the new word. "A taste of what is to come if ye continue to pursue this path. I'm no' asking for the whole thing to be shut down—though God knows it should be. I'm no' even asking for ye to consider the morality of what ye hae done."

"What do you want, then?"

"I want ye to gi' up this madness and leave Mrs. Manning alone. She hae done nothing to threaten yer project or its future."

"And what about you?"

"What aboot me?"

"Don't you want to go home?" Nichols said silkily. "I can send you there."

Hugh froze but only for a moment, saying decisively, "I can buy my own plane ticket."

"No, to your real home," the INSCOM agent baited the hook further. "I was just explaining to Mrs. Manning that the problem has been fixed. All *negative* side effects of the project can be remedied. You can go back where you belong."

XXXXX

Hugh didn't even twitch at the offer. Home. Was it surprising that he did not miss it? Or was it simply knowing that the Scotland he would reach was not truly his own?

"I am where I belong. There is no place I would rather be," he said firmly. "If we were to come across any of your negative side effects, however, we will be sure to let them know about your generous offer. Now is that all?"

A reluctant smile curved the corner of Nichols' lips. "I had to try, you know? I was never worried about this, not like Jameson was. I figured that the escapees would simply walk in front of a car or something and the problem would solve itself."

"It was probably a freight train," Hugh said, since he had

felt rather decimated on occasion since his arrival. "Either way, I would wager that yer problem is completely taken care of … except for the matter of the project information leaking to the public. Nasty business that."

"Yes," Nichols nodded thoughtfully. "I would hate to see that happen."

"Sir!" Jackson appeared at the door, panting for breath, as he looked frantically between Hugh and Nichols and down to Jameson, still unconscious on the floor.

"No need to worry, Jackson," Nichols held up a hand. "These two were just leaving."

"But sir!"

"Let them pass, Jackson."

"Do we hae an accord then, Agent Nichols?" Hugh asked, taking Sorcha by the hand.

"I would say we do," the agent nodded. "I am retiring soon, but I will see that the case is closed and all other *impediments*,"—he glanced down at Jameson with a grin—"to your continued freedom are taken care of before I go."

"I would appreciate that."

"And I would appreciate retiring without a flaw on my record."

)()()()()(

"What were you thinking?" Claire asked as soon as they were clear of the van and the rousing agents. "You were supposed to be going to Canada this morning."

"And ye were supposed to be going wi' me," Hugh answered sternly as he towed her away.

"I was trying to save you."

"And I had to save ye as well."

Hugh tugged her around the corner and behind a tree. "Ye foolish, foolish thing. I've ne'er been so angry as I was when I woke and found you gone. Promise me ye'll never do anything so imprudent again."

"But Hugh ..."

Raking his fingers through her hair, he tilted her head back until she was able to look into his bright blue eyes fully and read the warmth and caring there. "I could no' lose ye when I hae lost all else," he whispered in his husky brogue, stroking his calloused thumb against her cheek.

"I'm sorry I couldn't go with you."

"I dinnae mean to pressure ye," he told her. "I only wanted to share my new life wi' ye."

"Oh, Hugh ... but what if Nichols's offer was genuine?" she asked, her heart racing. "What if he could have sent you home?"

"Did ye believe him? I dinnae."

"So you would go home, if you could?"

"Nay, Sorcha lass, my place is wi' ye now," he whispered earnestly. "If ye'll have me."

"But I want you to have what you really want," Claire protested. "I want you to be happy."

"Remain by my side, my love, and I will be."

"You don't have to say that."

"Lass, look at me," Hugh commanded. Claire met his eyes and read the sincerity there. It echoed everything that burned in her heart, everything she had refused to voice. Everything she had feared feeling once more. "Ye are what I want, my love. Wi' ye I hae found everything I need."

"*Mé gráigh tú?*" she asked, stumbling over the foreign words that had lingered in her thoughts.

"I adore ye," he translated softly.

Claire's heart skipped a beat. "*Mé adhradh tú?*"

Hugh lifted her hands, pressing a tender kiss against her

knuckles. "I worship ye."

"Mé gr-gray..." She started with a mispronunciation.

"*Mé grá tú, mo Sorcha. I gcónaí*," he corrected and finish for her. "Can ye nae guess?"

"I couldn't bear the thought of losing you, Hugh," she whispered, her throat tight with tears. "Anywhere you go, anything you need, I will be there for you. I love you. So much."

"And I love ye, my Sorcha," he whispered, bending his head to hers. "Always."

)O)O)O)(

Darth Vader's *Imperial March* blasted from Danny's phone, and he looked down in surprise at the image of the iconic Rolling Stones emblem of a red tongue sticking out at him that served as his avatar for Claire's incoming calls. *What the hell?*

"What are you doing?" he asked by way of answer.

"Calling me from your own GD phone?"

"Where are you?" she asked by way of an answer.

Danny growled with some frustration and hung up the phone. There couldn't be two people in the world that could be so freaking foolish as first Hugh and now Claire were being. God help him if he ever became such a fool for som—

Darth Vader began marching again and Danny bit back a primal scream and snarled into the phone as he pressed it to his ear, "You know if they can track you on that damned thing, they can track whom you're talking to, too."

"Would you just come and pick us up?" was all she said.

Danny blinked at that, any thoughts of the NSA tracking her signal having fled his mind. "You mean it worked?"

"Of course, it worked. Did you think it wouldn't?"

"Of course not," Danny lied blithely. "I was so sure it

would that I figured you could just take your own car."

Claire laughed, and he heard her repeat the words to Hugh before his laughter joined hers. "Sorry, I forgot it was here. Thanks, Danny. For everything."

"Anything for you, Sis."

"Really? In that case, can you book me two tickets to Edinburgh?" she asked merrily.

"Sure," he said, just as flippantly. "Window or aisle?"

"Oh, aisle, I guess," she said. "I doubt Hugh will be too anxious to see what's coming. And make sure you get us in first class. I would hate to tarnish the entire experience for him the first time 'round."

Claire said something else to Hugh and they both laughed once more, and Danny rolled his eyes in disgust. If love could turn two of the most intelligent people he had ever known into raving lunatics, he would be content to restrict his affections to a lifetime love affair with his laptop.

Much can be excused if it's done for the right reasons, Danny thought with a wicked grin after they said good-bye. If he was actually going to go to the trouble of booking their flight for them, he was going to give them the longest red-eye available because a little sibling revenge was always the best reason for everything.

Epilogue

Breamar Highland Games
September 2013
Where Freedom has become a Love Affair

The crowd cheered and Claire joined them enthusiastically as Hugh successfully heaved the fifty-six-pound weight into the air and over the bar currently set at fifteen feet high, his ancient Urquhart plaid flapping about his muscular thighs. Directing a cocky salute and a wink to Claire, he turned and strode back to the group of competitors waiting for their next turn as the renowned heavy eventer, Hamish Robb, held out his hand in congratulations. Hugh accepted the compliments and whistles from the crowd with a wave of his arm and a broad grin that only served to amplify the delighted onlookers.

The Breamar Highland Games were the oldest and most prestigious of the many highland games held throughout

Scotland, but surely they had never had such a genuine participant in the heavy events as Hugh. Some might have commented on the remarkable accuracy of Hugh's kilt in the blue, green, and red of the Urquhart plaid, his leather shoes, and even his stockings, but none would ever know how truly authentic a Highlander he was, or that he had roamed Scotland long before the first of the modern Highland Games.

Obviously Hugh was in his element. He'd already broken the games' record in the twenty-two-pound Scots hammer, throwing over thirty-five meters, and was well on his way to proving himself victorious in many of the other events as well. And it wasn't merely the traditional events themselves that had such satisfaction gleaming in his eyes. It was the pipes, the fiddle, the traditional dance, and the ancient castle that hosted it all that, in spite of the modern tents and food vendors interspersed among it all, reminded him of another time in a way that the busy streets of Inverness had yet to achieve.

Scotland really was the most magical place Claire had ever been, and it was easy to appreciate why Hugh had longed for it so. It was wild and untamed yet majestic and elegant. Just like him.

Over the past few weeks, they'd found time to rediscover the more remote and unpopulated areas of Scotland where only minimal change could be found. They had roamed ancient villages that looked as out of time as Hugh was and walked hand in hand across endless moors where the rolling hills of verdant green stood in vivid contrast to the turbulent grey clouds suspended heavily above them. They had picnicked on the banks of turbulent rivers still swollen with the late thaw and on the barren beaches of the Cromarty

Firth, wanting only the shadows of Rosebraugh over them for Hugh to feel truly at home.

And she did as well, with Hugh at her side.

They were making a new home together. Both of them putting the past where it belonged and looking forward. Claire had returned her focus to environmentally responsible research and had taken a job at the small propulsion lab near Inverness. Hugh was taking small steps into investments but had also taken her offhanded suggestion to write about his time with Voltaire to heart. He'd had the idea to write it as a work of fiction, taking his conversations with Voltaire, Hume, Frederick and others of that time into round table debate that could have never taken place but for Hugh's interactions between them. His tentatively entitled "Conversations Among Men" had already received notice from the Oxford Press.

"Well, well, well, Mrs. Manning."

Claire stiffened at the regrettably familiar voice and looked over at the man who had appeared at her side. His dark suit and tie were such a ludicrous contrast to the casual attire of the crowd and the kilted participants in the games, she might have laughed aloud had it not been for the dread and nerves that suddenly knotted her stomach. She hadn't been so shaken for weeks, but she forced the anxiety away, silently assuring herself that there was no reason now to worry. She was safe in the thick crowds, safe with all the security that accompanied the Queen's presence. "What? No kilt?"

"I'm not here to participate, Mrs. Manning," Phil Jameson said softly.

"No? Then what brings you to Scotland? Vacation?" she asked. "Because I'm sure it can't be anything else."

"You do think this false naïveté is humorous, don't you?" he asked rhetorically. "No, your trip through customs raised a red flag on my notifications, so I thought to come and see what you were about for myself. I was surprised to learn that you'd moved out of your townhouse in Spokane."

She had packed Matt's things carefully into a box with Hugh at her side but had taped that last box shut with no guilt. Perhaps one day she might bring one or two of those items out once again but she'd learned that life was for the living. She had promised herself once that she would mourn her husband for the rest of her life but it had taken recent events and even Phil Jameson himself to make her realize that her own life hadn't ended.

When her parents and brothers and even Robert and Sue had come to help them pack her belongings away into storage, only one of them knew that Hugh Urquhart wasn't the only one who should be thanked for drawing her from the darkness that had enveloped her.

"I guess I should have sent a note, but, you know, a little bird told me that you had been demoted and put on desk duty so I didn't think you'd mind if I carried on without your okay." From everything Danny had been able to dig up for her, she knew that Jameson had been officially reprimanded for the excessive and borderline illegal measure she'd taken during the search for both Hugh and the Native American escapee. "How did you even come across me here so conveniently? There are a thousand places I could have been today."

Jameson only frowned, ignoring the taunt, and stared across the field, taking in the competition on the field. "You are still a difficult woman to run to ground. Thankfully, your new neighbors knew where you had done this weekend. Tell me, which one is he?"

"Can't you guess?" She waved her hand at the field of men dressed in kilts. "They all look alike, don't they? So you tell me. Which one is your savage?"

"Shall I bring them all in, then?"

"Call me a skeptic but I don't think the NSA has that kind of power over here, even if you were still on the case ... oh, that's right. The case is closed, isn't it? Yes, I know that and more," Claire went on boldly, refusing to let Jameson's appearance fluster her. There was little chance that his superiors had endorsed his search for her, which meant that Jameson had taken up a personal vendetta against Hugh. "Even if you still had the authority, how would you explain yourself? Explain who you were looking for?"

"I could just take in the first undocumented highlander I come across."

A slow smile curled her lip. "You do that."

He turned to look at her with a furrowed brow that spoke clearly of his frustration. "He's not what you think, Mrs. Manning."

"So you've said a dozen times, but let's agree to disagree, all right?" she said. "There is no threat officially or unofficially any longer. Your director saw to that, didn't he? Stop wasting more taxpayer money ... or your own, since I'd be willing to bet that your director doesn't know you're here. Should we call and ask?"

Jameson just frowned and shook his head. "I can't leave, knowing what I know. You wouldn't either, if you knew."

"I've read the files and can even read between the lines, Phil."

"Then you know he's not human."

"He's incredibly human," Claire whispered, turning her

head as Hugh's warm laughter joined that of the other men in kilts, pretenders to the Highland legacy. He belonged here. This wasn't his home but it was the closest he would ever have. She refused to let Jameson ruin that for him. "You're a fool to pursue this, Phil, and you're even crazier if you think that a little world politics is all that would blow up if the magnitude of what Fielding did got loose. You should consider yourselves lucky to have gotten off with just a slap on the hand … so far, of course. Could be worse for you if it all somehow managed to get out … and it will if you don't leave it alone. What would Nichols say, with his impending retirement and all?"

"Still trying to blackmail me?"

"Merely attempting to make you see that you're jumping at shadows. Stop trying to pretend that you know more than the scientists, Phil. If there was any real danger to the world at large, as you seem to think, Fielding's entire office would've been sealed off as a biohazard right from the beginning; did you ever think of that? Just be glad your moneymaker is still intact and everything that resulted from it has been deemed safe."

Hugh's biceps bulged against the short sleeves of the T-shirt he wore with his kilt as he lifted the heavy weight once again and flung it over his head with an audible grunt. Up it went over the high bar again, embedding itself with a solid *thud* into the moist ground of the field. The crowd roared and Claire joined them in their applause as Hugh's gaze once again searched her out, eager to share his triumph at the accomplishment, but the brash smile slipped away when he saw the man at her side, and a frown took its place as he turned in her direction.

Claire shook her head with a glower of her own but

Hugh kept coming. "By the way, it's not Mrs. Manning any longer. It's Mrs. Urquhart. I remarried recently. I thought with your connections, you would've known."

Jameson gaped. "To the savage?"

"No, to that wonderful Scottish man who you missed meeting a few months ago when you ran into his fist. He's a commodities trader in Inverness. That's why I'm here, actually. Not here as in these games, but here in Scotland. I moved here with him." She continued as Hugh neared, aware that the NSA agent was still staring at her in astonishment, "You're not going to find what you're looking for here. Go home, Phil. Find another hobby before I have you arrested for stalking me."

Hugh jogged up to them and slipped an arm around Claire's waist before transforming his scowl into a politely inquiring look. "Who's this, Sorcha?"

"This is Special Agent Phil Jameson from the National Security Agency in the United States," she said.

"*Ah*, I dinnae recognize ye… conscious, that is," Hugh said with a raised brow as he looked the agent up and down speculatively before addressing him directly in the most cultured and regal tones Claire had yet to hear from him. "I thought Agent Nichols had agreed that ye wouldnae be bothering us any longer, Jameson."

"I can't just let it go. I know who you are."

Hugh's voice dropped to an icy chill. "And I know that if ye willnae let Claire live her life wi'out yer constant interference, I will do more than see the details of yer project spread to the ends of the earth. I will show ye pain such as ye've ne'er imagined before I break yer neck wi' my own two hands."

"You can't threaten me. I am a federal agent."

"And I'm a verra angry and protective Scotsman," Hugh shot back. "Ye hae nae reason other than yer own paranoia to pursue this. Only Claire's benevolence saved ye the first time. Leave now before I override her wishes and ye die most ... savagely."

Jameson gaped, his mouth opening and closing as his hand went inside his jacket as if he'd forgotten that there was no longer a pistol holstered there. "I will find something, someday to put you back in prison where you belong."

"Good luck wi' that," Hugh mocked as Jameson turned away, knowing that with Danny's good work there would never be anything for Jameson to find. The agent's threats were empty ones, while his were not. If Jameson came within a hundred meters of them again, Hugh would happily find a more permanent solution to his meddling in a manner that harkened back to his savage roots.

Hugh gathered Claire into his arms. "Are ye all right, then? Did he threaten ye?"

She had to smile at that. "No, but you did a good enough job on him. I doubt he'll be bothering us anymore."

"Good," he said, tracing a light caress down her temple and cheek before slipping his fingers along her jaw and threading them into the hair at the base of her neck. His other hand slid down to splay across her flat abdomen. "Because, I hae a whole new life to look forward to with the woman who saved my life."

She laughed, feeling joy warm her heart and soul as she snuggled into Hugh's loving embrace. "I only *tried* to save your life, but in the end, it was you who saved me, my handsome Highlander. You brought purpose and laughter back into my life... No, let me amend that. You brought *life* back into my life. I love you."

"I love ye more," Hugh whispered feathering a kiss across her lips.

"I loved you first," she argued between kisses.

Hugh smiled against her lips. "I said it first."

"Yes, but I said it first in Engl..."

Catching her tightly in his embrace, Hugh cut off Claire's playful arguing with a passionate kiss, stealing the words away until they faded into a soft moan of delight. A thousand such arguments might await them in the future but the number paled in comparison to the millions of kisses waiting to be taken.

Find out what happened after Hugh disappeared from the Culloden moor in Angeline's latest time travel romance...

Love in the Time of a Highland Laird

AUTHOR'S NOTE

I hoped you enjoyed this different approach to time travel romance. It's not often the hero is the one to make the leap through time but even less often that it is the present the story is presented in. I thought it'd be interested to take a strong alpha man out of his element and see how he reacts to perhaps not being entirely in control of his life. The future is certainly outside of Hugh's comfort zone!

This is also a tale in which the method of the transportation through time is achieved through a more probable process than the magical sort. My husband is a huge fan of quantum physics, a big believer in reality. It is one of his theories I present combined with others he's read that comprise the Mark-Davis project. I hope you find the change refreshing.

But no good Laird for All Time series novel would be right without an appearance by Auld Donell. I hope you recognized him as the custodian Claire runs into at the lab. He doesn't have much to say, but his reasons for being here and the influential role he plays in bringing Hugh to the future are more thoroughly explored in *Love in the Time of a Highland Laird*.

As for his big picture plan? You'll just have to wait and see.

Also, while success for me personally is measured in bringing you joy, a moment of emotion, and escape from the hectic thing that is life, it is also measured by the quality and quantity of the reviews my books receive. They don't just help other readers decide to spend their time and money on a book, they help me, too. I read each one that is posted. I take what you say to heart and use it to improve and grow.

If you would take a few minutes of your time to leave a review, I'd be forever grateful.

Angeline

ABOUT THE AUTHOR

Angeline Fortin is the author of historical and time-travel romance offering her readers a fun, sexy and often touching tales of romance.

Her 2015 time travel romance, Taken: A Laird for All Time Novel, was awarded the Virginia Romance Writers 2015 Holt Medallion Award for Paranormal Romance. She is a PAN member of the Romance Writers of America and Midwest Fiction Writers.

A Question of Love, the first of her Victorian historical romance series Questions for a Highlander, was released later that year and quickly followed by series additions *A Question of Trust* and *A Question of Lust*. The series primarily follows the siblings of the MacKintosh clan. Ten brothers and their lone sister who end up looking for love in all the right places.

While the series continues on with familiar characters well known to those who have read the entire series, each single title is also a stand-alone tale of highland romance.

With a degree in US History from UNLV and having previously worked as a historical interpreter at Colonial Williamsburg, Angeline brings her love of history and Great Britain to the forefront in settings such as Victorian London and Edinburgh.

As a former military wife, Angeline has lived from the west coast to the east, from the north and to the south and uses those experiences along with her favorite places to tie into her time travel novels as well.

Angeline is a native Minnesotan who recently relocated back to the land of her birth and braved the worst winter recorded since before she initially moved away. She lives in Apple Valley outside the Twin Cities with her husband, two children and three dogs.

She is a wine enthusiast, DIY addict (much to her husband's chagrin) and sports fanatic who roots for the Twins and Vikings faithfully through their highs and lows.

Most of all she loves what she does every day - writing. She does it for you the reader, to bring a smile or a tear and loves to hear from her fans.

You can check out her website www.angelinefortin.com for summaries off all her books, companion information and sign up for her newsletter for news about upcoming releases. You can contact her at fortin.angeline@gmail.com.

Or you can follow her just about anywhere!

Facebook: http://on.fb.me/1fBD1qq
Twitter: https://twitter.com/AngelineFortin
Instagram: https://www.instagram.com/angelinefortin/?hl=en
Goodreads: https://www.goodreads.com/author/show/4863193.Angeline_Fortin
Google+: http://bit.ly/1hWXSGB
Tumblr: https://www.tumblr.com/blog/angeline-fortin
Pinterest: https://www.pinterest.com/angelinefortin1/

Made in the USA
Coppell, TX
13 August 2024